W9-DHN-399

DATE DUE

SEP 3 0 2009			
NOV 0 1 2010			
NOV 2 9 2010			
NOV 2 9 2010			

Demco

Bewitching Season

Bewitching Season

Marissa Doyle

HENRY HOLT AND COMPANY

New York

Henry Holt and Company, LLC
Publishers since 1866
175 Fifth Avenue
New York, New York 10010
www.HenryHoltKids.com

Henry Holt® is a registered trademark of Henry Holt and Company, LLC.
Text copyright © 2008 by Marissa Doyle
All rights reserved.
Distributed in Canada by H. B. Fenn and Company Ltd.

Library of Congress Cataloging-in-Publication Data
Doyle, Marissa.
Bewitching Season / Marissa Doyle.—1st ed.
p.   cm.
Summary: In 1837, as seventeen-year-old twins, Persephone and
Penelope, are starting their first Season in London they find their
beloved governess, who has taught them everything
they know about magic, has disappeared.
ISBN-13: 978-0-8050-8251-7 / ISBN-10: 0-8050-8251-4
[1. Twins—Fiction.   2. Sisters—Fiction.   3. Magic—Fiction.
4. Missing persons—Fiction.   5. London (England)—History—
19th century—Fiction.   6. Great Britain—History—William IV,
1830–1837—Fiction.]   I. Title.
PZ7.D7758Be 2008   [Fic]—dc22   2007027317

First Edition—2008
Book design by Laurent Linn
Printed in the United States of America on acid-free paper. ∞

1   3   5   7   9   10   8   6   4   2

*To Mom and Sherry and Liz and Hal and my Write Sisters
Janet and Doreen, who never said "if," but "when";
to my agent, Emily Sylvan Kim, who made the "when" into "now";
to Dick—my only sadness is that you're not here for this;
and most of all, to Scott*

*M*y God, Persy, you killed him!"

"I did not!" the Honorable Persephone Leland snapped back at her twin sister, Penelope, who was perched on the battered schoolroom table. She rubbed her damp palms on her apron—they still tingled, the way they usually did after she'd cast a spell—and looked anxiously at her little brother, sprawled pale and motionless on the faded Turkish carpet in front of her. What would she say to Mama? "I seem to have killed Charles during lessons this morning" would probably not go over well as a conversation starter at lunch. She turned to her governess. "Oh, Ally, I did it just like the other times!"

Miss Allardyce had assigned them halting spells today. While Pen watched, Persy had stopped Charles in his tracks a dozen times with her command of *repellere statim!* But this time her spell's force had not only halted him but also knocked him over backward. She dropped to the floor and grabbed one of his limp hands. "Charles, please, are you all right?"

Miss Allardyce sighed. "Penelope, do not take the Lord's name in vain. A true lady is known by her conduct under trying circumstances. And Charles, get up before your sisters have hysterics. I know you're hoaxing us." She bent and gave one of his brown curls a sharp tug.

Persy exhaled in relief as her brother opened his eyes and gave her an impudent grin. "Got you, Persy." He sprang up and held out a hand to her. "Tell me you weren't just a little worried."

She was, but she'd never admit it to him, the little beast. Ignoring his hand, she scrambled to her feet and shook out the creases in her pink morning dress.

Honestly, why did Ally let Charles sit in on their magic classes when he was home from school on holidays? Yes, it was helpful to have someone on whom to practice spells like this one, and they couldn't very well ask any of the servants. Magic was not something one advertised, as Ally frequently reminded them. It was risky enough having their lessons in the schoolroom, but Ally had set up a warning spell at the end of the corridor in case the footman came up with more coal for the fireplace. Still, practicing on *Charles* was sometimes too much.

"I wasn't worried. In fact, I rather hoped I'd found a spell to knock you unconscious. It would have been terribly useful," she said, looking down her nose at him. He grinned again and stuck out his tongue at her.

"Persy," Ally chided. "Is that a commendable sentiment?"

"No, but it's an honest one." Persy collapsed on the yellow brocade sofa Mama had sent up here when it became too disreputable for the morning room. Between practicing that halting spell and the hour of object teleportation and manipulation before that—not to mention Charles's shenanigans—her head was starting to pound. Hard magic practice always did that to her. "I think I've had enough for one morning, please, Ally. It's Pen's turn."

Miss Allardyce frowned as she consulted the watch at the waist of her neat maroon dress. "You have another ten minutes scheduled—"

Persy groaned and began to rise.

"—but I shall excuse you for this morning." She bent over Persy and brushed her fingers across her forehead. "Better?" she added softly, belying her stern look.

"Yes, thank you." Persy closed her eyes and sighed. She would have to learn Ally's headache-curing spell one of these days.

Pen shook her head as she rolled up the sleeves of her dress. "You're such a goose, Persy. If you didn't stay up late every night reading Ally's spell books, you wouldn't get the megrims."

"But if I don't study them now, when will I be able to? We leave for London next week." Persy kept her eyes closed so that she wouldn't have to see Pen's face light up at the mention of London.

"I know." Pen's voice was dreamy. "I can't wait. Balls and parties and getting presented at court—"

"—and having to be polite to witless boys who talk only about clothes and boxing matches—" Persy grimaced as she thought of it.

"—and men with exquisite manners asking us to dance—" Pen ignored her.

"—and nasty mamas who scowl if you're asked to dance before their daughters are—"

"—and society beauties in the latest fashions—"

"—and boring conversation about who cut whom dead at Lady So-and-So's reception—"

"—and maybe finally seeing the princess." Pen finished triumphantly.

That stopped Persy dead. If she had to "come out"—go to London and be presented to Queen Adelaide and attend balls and be a proper society miss looking for a husband—then the least that should happen was that she get a glimpse of Princess Victoria. Ever since they'd learned that they shared the princess's May birthday, she and Pen had scoured the illustrated papers for pictures and snippets of information about the girl who would someday be queen of England. Imagine, someone just their age—and a girl, *just like them*—as queen . . . after so many decades of disreputable old men ruling the country, it was fascinating to contemplate.

"Do you think we ever *will* see her?" she couldn't help asking.

"Just think . . . if she should become queen tomorrow." Pen's voice was breathless. "Then we'd be presented to—to *her*!"

"Girls." Ally stepped forward, shaking her head but smiling. "That would presuppose the death of our present king, which is hardly kind or proper. And if Princess Victoria were to become queen before she turns eighteen, it is more likely that you'd be presented to her mother as the queen's regent."

"Oh." Pen sounded disappointed. "Well, it was just a thought. But maybe we will see her, just the same . . . they say she's ever so tiny, but has the most beautiful blue eyes. Do you remember the sketch of her Grandmama sent us last year? I wonder how she wears her hair now? Do you think it's like that illustration we saw in—"

Ally cleared her throat. "Might we continue with our lesson before the bell rings for luncheon? Charles, if you will . . . Charles?"

A snoring sound issued from under the sofa. Persy started, and peered under its edge.

"I got bored and went to sleep while you talked about that girl stuff," he said, opening one blue eye and squinting at her.

Eleven-year-old boys. What else should she expect? Persy poked him. "Come on out, Chucklehead."

"Don't want to. I'm tired of getting pushed around while you practice magic on me. Why can't I learn too, Ally?" He rolled out from under the sofa and glared up at them. "I'm stuck going to rotten old Eton while you two have fun here doing spells all the time."

Ally shook her head at him. "I've told you, Charles. Boys your age don't usually have the capacity for magic. And in your family it has been the girls who possess it. Attending Eton is a privilege that only you, as a boy, can enjoy. Don't begrudge your sisters their education."

"*You* get to learn Greek," Persy said glumly. Oh, how she'd love to learn ancient Greek, and be able to read *The Odyssey* in Homer's own words.

Pen made a face at her and strolled to the ivy-shrouded window. "And fencing. Now *that* would be exciting. Come on, Chuckles. Let's get busy. It looks like the rain's finally stopped. After lunch you can go outside and play and not endure the torture of watching us anymore."

Crossing the dark-paneled hall on her way to the midday meal, Persy glanced up at the great family-tree mural painted on one wall. When twin girls were born to James Leland, thirteenth Viscount Atherston, and his wife, Lady Parthenope, it was reckoned the joke of the season: no daughters had been born in the direct Leland line since King Henry created the title in the 1530s.

What few remembered after such a long time was that Leland women were known for their magical abilities. It was only thanks to Ally, whose mother had traced the histories of the magic-possessing families of England, that the Leland girls had learned to use their power.

Lord Atherston was a quiet, scholarly man who took great joy in finding two perfect classical names for his two tiny perfect daughters. Though Mama had told them that she'd protested, citing the tears she had shed in her early schoolroom years learning how to spell her own classically derived name, he was adamant.

And so the names Persephone and Penelope had duly been painted onto that wall, to be joined six years later by that of Charles Augustus, or Chuckles, as his sisters had christened him. Eventually Charles's name would be outlined in gold as the fourteenth viscount. Rather sooner, hers and Pen's would be joined by other names, names that belonged to eligible young twigs from other family trees.

Persy's mouth went dry at the thought. Why couldn't she stay a child forever, having magic lessons with Ally and sneaking books out of Papa's library to read and avoiding the agony of coming out and balls and meeting strangers? She shivered and averted her eyes from the wall as she followed Pen into the breakfast room.

Papa stood by the marble fireplace, toasting his backside and reading a small leather-bound volume of Virgil's *Eclogues*. Their mother, Lady Parthenope, as she was still called—she had never quite been able to forget that she was a duke's eldest daughter—stood by the window with Miss Allardyce, who always joined them for family meals.

Mama looked at the clock on the chimneypiece. "Where is your brother?"

"I don't know. He left the schoolroom before we did," said Persy. She did not add that he had done so in a temper, tired of Pen's spotty success at halting spells: After he'd been jerked back and forth half a dozen times as her spell faded in and out, he had fled.

"It is fortunate that he will return to Eton in two days," offered Ally. "He is getting restless. Shall I ring for him?" She turned toward the bellpull.

"No, no. Let him miss a course, and then we shall see if he pays attention to the bell next time," Mama replied as she took her seat at table. "James, dear?"

"Of course." Papa slipped a ribbon into his book and put it on the table next to him, where he kept glancing at it longingly as Harry the footman brought in a platter of cutlets, followed by Mrs. Groening, the housekeeper, with a bowl of beetroot salad.

"Girls," said Mama as Harry served her, "now that Easter is past we will be leaving for London to shop for your clothes. Mrs. Albee has done an adequate job on your daytime dresses, but of course your party and ball dresses must be made in town. On Wednesday Miss Allardyce will go up to London to help open the house and start seeing about your wardrobes. We shall follow along in a few days—"

"But that means we'll miss lessons," Persy interjected.

Mama looked nettled. "Persephone dear, you would do well to put more effort into your dancing and less into Latin. I do not want you being called a bluestocking before you are even out."

Before Persy could open her mouth, Ally chimed in. "Mrs. Forrest was saying just last week at their party how well Persephone carried herself while dancing. The vicar's wife agreed, and she is the daughter of a baronet and was presented at court."

"Did she? Well . . . " Their mother picked up her fork again, mollified. "However, you must show me your court curtsies. I will get a sheet from Mrs. Groening after luncheon and see how well you can do them with a train." She looked again at the clock. "Now, where could that boy have got to?"

"He'll remember hot cutlets regretfully enough when he's on the coach back to Eton and has only cold bread and meat to eat," said Papa, helping himself to seconds at the sideboard. "When I was his age—"

"Oh, dear," said Ally, rising and hurrying to the window. Mama rose too and gasped.

Just then Persy heard it—a thin high wail, rather like the sound the enormous copper boiler in the kitchen made when Mrs. Groening was putting up marmalade. She and Pen rushed to the window after Ally.

The strange wail was coming from Charles, being carried up the terrace stairs by the head gardener. His brown curls were damp and matted with leaves, and his left arm had been hastily wrapped in what looked like the gardener's coat.

Mama was not a duke's daughter for nothing. After that one shocked intake of breath, she glided—albeit quickly—through the connecting door to the morning room, where doors to the terrace were open in the spring sunshine.

Persy and Pen exchanged anxious looks. Charles was a great boob sometimes, but if anything had happened to him . . .

"Sit, girls, and finish your meal," Ally enjoined them. "Your mother and I will deal with this. I rather doubt Charles will be returning to Eton anytime soon." She rang the housekeeper's bell vigorously and followed Mama into the next room.

"Ow! You're tugging too hard!" Pen squirmed in the chair before the looking glass.

"I'm sorry. I didn't mean to. Just thinking." Persy made a face in the mirror over her sister's head and kept on brushing the wavy honey brown veil of hair. Pen's hair was so thick and beautiful. Brushing it out was always a soothing and absorbing task for Persy, but one that left her feeling vaguely unsatisfied with her own hair. Even if it were exactly the same color and texture as her sister's.

Ally chided her for thinking Pen prettier than she, but Persy couldn't help it. Maybe it was Pen's lively, outgoing nature that added that extra sparkle to her blue eyes and animation to her features. Whatever it was, Persy felt like a pale, washed-out version of her sister.

"Thinking about what? Chuckles?" Pen set down the book she'd been squinting at in the dim candlelight.

"About Charles, and other things. He told me while Mama was getting the poppy tincture that he'd climbed the ivy vine so that we'd think he was doing a hovering spell outside the schoolroom window. We weren't even in the schoolroom anymore, which he might have deduced if he'd looked at a clock. Watching us practice magic and not being able to do it himself bothers him. One plait or two?"

"One, please." Pen bowed her head and sighed as Persy started braiding. "And now Mama won't let him go back to Eton until his wrist heals. All she needs is a fretful boy to deal with while she's getting ready for our coming out. Really, Perse, we had more sense at two than he does at eleven."

"He's a boy. They don't learn sense until they're thirty. If then." Persy scowled at the thick braid forming under her fingers, then tied it off with a ribbon. Boys! And now they would have to go to London and deal with *crowds* of them.

"Stop frowning. It gives you wrinkles." Pen jumped up and pushed her down into the seat. "Anyway, we won't be doing lessons with Ally gone. Chuckles won't have to fret too much. Oh, Persy, London dresses! And Ally will be helping with them, so they're sure to be perfect."

"But then we have to go out and wear them in public."

"That would be the general idea," agreed Pen. She bent and put her face close to Persy's so that they were reflected side by side in the mirror. "Very well, Persephone Augusta Caroline. Tell me that you're not the least little bit interested in going to London. *Swear* it."

Persy shifted in her seat and averted her eyes. "Stop that. All right, I can't. I *do* like the thought of wearing pretty new gowns and being presented to the queen and seeing—seeing everything. London. The streets and the shops and the people. The parties and balls and the people in their jewels being gossipy and fascinating. Even the princess, if we're lucky. I just wish I could be invisible while I do it. Don't you understand? When I'm at a party my mouth goes dry and all the scraps of conversation about the weather I've planned out beforehand vanish. And my gloves get damp because my hands are sweating, and I can't remember anyone's name even though they've just been introduced to me. And that's just at the little country parties we've been to. What will it be like at a London ball?"

"Hold still. You've a nasty knot here."

Persy gritted her teeth as the brush tugged at her hair. The scent of lavender oil drifted past her; Pen had drizzled a few drops onto her brush to help smooth out tangles. She closed her eyes and inhaled. She usually found the scent of lavender calming, but tonight it didn't seem to work.

"You know you can't stay here and hide forever," Pen said after a few more strokes of her brush. "Life is full of challenges, as Ally's always saying."

"Studying magic is a challenge too. It just happens to be a challenge that I'm not afraid of meeting."

"Then it's not much of a challenge, is it?"

"Oh, hush. You're not Ally. You can't get away with saying things like that. I've got an idea, Pen. You can go to London and come out for both of us. We're twins, after all. You'll do it beautifully. Then Papa can tell suitors, 'If you like this one, there is another just like her at home.' Or better yet, he can tell them I'm a frightful bluestocking, spend all my time with my nose in a book, and can only speak Latin, so they're best off forgetting about the other Leland twin."

Pen laughed and shook her head. "Shall I tell Papa that?"

"I was joking, goose. I know I don't have a choice. I'll just be dreadful at it and disappoint Mama sorely and be miserable for the rest of my life." Persy grimaced at her reflection.

"You won't be dreadful. You'll be fine. Besides, what would you do if you didn't go to London and come out?"

Would Pen laugh if she told her? "Oh, I don't know. Anything."

She took a deep breath and spoke in a rush. "Be a teacher like Ally, and find children to teach in families that have a history of magic, like she did with us. Or go to a university and study. I'd love to do those things more than anything."

Pen shook her head. Persy could read the skepticism in her eyes. "Persy, that's—that's very noble and everything, but it's not what we are. Papa's a viscount. Viscounts' daughters don't become governesses or scholars or anything. They marry men of their own class and have babies and run their husbands' houses. Now, stop looking so grim. It will be all right. We'll be doing London together, remember?"

"Are you two *still* talking about London?" Miss Allardyce, wearing a flannel night robe and an indulgent smile, came into the room.

Persy turned in her seat. "I wish I could come with you on Wednesday and visit your family's bookshop. That would give me something pleasant to look forward to."

"I promise to take you there when you arrive next week, if you are not too busy shopping." Ally took the brush from Pen and finished brushing Persy's hair. Persy saw her smile in the mirror become pensive. "I shall miss you, you know. I have enjoyed my years with you very much."

"But you'll only be gone a few days—" Pen began, then stopped. "Oh. I'd not really thought about that."

Persy's melancholy deepened. She and Pen were about to take their places in society as adults. There would be no reason for Ally to remain as their governess once they were out. But Ally had been with them for ten years, since they were small. She was practically part of the family. What would they do without her?

"Just because we're coming out doesn't mean that we want you to leave us," she added, to fill in her sister's abashed silence.

"Thank you. However, your parents might find my continued presence superfluous." Ally put the brush down on the dressing table and plaited Persy's hair.

"But we're just now really getting good at magic—at least, Persy is. I should have worked harder. I somehow never thought that you'd have to go away someday." Pen gave her a stricken look in the mirror.

"Not many young wives take their governesses with them when they marry," Ally teased gently. "How would you and Persy decide who got me? Or will you take a leaf from Solomon's book and divide me in two?"

"If anyone could manage that, it would be you," Persy said.

"Ah, if you think I am powerful, you should have met my grand-mother. You read her grimoire, Persy. Couldn't you feel her power in it?"

"Yes, especially when the pages turned themselves to where they thought I should read," Persy agreed.

Ally nodded. "I doubt another witch of her time was as power-ful as she."

"What about you today? How many witches are there in England who can do half of what you can?" Persy demanded.

"As the first tenet among witches is to conceal their powers, I could not say." Ally's voice was prim, but Persy caught the note of pleasure in it. "You would do well to remember that, especially as you enter society."

"We *know*," said Pen. "You've told us before."

"I shall say it again, and it will not be the last time. Consider it in this light. The last execution for witchcraft in Great Britain occurred less than a hundred years ago. I know that sounds like a very long time ago at age seventeen—"

"Almost eighteen," Pen reminded her.

"—but in terms of how far the nation has come in overcoming superstition, it is no time at all. Most of the people who were executed as witches probably weren't witches at all, but that did not matter, did it?"

"But as you said, no one's been executed for witchcraft for a hundred years. I don't see what you're so worried about. We'll be careful," Pen protested.

"No one's been executed. But there are other ways to die, ones that do not involve bloodshed. Think about what would happen if it were to become known that you were witches. You wouldn't be burned at the stake, no. You might even find yourself popular with those who would try to manipulate you into using your power for their benefit. But the greater part of society would shun you. Carriages would speed up when they drove past your house, to avoid contamination. You would never be welcome at court. And all your suitors would vanish like fog at sunrise. It would not matter that you are both lovely, charming girls. The assumption would be that you are somehow evil."

Even Persy felt stricken at the picture Ally painted. "But we aren't evil."

"Of course you aren't. But in the face of popular perception, truth has little power. Do you see?"

Pen's face was pale, even by firelight. "Then I suppose it doesn't matter that I'm not very good at magic, since we can never use it," she said in a small voice.

"I didn't say that you couldn't use it. Listen to me, girls. So long as you keep it secret, you *will* be able to use it to accomplish good things, useful things."

"Such as?"

Ally sighed. "I am not a seer, Persy. But your parents and I raised you to be moral, honest, upright women. Someday you will be able to use your magic in moral and honest ways. Until then, watch and wait. And keep your secret."

"Have you ever done anything great and good with your magic, Ally?" Persy leaned back against Ally's side. She remembered why she found the scent of lavender so comforting: Ally always smelled faintly of it.

There was a smile in Ally's voice. "I've taught you. Does that count? My grandmother once said to me what I just said to you. Becoming your governess was one way to do good. Maybe I will be able to do more someday. In the meanwhile, it was a more interesting prospect than marrying any of the young men who came calling at my father's shop."

Persy felt a faint flicker of envy. If only *she* had the option of going out to teach, rather than to dance and flirt and look for a husband . . .

"Did young men *really* come to your family's shop to see you?" Pen asked.

"Yes." A faint pink suffused Ally's face and the corners of her mouth turned up. "They still do, though my sister has little patience for them, either. I simply never met a man who was more interesting to me than my profession as a teacher."

"Doubt I will, either," muttered Persy.

"But if you did—" Pen began.

"*Quite* enough. I have left a list of spells for you to practice.

When you arrive in town we can move on to new work. Penelope, your sister will be happy to help you with any that cause you trouble. And Persy—" she hesitated.

"Yes, Ally?"

"*Do* practice your dancing with your sister. I regret having had to fib to your mother about your dancing skills at luncheon today." She smiled and kissed them both good night, then took up her candle and glided from the room.

2

"Come on, Persy. I spent the morning practicing magic. Now you have to practice dancing. Ally said so again just before she left yesterday. Help me move this out of the way." Pen took hold of the schoolroom table and dragged it a few feet to one side, grunting with effort.

"Must we?" said Persy, closing her book but not moving from her seat by the window.

"Yes. We promised Ally that you would practice dancing, remember? I did that distracting spell all morning until *I* felt distracted. Now you'll have to waltz with me till you're dizzy. Come *on*, this is heavy."

"I'll be dizzy in five minutes," Persy grumbled as they finished moving the table and rolled up the carpet.

"Nonsense," said Pen in her best Ally voice. "If you would just pay more attention during the turns—"

"I do. That's why I get dizzy."

Pen sighed as she dusted off her hands. "That article in *Lady's Magazine* says that Princess Victoria loves dancing and excels at it. If it's good enough for her—"

"I know, I know. Then it's good enough for us," Persy finished. It wasn't that she disliked dancing. It was everything that went with it that bothered her. But Pen was impossible to distract once she got an idea in her head. Distract—hmm . . .

"And don't think about trying the distracting spell on me. I know it too well now," Pen said with a grin. "May I have this waltz, Miss Leland?"

"But there's no music! I'll feel silly." Persy stepped back a pace, pink in the face at Pen's reading her half-formed thought.

Pen snatched the ends of her broad collar and tugged her back. "We'll hum. And won't you feel even sillier when you're at a ball and a fascinating young man asks you to dance and you have to refuse because you're afraid of breaking his toes? Better still, *I'll* hum, so you can pay attention to what you're doing. Now!" She took Persy's hand and put her other on her sister's waist.

Persy concentrated on her feet as Pen led her about the room in smooth, sweeping arcs. "Must you turn so often?"

Pen stopped humming. "Yes, unless you want to crash into the walls. Ally's not taught us how to dance through them yet. There, that's not bad. Don't hold yourself so stiffly."

"My hair is coming unpinned." Persy hunched her shoulders.

"So let it. We'll fix it later. Now, there—and there—and there—"

"Oh, there it goes! How am I supposed to see where I'm going with my hair in my face? I said I would be dizzy in five minutes."

Pen sighed. "You're not allowed to be dizzy. Don't watch the room, watch my nose. You should be listening to your partner's conversation with a look of total absorption on your face when you dance at a ball, anyway."

"How can I see your nose through my hair? And I can't dance and converse at the same time!"

"You don't have to. Simply look enthralled by what your partner says, and he'll think you're the wittiest and most enchanting creature in the room."

"You're a cynic, Pen."

"Well, that's what I heard Mama say once. Now hush. I can't talk to you and hum at the same time."

"Now my hair's completely down."

"You didn't pin it well enough this morning. Stop fussing and pay attention." Pen pulled her into a series of spins so that she had to concentrate on dancing through the cascade of hair that tumbled and bounced in her face.

"*Dum*-da-da, *dum*-da-da, *dum*," Pen hummed, and reversed. "Very good, Persy! We will turn you into a dancer yet!"

"Don't do that again! It was beastly!" groaned Persy, trying to regain her rhythm.

"Well, true gentlemen don't reverse. But you need to know how to deal with it if they do."

"Break their toes, most likely. Pen, how do you remember these things? Did Ally give you extra dancing lessons when I was busy with something else?"

"Of course not, goose. Stop looking at your feet."

"But if I stare at your nose, I'll laugh."

"Then close your eyes for a while. That'll force you to concentrate."

Persy closed her eyes. "You won't reverse again?"

"I promise."

With her eyes closed, Persy could better feel the subtle pressure of Pen's hand on her waist communicate direction. "Why, that helps! Can't I always dance with my eyes closed?"

"Excuse me," said a voice. "May I have the next waltz?"

Persy staggered as Pen abruptly halted. She opened her eyes.

A tall, fair-haired young man stood before them, dressed for riding in a deep blue coat, tan buckskin trousers, and shining boots. He seemed to be having a difficult time keeping the corners of his mouth in order, and his hazel eyes under extravagant dark lashes twinkled at them. In the doorway, Charles leaned against the jamb and held his splinted arm against his stomach as he giggled and snorted.

"Please pardon our intrusion. Your brother was sent to bring you down to the drawing room, and I came with him. You didn't hear us knock," the man explained gravely.

Persy pushed back her tumbled hair and stared. Dear heavens, it couldn't be *him* . . . but who else had those eyes, changeable as the sea, that had always seemed to see straight into everything . . . including her?

"It can't be," Pen said, a slow smile spreading across her face.

"Well, it could," said the young man, grinning openly at last. "At least, I think it could, if I am who you think I am. If you know what I mean."

"Lochinvar Seton, what are you doing here?" Pen stepped toward him, hand outstretched. "I thought you were touring on the continent?"

Persy felt the thudding of her heart all the way to her knees. Of course it was Lochinvar. How long had it been since she had seen him? She did some rapid mental counting. Four years, at least—time enough for him to turn from a gangling youth into the most handsome man she'd ever seen.

She remembered the towheaded boy who had frequently ridden over from the neighboring estate with his father, Papa's best friend, Lord Northgalis, and who had barely been able to say two words to them when they took him to play in the gardens. And when he had been able to speak, he'd been utterly beastly and teased them mercilessly. At least he had until his last visits, just before he left for Cambridge. Would he remember those afternoons now, when he'd shown Persy a different side of himself? She swallowed and wished her bone-dry tongue didn't all at once feel too large for her mouth. How could Pen be so calm, greeting this beautiful young man?

"I *was* on the continent, with friends from Cambridge. I got to Galiswood yesterday and father insisted we visit as soon as possible. Let me see if I can tell you apart. How are you, Pen—er, Miss Leland?" He bowed over her hand.

She smiled prettily. "So you can tell! I'm very well, thank you. Persy and I were just practicing our dancing. We leave for town next week for the season."

"Then I'll see you there. We go down in a few days as well." He turned, and Persy saw a flash of eager expectation in his eyes as he looked at her. Her own heart leapt in response. Did he remember those days after all?

But what must she look like right now, with her hair tumbled around her shoulders and her apron stained with ink from absent-mindedly wiping her pen on it? Certainly nothing like all the sophisticated, interesting people he must have met on his tour. Though she could feel that her cheeks were flaming, her vocal chords seemed to have frozen, along with her brain.

"How do you do, Lord Seton?" she finally said in a chilly voice, extending her hand. It was the only thing she could think of to say.

He stared at her for a moment as the eagerness drained out of his expression and his eyes flickered to his feet. Persy's heart plummeted to the floor as well.

"I'm very well, Miss Leland," he said to his gleaming boots. Then he looked up again. "But in desperate need of polishing my own dancing before we go to London. May I have this dance, if you please?" He bowed and took the clammy hand she still held out.

Oh, why wasn't Ally here to tell her what to do? The situation was absurd. He wore riding boots with spurs. Her hair tumbled about her like a shaggy pony's. They were in the schoolroom with the furniture pushed about higgledy-piggledy. But in that instant, she would have danced a fandango with a rose in her teeth if Lochinvar had asked her to. The hazel eyes had cast a spell on her more powerful than any she had ever studied with Ally. She stared at him, transfixed.

To her surprise, it was Charles who rescued her. "Mama says we are to come to the green salon for tea, Perse," he said anxiously. "She'll send me to bed if I don't get back down and lie on the sofa again, and I'll *die* of boredom if she does that."

"Mama's right, you goose. You *should* be in bed," said Pen. She glanced at Persy and her disreputable apron, then turned to Lochinvar. "Shall we go down? You must be thirsty after your ride."

Persy understood the silent message in Pen's glance. She waited until Lochinvar had followed Pen into the hall, then yanked off the apron and darted to retrieve her scattered hairpins.

"Are you coming, Miss Leland?" said Lochinvar, sticking his head back in the door as she tried to recoil her hair without benefit of a mirror.

"Mmm-hmmm," she said brightly, mouth full of pins.

He gave her a look she couldn't decipher, and vanished.

"Well, you two looked a sight," Charles said, still lounging in the doorway.

"I thought you had to go lie down?" snapped Persy from the corner of her mouth.

"What? Oh, right. Hey, isn't Lochinvar something? I'd—"

"His name is Lord Seton, Chucklehead." She drove the last pin straight into her scalp and winced.

"Lord Seton? But we never called him that before."

"He's a grown man now. You cannot call him by his Christian name the way you could when you were small and didn't know any better."

"Yes, Miss Leland," said Charles, pretending to cringe. The movement made him flinch and cradle his injured arm, and Persy bit back the scolding she had been about to deliver.

"Let's go, Chuckles. You *should* be in bed, you know," she said gently. "I wish Ally were here. Maybe she'd know a spell to keep your wrist from hurting so much." She put an arm around him as they walked down the hall to the stairs, and for once he did not squirm away from this overt display of sisterly affection.

But she couldn't help agreeing with him—Lochinvar *was* something. His mother had died when he was only six, and his father had brought him over frequently during his vacations from Eton. He was five years their senior, and had been as much tormentor as playmate for them. He would ride with them and either spur them into jumping terrifying fences or take off across country and lose them for hours at a time. Then there was the time he dared them to climb one of the enormous oaks in the park with him, and then shinned down to the ground and stood at the foot of the tree, gazing up at them with a look of devilish innocence as they tucked their skirts about them and tried to think of a modest way to get down. They had gotten their revenge by pelting him with acorns, but he had found something equally loathsome to do on his next visit.

"You must be kind and set him an example," Mama said when they complained. "He has no mother or sisters to help teach him moderation."

"I'll be happy to teach him a lesson or two," Pen always replied, but Mama would look stern and shush her.

One summer day, though, Persy had seen a different side of him. When the maid announced the Setons' arrival, she had scurried with her book to Grandfather's Folly on the far edge of the lawn, hoping the warmth of the day would keep Lochinvar in the house with the adults and her safe from whatever new mischief he had thought of. Pen went to hide in their room, claiming a headache and even allowing Mrs. Groening to dose her with her evil-tasting universal headache remedy. "Anything's better than an afternoon with *him*," she'd whispered to Persy on her way upstairs.

Persy had settled herself against a column on the far side of the little classical Greek-style summerhouse and thought about casting the concealing spell she had read recently in one of Ally's books. But it was too hot for magic, and surely she'd be safe out here. She yawned and opened *Northanger Abbey* again. The August warmth and the hum from a wasps' nest in the roof made her eyes heavy despite the chilly gothic rain that beat down in the pages of her book.

She was startled awake by something brushing across her bare head. Her eyes flew open. Lochinvar stood over her, handkerchief in hand.

"There was a wasp in your hair. I didn't think you'd want to find out the hard way if he was in a good mood or not," he said, shading his eyes with one hand as he looked down at her.

"Er, thank you," she said uncertainly, and scrambled to her feet. Had Charles given away her hiding place, the little beast? If he had . . .

"I didn't mean to disturb your nap. Is your book so dull?" he asked, holding out a hand for it.

Would he snatch it and run away, just to plague her? She thought about hiding it behind her back, but that might give him ideas. "Oh, no. Well, it's a little silly, but it's supposed to be, I think," she said, relinquishing it to him.

He smiled to himself as he read the title. To her surprise, there was no trace of mockery in his hazel eyes when he looked back at her. "Do you like Miss Austen's novels? So do I."

Persy nearly sat down again in shock. Was Lochinvar talking to her? Not calling her Persepolis or Persnickety, or pretending to think she was Pen, but actually *talking* to her . . . and about a book? She swallowed hard. "This is only the second one I've read, and Papa said I shouldn't let Mama see me reading novels because I'm too young—"

"Do you like them?"

"Oh, yes! I loved *Pride and Prejudice*! Wasn't Elizabeth wonderful? And I think that I shall try *Emma* next."

"Then you aren't too—how old *are* you, anyway?" He looked at her, head cocked to one side, the sun sparkling on his bright gold hair.

"Thirteen this past May."

"That's right. You and Pen were born the same day as Princess Victoria." He squinted into the Folly. "I hear the wasps. Let's walk in the shade."

So she had followed him to the edge of the lawn, strolling back toward the house in the shade of the trees, and listened to him talk about the books he was reading now before he entered Cambridge in the autumn.

"I'm reading for pleasure all summer, because after Michaelmas I won't be able to," he confessed. They talked about the Waverley Novels, some of which she'd read, and Miss Burney and Miss Edgeworth, and Persy found herself promising to ask her father to let her read the Persian novels of Mr. Morier, if they could be found, and the American Mr. Cooper's *The Last of the Mohicans*.

She stole quick looks at him as he enthusiastically suggested what books she should read next. What was making him so pleasant today? Why, his last visit at Easter had been when he took them riding through every brook, ditch, and puddle he could find. It had taken her and Pen *days* to sponge the mud out of their riding habits. She almost tiptoed at his side, waiting for him to somehow twist their conversation into some opportunity to tease. But he never did.

As they approached the stairs up to the terrace, Lochinvar paused to gaze back out over the lawn toward Grandfather's Folly. Persy shaded her eyes with her hand and looked hard at his face, to see if she could see what had changed him since that spring.

It still looked like him—same thick blond hair and dark-lashed eyes. But—she saw with a funny feeling in the pit of her stomach—he *had* changed. His voice was deeper, no longer cracking and awkward. The round boy's face had grown planes and angles. And was that fuzz on his upper lip?

"I never knew you liked to read," he said, and she realized that he had been watching her stare at him.

"You never asked," she blurted out.

But he only laughed. "No, I don't suppose I did. But then I never see you alone without Pen."

"She reads too, you know," she couldn't help saying pertly. "And you could have told us that you like to read."

"With a name like Lochinvar, how could I not? I've been reading Sir Walter Scott since I found my name in the book of his poems in our schoolroom."

"'So faithful in love and so dauntless in war,/There never was knight like the young Lochinvar,'" Persy quoted. "Well, the war part was certainly right, at least as far as we were concerned." She tensed to run but he laughed again.

"I hope we can call a truce now, Persy."

She had seen him only twice more after that, when he was down from Cambridge. Both occasions had been more formal ones, over tea in the salon with Mama and Papa and Lord Northgalis, but he had chatted with her about what she was reading and studying with Ally. She did not tell him that she had pestered her father to find every book he mentioned, both favorably and unfavorably, so that she could read them. Or that she replayed their conversations in her head over and over again, for weeks afterward.

Now, walking down the stairs with Charles snuggled under her arm, Persy's mind raced. Lochinvar had been nicer to her that summer because he had grown up. Because it had become more amusing to talk about books with her than chase her bellowing about the garden with a fat toad in each hand.

But she'd grown up, too. Would he still care to talk about books with a young woman, the way he had with a girl? Or would he think her overeducated? Young ladies in society were supposed to flirt and giggle, not discuss literature and philosophy. Now he'd surely think her a dreadful bluestocking.

He'd never think that about Pen. Persy thought about the pleased smile Pen had given him just now when she held out her probably nonsweaty hand to him. Did Pen recall how awful he had been as a boy?

She had laughed when Persy had told her about their bookish conversation in the Folly, and said she'd been glad she'd had the headache. Persy never told her about their subsequent discussions, and Pen had continued to make herself as unobtrusive as possible whenever he came to visit.

She hadn't today.

How did Pen do it? Their interactions with young men had been limited to the few neighborhood parties that Mama had let them attend. Pen had claimed to find them as excruciating as Persy had. But she had been perfectly natural and gracious with Lochinvar just now.

"Well, we *have* known him forever," Persy could almost hear her say.

But they hadn't. He wasn't the awful boy they had once known, but a grown man . . . a very handsome grown man—

"Ow, don't hug too hard!" Charles protested.

"I'm sorry." Persy yanked her attention back to the present.

"Do you think Papa will let me travel on the continent someday, like Loch—Lord Seton?" Charles asked as they walked down the gallery to the green salon.

"If it means you turn out like him, I don't see why not."

Charles looked up in surprise. "How do you know how he's turned out?"

"Oh," Persy floundered. "Well, he's picked up a lot of polish on his travels, don't you think? He looks very well."

"But he's always looked—ooh, Persy thinks he's handsome!" Charles grinned up at her and danced away, his voice rising. "Persy thinks he's—"

"Quiet, brat, or I'll tell Mama you slid down the banister just now!" Persy lunged for him. "And I'll find a spell to make your good arm itchy all the time, and you won't be able to scratch it with your hurt one."

To Persy's relief they'd reached a truce by the time they came to the green salon's door. She gave him one last warning glance as they entered.

"There she is!" boomed the Earl of Northgalis. "How's my Persephone?"

Persy hurried over to make proper greeting to him, but he scooped her into a hug, then held her at arm's length to scrutinize her from under his bushy brows.

"Just as pretty as her sister," he proclaimed. "Or is it that her sister is as pretty as she? No matter. Haven't they grown into a handsome pair, Lochinvar?"

"There was never any doubt they would, sir, as they resemble their mother so nearly," replied Lochinvar, seated next to Pen on the other sofa by the tea table.

"Listen to him!" said Mama with a pleased chuckle. "He'll have the London girls eating out of his hand." She began to turn back to Lord Northgalis, then paused. "Goodness, Persy, sit down and stop looking so forlorn. Charles, you really ought—"

"I'll go back to bed later, I promise!" Charles sat himself down on a chair and gripped its arm with his good hand as if fearful of being dragged away.

Persy turned away from Charles's wheedling. Pen and Lochinvar—*Lord Seton,* she reminded herself—took up most of the sofa, so she sat on one of the tiny gilt bamboo chairs that Grandmama had bought after a visit to the Brighton Pavilion, and prayed she wouldn't fall off it.

"Won't you tell us a little about your travels, Lord Seton—" Pen began.

He interrupted her. "If you call me that again, I shall either laugh or refuse to answer you, as we've known each other since before we could even pronounce each other's names properly. I'm Lochinvar, Miss Leland."

Pen colored slightly. The pink flush made her eyes seem even bluer. Persy was sure that if *she* were sitting where Pen was, she'd be positively gibbering.

"Lochinvar," Pen agreed, and smiled down at her hands. "Now, tell us about your tour. What cities did you visit? We want to hear everything!"

3

$\mathscr{F}$our days after the Setons' unexpected visit to Mage's Tutterow, Melusine Allardyce walked briskly down London's busy Oxford Street, the last item on her list of errands completed. Examining Madame Gendreau's sketches and fabrics for the girls' dresses had taken the most time, and had in its turn generated a new list for the next day: visits to purveyors of gloves, fans, and other sundries, to match the snippets of fabric in her reticule.

But Miss Allardyce felt more than equal to the task of organizing wardrobes for Persy and Pen, and knew that Lady Parthenope would approve her choices when she arrived in London in a few days. She and her employer shared a strong mutual respect, born of their similar managerial abilities and efficiency. Pen had been known to refer to them as General Marlborough and General Wellington behind their backs, much to Miss Allardyce's secret amusement.

Oxford Street was crowded with shoppers scurrying homeward for the coming supper hour. She dodged the rude and the oblivious with ruthless politeness while managing to keep her slippers free of the worst of the filth of the streets. London did not suit Miss Allardyce's sense of order and decorum; she could not see herself returning to her parents' home here after leaving the Lelands. A position with another country-based family would be preferable.

But for now, she would enjoy the melancholy pleasure of helping launch her two pupils into society. Both girls would do well. They had been apt and obedient students, and Persy in particular had shown a real love of learning that had been most gratifying. A pity she would never have a chance to display the depth and breadth of her knowledge. And as for their magical abilities . . .

Miss Allardyce sighed as she twitched her skirts from the grasp of a grubby street urchin, then extracted a penny from her purse for him. She knew well that the girls could never display their magical accomplishments to the world. But she was proud to have developed their talent, and proud that she had helped form their strong, upright characters. The good Lord knew that many people with the talent were not always equally as moral.

She squelched the sadness that welled, like blood from a cut, when she thought of leaving them. There would be time enough to grieve when she actually left. Professional governesses could not afford the luxury of too much affection for the children they taught. But then a memory of Pen's stricken face when she mentioned leaving them last week melted her steely resolutions. Dear girls. She patted her reticule, which held the letters from them that had arrived in the morning's post. Pen's had been particularly amusing.

Dearest Ally,

Such alarums since you left here last week! Everyone and everything is in a state of disruption as we pack for London. Charles mopes about now that the fun of being cosseted has worn off and he realizes that coming to town and listening to us talk about clothes and parties will be just as bad as listening to us talk about magic. And Persy is a total dolt. Let me tell you why.

Lord Northgalis came for a visit this afternoon, and whom do you think he brought with him? Lochinvar, back from his grand tour! He and Chuckles walked in on Persy and me dancing in the schoolroom, much to his amusement and poor Persy's mortification, as her hair had come down in our exertions.

He is much improved by age and travel and has become a very personable young man, nothing like the dreadful boy he used to be. I practiced my conversation on him quite successfully, I think. Persy sat dumb until he started to describe his visits to some Roman ruins in Italy, when she brightened considerably but would not open her mouth. He saw her interest too and kept steering conversation around to similar topics, but she still would not speak. I was quite out of patience as she would have been better able to discuss the topic than I (don't scold, but I admit I found his gossip of persons and foreign customs more fascinating). As it was I would have liked to nap while he went on about Latin graffiti and Etruscan tombs.

Only when they were about to leave was he able to get a peep out of Persy by asking what she was reading. It *seemed to strike some spark from her, for she finally looked up at him with a hint of warmth in her expression, but just then Lord Northgalis fell upon us and whisked a very disappointed-looking Lochinvar from our midst. The whole visit was most provoking, and Persy even more so when I scolded her for being such a statue. She only mumbled something about wishing she were thirteen again. What will we do with her? I rather suspect Lochinvar has taken an interest in her, but how will we ever find out if she won't even look at him?*

At least the Setons will be in London for the season as well. It will be good to have a few familiar faces about when we start going out into society. They have promised to call as soon as we are all settled in town. I hope that Persy will be better behaved when they do.

Oh, Persy. Miss Allardyce sighed to herself and shook her head in exasperated if gentle reproof, causing a passerby to jump and give her a guilty look. If only there were some way to help the child see herself as others did, to see the fine, intelligent expression of her soft blue eyes and the sweet generosity and spice of humor in the quirk of her mouth.

"Melusine!"

She started and looked up. Her father stood on the pavement before her, looking at her in amusement. He wore the old-fashioned soft canvas coat and gloves he always wore when arranging merchandise, and she realized that she was home. How had she made it here so soon? She glanced up at the familiar sign over his head, recently and brightly repainted.

For once Miss Allardyce let her exquisite correctness lapse and became again the girl who adored her papa. She kissed his cheek right there in the middle of Oxford Street, with nary a blush or look around.

He chuckled. "You were thinking some deep thoughts, it looks like. Come tell me what you think of these new window dressings."

He held out his hand and she took it with a gentle squeeze, then stood by his side to survey the shop front.

Lengths of green velvet had been draped in the windows, and a scattering of botanical books, open to their prettiest plates, completed the cheerful, springlike picture. A few silk flowers were scattered among them.

"It's lovely, Father! Did you think of it?"

"No, your sister did. Lorelei insists it will bring in more custom if we follow the season with our displays. It looks more like a milliner's window than a bookseller's, but there *have* been more browsers since yesterday." His voice was grudging, but his eyes smiled. "At least she's taking notice of something other than her sewing and her potion brewing. You look well, daughter. Your mother said you'd be home for tea tonight. She was quite put out about it because she had promised to visit Aunt Parris today, but she baked you a cake. Your brother's gone with her for the day."

"I'm sorry to miss her and Merlin. You look well, too." She smiled at the tall, stooped man. "I'm afraid I can't stay long. But I'll be in town till early August. The girls will be here in a few days, and have already asked to visit. Mother can do a big tea for them."

"That should make her feel better." He opened the shop door for her.

At the tinkle of the door's brass bell, a petite girl seated behind the store's counter looked up. "Melly! You're here!" she exclaimed and hurried across the room, bumping into a customer who pored over a stack of books on the counter. "Pardon!" she called over her shoulder and launched herself at Miss Allardyce.

"Lorrie!" The sisters clung together for a moment, and Miss Allardyce surprised herself with a trace of mistiness in her eyes. Lorrie—the Lorelei who had decorated the windows so cleverly—was the baby of the family and had been her pet growing up. She held her at arm's length to have a good look at her. "How are you? Are you still studying? Your window dressing for Father is lovely."

"Thank you." Lorrie let go of one of Miss Allardyce's hands and waved it in a spiraling pattern. A strong scent of violets and new-mown grass filled the shop. The customer at the counter looked up, startled.

"How's that?" she asked, grinning. "I've just had flowers on the brain lately. Spring, I guess."

Miss Allardyce shook her head but smiled. "Discretion, Lorrie," she murmured, with a glance at the man by the counter. "You shouldn't do that sort of thing in here."

"Pooh," Lorrie stage-whispered back. "I get bored when it's my turn to mind the shop, and think these spells up. I can do roses, eglantine, and lilac too. I tried to do lavender for you, but it's not quite right yet."

"Melusine cannot stay long, Lorrie. Would you mind putting on the kettle so we can have some tea?" said Mr. Allardyce. He turned to the customer, who was watching them keenly. "May I help you, sir?"

"Oh, ah, not just now, thank you," said the man, looking away. An Irish lilt tinged his speech though his accent was cultured, and Miss Allardyce saw that his hair under his silk hat was a beautiful dark auburn. "I'll just browse, if I may."

"If I can be of assistance in finding anything—"

"Indeed, sir, I'll ask." The man went back to his book.

Miss Allardyce untied her bonnet and hung her cloak on the rack behind the counter where her father kept his working coats. She sat down in the chair her sister had vacated and looked around the shop in satisfaction. The delightful chaos that had reigned in it all through her childhood, despite her and Mother's efforts to organize it, had vanished. Now all the books were off the floor and in cases, and small, neatly lettered signs at the top of each tier of shelves indicated subject matter. Here and there velvet-covered stands displayed particularly handsome or quaint volumes. "It looks very nice, Father. I like how you have rearranged it all."

Mr. Allardyce looked sheepish. "That's Lorrie again. I could never have done this. She cannot be troubled to open a book other than a novel, but she does enjoy arranging them. Your brother gets irritated, but she keeps the shop so well dusted and swept as well as organized that he cannot fault her. I don't think a bookshop's the place for her, but your mother and I don't know what else to do with her. Especially after that business with Mrs. Thibault."

Miss Allardyce nodded gravely. Lorrie's design talents had led her parents to apprentice her to a nearby milliner, Mrs. Tibbs—or Thibault, as she had taken to calling herself in hopes of attracting a more fashionable clientele.

All had gone well until the milliner had entered her workroom unusually early one morning to see her new assistant standing before a row of hats, arms raised like an orchestra conductor's, watching them trim themselves under her airy guidance. Fortunately for Lorrie, Mrs. Thibault had had a tumbler of gin along with her morning bread and egg, and it hadn't been hard to convince her that a different choice of breakfast beverage would be wise if she didn't want to keep "seeing things." But she had never been comfortable with Lorrie after that day, and had released her without argument when she cited family needs and came back to work at the bookshop.

"We've all rather spoiled her, haven't we? You know that I will be leaving Lord Atherston's employ sometime this year. Maybe I can find a suitable situation for her when I start looking for myself," she said, patting his hand.

"How are Miss Persy and Miss Pen?" asked Mr. Allardyce, looking happy to change the subject.

"Very well. Excited about their coming out. At least, Penelope is. Oh—before I forget—" She opened her reticule. "Here's Grandmother's grimoire that you sent me last winter."

"Ah." Mr. Allardyce took the little book and stroked it reverently. The pages rustled, like a preening bird settling its feathers. "Thank you. You've treated it well. How did the girls like it?"

"Persy was quite fascinated by it. Her progress is most gratifying." The grimoire rustled again.

"It agrees with you," said Mr. Allardyce. "Perhaps—"

A sudden thud made them both jump. The auburn-haired customer bent down to retrieve the book he had dropped. "Your pardon," he muttered, not looking at them. "No damage to it, sir."

"Certainly," said Mr. Allardyce, nodding. He turned back to Miss Allardyce and the grimoire, then clapped himself on the forehead. "Lucca's beard, I nearly forgot! Lorrie!" he called. "Where is that book for your sister?"

Miss Allardyce heard a muffled reply from the back office, ending in something like "counter."

Mr. Allardyce frowned. "Are you sure?" he called back.

Lorrie appeared, wielding a knife with sticky dark cake crumbs stuck to it, and strode to the end of the counter.

"Mother said Melly was coming, remember? I left it out here so we wouldn't forget it. Hold this a moment, please." She handed the knife to the auburn-haired man, who still stood there. He jumped and looked alarmed, but she ignored him as she riffled through the pile of books he had been examining.

"Here!" she said, and pulled out a small one bound in faded blue kid. She handed it to Miss Allardyce with a triumphant flourish, took the knife back with muttered thanks, and strode into the office. A faint "tea in five minutes" drifted down the hallway in her wake.

Miss Allardyce turned the book over. The remains of gilt lettering could just be seen on the spine, but it was impossible to tell now what the title was. Had been. She rubbed them with a finger and they began to glimmer faintly, until she was able to read *Mary Dalzell Herr Booke* in old-fashioned, crooked letters.

Another grimoire! Miss Allardyce had quite a number of them stored in her trunk at the Atherstons'. Sometimes in the evening she would open it and listen to the old spell books rustle and whisper to one another as she carefully wiped their bindings and read a page or two of the queer cramped writing their owners had written in them. This one looked older than most of the others she had, though. She smiled up at her father. "It's lovely!"

"Excuse me," said the man at the counter, who still stared after Lorrie. "I had thought to purchase that book."

Mr. Allardyce bowed again. "My apologies, sir, but it isn't for sale. It should not have been on the counter, but my daughter is young and thoughtless. It was intended for someone."

"But . . ."

"I had meant it as a gift for my elder daughter here, who is a teacher and scholar of no little erudition. You will, I am sure, understand," her father continued with an apologetic smile.

The book quivered in her hand. Even with gloved fingers Miss Allardyce could feel the magic inside it. Had this man felt it too? She looked at him again and saw his eyes were now fixed on her. Though pleasant of appearance, clean-shaven, and well if somberly dressed with a very plain, very white cravat, there was something disquieting about him. With a faint thrill of surprise she realized what it was. His eyes, wide-set and clear, were of different colors: the right one blue, the left brown.

"Is she?" he said softly in his lilting accent.

His gaze never wavered as she stared back at him, and she knew, with complete certainty, that this stranger also had felt the power that resided in the little book because . . . because . . .

The man was a wizard.

"I'll just go help Lorrie with the tea," she said, rising and hurrying down the short passage to her father's office, the book clutched in her hand.

Lorrie was muttering to herself as she set out cups and the plate of Mother's dark spicy cake on the crowded table. Miss Allardyce ignored her and sank into the chair at Father's desk, distressed by her surprise and confusion. They were not emotions she was accustomed to feeling.

How had she not known at once when she walked into the shop that the handsome stranger at the counter was a wizard? Power had fairly radiated from him when she met his eyes just now. Had he kept it cloaked until his surprise made him reveal it? For, just as strongly, she had felt his surprise as he looked at her. He, too, knew what she was.

Miss Allardyce shivered. Who was he? Mother was the acknowledged historian in the family, keeping track of the families in England known to possess magic ability. She might know something of him, if only there were some way to find out his name. . . .

Just then the shop's bell tinkled, and Mr. Allardyce came into the office a moment later. "There. We can hope no one else will come in while we have our tea." He removed a pile of books from a chair, pulled off his gloves, and sat down with a grunt of relief.

"Do you know him?" Miss Allardyce asked before he had even finished seating himself.

"Who, the man who just left? Never seen him in here before. Irish, sounded like. We don't get many Irishmen coming in for books." Mr. Allardyce took the cup Lorrie handed him and poured some tea into his saucer to cool it.

Then Mother would probably not have any idea of who he was;

her knowledge of magically gifted families did not extend past England's shores. "He was a wizard, Father," she said aloud.

"Was he? Hmmph. Lorrie, you cannot leave magic books out on the counter for anyone to pick up. You know that."

Lorrie's lower lip quivered, but she only said, "I'm sorry, sir," and dropped an extra spoonful of sugar into her cup.

Miss Allardyce drank her tea, but she could not eat any of Mother's cake despite it being a favorite of hers. The stranger's eyes had unsettled her. He had looked at her with an interest that had gone first from friendly admiration to speculative intensity, and then—

"It's getting late. I should leave now," she said, and rose abruptly.

Lorrie looked up at her in surprise. "But you've not even touched your cake."

"I know. Wrap it for me and I'll have it tonight. I'll come back in a few days when Mother and Merlin are home, and bring Miss Persephone and Miss Penelope with me next week. They can tell you about their presentation dresses. If I hurry I can catch the omnibus and save walking."

"Are you well, Melusine?" said her father, looking at her with knitted brows.

"Quite well, only running later than I ought. Thank you for the book, Father. I'll come again on Thursday. Will that do?" She kissed them both, retied her bonnet, and hurried back into the shop.

Lorrie came after and helped fasten her cloak. "I'm glad you're back in London," she said, with a frown at the frog fastenings. "It's so dull without you."

"Silly child, I've been gone for years." Miss Allardyce tempered her words with a quick hug.

"I know. But I think I miss you more now that I'm twenty than I did when I was small. I love Mother and Father, and even Merlin when he's not being a prat—"

"Lorrie!"

"—but I don't want to spend the rest of my life dusting books and arranging the windows. I want to . . ."

"What?"

"I don't know!" Lorrie half sobbed.

Miss Allardyce took a deep breath and stifled her impatience. "You know that I'll be leaving the Lelands' employ soon. I already told Father that when I look for a new position, I'd look for something for you as well."

"Like what?" Lorrie's face brightened.

"I don't know yet. Be patient. We'll talk when I come back." She hugged her again.

"Bring that cloak with you when you come," Lorrie called after her as she reached the door. "Those frogs went out of fashion ages ago. I'll rip 'em off and put something a little less medieval on for you."

Miss Allardyce laughed and shook her head, then slipped out the door.

Oxford Street was busier than ever. Tradesmen's wagons, drawn by tired horses, clomped by in the late-afternoon light. Anxious women in sober cloaks and bonnets hurried past with full baskets on their arms, occupied with thoughts of supper. Even a few elegantly dressed women, with servants in tow, ambled by. Street vendors still cried their wares but their voices were hoarse and half-hearted at this hour, their vegetables and flowers wilted.

Miss Allardyce stepped to the outside edge of the passing crowds on the pavement, where fewer dared walk for fear of stepping in something smelly and unpleasant. It was more hazardous, but also faster. Right now all Miss Allardyce wanted was the peace of her small room to mull over the afternoon and the unsettling man in the shop. Why had she been so troubled by him? Why had he looked at her so strangely?

A large horse-drawn omnibus rumbled past. Surely there must be one that she might catch to save her this perilous walk. She had confidently thrown the comment out to keep Lorrie from fussing at her departure, but it had been years since she had lived in London. She paused to take her bearings and realized that she had been walking in the wrong direction. Flustered, she looked around.

Just then a closed carriage, painted a shining dark green, drew up beside her. She looked up in surprise as the door opened.

"May I offer you a ride?" said a polite voice.

Miss Allardyce started. There was a soft lilt in those words that she knew. She stared dumbly as a face appeared in the doorway, a face from which two eyes, one blue and one brown, surveyed her.

"No," she whispered. An impulse to run seized her, but she wasn't sure that her legs could obey it.

"But I insist, Miss Allardyce."

She had not seen a carriage like this outside the bookshop when the strange man was there. Was this elegant equipage really his? Then she became aware that two footmen in discreet livery had jumped down from their perches at the back of the carriage and now stood close behind her. Sudden indignation helped her regain her customary aplomb.

"As I have no idea of your purpose or destination or even your name, I should prefer to walk, if you please," she said, stepping back just enough to tread hard on the toe of one of the tall footmen. She heard him curse under his breath and took advantage of his momentary inattention to try to dodge out of his way.

The other footman lunged and blocked her. She glared up at him and said loudly, "What is the meaning of this? Stand aside or I shall scream."

The odd-eyed man sighed. "Edmund, James, if you please."

Miss Allardyce froze as she felt something hard shoved against her side. She glanced down and saw that it was the barrel of a pistol, held by the footman whose toes she'd trod upon.

"Into the kerridge, please, miss," said the other, taking her arm. "And please, no shoutin'. We don't likes shoutin', we don't." He nodded to his colleague with the gun, who grinned and gave her a shove. She stumbled into the carriage and felt him climb in after her.

The interior of the carriage was as elegant as its exterior, with polished wood fittings and green leather seats, well padded. The man from the shop had politely moved to give her the forward-facing seat.

"You must forgive our, er, insistence. But it is quite vital that you accompany me back to my master at once," he apologized. The footman settled next to him, pistol still pointing at Miss Allardyce as she shrank into the corner of the seat.

"Where are you taking me? I demand an explanation!" she replied. Thank heavens her voice didn't shake too much.

"Do not fear, Miss Allardyce. You will be well looked after. All I am at liberty to communicate to you is that your unusual talents are required right now for an urgent matter at the highest levels in the kingdom," the man said, seeming to choose his words with care.

"My talents? I have no idea what you are speaking of," she prevaricated. A knot began to tie itself somewhere in her midsection, and her hands felt icy inside their neat gloves.

"On the contrary, I think you do. It's not difficult for one who shares it to see that you possess a great deal of talent indeed." The odd-eyed man waved a hand in the air and murmured a word. A fresh sprig of lavender appeared from nowhere in his long fingers. He held it out to her with an almost contrite air.

A whiff of its sharp fresh scent reached her as she stared at it, her mind awhirl. The footman beside him eyed it nervously and moved a cautious inch or so away from him on the seat.

"You see, Miss Allardyce? I am a visitor to London, as you might have guessed. When I have a spare moment I enjoy visiting the booksellers' shops. There was an aura about your family's that drew me immediately—an odor of magic, if you will. I thought perhaps it was from the books until I overheard you and your sister. Her trifle of a spell startled me. She has talent, but it does not have the discipline or depth of your own. I can tell that just by being near you." He smiled down at the flower in his hand.

"You still haven't told me the meaning of this—this—outrage," she stammered.

"No, I realize I haven't. Nor am I permitted to. That is for my master to do." His lip curled slightly, whether in amusement or distaste she could not read. "I don't approve of his methods, and I hope you will forgive me and understand I don't do this of my own free will. I should much rather have made your acquaintance in happier circumstances, for I've never encountered such powerful or elegant magic in anyone outside of my homeland. But I have my orders, and am constrained to follow them. I am as much a captive as you."

"I find that hard to believe," she retorted, looking at the footman with the pistol.

"Do you? Do I look like a rascal who enjoys snatching innocent women off the street? Given my choice, I would be home in Cork tutoring and studying magic myself. But a family debt has forced me here to this great dirty city and this equally dirty task." His wide mouth twisted into a bitter line. "Believe me, Miss Allardyce. My dislike of this situation is as great as yours. Greater, in fact. You are an innocent victim. I am villain and victim both."

"My employer, Lord Atherston, will have something to say about this, I assure you!" she protested. To her horror, the tears she had been blinking back began to leak out, one at a time, as she sat stiff and upright in her seat. But when she reached for her reticule to extract a handkerchief, the footman raised his pistol.

"Really, Edmund. She's not about to turn you into a newt, though I wouldn't blame her if she did." The wizard shook his head in disgust and handed her a square of snow-white linen. Then he produced a notebook from his pocket and made a quick notation in it. "Lord Atherston, you said? Hmm." Raising his voice, he called, "Quickly!" and rapped on the wall above his head.

Miss Allardyce felt the carriage lurch as it plunged into the flow of traffic heading west down the busy street.

Persy awoke, clutching her blankets and breathing hard, and stared from her high bed into the recesses of her room. The setting moon

cast a dim silver light on the half-filled boxes and trunks that stood around, creating weird silhouettes that gave her the shivers despite the fact that she was drenched in sweat. That was the third time tonight that she'd had that dreadful dream, and there was no way she'd be able to get back to—

"Persy!" a voice hissed.

Persy nearly shrieked and dove under her covers. Then she realized who it was. "Pen! You all but killed me," she scolded, emerging from the blankets. "What are you doing in here?"

Pen hurried across the room, barking her shins on an open trunk. "Blast!" she muttered, kicking at it irritably, then flung herself onto Persy's bed. "I couldn't sleep. I keep having this awful dream," she said, huddling under the blankets. Her voice sounded as if she were close to tears.

Persy felt another chill as she put an arm around her sister's shoulders. "What was it?"

"I—I'm in an enormous house, all corridors, and hear Ally calling for me to come and help her before it's too late. I run up and down the passages and try the doors, but they're all locked, and her voice sounds more and more desperate as she calls for me. It's horrible, Perse. There's such an air of menace, a feeling that if I don't find her quickly something dreadful will happen." She swallowed a sob.

A feeling of unreality washed over Persy. "And you can't tell which direction her voice is coming from, either. And it's night, and there aren't any gaslights, only lamps here and there on little tables—"

"Yes! How did you know?" Pen grabbed for her hand.

"Because I've had the same dream three times in a row tonight, and it *is* horrible. What could it mean? You don't think that . . ." Persy's voice trailed into uneasy silence.

"That there's something wrong with Ally? And she's trying to let us know? That's what I am afraid of, if you're having it too. What else could it mean?"

"That maybe we have both been reading too many of Mrs. Radcliffe's gothic novels?" Persy groped for rationality in the face of Pen's dramatic words. "Surely if there was something wrong we would hear from her or somebody at the town house. . . ."

Pen snorted in disgust. "Do you think we're both imagining things, Persy? Is that why we both dreamed the same thing? What if nobody knows there's something wrong, apart from us? All I can say is that I won't be happy until we get to London and see for ourselves that Ally is all right."

4

 everal days later Persy and Pen, noses flattened against the windows of the coach, gazed out at the streets of London. For once Lady Parthenope did not scold them to resume their seats and comport themselves like the adults they nearly were. Instead she smiled at their exclamations and answered their breathless questions with indulgent patience.

"After all, they haven't been in town for years," she said to Papa. "I can still remember arriving in London at the start of my first season."

"And last," he replied, patting her hand and smiling. "You were far too pretty to have had a second season. I was lucky to have got in to speak to your father before anyone else did."

"Piffle. I didn't want anyone else, my dear. I knew at my second assembly at Almack's that you were the catch of the season as far as I was concerned. . . ."

Persy continued to look out at the sights, but her parents' conversation somehow took the zest out of the moment for her. Mama and Papa had married for love, though of course their match had been quite suitable and approved by their families. Somehow she couldn't see herself being so lucky. Not that she'd even have the chance to meet anyone of whom her parents wouldn't approve—that was the whole point of the season. But it seemed impossible that anyone would fall in love with a girl as shy as she was.

Well, Pen would surely find someone perfect within minutes of their first ball and be engaged by June. That would keep Mama occupied until next season, and camouflage the fact that Persy was a complete failure. A picture of a radiant Pen in a beautiful dress and veil, walking down the aisle of a grand London church on the arm of a tall man with hazel eyes and bright gold hair, flashed across Persy's mind. She winced and quickly thought of something else. Fortunately at that moment, the carriage slowed and halted.

"It's not as big as I remember," Charles said, staring out the window next to her. Persy looked over and saw the gray stone façade of their family's London house.

"Of course it isn't. Pen and I were—what, ten, last time we came to town? When we came to see the last king's funeral procession? Which means you were just four," she said.

"I suppose," he agreed gloomily.

Pen laughed at him. "Try not to die of excitement, Chuckles." Then she turned and grinned. "Oh, isn't it exciting, Persy? London!"

But Persy still looked at her brother. His face was white and tired. The coach, though relatively new and well sprung, had still traveled rough on the roads damaged by an unusually severe winter. Charles had not complained much, but Persy could see that the constant jolting had been hard on his injured arm. She and Pen had tried to sit as close as possible to him to help absorb the worst of the ride, but an eleven-year-old boy could take only so much snuggling from his elder sisters. Persy hoped Ally would be able to do something to ease his discomfort.

The footman came round and opened the door for them. As Persy alighted on the brick pavement outside the house, trying to ignore the small crowd of passersby that had gathered to see what new grand family had arrived for the season, the front door of the house opened. Kenney, the town house butler, smiled out at them in as warm and welcoming a manner as his dignity would permit. Persy caught her sister's expression. *Where was Ally?* it asked.

Persy shook her head. "Wait," she silently mouthed.

In the chilly and highly polished front hall, Mama accepted the town staff's greetings calmly as Kenney took their wraps. "The journey was pleasant, thank you, though I think Charles is fatigued. If you could have some tea brought up to the morning room—then I think a little rest for all of us before dinner. Tomorrow will be a busy day, I'm sure. Please ask Miss Allardyce to attend us for tea."

Kenney was already halfway across the room to the bell, but he stopped at Mama's last words. "Oh, my lady. Miss Allardyce is not here."

"Not here?" Persy echoed, with a sinking feeling in her chest. Pen made a hissing sound and seized her arm.

Lady Parthenope glanced at them but did not scold. "Where did she go?"

"I believe she went to visit her family the other day after doing her errands—she told me she'd be stopping to see them. Then at the time I was expecting her back for supper, a boy stopped in with a note, saying it was from her. It wasn't addressed, and I'm afraid I took the liberty of reading it, not knowing what it might contain." He felt in a pocket and produced a piece of paper, which he held out. Persy and Pen hurried to read over their mother's shoulder.

My dear Lady Parthenope,

I must beg your forgiveness and indulgence, but an illness in my family has necessitated that I take a temporary leave from your service. Only the gravest and most sensitive of situations would persuade me to pursue such an action. I do humbly ask your forbearance, and promise to communicate with you as soon as circumstances permit.

> *Your obedient servant,*
> *Melusine Allardyce*

"Well!" said Mama, and handed Lord Atherston the note.

"Where's Ally?" said Charles, his voice plaintive. "My arm hurts."

"There, lamb." Mrs. Huxworthy, the cook, stepped forward and patted his good hand. "Shall I take Mr. Charles down to the kitchen and see if I can't find him something to make his poor arm feel better?" Charles was rather her pet, and she clearly relished the thought of having him to herself without Miss Allardyce's admonishments concerning too-rich treats with his tea.

"May we come too?" asked Pen.

Persy looked at her. Clearly she hoped to question Mrs. Huxworthy. But Lady Parthenope frowned.

"Certainly not, dear. You're too old to take tea in the kitchen. Yes, Mrs. Huxworthy, you may take Charles down. Kenney, was there any other message with this? When did it arrive?"

"No message, my lady. The boy gave the note to the parlormaid and left without even waiting for a tip. It arrived about six on Monday. I had a look down the street for the boy, but he was long gone."

"I see. Tea, then, if you please, and hot water in our rooms after that."

Footmen began to appear with trunks and bundles from the baggage carts, so Mama swept them up the stairs to the morning room, looking vexed.

"I want to see that note," Pen whispered, taking Persy's arm as they followed behind. Persy nodded, too disturbed to reply.

What should they make of this? It was one thing if Ally had left to help take care of her family. But her mother and father were there to handle any family emergency that might arise. And besides, Ally's brother and younger sister were still at home. Why would they need to call Ally away?

In the blue and gold morning room Mama busied herself with taking off her bonnet and slowly removing her gloves, but it was plain to see that she simmered under her deliberate demeanor. She managed to restrain herself until the footman had brought up the tea tray and lit the fire. As soon as he had shut the door behind him, the girls could see her count to ten, to give him time to make it down the corridor to the stairs. Then she exploded.

"Why *now*? Why did whatever relation of hers have to choose this week to go into a decline? Could it be that the influenza epidemic is still about? I *need* Miss Allardyce here. I'm sure the note from the Lord Chamberlain will arrive any moment giving notice of the date for your presentations, and we don't have a stitch of clothing ready for you! I had thought that she would have all the groundwork laid so that we could just go have you measured tomorrow and—"

"Ally measured us before she left, so that Madame Gendreau could get started on our dresses," Pen assured her.

"And what are we supposed to do with Charles? I had assumed she would be able to give him his lessons and help keep him occupied while we were out!" Mama paced around the sofa in agitation.

"Now, dear, I can take him along to the visitors' gallery at Parliament sometimes with Harry or one of the other footmen to keep an eye on him," added Papa. He nodded to Pen to pour tea for her mother. "Miss Allardyce has been the soul of dependability for years. I'm sure she would not do this unless there was some very good reason."

"Pen and I can help with his lessons when we're not busy," Persy said. "And Mrs. Huxworthy in the kitchen can help watch him too."

But Mama did not want to be calmed down just yet. "Mrs. Huxworthy and Harry have enough duties of their own without having to looking after a fractious boy. It's the principle of the thing!"

"Have some tea, my dear," Papa said firmly, catching her in midstride and steering her to the sofa. He handed her the cup Pen had poured. "We're all tired, and perhaps matters won't seem so bad after we've rested. I myself am concerned for Miss Allardyce's family. I trust that her parents have not been taken ill."

"May we see her note, Papa?" asked Pen.

"Hmm? Oh, yes. Here you are." He pulled it from his pocket and handed it to her across the tea table. Persy huddled next to her to read it again.

"It looks like her writing," Pen said under her breath. "See the *L* and the *P*? But messy, as if she had written it in a hurry, or on an uneven surface."

"Or in a moving carriage," Persy added, rubbing the shoulder she had used to brace herself all morning.

Pen stared intently at the piece of paper, as if willing it to speak. "Look!" she said suddenly. "It's been torn across the top. As if someone had torn off a monogram or an engraved name to keep it from giving a clue."

"Or just tore it off the end of her shopping list, if she were in a hurry. What did I say about reading too many gothic novels?" Persy whispered back.

Pen snorted. Her lips moved soundlessly for a moment. Then she sighed. "No secret codes. I tried reading the first letter of each word to see if it spelled something, but it doesn't."

"Oh, Pen. Here, let me see it for a moment." Persy took the note in her hands and closed her eyes. *Feel,* she told herself. *Listen.*

All at once a sensation of panic flooded her, and she gasped out loud. She could feel falsehood and fear emanating from the slip of paper, fear of injury and fear of—of—

"What *is* it?" Pen hissed in her ear.

"Are you all right, child?" asked Lady Parthenope.

Persy looked up and saw her sister and parents were staring at her.

"You made an odd noise," said her father, looking concerned.

"I'm s-sorry," Persy said, floundering. "This note, it—just gave me a—a paper cut, on the tip of my finger. It startled me."

"Gracious, child. If there is a way to have a mishap, you find it, don't you? Wrap your finger in your handkerchief. Don't bleed on your dress," Mama admonished, and went back to venting her indignation to Papa.

Pen still frowned at her. "What was it, really?" she murmured.

"Take the note. Listen to it." Persy shoved it back at her sister with shaking hands and reached for her teacup.

Pen held it and closed her eyes too. After a few seconds she inhaled sharply, though not loudly enough to disturb her parents. "I feel what you mean. Too many gothic novels, hmm?"

"All right, I apologize. I was just playing devil's advocate when I said that, to keep us from seeing things that weren't real."

"Ally's unhappiness when she wrote that was real enough. She knew she was writing lies, and she was terrified while she did it. So why?" Pen whispered, her voice fierce.

"May we be excused, Mama?" said Persy loudly, taking Pen's arm as she rose. "I should like to go wash off my finger, if I may."

"Of course, dear. You remember where your room is?"

"Yes, Mama. Thank you." Persy nodded, pulling Pen behind her.

They found Charles seated on the stairs up to the third floor, less white but still tired-looking. "The Hoaxer sent me up for a rest, but I don't know where my room is," he muttered at their feet.

"Come on. We'll show you. And don't call Mrs. Huxworthy the Hoaxer, Chuckles. It isn't polite," said Persy as she stepped past him.

"But calling Miss Allardyce Ally is?" he challenged.

"It's like us calling you Chuckles. It's a term of endearment."

"Where *is* Ally? I like the Hoaxer well enough but she gets up my nose after a while. She was all right when I was little." Charles stood up.

Persy hesitated, but Pen said, "We don't know where she is. And we don't like it."

"What do you mean?" he asked, sounding less peevish.

"Pen," Persy said in a low, warning voice.

"Why not tell him? It will keep his mind off himself for a bit," she whispered back.

"What? Tell me what?" Charles said anxiously from behind them as they climbed the stairs.

"All right, Chucklehead. But you've got to promise not to tell anyone. Not even Mama and Papa, unless we say you may," said Pen in a mysterious tone.

"I promise!"

"Anyone," echoed Persy.

"I swear on my—on my honor as a gentleman!" Charles said dramatically. He stopped on the stair and placed his uninjured right hand on his heart.

Pen's mouth curved in a grin, but she held her peace. "Good thing it's your left arm that's useless. I suppose we'll have to accept that, Persy?"

"So it seems. Come on." She led them up the rest of the stairs and down the short corridor. "That's your door, there, Charles. We're in here. London houses never have enough bedchambers, so we're sharing."

The fire had already been lit, taking the chill of disuse from the room. Pen motioned her brother into the low slipper chair by the grate and seated herself on the edge of the large curtain-hung bed. Persy sat on a nearby trunk. "We'll have to do the unpacking ourselves, without Ally," she observed.

Pen groaned. "I begin to understand Mama's dismay. What'll we do without her to help us dress for balls? I guess Andrews could help, but she'll be busy getting Mama ready. Mama will have to hire us a maid." She took off her bonnet, unpinned her coiled braids of honey brown hair, and began to brush her cheek absentmindedly with the soft end of one. Persy wa[...]

this childhood habit but didn't ha[...]

"What about Ally?" Charles ne[...]

"Quiet, Charlie-boy." Persy noc[...]

Pen quickly summarized the cor[...]

tions to it. "That just doesn't sound[...]

Charles looked dubious. "No, r[...]

Pen slipped the note from insi[...]

sneaking this out," she said, pulling[...]

novels can have its uses." She hand[...]

"Then you do think s[...]
"I don't know. I h[...]
I felt that note. O[...]
and told us w[...]
fist and f[...]

He read the note, then flattened it between his hands. A look of wonder filled his face. "You're right! I can feel it too!" he said, eyes enormous.

"Don't be silly, Chuckles. You cannot." Pen shook her head and took the note back from him. "Only witches can. So the question is, where is Ally? And why did she go? Did she go on her own, or was she forced?"

"Who could—or *would* force Ally to do anything? She's—she's a governess. It's not like she's a rich heiress who could be kidnapped and held for ransom or anything," objected Persy.

"Did too feel it," Charles muttered.

"Hush. So what do we do? Mama and Papa don't have any reason to question the note. Do we tell them what we know?"

"We don't *know* anything. Besides, if we do that, we'll have to tell them everything else," said Persy slowly. "About the magic tutoring and all. I don't know how they'll feel about that. What if they think magic is evil, and think it good riddance Ally is gone, and forbid us to have anything further to do with her or with magic? Or if they think we're lying? Then there'll be no one to help her."

ne needs helping!" crowed Pen.

d hoped we were being overimaginative until
n, why couldn't she have put a message spell on it
hat was really going on?" Persy leaned her chin on her
owned.

don't think she had time. You saw how rushed and untidy her
riting was. And she didn't put that fear and worry intentionally on
the note—it just absorbed what she was feeling. What do we do?"
Pen swished furiously with her braid.

"Why don't we go to her family's shop and ask if they know
where she is?" asked Charles.

Both sisters stared at him.

"Why not?" he said reasonably. "It would seem to be the first
thing to do."

Pen looked at Persy. "Why didn't we think of that?"

"Because you're too busy worrying." Charles had shaken off his
earlier peevishness and looked alert and happy. "It's obvious you
need a male brain to direct matters here."

"Spare me, Charles, or I might be ill," said Persy sourly. "And it's
not that easy, milord Brain. We can't just traipse down for a visit
there like it was one of the shops back home in the village. This is
London, remember? Pen and I can't go out alone, and pardon me,
but you're not quite old enough to be our chaperone despite your
vastly superior intelligence."

Charles looked sullen again. "Tease me all you like. But I'll bet
I'm the one who figures it all out in the end."

"And we'll be suitably grateful if you are," said Pen. "In the
meanwhile, run along before Mama comes up and explodes again."

5

At breakfast the next morning Lady Parthenope had regained her equanimity and had gone into full Wellington mode, planning the morning's shopping like a battle campaign. "We'll go to Madame Gendreau's first, and see what Miss Allardyce was able to accomplish before her defection," she announced to the girls when they came down. "We'll concentrate on your presentation dresses, since that comes soonest. And perhaps a simple, appropriate dress or two for small evening parties before then. Your presentation dresses will do for the first few balls, but she must have your other ball dresses ready soon after."

"The soonest?" asked Pen.

"Oh, didn't I tell you? No, I suppose I haven't had a chance. I received a note from the Lord Chamberlain this morning. You two will be presented to Her Majesty at a drawing room this Tuesday week."

Persy did some calculating and gulped. "In ten days?" she murmured.

"Indeed," said their mother briskly. "Which means we have a great deal to get accomplished. Eat quickly, girls, so we can arrive at

Madame Gendreau's as soon as possible. I've already rung for the carriage. Ah, Charles, my dear. How are you feeling this morning?"

"Good morning, Mama. Good morning, Papa." Charles sidled into the room, the morning sun shining in the window creating a halo of his untidy curls and making him look like a disreputable cherub. His braces flapped behind him.

"Do you not greet your sisters as well?" said Lady Parthenope, motioning him over and buttoning his suspenders in back. "What shall we do without Ally?" she sighed as she patted his good arm.

Charles circled around the table to where Persy sat. She stared as he took her hand and bowed over it.

"Good morning, sister," he intoned solemnly. Persy started to giggle until she felt a damp piece of paper pressed into her palm.

"Good morning, Chuck," she replied, sliding her hand under her napkin and glancing down at it. A note?

Charles made the same greeting to Pen. While her parents stared at him in bemusement, Persy unfolded his note and read: *Asked the Hoaxer about Ally. Will continue interragashuns.*

Persy managed to maintain a sober expression despite Charles's misspelled and overwrought choice of words. Wait till Pen saw this.

Fortunately for Madame Gendreau, she knew her client well and was prepared when Lady Parthenope swept into her shop like a general entering a subjugated city.

She led them into a fitting room papered in a pale pink moiré that reflected a flattering light onto its occupants. Mama took the small gilded chair offered her, accepted a cup of tea from an assistant, and fixed Madame with a steely eye.

"Ten days, Madame, until their presentations," she announced without preamble.

Madame did not bat an eyelash. "It will not be a difficulty. I think you will be pleased with what your Mademoiselle Allardyce chose for the young misses." She picked up a bell and rang it vigorously. "Now, which of you is 'oo? 'Ow do you tell them apart, my ladee?"

Pen rolled her eyes at Madame's accent. "We'll see how long she keeps it up," she whispered to Persy. "How much do you want to wager she's bellowing at her seamstresses in cockney when no customers are around?"

Persy barely nodded back. She had been silent during the carriage ride, gloved hands clutched together, thinking. Ten days until they made their curtsies to the queen. Ten days while she thought of everything that could possibly go wrong. She could trip over her train in front of the entire court. Or the required three white feathers in her hair could get lost. Or—

"What?" Pen prodded. "You haven't said a word since breakfast. You look like you're marching to your own execution." At a polite gesture from Madame, she took off her shawl and bonnet, and an assistant came around to unhook her bodice at the back. Persy did the same, trying not to let anyone see how her hands shook.

"I am," she murmured at last. "Pen, it's really happening. In ten days' time, I will die either of fright or embarrassment." Her eyes were hot and itchy with unshed tears.

"No you won't." Pen answered so fiercely that their mother paused in her conversation with Madame and looked at them. "You'll be fine. I know it."

"No. You'll have to keep away from me when we start going to parties," Persy whispered back. "I don't want to drag you down and give everyone the impression that both the Misses Leland are dull and awkward."

Pen started to reply, but just then three assistants laden with armfuls of white silk and pastel muslin and multiple fluffy petticoats marched in. Madame Gendreau turned to Pen and Persy. "If we could start with the court dresses, *s'il vous plait,*" she said. It was not a request.

Pen kept up a flow of excited chatter and exclamations to cover her sister's silence during their fitting, for which Persy was extremely grateful: Not even the excitement of their first silk dresses could rouse her from her despondency. The dresses were identical except for differing ribbon colors, with the requisite short sleeves and deep décolletage of presentation dresses, though less deep now at Queen Adelaide's more straitlaced court than would have been decreed at the previous king's.

Persy stared at the fine French carpet on the floor as the assistants mercilessly tightened her and Pen's corsets into the required slenderness. If they tugged any harder, she would surely pop and make a dreadful mess all over Madame Gendreau's pink walls. Either that or faint from lack of breath.

To her relief, neither happened. The assistant slid what seemed like acres of white silk over her head and arranged it around her. Only when Pen gasped "Persy!" did she look up into the mirror.

Her waist looked tiny above the bell of her skirt. The short sleeves were snug in the latest style, and the tighter corsets made her figure look unexpectedly mature. Good heavens, she *would* pop. And she looked like—like a woman. Well, she was one, wasn't she? Mama could have had them come out last year, but Ally had asked to let them wait a year longer so that they could keep studying. If she was nervous now, imagine what *that* would have been like.

She breathed gingerly, trying to find how deeply she could do so and not explode her dress. Wouldn't that be a splendid start to her society career? In her mind she could almost hear Pen sigh and ask, "What would be worse? Worrying about falling out of your gowns, or worrying that you'll rustle because you've had to stuff your corset with tissue paper so you don't look like a board?"

"My girls are grown up, aren't they?" Mama said to Madame. Persy could see that her eyes were unusually bright.

"They shall be the belles of the season, *n'est-ce pas?*" agreed Madame Gendreau, looking at them critically. "The bodice on thees one—take it in a leetle, like thees. . . ."

"Persy, you're—you're beautiful," Pen whispered as they stood side by side before the mirror while the assistants adjusted and basted. "Don't you see it?"

Persy shook her head. "No, I don't. But you are. You *will* be the toast of the town."

Behind them, Madame continued to survey them. She smiled and shook her head. "You are both *très* silly young ladees. Now . . ." She looked at them, head to one side. "Green ribbon for you, *oui?* And peach for you. These dresses will be ready nex' Friday. Will that do? 'As Mademoiselle Allardyce found you yet slippers and—"

"Miss Allardyce was called away unexpectedly, and has been unable to complete selection of those items. I hope to take care of them today." It was a measure of Mama's irritation with Ally that she had interrupted Madame. "Purchasing fans and gloves will be a simple matter. But I worry about their headdresses, with so little time."

Madame puffed her cheeks out and gestured to her assistants to help the girls out of their dresses. "A pitee, *oui*. Mademoiselle Allardyce—her taste was *très bon. Mais,* I can send you to a friend, but she is *très* busee, and I cannot guarantee that she will 'ave time. . . ." She shrugged elaborately.

Pen and Persy tried on several more dresses each, and Persy could not help but marvel at what Ally had been able to accomplish in such a short time before her disappearance. Mama approved all of them with minor modifications, and when keen-eyed Madame suggested that they take time now to order the first of the girls' ball dresses, Mama genially agreed, and even accepted another cup of tea.

Under cover of the entrance of the tea, Persy sidled over to Madame. It was time to risk a small interrogation spell to see what she could find out. "Excuse me," she murmured.

"Yes, *ma chère?*" Madame Gendreau looked up from her pattern book, already partway through a dress sketch.

"When Miss Allardyce was here to order our dresses, did she— did she say where else she was going?" Persy fixed her eyes on Madame's brown, slightly bleary ones and murmured *"Veritas mihi"* under her breath.

Madame blinked at her for a moment, then sniffed and patted her cap. "I do not 'ave the time to gossip with my clients—"

"Oh, not gossip!" Persy assured her. "I just wondered, you know, if maybe she said she was going to the milliner's." *Veritas mihi . . . veritas . . .*

The slight bristle in Madame's demeanor slowly smoothed as the spell rippled over her. "Let me see . . . it was afternoon when she came. . . ." She paused and delicately nibbled the end of her pencil. "Ah, *mais oui*. She was going next to her 'ome. I was surprised to 'ear that 'er familee was in trade, she seem such a refine' person. But they are booksellers, in Oxford Street, *non*? It would be where she gets 'er knowledge to be a fine teacher for you." She nodded sagely. "She did not go to the milliner's, then. But I tell you 'oo to see for your bonnets, to my colleague who makes the nicest—"

"Oh, thank you! Er, that is, I'm sure my mother will be happy to patronize your milliner friend." Persy glanced at Pen, who nodded slightly. Oxford Street. At least they knew where to start their search.

By the time they left Madame Gendreau's, Persy had begun to feel better. The excitement of ordering half a dozen new dresses in silk and other luxurious and grown-up fabrics couldn't help but raise anyone's spirits. At least, that was, until she thought again about why they were buying them.

Their next stop was just a few doors down from Madame's, for kid evening gloves and silk stockings and pairs of ready-made black satin slippers with the new elastic bands for evening. Lady Parthenope also bought them Chinese silk crepe shawls with deep fringes, and Chantilly lace ones, and beautifully embroidered Indian cashmere ones for chilly evenings. Then there were delicate reticules, beaded and smocked, and beautiful if impractical lace handkerchiefs, plain stockings in palest pink and blue and embroidered white ones, and yards of ribbon and lace.

By the time they were driving home for a late luncheon, both girls were chattering about the piles of packages heaped in the carriage, for Pen had insisted they take them now rather than having them delivered. Mama smiled at their excited prattle.

"Not a bad start to our preparations," she agreed, then winced as the carriage wheels bumped over refuse in the road. "But remind me not to drink so much tea at our first stop next time."

"Yes, Mama," Pen replied, smothering a grin. "Did you say 'not a bad start'? Will there be more?"

"Oh, yes. I just wanted to get done what you would need first. In a few days we'll return to Madame's to order the rest of your dresses. Once your presentations are past, we'll need more ball and party dresses."

Persy sighed and wilted once again at the mention of their presentation.

The next morning dawned clear and warm. Finished with his yearly springtime course of nature readings from the classics, Papa had decided that a pleasant ride in the country was just what he needed. Mama gently reminded him that as they were in London, rural pleasures would have to wait, but if he still wanted a breath of air and exercise . . .

And that was how Persy, eyes agog as London high society paraded around them, found herself and Pen trotting behind Papa in Hyde Park on their hired horses from John Tilbury's Mount Street stables.

Even here in the city, it was easy to sense that spring was well underway. A smell of damp earth was pervasive, not musty or moldering but rich with the promise of new life. The trees were all clothed in the delicate greens of spring, their new leaves fluttering in the slight breeze. Fluttering, too, in the soft springtime wind were the veils that trailed like wisps of smoke from the top hats of the fashionable ladies riding sedately up and down the sanded path in their snug habits, nodding and smiling to their male acquaintances and appraising with narrowed eyes their female rivals.

Despite these distractions, however, Persy and Pen were still carrying on an argument left from the night before, albeit quietly, as they followed their father.

"Mama will never let us go to the Allardyces' shop alone," Persy insisted. "Nor would we want her to go there with us. I say we send a note. Ooh, look at that lady's mount! What a lovely gray."

"Probably an ex–carriage horse. You should have seen that brown I pointed out before. Anyway, a note saying what? 'We were wondering if Ally really is undertaking family duties, or if she's lying and is off somewhere else'? Come on, Persy. How will that sound? And what if she really is in trouble? Her family will be frantic. Furthermore, I don't like to make them pay the threepenny postage if we send them a note. It wouldn't be fair," Pen finished virtuously.

Persy hated it when Pen was so self-righteously right. "I still don't know how you think we'd be allowed to go shopping in Oxford Street on our own. If only Charles were our elder brother, not our younger. I rather like that lady's habit—the deep green one, there. I've never seen one in that color."

"Mama would hate it, so don't ask her for one. She thinks black is the only proper color for a riding habit. My goodness, Papa, who's that?" Pen nodded toward a knot of wild-looking young men in very dashing coats and no hats, their shaggy locks flowing in the breeze. One in the center had dark flashing eyes and a fascinating air of danger about him.

Lord Atherston peered over at the crowd. "Goodness me. I do believe that's the Duke of Brunswick. The one in the center, with the large mustaches and dark hair. He was banished from his own duchy—his brother rules it now—and . . . well, one hears gossip." He shook his head.

Pen's eyes grew round as she stared at the group. "Might we ride a little nearer? I've never seen an exiled duke before."

Persy looked too, but it wasn't the disreputable duke that caught her attention. She drew her horse closer to Pen's. "He's not stuffed and mounted for display, goose. And he can't be very nice if he got kicked out of his own country. Never mind him, and look who's coming from over there."

Pen's cheeks turned pink and her eyes brightened. "Papa," she said, "that's Lochinvar Seton! Not far off from the diabolical duke. What good eyes you have, Persy."

Lord Atherston stopped his horse and looked around. "Where? Oh, yes, so it is. I say, my boy," he called and waved his crop. Persy saw Lochinvar lift his hat and wave it before spurring his horse toward them.

Pen gazed at him, the duke forgotten. "That's a lovely horse he's riding. I'll bet it didn't come from Tilbury's. However did you know it was him from so far away?"

Because, Persy thought. She didn't dare complete the sentence, even in her own mind. She took a deep calming breath, grateful that she was on horseback, where it was usually much harder to trip over one's own feet.

"Good morning, Lord Atherston!" Lochinvar called as he approached, hat still off. The sun glinted in his gold hair. "Father said he'd got your card, and that we must visit now that you were up in town. But I'm glad I don't have to wait. Good morning, Miss Leland.

Good morning, Miss Leland." His eyes twinkled as he bowed to each of them.

Pen laughed too. "You make it sound like there's just one Miss Leland who's hard of hearing. But I suppose we'll have to get used to it. And it relieves you of the necessity of guessing who is whom."

"Oh, I always know that," he said, smiling down at the reins held in one gloved hand.

Of course he did. Pen was the pretty, lively one. Persy looked sideways at her sister, and saw Pen look back at her with an odd expression. But before she had time to do much more than register it, it had gone.

There was a moment's silence as they began to walk their mounts again, Lochinvar turning his horse to walk with them. Persy's horse stumbled, and she groaned inwardly. It just figured. She couldn't trip over her own feet while riding, so her horse did it for her. She was not sure if she was grateful or dismayed that Lochinvar was on Pen's other side.

Then, mercifully, Pen spoke. "That is a very handsome horse, Lord Seton. His paces are quite fine."

"Thank you. He was a welcome-home gift from Father, waiting when we arrived in town. I'm still getting used to him, but I think he shall suit quite well as his manners are excellent. Perhaps you might have some suggestions for what I should call him."

Pen eyed the large bay next to her. "It will have to be something fitting for such a stately animal."

"I thought something from the classics would do. Pegasus, or Bucephalus, or something like that?" he suggested.

"Everyone's got a horse named Pegasus. He deserves better."

Persy surprised herself by speaking her thought aloud, then could have bitten her tongue in two at her dismissive tone. How rude had she seemed? Charles had insisted on naming his first pony Pegasus the Magnificent, much to their disgust.

"I should hate to name him anything dull and common. I always feel I should tip my hat to him when I enter the stable, he's such a polite beast," Lochinvar confessed.

"Then you must call him after Lord Chesterfield, if that is the case," said Persy, and blushed at her own daring.

"Of course!" Lochinvar's grin flashed at Persy. It made her feel dizzy. "That's the perfect name for him. Father will love it. He made me read Lord Chesterfield's letters when I was a boy. Chesterfield." He patted the bay's neck. "How do you like that, then? You must thank Miss Persy for naming you. I knew she'd do it. Thank you," he added, leaning forward to catch her eye.

"Oh." She waved a hand. Her horse flicked its ears nervously. "Anyone could have thought of it."

Papa drew up and consulted his watch. "We are expected home shortly, as I know your mother has another full day planned. Can we count on you stopping in for a visit, Seton?"

Lochinvar bowed in his saddle. "I would be delighted, sir. Chesterfield and I will call tomorrow, if we may." He touched his hat to them and trotted away.

"Handsome beast," commented Papa.

"Oh, yes," Pen said wistfully. "Isn't he?"

Persy sighed in agreement. But she wasn't thinking about the horse. Was Pen? She put aside that thought and tried to concentrate on the day's coming shopping. Even the prospect of delicately tinted kid slippers and French lace scarves couldn't dispel the gloom she suddenly felt. What good would beautiful clothes be to a tongue-tied bookworm like her?

Her father's voice broke into her thoughts. "Young Lochinvar's turned out well, despite everything," he said, almost to himself.

"Despite what?" Pen demanded. "Why shouldn't he turn out well?"

Lord Atherston shifted nervously in the saddle, making his horse shy. He patted its neck, and took rather longer than was necessary to soothe it before he continued. "Well, losing his mother at such a young age. I remember how very close he was to her, and how devastated he was when she died under such strange circumstances—"

"Strange how? I thought she died in childbi—I mean, after being confined?" Persy interrupted him.

Fortunately, Papa was less strict than Mama about proper gentility of phrasing. But he looked uncomfortable as he turned to her. "Er, well . . . I don't think I really ought to say—"

"Oh, Papa, you *have* to tell us now. You can't just leave us hanging," Pen wheedled. "What circumstances?"

Their father sighed and looked about them for potential eavesdroppers before he spoke. "Please don't tell your mother I told you this. But if you're to be seeing more of Lochinvar, you probably ought to know about it. Some people say—not I, or any rational person—but some people say that Lady Northgalis was killed by"—he glanced around them again—"by a witch's curse."

Persy felt her jaw drop. She closed her mouth and glanced over at Pen, who drew her horse alongside. "A witch?" she said, with a weak little laugh. "But that's ridiculous. There's no such thing as witches and magic."

"As I said, no rational person lends any credence to such non-sense. But the story went around that she dismissed a new house-keeper because she caught her performing some type of heathen ritual, and the woman cursed her with death within the year. When she died in childbed just a few months later along with her infant, the story spread like wildfire."

Persy was silent as they trotted back toward the park gate. Death curses were not only extremely difficult and time-consuming to do, but also required enormous amounts of power and training. It was most unlikely that a humble housekeeper would have had either. And childbirth was such a hazardous event for women. Poor Lady Northgalis hadn't needed a curse to kill her.

But a six-year-old Lochinvar wouldn't have understood that. He would have heard the breathless gossip of the maids and the other staff around him, and heard that his beloved mama had been killed by a witch. He must find the very mention of magic and witches abhorrent.

And if he held the idea of magic in such horror because of his mother's death . . . then he must never, *never* learn about her and Pen's abilities. Not that it made any difference for *her*. Lochinvar still saw her as the girl with her nose in a book. That was clear from the Lord Chesterfield discussion. But for Pen's sake . . . he would surely be interested in Pen, once they started attending social events—

"Persy, why are you squirming in your saddle like that? You nearly spooked my horse," complained Pen.

$\mathscr{L}$ochinvar called promptly at four the next afternoon.

Persy and Pen were helping Charles with his geography lesson, working with the globe and a folio of maps at a table set by his bedroom window, which provided excellent light and which just happened to overlook the front door. Persy blessed the inattentiveness of eleven-year-old boys to the nuances of female dress, so that he didn't notice their best day dresses and new lace berthas under their everyday aprons.

Persy was just going over the principal exports of the islands of the Caribbean Sea with him when Pen, lounging on the windowsill, sat up and cleared her throat. Persy looked at her, and she nodded.

"All right, Chuckles. I think that's enough. Shall we continue tomorrow?" she asked brightly, closing the folio and gathering pencils. Pen was already at the door, untying her apron.

However, Charles was more observant than she'd given him credit for. "Why?" he demanded. "You kept me at it till half-past yesterday. What are you two going to do now?" He squinted at Pen. "Why's she taking her apron off?"

Pen flushed. "Never you mind, Chu—"

The front door knocker sounded. Charles grinned.

"I know!" he crowed. "Someone's come to call for you, then. You were watching out the window, Pen, weren't you? Is it your beau? Does Mama know? Pen has a beau, Pen has a—"

"Stop it, Charles!" Persy snapped. "She has no such thing. You're being rude and unkind, and if you like you shall stay up here and write me out today's lesson while we have tea with Lochinvar."

"Is that who your beau is?" he asked, eyes innocently wide.

"Charles!" gasped Pen.

Without thinking, Persy reached over and yanked Charles by the earlobe. He howled in protest.

"How dare you!" she said through gritted teeth. "Pen and I are about to enter society as grown women. I think it is about time you started treating us with the respect due to your elders, even if we are only sisters. Now, apologize." She stood over him, feeling tall and intimidating.

The teasing light in Charles's eyes faded. He looked down at his shoes for a moment, then back up at her. "You're right," he mumbled. "I shouldn't speak like that to you. I'm sorry."

Persy stared at him and felt a sense of shame creep over her. Yes, she had been angry at Charles's childish chanting, and it *was* time for him to treat them with more respect. But what had made her angriest of all was his joking insinuation that Lochinvar was calling just to see Pen.

Well, why shouldn't he? Pen could actually talk to him like a sane and pleasant human being and not get tongue-tied and abrupt like she did. She cringed slightly as she thought about their conversation while riding yesterday. Pen had tried to assure her that she hadn't been rude when she vetoed his name choices—well, at least not very rude. But Pen was too loyal to ever say otherwise. Persy sighed and looked at her brother.

"Apology accepted. And I'm sorry, too. I should not have snapped at you like that," she said, holding out her hand to him. "Will you come down and have tea with us, if Mama allows it?"

"Could I? Thanks! Do you think Loch—Lord Seton will show me his horse? He sounds a right stunner," said Charles, almost dancing toward the door. Then he stopped and turned back to Persy. "You don't need to do anything, Perse. You look very nice just the way you are."

Persy followed him and Pen down the stairs, surreptitiously blinking back tears. Brothers. Just when you were ready to drown them, they said things like that to you.

Lord Northgalis had come with Lochinvar, and was already ensconced next to Mama on one sofa. Charles planted himself on the other sofa, next to Lochinvar. "Tell me about your horse," he demanded.

"Charles?" said Pen sweetly.

Charles thought hard for a moment. "Please?" he added, with an ingratiating smile.

Lochinvar smiled back. "Lord Chesterfield—or his equine namesake, rather—and Father both approved of your choice of name, by the way. They thought it perfect."

Persy sat down next to Charles and murmured "Thank you" at her lap.

"Anyway, Father bred him on the estate the year I left for Cambridge, intending him for me. If he had known he'd turn out so well, he probably would have kept him." He grinned at his father.

"Hah. If your riding hadn't improved so much of late, I might have." Lord Northgalis caught his words and laughed back at him. "Capital name for him, Persephone. Couldn't have thought of one better. You'll have to come round next year and name all the spring crop of foals for us."

"Father's interested in raising horses," Lochinvar told them. "He's brought some over from France and Hanover, and hired a man from Newmarket to oversee their training. He wants to have a winner at Epsom by forty-two."

Charles looked ecstatic. "Why can't Papa do that too? I'd help train 'em. Horses like me."

"Is that why Pegasus the Magnificent took a bite out of your ear that time?" Pen murmured.

"I was only six. And he was shockingly underbred," Charles informed her, tossing his curls impatiently. "Not like Lochinvar—er, Lord Seton's horses."

"I don't like to disappoint you, Charles, but I don't have anything to do with the horses. Right now I'm more interested in schools."

Charles looked disgusted.

"Schools?" said Persy, sitting a little straighter.

Lochinvar leaned around Charles to look at her. "The schoolhouse on the estate lost its roof over the winter—all the thatch was just picked up and blown away in one of the storms, Father said. I went to watch it being reroofed when I got back, and met the schoolmaster. He's got some unusual ideas on education, and I told him about a school I had seen on my tour in Germany, called a *Kindergarten*. He lent me a book by a Swiss teacher named Pestalozzi, and he wants to order the school along the precepts set out by him. I said I'd send along whatever supplies he needed from

London. Oh, and I must find a bookshop—there's a book by an Englishman about Pestalozzian schools he suggested I read."

"A bookshop?" Pen looked at Persy and raised her eyebrows. "As a matter of fact," she continued slowly, "we do know of a bookshop that comes highly recommended. Allardyce's, on Oxford Street."

Schools? He was interested in schools? Persy gave herself a mental shake. Had she heard him correctly?

Lochinvar felt in his pocket and pulled out a memorandum book. "Allardyce's?" he said, staring at the name after he had written it in his book. "As in your governess? Does it belong to her family?"

"Yes. We're rather interested in visiting it ourselves," Pen continued nonchalantly.

"Then couldn't she bring you there? Could I accompany you when you go?" Lochinvar looked pleased.

"Well, er—" Persy started.

"She can't," Pen said boldly, with another glance at Persy. "She's gone."

Lochinvar frowned. "Gone?"

"Yes. She left a note for us when we arrived that she'd been called away on family business. But we're not sure we believe it," she added in a rush.

"The note was scary," Charles declaimed. "You could feel it—she was completely *horripilated* when she wrote it—"

"Charles," Persy warned as she glanced at Mama and Lord Northgalis, but they were deep in their own conversation.

"And we're not sure if we should be worried or not, and we thought that if we could only go visit her father's shop, maybe we could find out if she's really all right or not . . . ," Pen continued, all in one breath.

"What if she's been kidnapped by Turks?" Charles whispered, looking around the room as if he expected a turbaned figure waving a scimitar to appear from behind his mother's sofa.

"What?" Lochinvar held up one hand and turned to Persy. "Turks? Could we start this again, please? What has Miss Allardyce got to do with the Turks?"

"Hush, Charles! Let me tell it," Persy commanded, but gently. Was it wise to take Lochinvar into their confidence, when they didn't even know if there was truly anything wrong? But it was too late now. She turned to Lochinvar, took a deep breath, and hoped she wouldn't sound too silly. If there were some way he could help . . . "Maybe we're just being foolish. But as Pen said, we were quite surprised that Ally wasn't here when we arrived in town. She left a note of explanation, but it—it somehow didn't sound right. Something quite dreadful had to have happened in order to make her just—disappear like she did. She's never been in the least irresponsible or flighty. The three of us wonder if she isn't in some difficulty."

"With the Turks? In London?" Lochinvar's mouth twitched.

"No, that's just Charles being dramatic," Pen put in. "It's a little hard to explain. But we would dearly like to visit her family's shop and make sure that she really is taking care of a sick relative."

"And if she isn't?"

Persy took a deep breath. "Then we must find her."

"We've been trying to think of a way to convince Mama to let us go to the shop without telling her why," Pen said into the silence under the murmur of their parents' conversation.

"Why shouldn't she know?" he asked. "Haven't you told her that you're concerned about Miss Allardyce?"

"Of course they haven't!" said Charles. "Then they'd have to tell her that they're wi—"

"—without any good reason for our suspicions," Persy interjected, stepping hard on Charles's foot under cover of her skirt. "She'll think we're being silly and childish, and anyway she's too wrapped up with our presentation at court to think of anything else."

Charles withdrew his foot from under Persy's and went to sit in the window seat nearby, where he stared out at the street and pretended to ignore them. Persy felt a little remorseful for shushing him so abruptly, but considering Papa's tale yesterday about the rumored cause of Lady Seton's death, Lochinvar was the last person who should know their secret. What would he say if she decided to make his hat, set on the floor by him, start dancing a jig? She could just picture the look of distaste that would have crossed his face if Charles had been allowed to finish his sentence. If Lochinvar found her unattractive now, how much more so would he if he knew about her powers?

Lochinvar's voice cut through her reverie. "Do you think your mother would let you go if we all went together? I do want to find that book I told you about. And after all, we'd be with your governess's family in a public place."

"Oh!" Pen clapped her hands. "That would be perfect!"

"Me too?" said Charles from the window seat. Clearly his wounded pride had not prevented him from listening closely to their conversation.

"Indeed, Master Charles. You must come along to chaperone your sisters," Lochinvar replied crisply.

"Oh, *really*," groaned Pen.

But Persy saw the hint of a smile in the corners of Lochinvar's eyes when he spoke, as well as the dawning hero worship in Charles's as he stared open-mouthed at Lochinvar. Charles probably had never considered the idea that he might ever have any abilities that his sisters did not. But recalling that he was, after all, their brother, and bound to protect them even if they were witches, it would ensure Charles's good behavior and more important, his silence. She smiled to herself at Lochinvar's cleverness.

In the end, it turned out to be easier than they had expected to convince their mother to let them visit the Allardyces. Pen was elected as spokesman, and she made their request shortly before the Setons took their leave.

"Well," Mama said slowly, "I suppose I could bring you there and take care of a few calls while you have your visit. If Miss Allardyce is there, you can find out how long she expects to be away and refresh her memory of her duty to you at this important time." The thought seemed to please her. "And we could stop at the milliner's on the way and see if your hats are done."

Lochinvar's smile became slightly strained at mention of the milliner's, but he bowed and said, "It will be a pleasure, ma'am."

They all accompanied Lord Northgalis and Lochinvar to the door on their departure. The girls stood with their mother and made their bows, but Charles wriggled around them and stuck his head out the front door.

"Oh, I say, you came in a carriage," he said in a disappointed voice to Lochinvar, after a good look up and down the street. "I was hoping to see Lord Chesterfield. Will you come again soon and bring him?"

"Will tomorrow do?" Lochinvar asked, while Mama frowned ferociously at her son.

"Rather!" Charles looked transported.

After the door had closed behind their guests, Lady Parthenope gave vent to her displeasure. "Really, Charles. I would expect a little more sense of decorum than thrusting your head out the front door like that. Pray in future refrain from such childishness."

"Yes, ma'am," Charles replied, hanging his head. But his eyes swiveled toward his sisters in an unmistakable wink. As soon as their mother had swept up the stairs, they pounced.

"What was that all about, Chuckles?" demanded Pen, taking his good arm and steering him into one of the empty reception rooms, where they could be sure of being at least momentarily undisturbed.

Charles shrugged and walked up to the fireplace, where he began making absurd faces at himself in the large pier glass that hung over the chimneypiece. "Nothing you need to know," he replied paternally. "He said I was to protect you, and I don't want you worrying yourselves."

"Worrying ourselves about what? That you've contracted a sudden incurable dementia? What was the winking about? Did it have anything to do with that folderol about wanting to see Lochinvar's horse?" Pen joined him at the mirror and made a threatening face over his head.

"Lord Seton," he reminded her. "And yes, it did. I thought it worth risking a scold from Mama to have a better look at the man who's been watching the house, as she won't let me out there on my own till my arm's healed."

"What?" Persy turned him to face her. "What man?"

"Oh, didn't you know? I spotted him the other day. I thought that was why you were so interested in looking out my window today before Lord Seton came. He's been there three or four days, lounging against the lamppost. Sometimes he wanders up and down the street a bit, and he's worn different clothes every day, like he's trying not to be recognized. The glass in my window is a little wavy, and I wanted to have a better look at him as he was right across the street when I was looking out the drawing room window just now. So I pretended to be looking for Lord Chesterfield. I thought it was a good plan," he said, looking smug.

Pen looked at Persy. "Do we believe him? Why should anyone be watching our house?"

Their brother scowled. "Fine! Don't believe me! Of course I'm making it up, because I'm so bored I'm seeing things. Maybe you aren't concerned about strangers staring at our house, but I am. It's up to me to keep my eye on you, remember?" He stalked out of the room. They heard the door down to the kitchens slam.

"Off to drown his sorrows in jam tarts." Pen laughed nervously. Persy shook her head. Was their house really being watched? And if so, by whom?

The next day, Persy and Pen waited anxiously as Mama stared from the carriage window at the front façade of the Allardyces' shop on Oxford Street.

"It looks respectable enough. Of course, it couldn't be otherwise, if Miss Allardyce's family own it," she said, half to herself. "Mr. and Mrs. Allardyce are quiet, well-mannered people." She sat up with a little shake. "Very well, children. I shall escort you in and be back in an hour's time. That will allow me to get two or three calls in quite handily." She rapped on the door, and the footman appeared.

When Lochinvar opened the shop door for them, Mr. Allardyce was seated behind the counter, marking prices on slips of paper and tucking them into books. A petite girl of about their own age, with a feather duster tucked into the back of her waistband so that she looked like an exotic and peculiar species of bird, arranged the books Mr. Allardyce had finished pricing. A shiny bell hanging from the door announced them.

Mr. Allardyce looked up at their entrance and stared for a brief second. Then he rose with a beaming smile, which, however, seemed to Persy to fade as he surveyed them.

"My goodness! Can it really be? Is it the Misses Leland? Though last I saw they were still just pretty little girls in short dresses. Oh, Lady Atherston, your pardon. These handsome young ladies rather flustered me." He came around the corner and bowed to them.

"How good to see you again, Mr. Allardyce," said Mama with a gracious nod. Her new visiting bonnet tottered alarmingly. "We were in the neighborhood, and the girls wished to stop by." She introduced Lochinvar and Charles, smiled when Mr. Allardyce pre-sented the girl with the duster as his youngest daughter, Lorelei, then turned back to Pen and Persy.

"Don't spend all your pocket money, Persy. Pray send my regards to Miss Allardyce, if you will. I hope we can count on her rapid return to us," she said with another nod to Mr. Allardyce before sweeping out again.

Mr. Allardyce frowned after her, the shop bell still tingling in her wake. "Her rapid what?" he said, more to himself than to them.

Pen stared significantly at Persy. Deflated, she nodded back.

"Excuse us, Mr. Allardyce," she began politely.

"Eh? I beg your pardon, but I'm not sure I understand what her ladyship said. It is an honor to have you visit, but, ah . . . isn't my daughter with you? She stopped in a week or so ago and promised to come back in a few days and bring you along for a visit. We haven't heard from her since then, but we assumed she was occupied with her duties. Is she ill?" He looked worried. The petite girl, openly listening, came to stand by her father.

"I think we need to discuss something with you, sir," said Persy.

Mr. Allardyce looked at their sober expressions and said a few quiet words to Lorelei. She nodded and moved into the back of the shop, reemerging with a straight chair. Lochinvar sprang forward to take it from her, then at her behest carried out two more.

Mr. Allardyce put up the CLOSED sign in the window, then took a long pole and rapped smartly on the ceiling. A brief rap answered him, and a moment later, footsteps descending stairs could be heard. A brisk, handsome woman with Ally's straight posture, luxuriant dark hair, and long nose came from the back of the shop, stopped in the doorway, and stared before breaking into a wide smile.

"Miss Persephone! Miss Penelope! How wonderful!" She looked beyond them, and her smile faded. "But where is . . . ?"

"We'd hoped you could tell us," Persy said gently. "We expected to find Miss Allardyce here, because we haven't seen her since we came to town."

Lochinvar discreetly moved to browse on the other side of the shop while Pen and Persy told their story to the shocked Allardyces. When Persy told of their dreams, Mrs. Allardyce turned very pale, and Lorelei red. Mr. Allardyce remained silent, only opening his mouth to ask to examine Ally's note. He too held it between his hands for a moment, then pressed his lips together.

"She's either run away or been kidnapped, and running away doesn't seem to answer what we know. Why else the horrible feelings in the note and the dreams?" Pen said in conclusion.

Mr. Allardyce frowned. "But who? And why kidnap an ordinary governess?"

"But she isn't ordinary, is she?" said Charles into the silence. Across the room Persy saw Lochinvar look up at them from the book he'd been examining.

Mr. Allardyce looked uneasily at Charles, then at the girls.

"It's all right," Persy reassured him. "Charles knows. He sits in on our lessons when he's at home. *All* our lessons. Ally—er, Miss Allardyce always permits him."

"'Ally'?" Lorelei giggled.

"But who besides you and us knows that there is anything out of the ordinary about her? And why would it matter?" Mr. Allardyce asked.

"That man knew. Remember, Father? The man in the shop that day when she came for a visit? The one with the Irish accent?" Lorelei prodded him. "He wanted to buy that old grimoire you were saving for her that I got mixed up with the other books. He kept looking at us and trying to listen to what we were saying. I thought I'd scare him off by shoving the cake knife at him, but it didn't work."

"Don't be silly, Lorrie," said Mrs. Allardyce firmly.

"But Melly said she thought he was a wizard! So why shouldn't—"

"Hush, Lorelei!" Mr. Allardyce interrupted. "Have you tried to do anything to contact her?"

"No," said Pen. "It's why we're here. We weren't sure that she might not really be taking care of a sick relative, after all."

"I have," Persy volunteered, in a low voice. "Tried to find her, that is."

Pen stared at her. "You have? Why didn't you tell me?"

"What method did you use, Miss Leland?" asked Mr. Allardyce.

"Scrying, in my washbowl. It, er, didn't show me much. Ally hadn't gone much into it with us yet."

Lorrie looked impressed. "You really can do magic? I thought that girls like you were just empty-head—" She flushed and sat back in her chair.

"That's enough out of you, miss," admonished her mother. She looked pale but determined. "John, this is more in your line. Why don't you see what you can find with the maps? Lorrie, some refreshments, if you please. And—" She glanced toward Lochinvar, back studiously to them. "Do you want him as well?"

Mr. Allardyce turned to the girls. "What my wife is suggesting is that I try to locate Melusine with a map-dowsing spell. Have you ever seen one?"

"No," said Persy, interested. "Ally's mentioned them, but we've not tried them. She wanted us to perfect our mental technique before we moved to manipulating with the physical."

"A good approach," he approved. "You should be able to control and utilize your own internal power before learning to use externals. Is milord Seton, ah, acquainted with your abilities?"

"No!" Persy replied urgently. "He doesn't know anything about it. He knows we're worried about Ally, but he accompanied us as a favor and to find a certain book. If maybe Mrs. Allardyce . . ."

"I'll keep him occupied for as long as you need. Go on. I'll manage." Mrs. Allardyce nodded at them, then moved toward Lochinvar with a bright smile.

The small back office looked more like Persy's memories of her previous visit to the shop, with piles of books stacked round the room. Mr. Allardyce set out two chairs for them, cleared several stacks and numerous sheaves of paper from the center table, then sorted through a pile of rolled parchment until he grunted in satisfaction and pulled one out. He unrolled it on the table, holding it down at the corners with books, and Persy saw that it was a map of England.

Next Mr. Allardyce rummaged in a drawer of his desk and pulled out a turned-brass plumb bob hanging from a short length of chain, and a long brass ruler. He stood over the table a moment, eyes closed, the pendulum hanging loosely between the thumb and forefinger of his right hand.

"Very well," he said, opening his eyes again. "This is what is known as map dowsing. I am going to move the ruler very slowly over the map while holding the pendulum above it, and ask the pendulum to indicate when it passes over where she is. We'll draw a line, and do it again from the other axis to find a point. Then we will change maps again, until we can locate her quite precisely. Do you understand?"

Pen nodded, eyes wide, and looked expectantly at the pendulum as Mr. Allardyce slowly began to slide the ruler over the map. When the brass weight began to circle counterclockwise frantically, he set it down and drew a faint line along the length of the ruler. The line ran directly through London.

So did the next. Mr. Allardyce looked both relieved and concerned at this turn of events. "It means she can't be far, which is reassuring. But there are a great many places in London where she might be," he said, riffling through the rolled maps until he came to the one of London.

Persy felt Charles's hand grip hers as Mr. Allardyce began to draw the ruler slowly across the closely printed page, first one way and then the other. Charles's palm was sweaty, but he looked more excited than she had seen him since before his accident.

"There," Mr. Allardyce said as he drew the second line. They all leaned forward to stare at the structure on the map, set in its frame of green, at the point created by the two lines. Persy looked up at her sister, knowing that Pen's face must be reflecting her own surprise, but Mr. Allardyce only looked more puzzled.

"Kensington Palace?" said Charles aloud. "Ally's at Kensington Palace?"

Lorrie came down the stairs then, holding a tray of wine biscuits and a decanter of deep red liquid. "Mother's strawberry cordial, from last year. It came out rather well, I thought." She paused and leaned over the map. "Done already? But what could she be doing at Kensington Palace? Are you sure, Father?"

"As sure as I ever am." He stared down at it. "Kensington Palace is out of my ability to investigate, I'm afraid. Is there any way you two might have reason to go there?"

"Us?" squeaked Pen. "Why, I don't know. We can talk to our father about it, though. I don't even know who lives there, apart from Princess Victoria."

"Don't some of the king's brothers and sisters live there too?" Persy added. "The children of old King George the Third who never married?"

"So I hear." Mr. Allardyce hunched his shoulders, looking baffled. "Kensington Palace," he murmured. "I don't like it. Why is she there? You young ladies were quite right about that note—why ever she's there, it isn't because she wants to be."

Mrs. Allardyce's voice could suddenly be heard from the next room, pleasant but loud. "So happy we were able to find Mr. Mayo's book for you, your lordship. Shall I have it sent, or would you care to take it with you?"

"I believe that means we should complete our business here," said Mr. Allardyce, motioning them back toward the shop. "Please, if you learn anything, send us a message. I doubt we'll either of us get a night's rest until we know what is happening. Kensington Palace," he murmured again. The furrow between his brows deepened. "What could the high folk want with us?"

Lochinvar looked happy as he stroked the spine of a book and listened to Mrs. Allardyce's monologue on the relative merits of calfskin and kid bindings. He glanced at them with an inquiring expression as they emerged from the back room, but he did not interrupt.

Lorrie set down her tray by her mother and strategically sat across from Pen and Persy, the better to study their clothes, Persy guessed. Mrs. Allardyce poured them tiny glasses of cordial and passed the sweet biscuits, her stream of chat never slowing, but it was easy to see that she was only half attending to her own words. Persy wished she could dispel the tension that whirled and eddied around them, and just talk about Ally. It was with great relief that she glanced out the window and saw the family carriage draw up and disgorge Mama.

Mr. Allardyce rose and opened the door. Mama looked thunderous as she swept in, though her greeting was courteous enough. She clutched a pair of hatboxes by their cream-colored ribbon ties.

"Have you had a pleasant visit?" she asked. Then, without waiting for an answer, she said, "Mrs. Allardyce, I would be most extremely grateful for a glass of your cordial. I have just had a most trying twenty minutes." She let the boxes fall carelessly to the floor.

"Madame Thibault," breathed Lorrie, staring at the name stenciled on them.

"You know her?" said Mama. "Then I trust that you will have the sense never to patronize her if you don't want a bonnet fit only for—for—" She drained the glass Mrs. Allardyce handed her and sighed. "I am sorry, girls. These were supposed to be your new visiting bonnets. What could Madame Gendreau have been thinking when she recommended that woman? She has all the millinery talent of a dyspeptic goat."

Lorrie sidled over to her. "May I?" she asked, gesturing at the boxes.

Mama looked surprised, but nodded. "If you want to. So long as I don't have to look at them again." She shuddered.

Lorrie took the lid off the first box and peered inside. Persy looked too and got an impression of a large bird, festooned with garish ribbon rosettes, that had had a fatal encounter with a plate-glass window. She stifled a giggle as Lorrie tsked and replaced the cover, then picked up the other box as well.

"Excuse me for a moment," she said grimly. "I think I have some work to do." She stalked down the hall toward the office.

"Lorrie was once apprenticed to Madame Thibault," Mrs. Allardyce explained to Mama, who looked alarmed at this news.

Persy felt a sudden tingle of magic in the air, emanating from the back room. She saw Pen glance that way, then back at her. A faint odor of burning feathers made Mama look even more apprehensive. Just as she opened her mouth to speak, however, Lorrie came back, looking satisfied. She handed the boxes to Mama.

"In future, you might want to buy your hats from Madame LeBlanc, your ladyship," she suggested.

"I do—that is, she's my regular milliner. But she is so busy just now . . ."

Lorrie inclined her head. "If you continue to patronize Madame Thibault, I would be happy to repair the worst of her work. But Madame LeBlanc drinks less, so I hear." She sat down, took a biscuit, and crunched it.

Lady Parthenope blinked.

"Mama," Pen ventured, "Lord Seton might have other commitments today."

"What?" Mama looked startled. "Oh, of course. Thank you so much for the cordial, Mrs. Allardyce. We are so sorry to have missed Miss Allardyce. Please convey our greetings and hopes that she will be able to return to us *soon*."

Mrs. Allardyce looked pale but bowed. "Of course, Lady Atherston. It was most kind of you to visit."

Mr. Allardyce held the door for them. "Write if there's news," he mouthed. Pen nodded.

"Or if you need more emergency bonnet repair," added Lorrie.

Persy was grateful that Lochinvar was so delighted by his book. At least he seemed to be as they rolled slowly down crowded Oxford Street. His animated conversation about schooling for young children filled the gap left by everyone else's silence as they contemplated Kensington Palace and the vagaries of milliners.

He had known at once that something had happened when they came out of the Allardyces' back room. Persy had seen the inquiry in his expression, but he had been far too polite to ask any direct questions. And now he could see that they were all preoccupied, and he was doing his best to make solo conversation so that they could be preoccupied in peace. It was an act of charitable gallantry that Persy, at any rate, was not too absorbed to notice.

When had he learned how to do this? Had the thoughtful, considerate man always been there behind the sometimes sullen, sometimes boisterous boy, patiently waiting for the boy to grow up? And his enthusiasm for founding the new school on the Seton estates . . . that was not feigned. He very clearly cared a great deal about it. Schools! Teaching! Oh, if only she could talk to him without tripping over her own tongue in embarrassment. Just think, they were both interested in the same things. . . .

But what did it matter if they were both interested in schools? That was the only thing they would ever share. Surely he'd forgotten about the talks they'd once had—and even if he hadn't, she'd been only thirteen then. He'd been humoring her, the funny little bluestocking-to-be. She shouldn't start fancying she felt anything for him, because handsome young viscounts didn't propose to girls who wanted to teach.

But what wouldn't she give to be able to discuss his new school with him, to talk of how to help children love learning, just as they had once talked about books. She closed her eyes and pictured herself and Lochinvar, snug by the fire in the morning room at Galiswood, planning lessons and making lists—

"Persy, I can't stand it anymore," said Pen, interrupting her daydream and Lochinvar's monologue on nature as classroom. "Open that box by your foot and let's see what Lorrie Allardyce did to those bonnets."

"Must you?" sighed Mama, closing her eyes. "Very well. She didn't have enough time to make them any worse, I suppose."

Persy lifted the box and untied the sturdy knot Lorrie had shut it with. She pushed aside the tissue paper and stared. The flattened bird had vanished, or had somehow been transmuted from ghastly to charming. Delicate feathers and ribbons in soft blending shades, along with a cluster of tiny silk rosebuds, greeted her delighted gaze.

"Oh!" she exclaimed, and rapturously lifted it out of the box.

"Persy!" Pen nearly shrieked. "It's wonderful! Try it on!"

"That's not the same hat," said Mama, staring also. "Or is it?"

Persy untied her old bonnet and set Lorrie's revision on her head. Pen leaned around their mother to look. "She's amazing," she breathed.

"How did that girl have time to do *that*?" Mama said in wonderment.

"I liked it the other way better," said Charles. "It was horripilatious."

Persy wrinkled her nose at her brother, then caught sight of

Lochinvar seated next to him. He too gazed at her, hazel eyes wide.

"It's a lovely hat," he murmured.

Persy felt her spirits rise at his words, then plummet. Of course it was a lovely hat. But that didn't mean she added anything to its beauty. "Thank you," she muttered. From her mother's other side, she heard Pen sigh.

$\mathscr{P}$apa, tell me about Kensington Palace," said Pen at dinner that night. Persy looked up and gave her an encouraging smile.

The three Lelands had huddled in Charles's room after Lochinvar left, trying to figure out their next step in finding Ally. As Persy pointed out, they needed more information. Asking Papa would be a safe way to get it, as he and Mama would assume it was another part of their continuing obsession with Kensington Palace's best-known inhabitant.

Lord Atherston's eyes twinkled. "Well, let me see. I believe a young lady by the name of Her Highness the Princess Alexandrina Victoria, heiress presumptive to the throne, lives there."

"We *know* that." Pen rolled her eyes. "But what else? What's it like? Do the king and queen live there too?"

"No. It hasn't been used as a royal residence since the time of George II, a good eighty years ago. Apart from housing your heroine"—he smiled at them—"it's mostly used as a home for superannuated royals. Many of the king's brothers and sisters have or had apartments there. The Duke of Sussex and his mistr—"

Mama coughed delicately.

"—er, the Duke of Sussex lives there, and the Princess Sophia as well. It's become rather run-down over the years, and was never as magnificent as most of the other royal residences. But it's a pleasant place—peaceful and countryish. The gardens are charming, I hear, though I haven't seen them in years."

"Might we visit them? Are they open to the public?"

"Well, I suppose we might if you wish. But you're not very likely to bump into the princess if we do. Her mother, the Duchess of Kent, is quite protective of her, and seems to see plots to harm her behind every shrub. And that comptroller of hers—Sir John Conrad . . ." Papa paused, brow furrowed. "No, it's Conroy. The duchess has relied on him since the duke died when Victoria was just a baby—perhaps more than one usually relies on an employee. He's been feeding the duchess's suspicions for years. According to Lord Melbourne, who's in a position to know, he's determined to get some advantage from his position as head of the princess's household staff. He's connived to keep the princess and the king and queen apart in order to preserve his own influence. There's very little communication between the court and Kensington Palace, so they say."

"That seems odd," Persy said. "Shouldn't the princess spend a great deal of time with the king, since she's heiress to the throne?"

"According to Lord M., the king thinks so. Both he and the queen are quite fond of the girl since they have no children of their own. But there's no love lost between the king and the duchess. There never has been. The things one hears about Sir John Conroy—"

"James! Are you repeating gossip?" admonished Mama.

"Oh, let him, just this once! We need to know," pleaded Pen.

Persy echoed her. This wasn't quite what they wanted to learn about, but still . . .

"*Need* to know?" said her mother, eyebrows raised.

"Well, want to know. The poor princess!"

Papa relented. "So long as it stays within these walls, girls. You must learn discretion if you're to be in society, and this will be good practice for you. From what I hear, the Duchess of Kent and Sir John are eager to maintain as much control as possible over the princess now that she's nearly eighteen and of age to inherit the throne when the king dies. The duchess's reasons are not to be wondered at. Her daughter is all she has in the world now that her children from her first marriage are grown and living back in Germany. But Sir John is ambitious. The Duke of Wellington thinks he stayed with the duchess after the duke died and ingratiated himself to her, gambling that no other heirs to the throne would be born and that Victoria would inherit. Then he'd have a position of power in her household that he could turn to profit once she became queen. I hear he's been angling for years to have her make him her private secretary or even to declare herself unable to rule and request a regency under the duchess—and him, behind the scenes—until her twenty-first birthday, or even longer."

"Goodness! You never told me that," Mama exclaimed, wide-eyed.

"You don't listen to gossip. Remember?" Papa smiled wickedly at her.

"How does the princess feel about this?" Pen asked.

"I'll leave that to your imagination. She's never liked Sir John, so it's said, but has been forced to spend little or no time with anyone else but his family. Sir John has convinced the duchess that the court is a wicked place and that the princess will be contaminated by contact with it. Of course, having the king's illegitimate children all over it doesn't help that perception—"

"James," warned Mama.

"—but Queen Adelaide is a model of Christian charity and forgives the king his past sins. It happened before they were married, after all. The queen is quite kind to them for the king's sake, but she does not permit any moral laxity around her. Nevertheless the duchess is quite sure that the court is a den of iniquity and uses it as her excuse to keep the princess away from it. It's very sad. The queen has always doted on the girl."

"So the princess must do as the duchess and Sir John say, even though she will be queen someday?" Pen looked indignant.

"I don't say that I approve of the duchess's actions," Papa said mildly. "But she *is* the princess's mother, and until Princess Victoria is of age then yes, she must do as her mother says. She is no different from you or any other girl in that respect."

"Our mama would never be like the duchess," Pen objected.

"The duchess is doing what she considers right under the circumstances," Mama chided her. "Don't presume to question your elders' judgment."

"But going against the king's wishes when Princess Victoria's going to inherit his crown someday, and keeping her prisoner in Kensington Palace—"

"Nonsense," said Mama. "She's not a prisoner. She's traveled extensively over England visiting a great many people and places. Your grandmama Leland met her two years ago at the Duke of Rutland's house, if you recall."

"But—"

"It is an unfortunate situation and has made a great many people unhappy," Papa said with finality. "I blame Conroy for the lion's share of it, and for coming between mother and child the way he has. But the princess has time on her side. All she has to do is be patient and steadfast. Sir John hasn't been able to force the girl into anything yet." He sipped from his wineglass and chuckled. "After all, he's not a sorcerer who can bewitch her into doing his bidding. He's merely an ambitious Irishman with a bent for self-promotion."

"Speaking of ambition, my dears," Mama said, looking happy at a chance to change the subject. "We've been invited to a musicale tomorrow evening by my friend Lady Gilley. I told her you weren't yet out, but she said it would be a private party, it being a Sunday. I thought it might be good practice for you, and Signora Albertazzi is to sing, which was quite a coup for the Gilleys. Thank goodness I had Madame Gendreau make up a few simple dresses, just in case something like this came up. It was perfect timing to have them arrive today."

Persy put down her fork. Somehow she wasn't hungry anymore.

"Oh, how exciting," Pen exclaimed. "Will it rain, do you think? I so wanted to wear the silk shawl we bought last week. And maybe the new black slippers—or should I save those for balls? How shall we do our hair?" She rattled on at great length until Charles ostentatiously gagged, blaming a fishbone when Mama scolded him.

Only after they had gone up to get ready for bed did Persy speak.

"We didn't learn much about Kensington, did we?" she said, helping Pen out of her stays.

"Don't sound so gloomy. We learned *something*. Poor Princess

Victoria! I had no idea. Wouldn't it be wonderful if we could just march down to Kensington Palace to bring back Ally and set the princess's matters to rights, too?" she said, inspecting her face in the mirror. "Drat, is that a spot coming on my forehead? Why now? It had better be gone by Tuesday. I don't want to curtsy to Queen Adelaide with spots on my face."

"If we survive tomorrow evening, that is," Persy couldn't keep from saying.

Pen turned and threw her arms around Persy. "Shh. You make it sound like we're going to be executed. Mama's right, you know. A musicale evening is the best way for us to start, because most of the time we can just sit and listen and not have to make conversation. At least not much. And we get to wear our new dresses. Besides, Mama won't let us stay late because she says we must get plenty of rest before Tuesday. It won't be that bad, really. Just smile a lot." She snatched a handkerchief off the dressing table and dabbed at Persy's eyes. "You'll be fine. I know it." Her face brightened. "Maybe that disreputable duke we saw in the park the other day will be there. Wouldn't that be exciting? Except that I don't want to see him if I've got a spotty forehead."

Persy leaned her head on Pen's shoulder. "I'm sure the Gilleys' drawing room will be crawling with dark and brooding Duke of Brunswicks, and spots or no spots, you're the one who'll be fine. Oh, why can't I just stay home?"

Persy was still wondering that in the carriage on the way to Lady Gilley's house in Grosvenor Square the next evening. Her hands, cased in one of the new pairs of delicate kid gloves, felt icy and sweaty at the same time.

Were Pen's hands feeling the same? Probably not. Pen's eyes sparkled with excitement though her expression was demure enough. She had chatted away as Mama's maid, Andrews, had helped them with their hair, and danced round the room in glee when Persy charmed away the offending pimple on her forehead. Now she sat in her white muslin dress with lilac ribbons and a wreath of ivy and violets over the soft bouncing ringlets Andrews had so carefully curled, looking like Spring. Persy knew that her own costume, with deep rose-colored ribbons and pink rosebuds, was just as attractive. But her face in the mirror had been pale and anxious, not smiling and eager like Pen's.

Mama too was anxious, but for a different reason. "I had assumed Miss Allardyce would be able to help the girls get ready for parties and such. Poor Andrews was run off her feet helping all of us with our hair and dressing. The only thing for it is to hire a maid for the girls," she said to Papa.

"As you wish, my dear. Unless, of course, you think Miss Allardyce will be back soon—"

"I don't care to speculate on when that will happen. Ingratitude seems to be rampant in this degenerate age we live in. Persy, why do you have that peculiar expression on your face?"

"No reason, Mama."

"Do try to appear a little more cheerful when we arrive at the Gilleys', dear. You look like you're on your way to a funeral."

Persy stifled a sigh. Oh, but she was—she was about to witness the simultaneous birth and death of her social career. Well, at least she could enjoy watching Pen be popular and admired.

As they drove up to the front door of Lord and Lady Gilley's house, brightly lit with the new hissing gas lamps, Mama gave them a last-minute going-over. She adjusted Persy's wreath and patted her cheek. "You'll be fine, dear. Don't worry. Won't they, dear?"

"Hmm? Oh, yes, of course they will." Papa peered past Persy to the carriage window beyond. "I wonder if Gilley could spare a minute to tell me about installing the gas in the house. I hear King William pulled all the gas lighting that King George had put in from the royal palaces. But wouldn't it be pleasant to have brighter light to read by in the evenings?"

"As we'll be spending the next few months away from the house in the evenings, I can't say it's high on my list of priorities just now," Mama replied crisply. "Heavens, dear, it's the *season*."

Pen took Persy's arm and squeezed it as they ascended the steps of the house behind their parents. "Start smiling now, so it's on your face when we go in," she whispered.

"I can't. My face won't move," Persy whispered back.

"Yes it will. Now."

The door was thrown open by a bewigged and powdered footman who bowed as they entered. The front hall was small but beautiful, with elaborate plaster moldings and tiled in alternating squares of black and cream marble. Through a tall set of doors she saw that the dining room beyond had been laid out for a post-concert cold supper buffet. The thought of food, even lemon ice or the daintiest meringue, made Persy's stomach contract in protest.

Guests chatted in small groups or promenaded up the staircase. Charles would have loved its curving balustrade and already been halfway up to test its sliding properties.

Beyond the footman who had opened the door for them was a small woman dressed in purple taffeta, with red cheeks and tall plumes in her gray-streaked dark hair. She greeted them with a broad smile. An equally compact, chubby man stood beside her, beaming.

"Parthenope! Lord Atherston!" Lady Gilley shook hands. "And heavens, these must be the twins. Such pretty girls. Wait till my Freddy sees 'em. You'll have a merry time on your hands this season. Now, which is which?"

Mama introduced them, and Persy felt her watch their curtsies with an anxious eye that relaxed after they didn't fall or otherwise disgrace themselves. Lady Gilley scrutinized them.

"Hmm. My, you are alike, aren't you? Better stick to memorizing ribbon color tonight till I've had a better look at you two. You can leave your mantles and tidy up in my boudoir, then go on into the drawing room. Signora Albertazzi is eager to begin on time tonight, as she's resting for opening night of a new opera later in the week. She's promised to sing one or two arias from it, which is a bit of a coup." She took a quick look around her, then leaned forward and confided, "D'you know, she's as English as you or me? Don't know where the fancy Italian name comes from."

Lord Gilley shrugged. "She can sing as well as any of those foreigners can, m'dear, so it's none of our affair if she takes one of their names to make herself sound grander."

"But 'Mrs. Smith' would be a sight easier to pronounce," Lady Gilley retorted. "Hope you enjoy her, girls," she added affably, drawing back and turning to the next arrival.

Persy and Pen followed Mama up the stairs. Behind her, Persy could hear her father saying, "I say, Gilley. Wanted to ask how you like the gaslights. Good, are they? Can you manage reading the papers by them?" She smiled. Dear Papa. If they installed gaslights he would probably read the night through and never sleep. Not that she would blame him . . .

"Perse, look up there," said Pen beside her.

"Hmm?" Still smiling, Persy looked up to the top of the stairs. Lochinvar Seton stood there, watching them ascend. Beside him another young man leaned over the balcony rail, as fair as Lochinvar but much shorter and very plump. He looked rather like a well-dressed sausage in his snug coat and high cravat. When he saw her smile he grinned back, then said something to Lochinvar, whose serious expression did not alter.

"Why didn't you warn me?" she muttered to Pen. And more important, why hadn't Lochinvar smiled back at her?

"Warn you about what?" Pen muttered back.

"Why, good evening, Lochinvar," Mama said, gaining the top step. "And Mr. Gilley. How pleasant to see you. Persephone, Penelope, this is the Honorable Frederick Gilley. Mr. Gilley, my daughters."

"How do you do?" said Pen. Persy echoed her. Her face tingled with warmth. Merciful heavens, couldn't she manage four words without turning red?

"We-e-ell, am I seeing double? There's far worse things to come in pairs, I daresay. Seton and I were just waiting to make ourselves useful. Might we take you into the drawing room after you've left your wraps off?" Mr. Gilley drawled. Persy looked up and saw that his eyes were on her. He was perspiring heavily in his tight coat and yellow brocaded velvet waistcoat. Lochinvar's waistcoat was of deep blue silk with fine stripes of gold thread. Persy knew which she preferred. She peeked at Pen and saw her shoot their mother a quick glance for guidance.

"You may go right now. I'll be along with Papa in a moment," Mama said with a smile, holding out her hands for their mantelets.

There would be no escape, then. Persy untied the bow at her throat and surrendered her short cloak, wishing she could throw it over her head instead and sit facing a corner for the rest of the evening.

"Do you care for music, Miss Leland?" asked Mr. Gilley, holding his arm out to her. His eyes, though twinkling and blue, were nearly swallowed in the creases of his plump face.

Persy tried to swallow, but her throat was too dry. "Oh, quite," was all she could manage. Then she realized that he was still looking at her expectantly, his arm crooked. Drat, drat, *drat*. She gulped and laid her hand on it, and let him lead her into the drawing room, which was scattered with dozens of small gilt chairs. Freddy Gilley steered her to a pair near the window.

"Beastly hot in here. Need some air," he muttered, mopping his forehead with a handkerchief then fussing with the window latch. "You and your sister are very like, you know."

"We're twins, Mr. Gilley," Persy managed to reply. A draft from the window wafted an odor of perspiration from her companion. Oh, when would the music start and put an end to the need to make conversation? And where had Pen and Lochinvar gotten off to?

"You're the elder, then?"

"Uh, yes, I am."

"Thought so. I can always tell with twins. Had two sets of 'em in my year at Eton, you know. Awfully funny thing. Of course, with the Ridleys we always knew because of the scar on John's forehead, poor bast—er—poor boy. But the Martins were impossible to tell apart, at least when they had their clothes on."

He rattled on at high speed, using slang that she'd learned from Charles and sometimes words she'd never heard before. It really didn't matter if she understood or not, for he never paused for a reply. To her relief, an occasional "Mmm?" or "Oh?" delivered alternately when he paused for breath seemed to satisfy him. But she couldn't very well look around for Pen and Lochinvar while Freddy was talking to—or *at*—her.

After what seemed hours Lord Gilley entered the room with a slight, dark-haired woman on his arm, followed by an elderly man clutching a sheaf of music. Lord Gilley led the woman to the piano, then waited for the last coughs and shuffles to subside before he introduced her as the signora.

"Oh, I say, that's too jolly bad," Freddy whispered loudly as the man settled himself on the piano bench. "I was just going to tell you about what Snarky Heddleston and I did to our tutor our last term. Nearly got us sent down, but it was a beauty of a—" He broke off as he perceived Signora Albertazzi glaring at him over the piano. Persy stared down at her lap in an agony of embarrassment until the first notes from the piano filled the room.

Was this what life was going to be like until the end of the season? Pretending to be enthralled by the incomprehensible and downright silly stories of young men she'd never met before, in hope that one of them would fall in love with her and propose? And if one of them didn't find her face and dowry attractive enough, doing it all over again next year . . . and for years after that, until she either found a husband or became an old maid?

It was a horrifying thought. Why couldn't she have stayed home with Ally, sitting by the fire and reading Miss Austen while toasting her icy feet? But home was miles away, and Ally mysteriously disappeared. Persy groped for the lace handkerchief at her waist and dabbed at her eyes.

Just then, the signora ended her song on a low, quavering note. Freddy Gilley leaned closer to Persy and murmured to her under cover of the applause.

"Smashing voice, hasn't she? You're looking a little leaky about the eyes there. Nice to meet a girl with artistic sensibilities. Felt a lump in my own throat too, at the end. Hanky?" He pulled out the one he'd used to mop his brow earlier and held it out.

"Ew . . . ah, no thank you, Mr. Gilley, I'm fine," Persy floundered, trying not to look too repelled by the moist square of linen he flourished at her.

Fortunately Signora Albertazzi launched into her next piece just then. Persy tried to concentrate on the music. At least while it went on, she didn't have to make conversation. The singer's lush voice washed over her like the incoming tide, somewhat smoothing the turmoil of her emotions. This time she was able to manage a small smile as she applauded at the end of the song. Ally had often hummed that particular tune over her needlework. Had Pen noticed too? Drat it, where *was* Pen? As the signora paused to consult with her accompanist, Persy did a discreet squirm and looked around the room.

At first she couldn't find her. Then she spotted the ivy-and-violet wreath, behind and to her right, with a gold head close beside it. Lochinvar was sitting beside Pen, leaning over to murmur in her ear. Lucky Pen, to have been able to sit with an acquaintance on her first foray into society, while she'd had to sit with the Giant Yellow Brocaded Sausage. Was Lochinvar counting himself lucky for having avoided the Stiff and Tedious Leland Twin? Watching them, Persy felt light-headed as a dreadful thought formed itself in her mind.

Was Pen starting to notice Lochinvar too?

No. Oh, no. A lump of misery rose in her throat. She swallowed hard and looked down at her slippers to try and regain her composure. Pen had always been outspoken in her disapproval of Lochinvar when they were children. But he was certainly a different person now—a handsome, well-spoken young man with excellent manners, heir to a solvent earldom and a close neighbor to boot. Compared to Freddy Gilley, he was a veritable deity. How could Pen not see that?

What did it matter that Pen's tongue-tied, maladroit sister had already fallen for the young man in question?

The signora sang another song, then rested while the pianist played a short piece by Mendelssohn. Persy struggled to look engrossed in the music, but a dull, throbbing ache had settled into her heart, and the image of Lochinvar's bright head by Pen's kept dancing before her mind's eye. After several songs and a few more piano solos, Signora Albertazzi took her last bow and left the room on Lord Gilley's arm, looking triumphant but tired amidst the enthusiastic applause.

"Bra-*vo*!" Freddy Gilley called, clapping hard. "That was something, wasn't it, Miss Leland? I say, Mother's got up a nice supper downstairs. Won't you let me get you some fodder? The butler's made a spiffing punch—tried it myself while he was mixing it." He winked as he rose and offered her his arm.

Persy looked around, hoping for an excuse to refuse. Pen was smiling up at Lochinvar as she took his arm. Beyond them she saw Mama smile again and nod to her as she walked out on the arm of a little old man in knee breeches and long coat. There would be no escape. She murmured her thanks and, with a heavy heart, took Freddy's arm again and let him take her down to the dining room.

Freddy brought her a plate laden with tiny cakes and slivered ham and strawberries and cream that looked delicious. But it all tasted like cotton wadding to her. Only the punch, cool and sparkling, reached her notice by bubbling up her nose and making her sneeze three times in rapid succession. To her dismay, Freddy offered her his handkerchief again. But he also brought her several more cups of the punch, which went down quite easily after her initial sneezing fit.

Between enormous mouthfuls—and sometimes even through them—Freddy told her the interrupted story of his and Snarky Heddleston's misdeeds in their last term, which led to the story of Snarky's elder brother's run-in with the cricket captain and the sheep, who'd had the same tutor—not the sheep, of course—which in turn reminded him of that tutor's favorite edition of Aristotle, bound in kid, that had somehow made its way into the vice-chancellor's privy. . . .

Aided by the curiously mellow feeling the punch seemed to give her, Persy let his words flow over her like a river in flood, murmuring small affirmative noises at appropriate intervals. Across the dining room she saw Lochinvar talking earnestly to Pen and looked hastily away.

Freddy brought her yet more punch, ate all the strawberries off her plate, and kept on talking. Numbness crept over Persy, starting at her ears but quickly spreading over the rest of her. At long last she heard a clock strike eleven. At the same time Mama swept up to them.

"Mr. Gilley, do forgive me, but it is time for us to bring Persy home. She's not officially out yet, you know," she said with an arch smile.

Before he could say anything else, Persy muttered a hasty "Good evening" and hurried a trifle unsteadily up the stairs to retrieve her wrap. Pen joined her, and in silence—blessed silence!—they found their cloaks and departed.

In the carriage Mama looked exultant. "Persy, you surprised me! In a pleasant way, of course, dear. Don't look so alarmed."

"What did I do?" Persy asked. A rosebud fell off her wreath and into her lap. Mama beamed at it.

"Oh, nothing much. Just made Freddy Gilley gush about what a fascinating creature you were and how much he'd enjoyed your conversation. I must say, I didn't expect you to make such a success of your first venture into London society. Gilley's not the brightest star in the firmament, but he's a start. He'll tell everyone what a charming girl you are so that when you're really out, it will be much easier for you at balls and such."

"What conversation?" Persy asked, baffled. "I never opened my mouth to say more than one word."

"There you have it. Well done." Mama leaned forward to pat her hand, then sat back and blinked. "Goodness, Persy, how much punch did you have? I can smell it on you. Do be careful next time. And what about you, Pen dear? What were you and Lochinvar talking about for so long?"

"Nothing much." Pen yawned, leaning her head back and closing her eyes. "His school, part of the time. It's late, isn't it?"

"Gilley says putting in the gas was the best thing he's ever done," Lord Atherston told them. "Said he can read the smallest print by it at any hour of the day or night, though the installation was a bit of a mess. Still, no more fussing with candles and scraping wax off everything would be a boon, wouldn't it?"

"Why don't we see how he likes it this time next year? We certainly can't think about tearing the house up now, just as the season's getting underway," Mama protested.

Papa sang the praises of modern advances for the rest of the ride home but Persy barely heard him. She'd just spent the evening wishing Freddy Gilley at the bottom of the China Sea, and found that he'd mistaken her silence for coquetry. And Mama had congratulated her for it, which was even worse. And what about Pen and Lochinvar? Why wasn't Pen willing to talk about her evening with him?

Once at home, she trudged after Pen up the stairs to their room, pulling off her ivy wreath and resisting the urge to trample it underfoot as she went. Upstairs at last, she helped Pen unhook her frock and release the laces of her corset, then turned for Pen to help her. Staring into the low-burning fire, she asked in a casual tone, "Did you have fun this evening?"

"It was all right," Pen replied in the same tone.

"So what did you and Lord Seton *really* talk about?"

Pen's hands paused, then continued unlacing her corset. "Oh, I don't remember now. A bit about the season, I suppose. Lochinvar said he was looking forward to seeing me at balls after next week. I'll bet he's a good dancer."

"You?"

"Us. Whatever."

This didn't sound good. "What about his school? You said—"

"Yes, he went on about his school for a while. I didn't find that part very interesting though, so . . ." Persy felt her shrug.

So what part of his conversation *had* been interesting to her? "Did you talk about going to the bookshop? Or Ally?"

"Yes, a little."

"Just a little?"

"Yes. I'm sorry, Persy. It's late and I'm very tired."

"But you two looked so wrapped up in—in talking. What—"

"There, you're all unlaced. Goodness, look at the time." Pen turned away from her and wiggled out of her gown and corset and chemise and into a nightdress. "I'm going to bed before I drop. Blow out the candles when you're done, please."

Persy undressed more slowly, watching from the corners of her eyes as Pen clambered into bed and made a show of fluffing her pillows and settling into a comfortable position. She was doing her best to avoid talking to her, her own sister. Surely that could only happen because someone else had come between them. She yanked her own nightdress over her head, threw a dressing gown over her shoulders, and, seizing the candle, fled the room. The last thing she wanted to do right now was lie down next to silent, evasive Pen.

The corridor was chilly. Persy shivered as she hurried down its dark length, not quite sure what to do with herself—but she had to do something. Anything. There had to be some way to relieve this tight, burning ache in her heart. Oh, why wasn't Ally here? She stopped, shielding the candle in her hand, then ran back the way she had come, past her room and toward Ally's small room at the end of the hall. She slipped inside, set the candle on the nightstand, and sat down on the smooth, neatly made bed. A ghost of Ally's lavender wafted up from the quilt. Persy threw herself down and buried her face in it.

Oh, Ally. It was horrible enough to have lost her. But now it looked like she would be losing Lochinvar as well.

That made her shake her head at herself. Since when had Lochinvar been hers to lose?

But in a way he had been hers, ever since that hot summer's day on the lawn at Mage's Tutterow when they had talked books together. So what if she'd been only thirteen? It was just as possible to fall in love at thirteen as it was at seventeen-almost-eighteen. It had struck her unbidden, like lightning from a clear sky, and she'd held him in her heart ever since.

She rolled over onto her back, trying to focus on the ceiling in the dancing light of her lone candle, but her eyes kept getting all fuzzy. Mama had been right about drinking too much punch. But it had made listening to Freddy a little more bearable. Drat it, why had it been him and not Lochinvar by her side all evening? How she would have loved to hear about what was happening with his school. It had all been wasted on Pen, who had as much as admitted that she had no interest in it.

But why now was she so interested in *him*?

Pen was her sister, her twin, her other self . . . but there was no way that she and Lochinvar—why, they had nothing in common. Pen had always loathed him when they were children, and she'd been skeptical when Persy had told her about their book discussion. No, there was no way she could be in love with Lochinvar now, even if Lochinvar was starting to like her.

But maybe Lochinvar didn't know that Pen wasn't the right Leland twin for him. Pen was so much better at being social than she was, but she was the one who shared Lochinvar's likes and his dreams. If only there were some way to make him see that . . .

Her candle popped and flickered. Startled, she sat up, and her eyes fell on Ally's trunk of spell books, tucked into an alcove by her wardrobe. A half-formed idea flitted through her mind, and she slid off the bed and knelt down by the trunk.

Ally had, just a few months back, taught her the word that unlocked this trunk's closing spell, which she'd put on to ensure that a snooping housemaid didn't see more than she ought to. Persy bent and whispered "Lord Nelson's syllabub" into the keyhole of the lock. It clicked softly, and the trunk's lid rose. The piles of spell books and grimoires inside it seemed to rustle and shift as the air struck them, as if they'd been holding their collective breath.

Was there possibly anything in here that could help her? Some spell she could do to help Lochinvar see their situation more clearly? She reached down and pulled out a book at random, letting it fall open in her hand.

"*To Keepe Maggots and Worms from Garden Plants*," she read aloud. No, not quite. She turned the page. "*A Charm to Prevent Horses from Casting Shoes*. Useful, but . . ." She put that book away and pulled out another. "*To Banish Troublesome Spirits*—perhaps I should try that one to counteract the Gilleys' punch. *To Bring Pain*—huh?" She squinted at the words. "Oh, I see. *To Bring Rain*. No, thank you. To either."

She went through several books that contained more of the same, and remembered Ally's comment that most witchcraft over the years had been used to help control the natural world. "Crops and harvests and weather were their life and their livelihood," she'd explained. "What else would the witches among the common folk weave their spells around?"

Evidently spells on how to bring befuddled young men to their senses didn't fall under any of those categories. She closed a grimoire that had evidently belonged to a raiser of prize sheep and stared at it glumly for a moment, then tucked it back into the trunk. A loose piece of parchment between the next two books caught her eye. She picked it up gingerly—it was very dirty and evidently quite old—and read the heading, which was written in queer, shaky letters:

To secure the Heart of your Beloved.

Persy stared at it until the words blurred and ran together. "A love spell," she whispered.

A love spell! Why hadn't that occurred to her before? Why fiddle about with anything else? Why not cut straight to the heart of the matter and make sure Lochinvar fell in love with her and not Pen?

She sat back on her heels and ran one hand through her hair as she thought. After all she'd be doing both of them a favor. Pen would be saved from having to tell Lochinvar she didn't like him and could go marry a duke or someone equally glamorous and become a famous society hostess, and Lochinvar . . . he would have someone who understood him and shared his interests: her. Wasn't that using her magic to achieve good, as Ally had exhorted them before they came to London?

She looked at the ingredients, written in the same hand: a copper basin, a cup of rosewater, a candle, ten silver spoons—why ten?—a pair of bootlaces . . .

Bootlaces?

She frowned and kept reading the spell. It sounded reasonable enough, apart from the slightly peculiar ingredients—and even the bootlaces made some amount of sense, tied together symbolically and so on.

But could she do this? Could she do a spell to make Lochinvar, who'd reputedly lost his mother to a witch's curse, fall in love with her?

Persy bit her lip. If this spell worked and Lochinvar eventually proposed to her, then she'd have to choose. And if it came down to a choice between her magic and him, then . . . then . . . A queer, dizzy feeling, not caused by punch, came over her. If she had to choose between being a witch and marrying Lochinvar, she'd take Lochinvar.

There. She'd admitted it. She'd choose love over magic. Persy straightened her shoulders and looked at the spell again. If she were very quiet, she could sneak downstairs and get a basin from the kitchen and the spoons from the butler's pantry, and there was a bottle of rosewater right on Ally's washstand. Thank heavens she'd had all that punch after all, despite the ferocious headache that was just starting to claw at the edge of her temples. Being slightly drunk was the only way she'd have courage enough to put a love spell on Lochinvar Seton.

$\mathcal{O}$n the morning of their presentation the following Tuesday, Mama came to wake them early. She bustled in and threw open their curtains, followed by three maids carrying the hip bath and cans of hot water.

"But it's hours until we even have to leave for St. James's." Persy yawned in protest as she looked at her gold watch on the bedside table. She and Pen had each received one as a Christmas present from Mama's mother, Grandmama Revesby. Wearing it these last months had somehow, more than anything else, made her feel like an adult.

"You must bathe and dress before the court hairdresser arrives at half-ten, and we must leave by one if we're to arrive at the palace in time." Mama peered into their faces. "No dark circles under your eyes, thank goodness. I knew I was right not to accept any invitations for last night. Come on, Persy. Hiding under the covers won't work." Then she bustled out of the room.

No dark circles. Now that was truly astounding. Ever since she'd cast the love spell on Lochinvar in Ally's room the night before last, Persy had been living on tenterhooks, wondering if the spell had worked. She'd also been almost ridiculously nice to Pen, prickled by a guilty conscience. Fortunately Pen had ignored her too-niceness, apart from a few strange looks.

Pen sounded painfully chipper this morning as she bounded out of bed. "This is it, Persy! We'll arrive at St. James's as girls, and leave it as women. Isn't it exciting?"

"All because we've got dressed up and curtsied to the queen, we're adults? Does that make any sense?" said Persy from under her heap of blankets.

"Hush. And yes it does, because that's how the world works. Ally always says that some people are born grown-up and some never get there. This is as good a way as any to decide who is and who isn't. Cheer up, Perse. We get to go out in the world and learn something other than from books."

"Books are safer. You always know what they're going to do."

"Oh, Persy. One day at a time." She felt Pen grope under the blankets until she found her hand. "All we have to do is smile and not trip over our trains, and Mama's made us practice that enough. Stop worrying about the rest of it. Want the first bath?"

"Mmrph." Persy snuggled under the blankets once more. If she were really lucky, she'd wake up from this unpleasant dream in a few minutes. Speaking of unpleasant dreams . . . she sat up in bed.

"Pen, I had the oddest dream last night. We were back at Mage's Tutterow playing hide-and-seek with Ally in the garden, only I'm not sure who was hiding and who was seeking—I kept calling to Ally and she to me, but we somehow could never meet."

Just then the maids came in with more cans of hot water and finished filling the bath and hanging clean towels on chair backs. Pen pulled off her nightgown and climbed into the tub after they left.

"I've had one like that too," she confessed, lathering away with the fine rose-scented soap Mama had bought at an outrageous price at that fancy apothecary shop last week. "Are you surprised? What do we want most in the world right now? To find Ally."

"Are you sure that's all? Do you think that she's trying to contact us through dreams?"

Pen frowned. "I suppose. But she said once that dream magic is very difficult to do unless the circumstances are exactly right for it. No, I think it's just wishful thinking . . . er, dreaming. Come on, lazybones, I'm nearly done."

Persy had barely finished her bath when the maids came in with breakfast trays. She choked down half a boiled egg on toast, and Pen didn't have appetite for much more. Mama came in and shook her head at them but did not scold.

"You'll make it up tonight, I suppose. Grandmama Leland is coming to dine along with her friend Lady Harrow." Her mouth made a funny little dip. Lady Harrow was their grandmother's dearest friend. She was also a very difficult dinner guest. "Drink your chocolate, and Andrews will be up shortly to help get you dressed."

Mama's maid had been with her for as long as Persy could remember. As she helped them with their silk stockings and slippers, chemises and corsets, starched petticoats and the luminous moon white silk presentation dresses, she sniffed occasionally.

"I can't believe you're old enough to go to court. Seems like just yesterday you were coming downstairs to dinner for the first time," she said, eyes misty.

Persy grunted, holding the edge of the dressing table. Even when she was busy waxing sentimental, Andrews could pull a corset tighter than their cook trussed her Christmas roast geese.

From downstairs she could distantly hear much bustle and movement: the florist arriving with their elaborate bouquets, footmen delivering invitations, Kenney admonishing giggling maids, Mrs. Huxworthy admonishing Kenney.

Then the court hairdresser arrived and unpacked his combs and pomades. Persy and Pen sat unmoving, not daring to quiver as he flourished his curling tongs, arranging clusters of curls on either side of their faces and pinning the required white plumes in their hair. Persy took a few experimental steps when he'd finished, feeling the weight of her train and the unaccustomed feathers nodding and earrings dangling at her ears. Their slight metallic jingle was distracting. Charles sidled into the room and stared at them in silence.

"What? No witty remarks? No 'You look like an escapee from the king's menagerie' comments?" she said at the solemn expression on his face.

"No. I was just thinking about when you scolded me about your being grown-up now. You really are, aren't you?" he said, looking at the feathers.

The court hairdresser laughed and patted him on the head as he left to go do Mama's hair. Then Papa came into the room and shook his head, staring at them with the same expression as his son.

"Do we pass muster, Papa?" Pen asked, practicing her curtsy before him.

"Oh, er." He fumbled in his pockets. Charles handed him his handkerchief, and he chuckled. "I won't deny seeing you girls looking like ladies isn't choking me up a little. But I was looking for something else." He felt in his pockets again and pulled out two small tissue-wrapped packets.

Persy gasped in delight as the tissue revealed double strands of opalescent pearls. Even Charles looked impressed as Papa clasped the necklaces around her and Pen's necks.

"Oh, thank you," she breathed, reaching up to touch their cool weight on her neck.

"Your uncle Charles Leland sent these for you last year when his ship was in China. He said that as Leland girls were a rare and precious commodity, they ought to be treated accordingly. Well, I'd better see that Kenney's called for the coach. Don't want to keep the queen waiting." Lord Atherston ducked his head and started toward the door, then came back and carefully kissed them both. Charles handed him his hanky again, and he left the room, blowing his nose.

It turned out that Mama hadn't exaggerated the dreadful traffic. Persy struggled not to lean back against the carriage seat, lest she crumple her train or disarrange her hair. "Why are the roads so crowded? Are that many people being presented today?" she asked.

"Oh, yes. But many come just to watch. Grandmama Revesby will surely be there, though I doubt we'll have a chance to do more than wave since she's on duty with the queen." Lady Parthenope was torn between pride in her mother's appointment as a lady-in-waiting at the largely Tory court and loyalty to her own husband's Whiggish leanings.

As the first hour turned into a second, even Pen's excitement began to flag. They couldn't even look out the windows, which were shut and curtained against the crowds that lined the road to St. James's on drawing-room days to examine and discuss, in loud detail, the clothes and appearance of the arriving presentees. But a rap on the carriage door startled them all. Mama peeked through the curtain.

"It's the court hairdresser. He stops at carriages to do any last-minute repairs to your hair or feathers," she reassured them as she opened the door to him. The hairdresser's sallow face peered in at them; he surveyed Persy and Pen, gave them an abrupt nod, and shut the door.

"I would suppose that means we're all right," Pen ventured.

"Thank heavens for small mercies," Persy muttered.

Much to their relief they pulled up to the entrance of the palace shortly afterward. Liveried pages pointed their way up long stair-cases and down longer corridors. Persy couldn't help but feel amused at the sight of so many girls all walking together with their feathers and trains over their arms, the required lace lappet head-dresses fluttering in the breeze of their passage, their pale-colored dresses differing but somehow still looking almost identical.

"We look like a flock of birds migrating south for the winter," Pen whispered to her.

"Birds, or lemmings about to go over a cliff?" she replied through stiff lips.

"Don't be ghoulish."

At long last they were ushered into the long gallery, immediately outside the Presence Chamber, where the queen would receive them. Dozens of girls promenaded up and down its length, while others clustered to compare dresses. A few looked close to tears; others chattered and laughed too loudly.

Another hour ticked by with maddening slowness.

"Our dresses are among the prettiest," Pen whispered after a while.

"Are they? Oh, good," Persy replied, staring into her bouquet.

"What are you doing?"

"Pretending I'm an Indian fakir, like the one Uncle Charles told about in one of his letters. You know, the man who could lie on a bed of needles without feeling any pain? Maybe it will make this all easier."

"My, what lovely pearls you're wearing," said a girl standing next to her. She was small and plump and looked like a tame mouse in her white dress with touches of silver-gray. Her complexion was a little gray, too, but maybe that was just the dress's stark whiteness. Slightly protruding front teeth completed the mousy image. "I envy you. Pearls look just dreadful on me."

"Thank you," Persy said, grateful for some distraction. "They were a gift from our uncle." This girl looked as nervous as she felt, which somehow made her feel better. At least she wasn't the only one. "He was in the China Sea with his ship and sent them to us."

"Us? Oh!" She squealed as Persy gestured to Pen. "Twins! What fun! I wish I had someone to be presented with, but all my female cousins are older than I am and my sisters younger. My name's Sarah Louder, but I'm called Sally. What's yours?"

Pen told her, and she shook her head in admiration. "What romantic names! I hate Sarah, and I hate Sally even worse. I should have liked to be named Euphemia, but I suppose it's a little late now."

"The Honorable Penelope Leland," intoned a lord-in-waiting at the door to the Presence Chamber.

"Oh, you're Honorables? My heavens. I'm just plain Miss. My papa's Sir Henry Louder. Good luck, then," said the girl.

Pen took Persy's arm and hurried her over to the door. The lord-in-waiting glanced at them, and an amused expression replaced the bored one he'd worn all afternoon.

"How do you two know which of you is which?" he said with a grin.

Persy tried to smile politely. Sometimes being a twin could be annoying.

"Let me see. Oh, the ribbons are different. Jolly good idea, or you'd never know who was who. Who's Penelope?" He consulted the cards in his hand.

"I am." Pen let her train, folded over her arm, drop to the ground. "Here I go!"

Persy watched while he handed the card with Pen's name to a page, who handed it off to a distinguished-looking man in knee breeches and with a beautiful jeweled sword at his side. Two other gentlemen-in-waiting spread Pen's train behind her with long sticks.

"The Honorable Penelope Leland," the lord chamberlain cried into the room, and Pen walked into the Presence Chamber, where the queen waited.

"Come on and watch your sister. You're next anyway," the lord-in-waiting whispered to Persy. She hurried into place and felt the men behind her arrange her train.

Pen made her way up to a platform, above which hung a cloth of state. Below it stood a small middle-aged woman with a large nose and heavy eyebrows, but with the sweetest expression in her brown eyes that Persy had ever seen. Her dress and bonnet, though made of rich materials, were disappointingly dowdy. Behind and to the sides of the royal dais were dozens of elaborately dressed courtiers, gossiping behind their fans as they watched. Was Mama somewhere among them, standing with Grandmama Revesby maybe?

Persy held her breath as Pen bent in her first curtsy. Queen Adelaide nodded to her as she rose and moved apace to curtsy to the next royal lady on the platform.

A loud "The Honorable Persephone Leland" interrupted her thoughts. She hurried forward after Pen, too intent to worry anymore, and started her curtsy to the queen.

The queen smiled when Persy rose. "Am I seeing double? A pleasure, since you're both so pretty. You must be my dear Jane Revesby's granddaughters. She said you would be here today. I am delighted to meet you."

"Thank you, ma'am." Persy barely was able to breathe. Grandmama had always loved the queen for her kindness, lamenting that few could see past her homely face and unfashionable gowns. Now Persy could see why she inspired such loyalty.

Persy shuffled sideways, looking for her sister. Pen had just finished curtsying to another elderly woman standing beyond the queen and was preparing to catch her train, thrown to her by a page, and back away. Persy curtsied to the woman, who peered at her with unexpected interest in her prominent blue eyes magnified by spectacles, then murmured something to the attendant just behind her. One of the king's sisters, perhaps? Probably; King George III had fifteen children, of whom the present king was one. Two of his daughters had never married. Papa had said one lived at Kensington. Princess Sophia, was it?

The mousy girl, Miss Louder, was just making her curtsy to the queen. Persy managed to catch her own train and backed away to the other door, where Pen was waiting for her.

"We did it," Pen whispered as she took Persy's arm. "I didn't even have to use the spell Ally taught us to make sure I caught my—"

"Hush—oh no . . . ," Persy moaned under her breath, staring back at the royal dais.

Sally Louder had completed her last curtsy, to the elderly princess. But whether due to nerves or shortsightedness, she had not properly caught her train when the page had tossed it to her, and was about to take her first step backward away from the royal presence directly onto it. Disaster, at least for poor plump Sally, was imminent.

Without thinking, Persy dropped her train and bouquet and held her hands outstretched before her, pointing at the hapless girl. The dragging fabric of Sally's train flipped up off the ground and hovered at knee height as, oblivious of her peril, the girl backed away.

"Goodness, Perse! That was quick thinking," Pen marveled.

"Thank you." Quick it had been, but had it been wise? Ally had warned them about using magic in public places. She glanced back up at the royal party where yet another girl was making her curtsy. Queen Adelaide was smiling her gentle smile at the white-feathered head bowed before her. But the woman next to the queen stared directly at her and Pen through her thick glasses.

Sally bumped into her, started, then smiled up at them over her shoulder. "I say, did you wait for me? How kind."

"You might want to check your train. It's dragging a little," Pen replied carefully. Beside her, Persy lowered her hands and exhaled in relief as she bent to retrieve her own train and her bruised flowers. The three eased out the doorway and back into the long gallery.

"Oh my heavens, I did it! Mama and Papa will be *so* happy. They were sure I'd do something disgraceful. I could never get my curtsy right when I practiced it at home, and Mama was afraid I'd end up showing the queen what my petticoats looked like," Sally bubbled as they stood in the hall.

"Excuse me," called a woman's voice from behind them. They turned.

The older woman with the prominent blue eyes was hurrying toward them, trailed by her surprised-looking attendant.

"Come on," Pen whispered to Persy and Sally, and sank into another curtsy.

The woman came up to them as they rose. Persy's heart pounded in her throat. She must have seen her spell to keep Sally from tripping on her train. Was she going to say something about it in this very crowded, very public place?

"Did I hear that you are Lelands?" the woman said, looking at Persy.

"Yes, ma'am," Pen said, "we are, ma'am."

"Then you must be the Duchess of Revesby's granddaughters. She is a good friend of mine, you know. I always look forward to her being in waiting with the queen. How lovely to meet you. You don't know who I am, do you?" She laughed a small ringing laugh, and the lavender ribbons in her cap fluttered. "I'm Sophia, the king's sister. What are your names again, my dears? Persephone and Penelope, isn't it?"

"That's right, Your Highness." Persy began to relax. Was this all? Had she run after them just because she was a friend of Grand-mama's? Maybe she hadn't seen her doing magic after all.

"Lovely names for pretty girls. I don't see many young people these days. Even my niece Victoria seems to be too busy to visit as much as she used to. Of course, with her birthday approaching I'm not surprised, but still . . ."

Persy felt Pen take a deep breath next to her. "Our birthday is coming too, Your Highness. It is the same day as the princess's," she volunteered.

The lavender ribbons quivered. "What an interesting coincidence! That settles it. You must visit me at Kensington and tell me more about yourselves. Will the day after tomorrow suit? I should so enjoy it."

Persy gulped.

"Really?" Pen squeaked. "You really want us to visit you, Your Highness?"

"Oh, yes. I shall expect you at three. We'll have a nice chat, and I shall make some of my rosewater biscuits. I love to bake, you know. Well, I had better get back before everyone wonders where I am. Good-bye, girls. I shall see you on Thursday." Trailed by her attendant, who cast them a curious look before following her mistress, Princess Sophia swept back into the Presence Chamber.

Sally Louder was nearly panting in amazement. "Why, you— you've just been invited to tea by the king's sister! My word! You've never met her before? And your grandmother's a duchess?" She looked like she was about to explode.

"Kensington Palace," Pen murmured, and her face grew pink. "Do you think we'll see her? Do you think there's any chance?"

"Well, I intend to go looking for her if I have the chance." Persy stared after the retreating princess.

"Go looking for Princess Victoria?"

"No! I meant looking for Ally."

"Invited to tea with Princess Sophia?" Frances Leland, dowager Lady Atherston, exclaimed that night at dinner after getting a complete report on the afternoon's events. "Did you hear that, Ann? How singular."

Persy and Pen, still in their court dresses and feathers but minus the trains, were dining with the adults that night. *No, wait—we are adults now,* Persy thought as she followed her family and Grandmama Leland's friend Lady Harrow into the dining room. *We're supposed to be here.*

Papa's mother was a slim, upright woman with a sharp eye and equally sharp tongue. When her husband died and her son inherited the title, she insisted on leaving Mage's Tutterow and purchasing a house for herself not far from London, where she could keep an eye on the foibles of her wide circle of acquaintances. Mama would sometimes read bits of her letters aloud to the girls, smothering her laughter when she came to a particularly amusing part—which always seemed to be too amusing for the girls to hear. Persy wondered if they would now be allowed to hear those parts, now that they were out.

Grandmama's best friend, Lady Harrow—or Lady Horror, as Charles had christened her—was a widow whose chief characteristics were her insatiable curiosity and her unvarying dark interpretation of events large and small. Persy looked at her plump form and wondered if Grandmama enjoyed her company in spite of or because of these attributes.

Lady Harrow took a sip of wine. "Sophia always was an odd duck, locked up in Kensington like that. All the old king's daughters were—those that didn't get away." She patted her upper lip, with its faint mustache, with her napkin. "Of course, there's her son—"

Mama cleared her throat slightly and gave Lady Harrow a quelling look.

"Nonsense, Parthenope. The girls are out now. They'll need to know these things, especially if they're going to mix in those circles," said Grandmama Leland, cutting into her quail with gusto.

"I suppose you're right," Mama sighed. "It's not easy to remember that they're grown women."

"Of course they aren't. They're still girls. But they have to start learning about the great wicked world."

"Is Princess Sophia wicked?" Pen asked, looking interested.

Grandmama Leland put down her fork. "No, my dear, just bored and lonely. The late King George was very fond of his daughters, you see, and didn't want to let them go. And there were not many potential husbands of appropriate rank and religion available for the princesses when they were young—this was in Napoleon's heyday, you know. So he and Queen Charlotte kept them sequestered and dragged them about from palace to palace, like a movable nunnery. When she was nineteen Princess Sophia caught the eye of one of her father's equerries, General Garth, and had an affair with him, which led to the birth of a son. It's not talked about, of course. She's continued to live her drab little life, back and forth between court and Kensington. I daresay you two were enough of a novelty to catch her fancy. It will not hurt anyone if you cheer her up for an hour or two."

"How romantic," Pen said when her grandmother had finished.

"Not at all, my dear," Lady Harrow interjected. "General Garth was a good thirty years her senior, and should have known better. It is pathetic and sordid if you ask me—"

"We didn't," Persy muttered to Pen. Mama shot her a look but remained silent.

"—and highly peculiar to invite a pair of girls whom she had never met, just out, to take tea with her. You will not let them go, Parthenope, will you? What business that dotty old woman's got with them is what I should like to know. Nothing savory, I am sure." Lady Harrow shook her head.

"Gracious, Ann! She's harmless. What unsavory business can she be up to?" snorted Grandmama Leland. "You see mischief and deception behind every tree. I suppose it makes life more interesting, but sometimes it's just plain silly."

"I rather think it will be good practice for the girls," Mama added coolly. "Surely no harm can come to the girls at Kensington Palace, of all places. And whatever rumors there might be around the princess, she receives at court with the king and queen—"

"Oh yes, the queen who allows her husband's illegitimate children to appear at court—" Lady Harrow sneered.

"—and that is good enough for me," Mama finished in her best duke's-daughter tone.

"Well, surely you will go with them, at least?"

"I wasn't invited, was I? No, the girls will go with my maid to wait in the carriage. Gracious, the Princess Sophia is probably still half child herself, in mind, what with the life she has led. I am sure they will get on quite well."

Lady Harrow tried one last time. "Well, I would not allow a daughter of mine—"

Grandmama snorted. "You have no daughters, my dear."

"But if I did—"

Just then, Lady Harrow's wineglass tipped over.

"Oh, Ann," Grandmama Leland remonstrated as a footman leapt forward with a linen towel. "It's a good thing we are not going anywhere else tonight."

Mama sighed and rang her bell. "More towels, if you please," she murmured as Kenney hurried in.

"Are you all right, Lady Harrow?" Papa asked, looking concerned.

"But I'd not even touched it!" Lady Harrow squeaked, watching wine drip off the tablecloth and onto her ample lap. Kenney appeared at her side, and she snatched a towel from him.

Persy looked at Pen, who was calmly eating her dinner. But there was a glint in her eye that gave her away. She gave Persy a tiny smile.

"Hmmph," said Grandmama Leland. Persy glanced up and saw her looking at Pen with a small frown.

As soon as dinner was over and they had gone up to the drawing room, Persy dragged Pen over to the piano. Under cover of choosing music, she whispered, "You knocked over that harridan's wineglass, didn't you?"

"I couldn't stand her anymore. She is just jealous because we were invited to take tea with royalty and none of her granddaughters ever has. I don't know why Grandmama keeps company with her." Pen made a disgusted face.

"Yes, and speaking of Grandmama, she gave you such a look after the wineglass fell. You don't think she thinks you had anything to do with it, do you? Pen, listen. What if there is something to what

Lady Horror was saying? Do you think it is usual for a king's daughter—especially one her age—to ask a couple of girls to tea? Just because she knows Grandmama Revesby? What if she *did* see me do that spell today?"

"What will she do, burn us at the stake? Stop worrying. Grandmama says she's harmless. Just think—we might get to meet Princess Victoria. And you said it yourself—what better chance will we have to look for Ally?"

"Are you going to chatter, or play?" called Grandmama Leland to them.

The rest of the evening, Persy and Pen took turns playing and singing while Grandmama Leland beamed at them and Lady Harrow looked disgruntled at their choices of songs.

But Persy's mind was not on their music. That was twice in one day that they'd done magic in a public place. Without Ally there to keep watch over them, they had become careless. They could not go on this way, especially now that they would be going out into society, or else they'd be levitating the musicians and changing the colors of the floral arrangements at balls by the end of the season.

Ally would have known about the temptations to do such things, and would have been there to remind them. She just *couldn't* have left them voluntarily, despite Lorrie Allardyce's fanciful suggestion that Ally had eloped with the Duke of Sussex and was in hiding with him in his enormous library at Kensington. And if she had not left them of her own accord, then she had been forced, and was at Kensington against her will. Persy decided that somehow, when they went to visit the princess, she must contrive to look for Ally.

At the end of the evening, as the two guests prepared to leave, Grandmama Leland embraced both Persy and Pen.

"Have a pleasant visit with Princess Sophia. I know you will be a credit to your family, girls. I shall call on Sunday so you can tell me all about it, shall I?"

"Alone, Grandmama, please?" whispered Pen.

Grandmama Leland smiled conspiratorially. "Alone," she murmured. "We don't want any more overturned glasses, do we? Good night, dears."

9

The very next morning, Pen and Persy joined their mother in leaving visiting cards with all her acquaintances in town. It was a tedious business, and Pen said so.

"Wait until we actually have to make visits, instead of just leaving cards," replied Mama with a sigh. Then she recollected herself. "But this is what is done, so you might as well get used to it. Especially if you want to be invited to balls and parties."

Actually, invitations had already started arriving in a blizzard of white pasteboard cards, all begging the honor of their presence at any number of balls, routs, drums, and parties of every stripe, sometimes several in one evening.

"I'm glad I won't have to do this sort of foolishness when I'm eighteen," commented Charles in smugly superior tones from a corner of the carriage. He had asked to accompany them that morning out of sheer boredom.

"Oh, yes you will," Mama answered him. "Perhaps not at eighteen, but as soon as you have taken your degree at Cambridge and are entering society. You will have to be presented and leave cards just as we do."

Charles winced, whether from his mother's words or from his injured arm banging against the side of the carriage as they hit a bump in the street.

"You ninny," Persy whispered to him, under cover of leaning forward to check his arm. "Going shopping will be as boring as staying at home, and is definitely more uncomfortable. Why did you come with us?"

"To see if I could get a better look at the fellows who've been following you every time you go out in the carriage. I thought maybe I could get closer to them while you were in the dressmaker's shop, pretend I'm a linkboy or something and offer to hold their horses for them."

"Like you'd pass for a street urchin? Don't even think about it, Chuckles." She tried to twist in her seat to peek out a window without attracting her mother's attention. Charles smirked at her and stood right up to look out.

"Please take your seat before you do yourself a worse injury, Charles!" Lady Parthenope scolded.

"Yes, Mama," he said, and sat, giving Persy a quick affirmative nod as he did so.

So they were still being followed. But why? Could this and the watch on their house have anything to do with Ally's disappearance? Certainly there was nothing else that smacked of intrigue in their lives. Not for the first time, Persy wished that they were all safely back at Mage's Tutterow and that there was no such thing as the London season.

"Biscuit, my dear? They're my own receipt."

"Thank you, ma'am." Persy took a cookie from the Lowestoft plate held out by the lady-in-waiting.

That afternoon, she and Pen were perched on the edge of a low Chippendale settee beside Princess Sophia, at her special request. The elderly princess had poured out their first cups of tea with her own hands while the lady-in-waiting silently passed plates of cakes and biscuits. The princess's sitting room was elegantly old-fashioned, but a strong smell of moldering plaster attested to Papa's description of Kensington Palace as run-down.

Princess Sophia was also elegantly old-fashioned, in a gown and headdress reminiscent of her youth at the turn of the century. Her gray hair was tucked into a mobcap, and a gauze fichu was draped and tucked over her shoulders. Her prominent blue eyes, legacy of her Hanoverian ancestors, were soft and dreamy behind a pair of thick spectacles, but hadn't missed a detail of the girls' faces or costumes.

"Very like your dear grandmama," she had said, peering into their faces as they rose from their curtsies after being ushered into her apartment by a slightly scruffy footman. "You have her coloring and build. Well, she is a handsome woman, so you are lucky girls." She motioned them down to the sofa. "How do you like the season so far?"

"We've not seen much of it yet, ma'am. We go to our first ball tomorrow night," Pen explained.

Persy remained silent, but the princess's attention swiveled to her at once.

"Don't worry, child. You will be fine. How I would have liked to go to balls when I was your age. But Papa did not think it proper." The elderly woman looked wistful as she removed her spectacles and polished them with her napkin.

Persy took a sip of tea to hide her awe. "Papa" was His late Majesty, King George III.

"At least my niece Victoria is being allowed to attend a few. 'Tis proper for her to become used to such occasions," Princess Sophia continued. "After all, she will be the head of society as well as queen someday. She should have some idea of how to conduct herself in public and not spend so much time with her governess in the schoolroom."

"Indeed, ma'am." It was strange to hear someone speaking of their goddess as if she were just a girl like themselves. Persy tried to imagine a small, regal figure seated in a schoolroom like their own at Mage's Tutterow, doing sums and parsing French verbs with a governess. It was impossible.

Just then, the door into Princess Sophia's sitting room flew open. Two men strode in, followed by the sheepish-looking footman. Or rather, one of them strode. He was tall, with dark side-whiskers and a narrow, shrewd face. He grinned familiarly at Princess Sophia and just sketched a bow as the footman intoned, "Sir John, Your Highness."

"Ah, you've got company. I hope you don't mind our popping in," said the man described as Sir John. He sauntered over and inspected the cake plate.

Persy saw Pen blink, and understood her sister's concealed surprise. This Sir John's manners were surprising, to say the least. Did one just "pop in" on a member of the royal family? And wasn't it up to the princess to address him first?

But Princess Sophia seemed untroubled by the man's breezy air. "How kind of you, Sir John. Will you not stop for tea?" she asked as he chose a biscuit and bit into it.

"Not today, ma'am. Michael and I have business to attend to. You know." His eyes slid over Pen and Persy, and Persy wished they hadn't. His examination of them was brutally thorough. Persy felt almost insulted by his close attention and the unpleasant quirk to the corners of his mouth as he crunched his cookie.

"My dear girls, may I introduce my excellent friend and advisor, Sir John Conroy? Sir John, these are my new friends, the Honorables Penelope and Persephone Leland. Their grandmama is the Duchess of Revesby." Princess Sophia had a peculiar expression on her face as she spoke, a sort of knowing simper. It wasn't attractive, and Persy averted her eyes from it. But looking at Sir John was even worse. Then she remembered. Hadn't Papa talked about a Sir John Conroy who was part of Princess Victoria's household?

"Pretty things, aren't they, ma'am? I could wish our dumpy little Victoria had more of their looks." Sir John was still staring at them. Then he turned to the man who had accompanied him into the room and remained quietly at his side, half a pace back. "My secretary, Mr. Michael Carrighar. What do you think, Michael? Will they do?"

Mr. Carrighar bowed. He was much younger than Sir John, in his early thirties perhaps, with deep auburn hair and a sad smile that didn't quite touch his eyes. Persy nodded to him, then nearly gaped at him. His eyes were two colors—one blue, one brown.

She reached for her teacup and hoped he hadn't noticed her momentary lapse of manners. Beside her Pen muttered, "'Dumpy'— how dare he?" from the corner of her mouth.

"Indeed, sir, I think they'll do." The man's accent was strange,

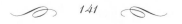

and Persy realized that he must be Irish. She looked at him again and saw that he stared quite openly at her, a slight line of concentration between his odd eyes. His stare was almost as disconcerting as Sir John's, but for different reasons. It was as if he were trying to see into her very soul. She tried to look away but couldn't. His strange eyes probed and searched her. It was a horrible feeling.

Sir John grinned. "Twins named Penelope and Persephone, eh? Two P's in a pod." He prodded his secretary in the ribs.

"Oh, Sir John, you are too clever." Princess Sophia giggled. "Now, pray do not tease my friends. It isn't nice."

Mr. Carrighar finally looked away. "They'll do quite well," he repeated softly.

Persy felt weak with relief when he turned his gaze. She glanced at Pen, and saw that her face was pale and concerned as their eyes met.

Sir John's unpleasant smile widened, and he clapped Michael Carrighar on the shoulder. "Well, we'll just be going, then, ma'am," he said, still smiling. "Business calls, and the duchess is expecting me. How delightful to meet two such fine young ladies, eh, Michael? I hope we see you again soon. Very soon." He snatched another cookie then bowed to them and to Princess Sophia.

"Give my regards to the duchess, and tell her I shall visit her later this evening," Princess Sophia admonished him as he swept toward the door, dragging Mr. Carrighar in his wake. "And my love to Victoria, of course."

"If I see her, I will. But I doubt she'll care to hear any words of love from this messenger, even if they're from you, ma'am." Sir John paused at the door as he spoke, gave them all one last grin, then left.

With a little sigh, Princess Sophia turned to Persy. "More tea?" She frowned. "Are you well, my dear?"

"I—I don't know," Persy whispered. What had just happened? What had that man done when he stared at them so intently? She involuntarily touched her forehead, convinced for one irrational moment that he had stripped the skin on it with the sharp blade of his regard.

"Please bring a handkerchief and some eau de cologne. I think our guest has the headache," Princess Sophia murmured to the hovering lady-in-waiting, who nodded and glided from the room.

"Please don't go to any trouble over me. I'll be all right in a moment," Persy protested feebly.

"It is no trouble at all. I am quite a martyr to headache myself, so I know how dreadful it can be. Now, just sit back and rest while Mary gets the eau de cologne. It always works for me." She patted Persy's hand, and when the lady-in-waiting brought the cologne, bathed Persy's forehead with it herself.

"Poor Victoria has been troubled by them too, lately. I always do the same for her if I happen to be near. Perhaps it is your age," she said soothingly. "All the excitement around the season—it is not to be wondered at."

Pen ventured a question. "Sir John is part of the princess's household?"

"Oh, yes, indeed. I do not know what her poor mother would have done all these long years without his strong arm to lean on. He and his family have been dedicated to her and Victoria ever since my brother died. Such a clever man—Sir John, I mean. He could have gone far in the army, if he so chose. But my brother begged him on his deathbed to look after his wife and child, and he gave up all prospects of a brilliant military career to keep his promise. So sad." Princess Sophia sighed and gazed into her teacup for a moment. "But Victoria is a dutiful child. I am sure she won't forget the enormous debt she owes Sir John for his years of selfless devotion to her and her mama, once she becomes queen." Her thin lips curved downward. "I'm *sure* she will not forget," she repeated.

"Has the other man—Mr. Carrighar—been with the princess a long time as well?" Persy asked.

"No, not at all. I believe he is some connection of Sir John's from Ireland. He has been here four or five months, perhaps. Sir John mentioned he had been a tutor at some university or other over there. Rather a strange young man, but Sir John assures me he's an invaluable help to him. Did you notice his eyes? They give me quite a turn whenever I see him. Perhaps it was that that gave you your headache. I recall having a dreadful one right after I saw an albino woman walking in the gardens once."

She prattled on, only pausing now and again to redampen the hanky on Persy's forehead or refill their cups. Only after quite an hour and a quarter had passed would she let them go.

"I cannot remember when I have had such a delightful visit. You must come see me again next week, girls, and tell me about the balls you have been to," she said as they prepared to leave.

"We couldn't think about taking so much of your time—" Pen began.

"But I want you to come. Perhaps"—Princess Sophia looked up at them shrewdly—"perhaps I could prevail upon my niece to stop in as well. I am sure she would be pleased to meet girls so exactly her own age. I will have to ask the duchess if that will be all right."

"Oh," said Persy, almost forgetting to breathe. Beside her Pen gave a little gasp.

"Next week, then." Princess Sophia gave them a regal nod as they curtsied and thanked her once again.

Pen looked as though she were scarcely able to contain herself until they were in the carriage with Mama's maid Andrews. "Wait till we tell them at home!" she bubbled. "Invited again! And maybe we'll meet the princess!"

Unlike Pen, Persy was quiet all the way home. Only when they were back in their room, dressing for dinner, did she break her silence.

"There was something not quite right about that Mr. Carrighar," she said to Pen as she fastened her dress. "Did you feel it? I felt as if he was trying to look inside my head. That's what gave me the headache. I fought it, but I'm not sure I was able to keep him out."

Pen shivered. "Me too. It reminded me of the time I lied about turning Charles's hair purple with that dyeing spell. Ally looked at me the same way, and I knew she could see that big black lie I was trying to hide."

"It did feel like he was using magic to examine us somehow. . . ." Persy trailed off and shook her head. "And we didn't even get to look for Ally while we were there."

"We'll be back there next week," Pen reminded her, but her optimistic tone sounded forced.

"Do you think we'll have any more chance then than we had today? No, Pen. We've got to do something!"

"Like what?"

Persy pounded her fist into her pillow. It was dreadfully unlady-like but she didn't care—there was no Ally to remonstrate with her. "I don't know!" she cried. "Something!"

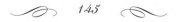

In her dim room at Kensington Palace, Miss Allardyce set down her fork and gently wiped her mouth with the fine linen napkin, then took a sip of wine. Across the table from her, Michael Carrighar peered at her plate.

"You didn't eat much," he said, sounding disappointed.

"I am sorry, Mr. Carrighar, but I don't have much appetite. Captivity can have that effect on some people." Miss Allardyce kept her voice cool.

"But I . . . that is, the cook went to a great deal of trouble over your dinner."

Miss Allardyce regarded him over the top of her glass. Mr. Carrighar had been most puzzling since luring her into that carriage on Oxford Street more than two weeks ago and bringing her here to this room girded with enchantments that would not let her leave, no matter what spell she tried. Although he refused to give in to her demands, her entreaties, or (though she disliked remembering it) her tears and set her free, he had been unfailingly polite at all times. She had not always been as polite in return when he tried to persuade her of the necessity of helping his employer, and remembering that was also disagreeable. "A true lady is known by her behavior under trying circumstances" was one of her favorite maxims. She comforted herself by reflecting that not many ladies had to withstand kidnapping and coercion to join sinister plots. Perhaps Mr. Carrighar understood her dilemma, and that was why he was always so kind and patient with her.

But over these weeks, his courtesy had evolved. It had begun taking an edge of warmth and interest that alternately pleased and alarmed her. Like it did now.

"Did you stand over her and glower while she cooked it?" she teased gently. To her surprise, he blushed and coughed slightly.

"I . . . well, yes, I did. Is there anything wrong with that? I want you to feel . . . well looked after. Like my honored guest."

Miss Allardyce's teasing mood evaporated. "But I'm not a guest, am I? I am your prisoner, until I agree to give your employer the help he wants. As I will never do that, this guest/host charade must eventually begin to grow wearisome."

"I could never find your company wearisome." Mr. Carrighar looked at her, his odd eyes intent. They still gave her a shiver when she looked at them, though it was no longer an unpleasant one.

After the first few days of her captivity, Mr. Carrighar had slowly shifted their discussions from his master's plans to other topics— her childhood, her magical education, her work as a governess— and sometimes let slip nuggets of information about himself. Miss Allardyce learned about his distinguished but irascible father and his disappointing but well-loved older brother, both in Ireland, and his own years of study and then work as a tutor at St. Kilda's College in Cork. She also learned about his swift, dry sense of humor, so like her own, and his enthusiastic study of weather magic, which she called showy just to watch his eyes kindle in indignation, until he saw that he was being teased. . . .

Mr. Carrighar sat back in his chair. "I met them today," he said abruptly, dropping his gaze.

"Met whom?" Miss Allardyce took another sip of wine, trying to drag her attention away from memories of Michael's—er—Mr. Carrighar's infectious laugh.

"Your pupils. Persephone and Penelope."

"What!" Miss Allardyce nearly dropped her wineglass. "Where? Are they all right?"

"They're quite well, and very charming girls. My master was quite taken with them." Mr. Carrighar was still staring at the table.

"What were you . . ." A horrible suspicion began to creep over her. "No. You can't drag them into this. I won't let you use them—"

Mr. Carrighar held up one hand. "No one said anything about using them, Miss Allardyce. They need not have anything at all to do with this—"

"—if I accede to your blackmail and give you what you want," she finished. The delicate wine she had been sipping with such pleasure—the wine Mr. Carrighar had brought for her—seemed to sour in her stomach. She made a gesture and the glass disappeared.

"That is a crude way to put it." Mr. Carrighar's voice was steady, but his hands betrayed him by curling into fists.

"Nonetheless, it's true." Miss Allardyce rose and took a few jerky, hesitating steps, then whirled back to face Mr. Carrighar. "How *could* you?" she shot at him. "They're innocent children."

He rose too. "They're trained witches, like you."

Miss Allardyce stared at him. Though his expression was composed, there was a flicker deep in his eyes. "They're moral human beings like me. Like you," she added softly. "How can you help him with this—this heinous deed? You're not an evil man."

He laughed. It sounded more like a cry of pain than amusement. "Aren't I?"

"No. I know you aren't. Don't let him use you this way. He can't force you . . . Michael." Her voice dropped as she used his name aloud.

Mr. Carrighar took a step toward her, and another, his face pale under his dark auburn hair. "Ah, but he can. He already has. I told you before that I too am his prisoner, and I did not lie. I have no choice but to help him if I don't want to see my family ruined and my father dead of a broken heart. Do you think I'm happy doing his bidding? Do you think I want to hold you here against your will?"

He closed the last inches between them and reached up to trace the line of her cheek with a trembling finger. "What does it concern us, the machinations and maneuverings of these people? Life will go on the same, no matter what happens. Life could go on . . . for *us*."

Miss Allardyce felt transfixed under his touch, but to her surprise her voice still retained its cool, dispassionate evenness. "No, it won't. We will have done ill, and ill would come back to us magnified. I beg you, don't help him. If we both stand against him—"

But he was shaking his head. "It's too late for that. I am bound to help him, and so are you."

"I? How?"

"The same way I am. Through the ones we love. He won't hesitate to use them to force you, just as he used mine to force me. If you would save your pupils, give me your word that you will help us, when the time comes."

$\mathcal{T}$heir next social event was a party at Lady Conyngham's. Persy did not care for the two chief occupations of the evening, cards and gossip, though she did enjoy a chat with Sally Louder and even managed to introduce her to Freddy Gilley without stuttering more than twice. Lord Northgalis sought her out between rubbers of whist to talk about his horses as they strolled around the room, laid out with potted orange trees to form groves in which card tables were situated.

Lochinvar was *not* there. He had come down with influenza, though Lord Northgalis assured her that it had been a light case and that he was already recovering. Persy could not help feeling relieved that he wasn't there so that she wouldn't be tempted to follow him about all evening, looking for signs that her spell had worked. She had been so wrapped up in their presentations and in the visit with Princess Sophia that she hadn't had time to think about it, but the thought of it had simmered in the back of her mind. If she were lucky, he'd still be convalescing in two days, when they would be attending their first ball.

"That's the last time I'll take any of Lady Harrow's recommendations!" Lady Parthenope declared again as they rumbled down Bond Street en route to Lady Whittendon's ball. "That woman was completely unreliable."

"We're sorry, Mama," Persy said once more. She hadn't *meant* to do magic in front of the new maid, really she hadn't. But what else could she have done with a pan of hot coals hurtling toward her sister's dress?

The maid had arrived that morning, a sturdy woman of forty with a bilious complexion and a stolid, no-nonsense air about her. Pen muttered that she looked like a superannuated nursery governess and that she would probably force-feed them barley water and gruel, but Mama seemed quite pleased with her.

"Lady Harrow recommended her," she whispered to the girls outside the morning room, just before they went in to meet her. "She said she'd be just the right influence on a pair of high-strung young girls."

"We're not high-strung," Pen had protested. "But we will be after a week of her in the house."

"Nonsense, girls. She's supposed to be an excellent hairdresser, and I'm sure she looks quite capable. Now mind your manners. I should think you'd be thrilled at the thought of having your own abigail." Mama fixed them with her steely Wellington eye that would brook no opposition.

On the whole, Persy rather looked forward to having a maid to help them. Though she and Pen were both tidy by nature, it would be nice to have someone to help keep in order the ridiculous amount of clothing and accessories required by young ladies in society.

So as they dressed for the ball in their presentation dresses, much poufed out with extra petticoats, she tried to be helpful and gracious. Or at least as helpful and gracious as her fluttering stomach and trembling hands would allow. To her relief the new maid was taciturn, speaking only when necessary. But to Pen, who tended to chatter when nervous, her silence was an affront.

"'Old your head just there, miss," the woman said to Pen as she wrapped a lock of her hair around a hot curling iron.

"These side-ringlets are so silly. I feel like a chandelier, with prisms bobbing around my ears," Pen complained to the room in general. The maid ignored her and muttered under her breath, counting.

"But they look so delicate and pretty on you." Persy had sat on the end of the bed, holding her own ringleted head as still as possible while trying to chafe some feeling back into her cold hands.

"They look no such thing," snapped Pen. She shifted impatiently on her chair, and her full skirt, overflowing the bench on which she sat, swept across the corner of the dressing table where the little brazier that heated the curling iron sat.

"Oh!" Persy squealed. The little metal bowl of hot coals seemed to fall in slow motion straight toward Pen's skirt as she stared at it.

"*Arreste!*" she had cried, pointing at it. The brazier froze in midair, righted itself, and drifted back up to the dressing table, where it landed with a quiet bump.

Then a louder bump made her jump. Their new maid had fallen to the floor in a faint. Persy still felt embarrassed recalling her wild-eyed look when she'd finally come around.

"I don't blame you, dear child," Mama reassured her. "It is evident that the woman was quite mad, falling over then running out of the house like that, without a word of explanation."

"Perhaps she suffered from fits," Pen suggested, concealing a grin behind her fan. Persy could not help being amused by the wickedly demure look in Pen's eye as she agreed with their mother. Pen had pranced around so gaily after the maid's precipitate departure that Persy had, only half-jokingly, accused her of knocking the brazier off the table on purpose.

"Indeed. Then all the more blame to Lady Harrow. It's a good thing Andrews had already finished with me and could help you, or we might have been late for the ball." Mama shook herself like a ruffled hen settling her feathers. "Now I shall have to start looking for a maid for you all over again."

At least the drama of the fleeing lady's maid had taken Persy's mind off the evening's main event—the ball. It wasn't until their carriage drew to a halt outside Whittendon House that she remembered that she would have to go into a hot, crowded room full of strangers and look like she was delighted to be there.

Pen took her arm and gave it a squeeze that was meant to be reassuring as they walked up the grand house's gleaming marble steps. She shot a quick look at Pen and saw that even her eyes were a little wider than usual and her cheeks a little paler. It was hardly a comforting sight. If *Pen* was nervous . . . she felt the anxious lump in her throat swell. At least Lochinvar would not be there; surely he was still recovering from his case of influenza. She could concentrate on getting though the evening safely and not on him.

As they entered the brightly lit foyer of the Marquess of Whittendon's palatial house, color and light and sound swirled through

Persy's senses and left her feeling light-headed. A kaleidoscope of gowns in every shade and tone, topped by headdresses sometimes charming, sometimes fearsome, swept by her in all directions as ladies who had probably taken tea together just hours before greeted one another with insincere shrieks of joy and cries of admiration. Upstairs in the ballroom the orchestra was already playing.

Then she was curtsying to the marquess and his elegant marchioness. She heard herself make polite replies to their kindly greetings. How was this all happening? It was like the real Persy was caught in a bubble, floating around above a large animated doll with her face and form that smiled and nodded and mouthed the right words. *I'm doing fine,* she thought a little incoherently. *I'd best keep out of my way and let myself get on with everything.*

She watched herself follow Pen and Mama up the stairs to the ballroom, smiling and bowing to Mama's acquaintances as they did. Still from a distance she greeted Sally Louder, who threw herself at them with delighted little squeaks and introduced them to her friends. It wasn't at all bad, really, this disembodied state. In fact, it was quite pleasant to be able to survey the beautiful ballroom and examine the ladies' dresses and coiffures in this distant, dreamy way—

"Good evening, Lady Parthenope," said a voice nearby.

All at once her calm departed as she turned and met the eyes of the golden-haired figure bowing before them.

"Good evening, Lochinvar," said Mama with a bright smile. "How nice to see you. Is your father here as well?"

"He is, ma'am. Lord Whittendon just sold him a mare, and they've become thick as thieves over their stable books. He wouldn't have missed tonight for anything, and neither would I."

It was, indeed, Lochinvar, in an exquisitely cut black coat and snowy linen. The darkness of his coat only made his hair shine the brighter, and his eyes were unusually vivid above the starkness of black and white.

Mama examined him. "You still look pale. Are you sure you're well enough to be out, my boy?"

"Er, well, mostly recovered, thank you." He nodded to Mama, but Persy thought that rather than appearing pale, he looked flushed. Even his ears. How funny. She could just see them blushing pink under his carefully combed hair. Now, why should Lochinvar be turning so pink? Then she realized he was speaking.

"Would you do me the honor of dancing with me, Persy— um—Miss Leland?" he asked, bowing to her again.

His ears had grown a deeper shade of rose, she noted. Some-times Papa's ears turned red right before he had a sneezing attack, as he frequently did when the autumn flowers began to—

He had said Persy and bowed in her direction. That meant he was talking to her, didn't it? He was asking her to dance. The sense of disembodied serenity that had started to creep over her again vanished for good. That was why he was blushing and stuttering. The love spell. It had started to work.

"Dance? Right now?" she blurted.

"Er, well, yes, that is, if you don't mind." The easy conversational tone that he had used with Mama had vanished, and his voice had become abrupt and a little squeaky. "It *is* a ball, and there's, um, music. Unless you're already engaged for this dance . . ."

Persy gulped, or at least tried to, with a throat gone dry as Egypt. Which was where she wished she were right now. Why couldn't he have asked her to dance later, when she'd had a chance to get over her initial fright at being at her first ball? Or better yet, have stayed at home with the remnants of his flu? With a quick, desperate look at Mama, who was smiling and nodding at her behind Lochinvar's back, she took his proffered hand and let him lead her into the crowd.

It was a waltz. Good. At least she wouldn't have to concentrate as hard as she would with quadrille figures. Her practice with Pen had paid off. As Lochinvar turned to her and placed his hand lightly on her waist, she found that her eyes were level with his mouth. That was reassuring too. She and Pen were tall enough that dancing with someone like Freddy Gilley, for instance, meant dancing eye to eye. Persy knew that she could never have danced with Lochinvar if she'd had to gaze into his eyes the entire time. Her feet would simply not have been capable of movement.

Oh, why couldn't she just close her eyes, the way she did when Pen made her practice? That made it so much easier to concentrate. She stared straight ahead at Lochinvar's unsmiling mouth.

Then again, maybe she didn't want to close her eyes. Lochinvar's upper lip was a little too narrow to be classically handsome, and his whole mouth held too stiffly just now, but the gentle upturn at the corners and that soft dimple in his chin were mesmerizing. If she closed her eyes now, she wouldn't be able to stare at it and think about what it would be like to brush her own lips across it.

Persephone! One part of her mind gasped in shock at such an unmaidenly thought, but she ignored it. This was her first waltz, at her first ball, and she was dancing with a man with the most imperfectly perfect mouth she had ever seen, and she would treasure this moment forever. What if she did suddenly pretend to lose her footing and collapse against his chest? Then he would gather her in his arms and—

Oh God, Persy, what have you done?

—and he would tell her that he loved her . . .

No! He couldn't!

Well, wasn't that what she'd wanted? Wasn't that why she'd cast that love spell on him? So that he'd fall in love with her and do something foolish and romantic like kiss her in the middle of a crowded ballroom?

So why was the thought of it making her cringe with embarrassment? Or was it really embarrassment?

Was it, just maybe, shame?

The night of the Gilleys' party, she'd been very unhappy and . . . well, perhaps just a little tipsy from all the punch Freddy had given her. Tipsy enough, at any rate, not to have been thinking clearly when she'd found that love spell in Ally's room. It seemed so clever, such a good idea, to make sure Lochinvar would fall in love with her and not Pen.

But was that really love?

What good was Lochinvar falling in love with her because of a spell? What kind of love was that? Did she want to marry him, to spend the rest of her life with him never knowing if he truly loved her, or if he'd been forced into it by magic? What if one day the spell wore off and he woke up and realized he hated her or, even worse, was totally indifferent to her?

She'd made a complete mess of everything.

The perfect lips were moving. Persy tore her gaze from them and looked up into his eyes. That was nearly fatal. The hazel eyes were examining her with far more intensity than she liked just now.

"It's your first ball," he stated.

"Yes," she agreed. Dear Lord, those eyes!

"It's my first, too, since I got back from the continent."

"Oh, indeed. How, um, agreeable." She winced inwardly at this inanity.

"Do you think you shall like the season?"

No, not at all. I shall hate every minute of it except when I see you, and then it will be even worse because I'll know that the only reason you're talking to me is because I manipulated you into it. "Er, I hope so."

He nodded, but did not reply.

Persy stole another look farther up his face, and met his eyes gazing down into hers. She blushed, and said quickly and without thought, to draw his attention from her pink cheeks, "I am sure Pen will have a pleasant time of it, though. She's the one who enjoys dancing and—and . . ."

"You don't care for it?" He smiled. "If I might confess . . . I'm not all that fond of it either, most of the time. But with the right partner it can be quite pleasant." He placed an unmistakable emphasis on the word "right."

Oh, heavens, now what should she say? More important, what should she *do*? That dratted spell really was working, wasn't it? And here he was, saying all the wonderful things that she'd longed to hear him say . . . and that he never would have, without her interference. There was only one thing for her to do.

"Well, I don't care for it in the least," she blurted. "I'm very bad at it, and don't get any pleasure from it at all. You were very kind to ask me, but I must confess that I don't enjoy it. Please don't feel you have to ask me in the future."

Lochinvar frowned. "But I—" he began.

Just then, the music ended. Persy curtsied to Lochinvar as was proper at the conclusion of a dance, forcing him to stop speaking and bow. She was not sure whether to be grateful or disappointed that he had been unable to finish what he was going to say. Probably grateful. Again she took his hand so that he could lead her back to their seats, hoping that he couldn't feel how sweaty her palms were through their gloves.

"What's this?" Lochinvar murmured.

Persy looked up from her glum reverie and saw that a knot of people, among them Freddy Gilley, had congregated around Mama and Pen. Evidently Freddy had brought several of his friends with him, mostly rather unfinished-looking young men with slightly too-vibrant cut-velvet waistcoats or oversnug trousers with gold buttons up their calves. Mama appeared slightly alarmed, while Sally Louder and her two friends and chaperones stood nearby, looking envious.

"Ah, there she is!" Freddy crowed when he caught sight of Persy and Lochinvar. "Sneaked in already, you sly dog Seton? But you can't keep her all evening. Here, Miss Leland, is the flower of London youth, dying to tread a measure with you." He bowed, hand on heart.

Persy gawked at him. Dear heavens, was this what Mama had meant that evening after the musicale at the Gilleys'? Would she be popular despite herself? The absolute last thing she wanted right now was this. She looked away from the blushing Pen and the chattering bucks, and her eye lighted on Sally Louder, still at the edge of their group.

Sally looked like a wilted flower, her round blue eyes watching the fun with the hurt, puzzled expression of a child locked out of a sweet shop that others freely enter. Persy felt her own pain recede in the face of the other girl's dejection. She wasn't the only one not enjoying this situation.

Without thinking, she leaned forward and pulled Sally into their midst. "Mr. Gilley, she may be *une petite fille,* but Miss Louder does not deserve to be overlooked by you and your friends," she heard herself say loudly.

Sally blushed as pink as her ribbons as Freddy looked down at her with a slowly spreading grin. "Good God, Miss Leland, you're right. How d'ye do, Miss Louder? I didn't see you there at first, you're such a dainty morsel." He took her hand and kissed it, leaving her looking stunned and delighted. Then Lady Louder, as small and mousy-plump as her daughter, stepped forward, and soon Sally's two friends had been introduced as well.

Feeling drained, Persy sank into a seat. But she was not long allowed to contemplate her misery in solitary peace among the potted palms before Freddy appeared to claim a dance. She found herself engaged for the rest of the presupper dances with the boisterous young men of Freddy's acquaintance.

One of the less boisterous ones, in his second or third season, was kind enough to point out some of the ball's better-known guests just before the midnight pause for supper and champagne. Persy tried not to stare as Lord Palmerston and Lady Cowper waltzed past, smiling into each other's eyes. Even she had heard of their long-standing affair, through Grandmama Leland's gossipy letters. And there was Princess Victoria's cousin, Prince George of Cambridge, a young man just her and Pen's age, but very short and sorely afflicted with spots.

"They say he shall make a match of it with little Vicky," her escort, Viscount Carharrick, whispered as he led her to the great staircase en route to the dining room. "Keep it in the family, you know. Myself, I wouldn't envy him."

"Nor would I envy *her*," Persy snapped back. How dare he speak so cavalierly about the princess? "She deserves someone who looks a little more like a prince."

"Like 'young Lochinvar come out of the west,' here? A bit more the handsome prince sort, don't you think? If you care for that sort of thing." He nodded toward a couple preceding them down the stair.

It was Lochinvar and Pen, gold head and honey brown bent together in conspiratorial fashion. As if he'd heard them, Lochinvar glanced back over his shoulder, straight at Persy. She froze in mid-step. But her escort, who hadn't noticed her pause, kept descending.

"Oh!" Jerked off her stair, Persy fell into him and felt her ankle twist. She hissed as pain lanced up her leg.

"Whoa there, Miss Leland," Lord Carharrick said, catching her. "Are you all right?"

Heart pounding, she gripped his arms, grateful for their solidity under her hands. Heavens, she'd nearly gone tumbling down the stairs, straight into Pen and Lochinvar. "Quite," she said, trying to catch her breath. "My foot slipped."

"Persy! What is it?"

Pen had started back up the stairs. Below Pen, others were pausing and looking up at them. Persy realized that she was standing in a near stranger's embrace in the middle of a crowd of descending suppergoers, and felt her cheeks start to burn. She pulled herself as unobtrusively as possible out of Lord Carharrick's arms as Pen and Lochinvar approached. "It's nothing. I just tripped, that's all." She set her foot down on the next step and winced.

"Why, you've hurt yourself." Lord Carharrick slipped an arm around her waist and pulled her against his side. "You must let me help you down."

"Really, I'll be fine," Persy repeated. Her face felt close to bursting into flame. Oh, why were they all staring?

"No, I insist. It was my fault. Don't worry, Miss Leland," he said to Pen. "I'll see that your sister is made comfortable." Lord Carharrick's voice was authoritative and sincere.

"Perse?" Pen sounded unsure.

Persy saw Lochinvar frown ferociously at him, and an idea clicked in her mind. "I'll be fine, Pen. Thank you so much, Lord Carharrick. You are too kind. And so *strong!*" She leaned against him to take the weight off her throbbing foot, then glanced up at him through her eyelashes in as coquettish a manner as she could.

"Umm . . . " Persy could almost feel Pen's astonishment in that one syllable. She ignored it, and after what seemed like forever Pen and Lochinvar turned away.

Persy concentrated on her feet the rest of the way into the dining room. Lord Carharrick led her to a small corner table surrounded by banks of drooping purple delphiniums and ferns and insisted on carrying over an extra chair to set her injured foot upon. Then he brought her a glass of champagne before disappearing to the buffet table.

Persy fanned her hot cheeks and sipped the champagne. The

icy cold effervescence soothed her burning throat. She'd made a total muff of everything, but perhaps she could fix it. All she had to do was rebuff Lochinvar at every turn and make it clear she had no interest in him. Surely he would eventually take the hint, even if he was under a spell, and find another girl to fall in love with. At least he'd be doing it of his own free will. Pretending to flirt so outrageously with Lord Carharrick was an excellent beginning—she'd felt Lochinvar's surprised disapproval as well as Pen's. . . .

Pen. She couldn't—just couldn't—admit to Pen what she'd done. So she'd have to pretend with Pen, too. The thought of having to dissemble with Pen—her twin, her confidante in everything . . . But it was all for the best. Pen would thank her someday, when all this was past.

Lord Carharrick reappeared, bearing plates heaped with pineapple ices and sweetmeats. "I hope I found something you'll like," he said, setting her plate down carefully. "How's your injury? Shall I try to find some ice for it?"

"Oh, no, thank you. It's not badly sprained, I don't think. I am sure it will feel better quite shortly," Persy replied, coloring again. "I'll just sit out the rest of the dances and I'm sure it will be better in a little while."

"Then I shall sit with you, if you will allow me," he said, with a little bow.

Persy took refuge behind her fan. Didn't he have other dance commitments to keep? It didn't seem proper for a man to sit out the entire evening with a girl if she wasn't dancing because of a sprained ankle, but neither Mama nor Ally had ever discussed this contingency. And if it were all right, she didn't want to give offense by asking him not to. She'd already been tactless enough for one night.

"That is most kind of you, sir," she said carefully, hoping that it was a sufficiently gracious, yet noncommittal, reply.

After that, she found that she could actually begin to relax, just a little. The pineapple ice was deliciously tart and the champagne refreshing, and Lord Carharrick's conversation was entertaining enough that she could fall back on her strategy of encouraging nods and murmurs of agreement and actually mean them. Perhaps it helped that there was nothing about him to remind her of Lochinvar. His hair and eyes were brown, with full curling side-whiskers and dark straight brows, and his figure was shorter and stockier. She might have thought him quite handsome, if she didn't know Lochinvar.

When he gently helped her rise after she had finished her ices, she was able to smile her thanks without blushing too badly. And when he brought her back to her seat in the ballroom and explained her accident to a startled Lady Parthenope, he made it sound like it had been entirely his fault. He was so charmingly contrite that Mama invited him to sit with them.

"And how is your dear mother?" she asked him. "I have not had the pleasure of seeing Lady Camborne yet this season."

"Mother's still with Father down at the manor, unfortunately, due to a new hunter that did not have the manners Father thought it did," Lord Carharrick replied. "Threw him against a fence and gave him a broken leg and a dislocated shoulder. I rather doubt you'll be seeing either of them this year, as it's such a long and uncomfortable ride from Cornwall."

"How dreadful! So you are alone in town? You must dine with us some evening. Lord Atherston shall write," Mama said with a sympathetic cluck.

"Well, I can't call staying at my club being quite alone, ma'am, but I would be most delighted to dine with you any evening. And I'll endeavor not to trip Miss Leland up on the stairs again if I am invited," he said, eyes twinkling.

Mama laughed. "It's hardly the most auspicious way to go about meeting young ladies, Lord Carharrick, so I should hope that you don't."

"Even when it gains me such pleasant company?" His eyes were warm on her again. She laughed and hid behind her fan. If he wanted to stay and flirt, that would suit her very well. Anything to contribute to putting Lochinvar off.

She spent the remainder of the evening listening to him and Mama chat, managing now and again to insert a word or two without mumbling or stuttering. Pen came and went as partners arrived to claim dances, and Persy was even able to pretend not to see Lochinvar hovering not far away. She couldn't help watching him from the corners of her eyes, though, and gradually the ache in her heart overtook the one in her ankle. If she hadn't been so stupid, she might have enjoyed dancing with him tonight, perhaps more than once. She could have sent him little glances from across the room, communicating her interest. Instead she'd put him beyond her reach forever.

Just before the evening ended, Sally Louder sidled over. "I should like to thank you," she said, seating herself by Persy and giving her arm a squeeze.

"What for?"

"For making Freddy Gilley notice me. I thought tonight would be horrible, but thanks to you it's been the most wonderful evening of my life. Do you know, I danced twelve times? Twelve! My cousin Caroline only danced twice at her first ball, and she's taller than me and has black eyes like a gypsy's. Mr. Gilley asked me *twice*." She sighed happily.

Persy opened her mouth, but Sally was not finished.

"After all, Mama says he's well-off—ten thousand a year, probably," she murmured, looking at Persy very seriously. "And he's so—so . . . " She sighed again and smiled a small dreamy smile.

Persy bit back the mocking reply that sprang to her lips. "He's so perfect for a certain girl I know whose name starts with an *S*," she said instead.

Sally rewarded her with a brilliant blush and another little sigh. "Do you really think so? You mean that you don't—that you're not, er . . . interested in him?"

Good heavens! "Not in the least," Persy assured her. "Don't worry. All we ask is that you invite us to your wedding."

Sally giggled. "Well, good night." She leaned toward Persy and pecked her cheek, then was gone.

It was nearly three when they finally arrived home. Pen helped Persy up the stairs, but both girls were too tired to speak much. Andrews helped them undress and wrapped Persy's foot in a bandage, and they climbed into their bed.

"Does your foot still hurt?" Pen asked after a moment.

"Not much," Persy replied, yawning and hoping she sounded careless.

"I'm sorry it had to ruin your first ball." Pen yawned too then added, just as carelessly, "But you seemed to have a good time with Lord Carharrick."

"I suppose. Mostly he and Mama talked." It felt like she and Pen were doing a delicate conversational dance, stepping gingerly around the topic with careful words. They should be giggling and comparing notes on the high points of the evening, both humorous and horrible—in other words, acting like sisters.

"I thought I heard him ask if he could call tomorrow to see how you are?" Pen persisted.

Drat. So she *had* overheard that. "Yes, I think he did."

"He seemed quite charming."

Persy stared into the dark. "He was very kind about my ankle" was all she could trust herself to say.

"Well, you certainly seemed to be taken with him." Pen's voice went up at the end, almost as if she were asking a question.

Persy came very close to saying, "No, I'm utterly indifferent to him." But then she'd have to explain why she'd pretended to flirt with him. Instead she made a noncommittal noise and turned it into a yawn. "Heavens, I'm sleepy. Good night, Pen." She rolled over and tucked the quilt around her ears.

But sleep was a long time coming. She'd survived her first ball. Sort of. Now all she had to do was alienate the man she loved, keep secrets from her beloved twin sister, and find her governess without even knowing how to start.

Flying to the moon might be easier.

$\mathcal{I}$n the morning Persy's foot felt much better, despite Charles's landing upon it when he stomped into their room and jumped on their bed at half past seven, demanding to hear how their evening had been.

"Ow!" she cried.

"Honestly, Persy, one injured member of the family's enough, don't you think?" he demanded, patting his sling. "How did you do for your foot, goose?"

Persy groaned and hid her head under her pillow. "How did you know?"

"News travels fast in London." Charles raised an eyebrow and tried to look world-weary. "The Hoaxer already has a poultice ready to put on it. It didn't smell too horripilatious, for a change. She takes a great interest in this sort of thing."

"Lord Carharrick seemed to take great interest in Persy, too." Pen yawned. "Now run along, Chuckles, or I'll practice halting spells on you again. Come back in about three hours with tea and buttered toast, and we might be willing to tell you about last night."

"Lord Carharrick?" Charles paused at the door and frowned. "Who's he? But Persy, I thought you liked—"

"*Repellere stat*—" Persy cried, emerging from her pillow.

"I'm going, I'm going!" The door clicked shut.

Getting any sleep after that was impossible, because her mind was occupied with trying to figure out how to murder Charles without upsetting Mama and Papa. She was still smothering yawns that afternoon in the drawing room with Charles, trying to get him to attend to lessons, when Kenney announced a visitor. To her dismay, Lochinvar walked in.

"Heigh ho!" Charles bounded over to him. "How's Lord Chesterfield? Did you ride him today?"

"Of course," Lochinvar said, ruffling Charles's curly hair. "And I promise you may come out and visit him, if your mother says you might."

"She will. Let's go!" Charles danced toward the door.

"Well, if you don't mind, I'd planned on inquiring first about your sister's health." Lochinvar glanced up at Persy. She swallowed.

"My sister's what? Oh, her ankle. She's fine. It hasn't kept her from plaguing me with maths, anyway. Come *on*!" Charles looked like a retriever waiting for his master's signal to bolt for a downed bird.

"Thank you, Chucklehead," Persy snapped at him, forgetting Lochinvar for a moment. "If you want to be behind your entire form when you go back to school, it won't be my fault."

"What maths?" Lochinvar set his hat down on the floor by the sofa and moved over to the table. He picked up Charles's book.

"Dusty old algebra. What's it got to do with anything important, like horses?" Charles rattled the doorknob.

"Many things, really. My father uses maths all the time for a lot of things. Including the stables."

Charles wandered back over to the table and peered at the book. "How?" he demanded, looking interested in spite of himself.

"Look." Lochinvar took a pencil and scribbled some figures in Charles's copybook. "Say you want to build a paddock for Lord Chesterfield's first foal."

Charles looked transported.

"And you've got, umm, ninety-five yards of fencing. What's the biggest paddock you could build, and what shape would it be? You'd have to use algebra to figure that out. So you see? Even for horses you'll need maths."

Charles stared down at the book and nodded slowly. "Persy said something like that. But it's different when *you*—oh, sorry, Perse." He flushed and took up his pencil. "Watch me. I'll solve this one."

Lochinvar sat down next to him and looked at her across Charles's bent head. "I'm impressed, Persy. Not many ladies have the least idea how to do more than count place settings at a table. I wish I could find a schoolmistress as knowledgeable as you for the children at the new school at Galiswood."

Persy flushed and tried to smother the pleasure his words gave her. "Actually, I hate maths," she said, making a face. "And I'm usually terrible at it, too. I'm just helping Charles because—er—because I—"

"What are you talking about, Persy?" Charles gawked at her and scratched his head with his pencil. "You love maths! And Ally said you were as good at it as she was. Are you feeling all right?"

She could feel Lochinvar staring at her, waiting for her reply. Fortunately, Pen and Mama came in just then and saved her from having to think up one. Mama greeted Lochinvar warmly and rang for tea. "What news of home?" she asked him. "How is your school progressing?"

Persy did her best to look bored, but that was precisely what she would have liked to ask. She could still feel Lochinvar's eyes on her as he replied, "I'm in regular correspondence with Mr. Chandler, the schoolmaster. He says the building is nearly finished, and is working with our carpenter on designing special tables for the pupils." He pulled a letter from his coat pocket and unfolded it. "He's asked me to look for some beginning maths primers that wouldn't be too intimidating for younger students, too."

"Got it!" Charles shoved the copybook at Lochinvar. "How's that?"

Lochinvar glanced at the page. "Well done, Master Chuckle-head. One more and you'll have earned your visit with Lord Chesterfield." He grinned at Charles, then turned to Persy. His grin faded. "I'm sorry to hear that you don't care for maths. I'd hoped . . . you seem to understand what would be suitable. Maybe you'd . . . if I could impose on you to look over some books with me?"

Pen laughed. "Persy not like maths? What has she been telling you? She's brilliant at it. Why, just the other day she said she wished she could have been a teacher."

Persy restrained an urge to shove a teacup into Pen's mouth. She glanced uncomfortably at Lochinvar and saw that he was regarding her with a perplexed frown. "Why, Pen, I said no such thing."

"But you did—"

A slight cough interrupted her. Kenney had appeared in the

doorway again and was trying to catch Mama's eye. "Lord Carharrick is downstairs, my lady. He wishes to inquire about Miss Persephone."

"Well, goodness, Kenney. Do send him up. And bring some more tea and tarts, please." Mama looked pleased and smiled a small, private smile at Persy.

Before Persy could panic, Lord Carharrick was there. He wore one of the newly fashionable tailless box coats, fawn-colored, with striped trousers. He bowed to the room in general, then came to Persy and held out a large bunch of sweet violets. "I'm so glad to see you up and around, Miss Leland. Then I take it you suffered no lasting harm from my clumsiness?"

Yes! Here was a golden opportunity to change the topic of conversation and put Lochinvar off. She took the flowers he held out to her and sniffed them rapturously. "Oh, how lovely, Lord Carharrick. My favorite! How did you know? Yes, I'm feeling much better today, thanks to your prompt attention last night."

Pen made a noise that could only be described as a snort. But Lord Carharrick looked delighted. He took the chair nearest where she sat with Lochinvar and Charles and looked at her. His waistcoat was violet, too, just like the flowers—and just like the ribbons on her dress last night, which was somehow annoying. She tried not to think about it and gave him a radiant smile.

"Got that one too," said Charles, and flourished his book at Lochinvar before turning to the newcomer. "Did you ride here?" he asked, looking him over.

"No, I took my carriage," Lord Carharrick answered, looking puzzled. "Why do you ask?"

"No reason." Charles turned to Lochinvar. "Well, can we go see Lord Chesterfield *now?*"

"I think now would be an excellent time," Lochinvar replied, unsmiling. "Might I take Charles down to see Lord Chesterfield, Lady Parthenope?"

"Yes, of course, as long as he doesn't cony-catch you into letting him ride him." Mama looked hard at Charles, who turned dull red and slouched to the door.

Lochinvar followed him, only pausing to bow and say in an unnecessarily loud voice, "Thank you for the refreshments, ma'am. Good-bye, Pen. Persy." He nodded shortly to Lord Carharrick, and disappeared after Charles.

Mama turned to Lord Carharrick. "Viscount Seton is a neighbor and the son of a dear friend. He and my daughters more or less grew up together."

She was trying to explain Lochinvar's familiar use of their names, Persy realized. Well, it *had* been rather noticeable.

"I see," Lord Carharrick said politely. Then he turned to Persy. "Since your foot feels better, I trust that I will have the honor of dancing with you tomorrow at Lady Brampton's ball?"

"Lord Chesterfield's incredible, Perse. He's—he's the most wonderful thing in the world!" Charles declaimed from the hearthrug, hugging his knees in ecstasy. He had been able to talk of little else since Lochinvar left that afternoon.

"Restrain yourself, Chuckles. His name is Lord Chesterfield, not Lord God Almighty, and he's just a horse," Persy replied as she peered into her hand mirror. They were due for a dinner party at

Lady Dowlett's that evening, and were waiting for Andrews to finish Mama's hair before she did theirs. Pen was still brushing out hers at their dressing table.

"And speaking of horses." Pen put down her brush and stared at Persy through the mirror. "What manure were you slinging about this afternoon, Persephone Leland?"

"I don't know what you're talking about." Persy pretended to be absorbed in her reflection.

"And Lochinvar promised that when my arm had healed and we were all back home again, he'd let me ride him in the paddock." Charles flapped his bandaged arm like a crazed chicken.

"Since when do you hate maths? And since when do you make eyes at people like Lord Carharrick? You looked like a heifer with indigestion whenever he looked at you today."

"Lochinvar said he looked like a wilted violet with that purple waistcoat," Charles added with relish.

"Charles!" Persy said severely.

He looked at her and shrugged. "Well, he did."

"Persy, there's something going on here." Pen sounded alarmingly like Ally for a moment.

"You're right, there is. Since when do you call Lord Seton by his first name, Chucklehead?" Persy asked.

"He told me to call him Lochinvar! He did!" Charles protested. "He said we'd known each other too long to be formal. Sometimes I just call him Seton, and that's all right too."

"You two have become best chums, haven't you?" commented Pen.

Persy relaxed. Good. Her distraction ploy had worked.

"Well, why not? We men have to stick together, if anything's going to get done." Charles sniffed. "By the way, he wanted to know if we'd heard anything about Ally and when we were going back to the Allardyces' shop."

Persy busied herself with her mirror again, but the reflection that looked at her was troubled. She'd been so tangled up in her own troubles the last few days that she had given only passing thought to Ally—mostly wishing that she were there to help her sort out her chaotic emotions. If Ally were here, she'd surely be able to tell her what to do.

Or would she? What would Ally say if she told her about the love spell? The thought made Persy wince, but she'd been presented to Her Majesty and was now, in the eyes of the world, an adult. Ally could no longer make her decisions for her. And just because she'd made a bad one in casting that spell on Lochinvar didn't mean she couldn't try to do better.

"You're right, Chuck. We do owe it to the Allardyces to let them know what we've been doing about looking for Ally," she said aloud.

"Which is precious little." Pen looked uncomfortable. "We'll ask Mama if we can go see them again."

Another invitation to tea with Princess Sophia at Kensington Palace briefly helped raise Persy's spirits. This time she paid more attention to the old palace's layout, though what good this would do them, she didn't know. There was no way she'd ever be able to wander about it looking for Ally. But it made her feel as if she were trying to help, at least.

Princess Sophia was more than cordial, kissing each of them on their arrival. "How kind of you young ones to come back and visit a quiet old lady like me!" she exclaimed, and sat them on either side of her on the sofa. Her old-fashioned chemise dress and tiny neck ruff made her look like a dressmaker's doll, lost and forgotten for years in a bureau drawer among faded sachets and old lace.

"I had invited the duchess to bring dear Victoria to meet you today, but alas, she was already engaged. It is a most busy time of year, as I'm sure you know," she continued.

Pen looked disappointed but said, "We enjoy visiting you, ma'am. You are most kind to honor us with the invitation."

"And you are most kind to come!" Sophia clapped her hands like a delighted child, and Persy remembered Mama's assessment of her that night at dinner with Grandmama Leland. The elderly princess *was* like a bored, lonely child, grateful even for the diversion of having a pair of unsophisticated girls to tea. It was a wonder that she hadn't turned into a gossiping intriguer out of sheer ennui, but remained simple and kind. Persy's heart warmed to her.

The princess poured them both chocolate and nodded to her lady-in-waiting to pass the plate of biscuits. "Now, you must tell me about your balls. Have you made any conquests yet? Any devoted beaus?"

"Persy has," Pen said.

Persy's jaw dropped.

"I knew it! And who is the young man? Is he handsome and wealthy? Or is he a too-charming younger son?" Princess Sophia looked even more delighted.

"It's Lord Carharrick, the Earl of Camborne's heir. He's been most attentive to my sister at every ball we've been to, always doing his best to get the supper dance, and the last waltz when he can. Isn't he smitten?" She leaned past the princess and stared hard at Persy.

Well, what should she expect Pen to think? But did she have to start talking about it in front of Princess Sophia?

"Ooh, she's blushing! You must tell us all," Princess Sophia urged.

Pen suddenly seemed to change her mind about needling Persy. "Speaking of blushing, you must hear what happened to a Miss Mullet at Lady de Courcy's ball. It was shocking!" she said in a dramatically conspiratorial tone that distracted Princess Sophia immediately. Persy was left to swallow her pique in silence.

On the carriage ride home, she turned to Pen. "What was that about?"

"What was what?" Pen asked, looking out the window and away from her.

"Telling the princess that Lord Carharrick is my beau." Persy did her best to keep her tone even.

"Well, isn't he?" Now Pen turned back to her. There was a speculative light in her eye that Persy had never seen before. "He certainly seems to be with you a great deal."

"He is not! Well, not that much."

"No?" Pen looked like a stranger all of a sudden.

"Well, what's wrong with it if he is?"

"What's wrong is that you make an absolute noodle of yourself whenever he's around, but you never even mention him at any other time. There's something funny going on here and you're not telling me about it." Pen still stared at her.

"I am not!"

"Girls, please!" Andrews put down her book and looked at them severely. They had almost forgotten that she was there, waiting for them during their visit to the palace. "I've never heard you quarrel like this before. Now that you are grown, is it time to start?"

"Sorry," Pen muttered. She gazed out the window at the passing street the entire trip home, while Persy sat feeling more wretched and alone than she ever had in her life. Ally had vanished, and she'd been able to do nothing to help her. She would never have Lochinvar, but did she have to lose her sister too?

12

*M*ama was quite happy to bring them and Lochinvar for another visit to the Allardyces'. Now that they'd shown themselves to be popular at parties and balls, most of her anxiety had melted away. She was relaxed and genial, especially to the mothers of girls who were not asked to dance as frequently as her daughters were.

Once again she dropped them at the bookshop door, promising to return for them after she called at Madame Gendreau's and Madame LeBlanc's. Lorrie Allardyce was in the window dusting and surveying the passersby when they drove up. She peered out at them, waved cheerfully, and vanished. An instant later Mr. Allardyce was opening the door for them.

"Lady Atherston, Miss Persy, Miss Pen, we are honored," he began, with a courtly bow for Mama's benefit. But Persy caught the anxious inquiry in his eye when he straightened. She shook her head slightly, and his shoulders slumped in disappointment. "Will you do us the compliment of taking a glass of Mrs. Allardyce's cordial?" he continued, still gracious.

"I should be delighted to when I come back for the children. Charles, I shall expect a good report of your behavior from your sisters and Lord Seton when I return." Mama fixed him with her eye as she turned back to the carriage door, held open by a grinning footman.

Charles smiled angelically. "Of course, Mother dear."

Mama snorted and left.

Persy's attention was caught by another figure, tall and slightly stooped and dressed in a canvas coat like Mr. Allardyce's. By the similarity of his features to Ally's, she guessed that this must be her brother, Merlin.

Mrs. Allardyce hurried forward to introduce him. As she came to Lochinvar she said, "And your book on foreign schools, Lord Seton? Was it what you had wanted? Merlin, won't you show Lord Seton those other books that came in on Tuesday? You can reach them more easily than I. Top shelf, near the front window." She bustled the girls and Charles back toward the office. Lorrie drifted after them, still pretending to dust.

"Lorrie! Where do you think you're going? I thought I'd told you to polish the lamps?" Merlin Allardyce called after her. To Persy's amusement, Lorrie pretended not to hear him and followed them back to the office.

Mr. Allardyce was already there, setting out chairs. He did not waste any time on niceties. "Any news?"

Pen spoke. "We've been to Kensington Palace twice but haven't been able to look around at all." She explained about meeting Princess Sophia at their presentation and being invited to visit her. "It's so frustrating to be there and not be able to do anything. I've wondered if we should not confide in the princess and ask if she would search for us."

Persy bit her lip. She had been having the same thought but hadn't voiced it because she and Pen were barely on speaking terms.

Mr. Allardyce rubbed his chin and frowned. "Do you trust her?"

"Why shouldn't we?" Pen looked puzzled. "She's a harmless old dear."

"Well, you know the lady. Maybe you could ask her for a tour of the palace, if she invites you again?" he suggested, brightening.

"Why don't you bring me along next time?" Charles piped up. "I could sneak into the palace while you're taking tea and search it."

Pen rolled her eyes. "You'd be lost in three minutes, and we'd never find you again. Besides, there are maids and footmen everywhere and probably guards, too. Princess Victoria lives there, remember? Now stop interrupting. We had to bring Chuckl—I mean Charles—today, or he would have burst," she explained to the Allardyces. "Now that his arm is healing, he can't sit still. I'm looking forward to you getting shipped back to Eton in June, Charley-horse."

"Well, it was only a suggestion," Charles snapped. "You don't have to—to . . ." He glowered at Pen and turned his chair away from her.

"We're sorry we're so bad-tempered," Persy apologized. "Between not being able to help Ally and trying to get through all the social commitments we have without a maid or anyone to help, we're rather in a way. Poor Mama—"

Lorrie Allardyce made a strange, strangled sound. They all turned to look at her.

"It's nothing. I had a sneeze that got stuck," she said with a dignified sniff. Her eyes, however, were bright and thoughtful.

Mr. Allardyce gave her a quelling look. "Whatever you decide to do at Kensington, please be careful. Anyone who would kidnap an innocent young woman—"

"Whoever kidnapped my sister won't be likely to stop there," Lorrie interjected. "You two ought to be more on your guard. Honestly, don't you think I ought to go along with them to Mayfair to keep an eye on them? You could—"

"Really, Lorrie!" Mr. Allardyce said sternly. "That is an inappropriate, not to mention silly suggestion."

"Fine," Charles said. "So maybe Persy and Pen ask Princess Sophia for help in looking around at Kensington Palace. Is that all? Isn't there *something* else we can do to help Ally? Can't Papa ask the king to help?"

Mr. Allardyce smiled. "I wish he could, Master Charles, but I don't think it will get us very far. No, all we can do for now is ask the princess's help, if your sisters deem it safe to do so."

Merlin was just wrapping up a book for Lochinvar when they filed solemnly from the back room of the bookshop. He glowered at Lorrie and jerked his head toward a basketful of sooty lamp chimneys waiting on the counter. Mama arrived a few minutes later, and after a small glass of Mrs. Allardyce's pomegranate cordial, they left.

"What book did you buy?" Charles asked Lochinvar, after they had rumbled along for several minutes in silence. "Something about horses?"

"No, nothing so exciting," Lochinvar replied, with a hint of a smile for Charles's eagerness. "Just another copy of the Mayo book on Pestalozzian schools. I sent my copy on to Mr. Chandler back at home, and wanted another. I'd hoped your sister might find it interesting."

Mama regarded him with an appraising look. "That was most kind of you, dear boy."

Persy looked quickly down at her gloved hands.

"Perse!" hissed Charles.

"Hmm?" She looked up and saw him jerk his head toward Lochinvar, who held something out to her.

The book.

"F-for me?" she stuttered.

"I—I rather hoped you would . . . if you're not too busy." Stuttering seemed to be contagious.

Persy stared at the book in his outstretched hand. There was nothing she would love better than to take the book and devour it, then spend hours discussing it with him so she could watch the way he leaned forward, his eyes wide open with enthusiasm, or the absentminded way he ruffled his hair when contemplating a question. If only Lochinvar were giving it to her because he *really* wanted to . . . oh, why had she been so stupid and put that spell on him?

"No, I . . . no, thank you, Lord Seton. Surely you might, er . . . find someone with more knowledge and interest—"

"Persephone!" Mama sounded outraged. She didn't say anything more but it wasn't necessary. Persy gulped and, feeling as if her hand belonged to somebody else, reached out and took the small book from him. Their fingertips just grazed each other, and she was sure that the book would burst into flames under her hand, so incendiary was the fleeting contact even through her gloves. She stole a glance at Lochinvar. A faint flush had crept up his cheeks, making his eyes appear very bright. They were fixed on her.

That week Persy survived, in addition to the usual round of social calls and appointments with Madame Gendreau, five balls, four dinners with either cards or music afterward, three parties, two breakfasts, and the abrupt departure of another new lady's maid.

This time, frightening her off was intentional. In a way, Persy was grateful that Potts was so awful, for it gave her and Pen a moment of camaraderie and common purpose as they had not shared for weeks.

"Persephone, Penelope, this is Potts. She comes most highly recommended, and I am sure she'll suit you just fine," said Mama as they entered the morning room. Her voice was warm, but there was a dubious set to her mouth.

It wasn't hard to see why. In contrast to the last maid, Potts was closer to their own age, in her early twenties, and pretty in a sharp-featured way. She examined each of them as Mama continued to wax effusive. Persy could almost see the figures tallying in her prominent eyes as she assessed every detail of their dresses in pounds and shillings.

When at last Mama sent them upstairs to show Potts their room, the new maid picked up where their mother had left off. "I am sure I shall like it here. Milady Atherston is extremely kind, isn't she? Of course, she is your mother so you'd have to say so. But she is quite well dressed, and you two aren't too bad, either. Though I must say, Miss Penelope, that shade of blue doesn't suit you as well as it might. It would look better on someone with my coloring, don't you think? I've always been quite fond of it as it looks so well on me. You must show me your gowns so I can start seeing what needs work. So you have a ball tonight, do you? Are there any beaus you're trying to charm who will be there? I've got some ideas for hair that I'm sure will just become the latest thing." She winked.

Persy looked away with a sinking feeling in her stomach and caught Pen's eye. There was a wicked sort of gleam in it that she thought she recognized.

"My, so this is your room? Well, I must say I'm a little surprised it's not bigger. Still, I don't suppose you're here much, what with your social commitments." Potts spoke with strange, rounded, drawn-out vowels, and Persy realized she was trying to imitate what she thought was an aristocratic accent.

The maid marched over to one of their clothes presses and threw open the doors. "Mmm-hmm . . . not bad . . . ooh, I rather fancy that one . . . ," she mumbled as she riffled through piles of neatly folded dresses.

"Perse!" Pen hissed in her ear. "Are you thinking what I'm thinking?"

"Probably. But what can we do? We need a maid. Mama can't spare Andrews anymore," Persy whispered under cover of Potts's happy monologue. "She's been run off her feet these last evenings."

"The entire household will be even more unhappy if we let this one stay long enough to properly set her hooks in us. We'll be doing everyone a favor if we get rid of her now," Pen returned fiercely. "What do you say?"

Persy looked over at Potts, who had pulled down one of their new evening dresses, of pale green striped silk, and was holding it against herself with a dreamy expression. "Why, that's my favorite one!" Persy protested feebly.

"You watch. In a moment it'll be, 'Miss Persephone, green really isn't your color, you know,'" muttered Pen. "Come *on*, Persy!"

"It's a lovely dress, but green can be so hard on some complexions," Potts said, holding the dress out at arm's length and peering over it.

Persy would have liked to laugh, but this was more than she could handle. She drew herself up and muttered a string of words.

A sleeve unfolded itself from out of the press and fluttered at Potts, trying to tap her on her shoulder.

"What?" Potts whirled around. Another dress snaked out its sleeve and snatched Persy's green dress out of the maid's hands. Pen started to snicker.

"Wh—wha—" Potts didn't seem to know whether to look at the clothes press full of shivering, shifting dresses or at Pen, clutching her sides and nearly shouting with mirth. Her mouth opened and closed as her head swung back and forth between the two, and Persy was reminded of a beached fish. She narrowed her eyes and spoke a few words more.

Faint thuds issued from the bottom shelves of the press, and Potts squealed again as riding boots and shoes walked their way out and began to kick her in the ankles and shins. The dresses that had sleeves long enough reached out to pummel her, and a shawl tossed over the edge of the press door flapped menacingly. Pen nearly howled as Potts gave them one last wild-eyed look and fled the room. A few seconds later they heard the front door slam.

Pen dropped to their bed. "Oh, Perse, that was wonderful. Her face . . ." She dissolved into fresh gales of laughter.

Persy grinned at her but felt a sudden twinge of guilt when she thought of Potts's horrified face. Mama would not be pleased. She was trying to find them a maid so that poor Andrews wouldn't be overworked helping the three of them. This was the second time she'd done magic without thinking it through and regretted the results.

"Come on, Pen," she said. "Help me put these shoes away and come up with an excuse for our latest maid's abrupt departure."

Persy was so happy to have spent a few unstrained minutes with Pen that she forgot to be nervous before the de Courcys' ball that evening. Or maybe she was just getting more used to being out in society, after all the events they had attended lately.

Lochinvar had claimed the first waltz with her, as he often did. He didn't ask if she'd read the book about schools yet and she did not mention it, though she had indeed already read it—twice, in fact. The memory of the touch of his hand on hers still burned and tingled, which was silly . . . after all, they had waltzed at several balls, and waltzing meant placing her hand in his. They were waltzing right now, for heaven's sake. But there had been something different about that touch in the carriage, something far beyond the simple contact required in dancing. She still wasn't sure what it was. Maybe she'd just imagined it. All she could do was hope that he hadn't felt it too.

When Lochinvar brought her back to her seat, Gerald Carharrick was waiting with Mama as usual, to claim the first of his dances of the evening. Persy remembered Pen's horrid comments about his being her beau and bit her lip.

At least Lord Carharrick's manners were excellent. He didn't linger by their seats, discouraging other young men from asking her to dance by his presence. But he always seemed to be nearby, so that if a fan were dropped or a chair required shifting, he was at her side almost at once to render assistance. And whenever she danced a cotillion he always seemed to be in place behind or in front of her, so that he could smile and nod to her as they moved through the figures. Might it be possible that she'd encouraged him a little *too* much?

Persy brooded over that thought for the next hour. She didn't want anyone trying to engage her already-engaged heart. When Lord Carharrick took her into the dining room for refreshments after the supper dance, she found herself studying him. He was as prompt as always in finding her a comfortable seat where she might see as much of the room as possible, and where the glare of candles would not dazzle her eyes nor a cold draft chill her. And as usual, she let him choose her a plate of such dainties as were offered, for this duty seemed to please him. Did he gaze at her with an unwonted tenderness in his eyes, or was he simply shortsighted? She scrutinized him as she spooned her coffee ice, letting his conversation wash over her as she did.

Unfortunately, her inattention to the matter at hand—the coffee ice—led to trouble. A quick movement made her look down at her lap, where a small light brown drip looked back up at her like an accusing eye.

"Oh, botheration!" She set down her glass just as another drip landed next to the first.

Lord Carharrick followed her gaze and at once whisked out an immaculate square of linen handkerchief. "Please," he said, offering it to her.

"No, it's not that bad," she said. "It just got my gloves, that's all." She held them out to him in demonstration, feeling almost giddy with relief.

Her white embroidered muslin gown had just arrived from Madame Gendreau's the previous day and Mama would be irate if she'd dripped coffee ice on it, especially now that they were maid-less once more and Andrews had to help take care of their evening dresses. But the gloves were new, too, with a delicate touch of embroidery around their hems and her initials worked in fine gold thread. At least it was not as expensive to replace them as the dress would have been, and white dancing gloves had to be changed frequently, anyway. But she'd brought only a plain pair along just in case, and these had looked so well with her dress.

"A pity. They're very pretty." Lord Carharrick took one of them from her and smoothed the embroidery under his fingers. "I wonder . . . ," he began, then hesitated.

"Yes?"

"I wonder if I might keep this glove to show my—my sister. She has a fondness for pretty gloves, and I'm sure she'd love to see this one and learn where you got it from."

His face was slightly pink as he spoke, and Persy found herself warming to him. Not all brothers would have bothered remembering such a thing about their sisters. Would Charles grow up to be as considerate? She could just hear him now: "I say, that's a very interesting spell book you have there. My sister Persy would be most . . ."

"How kind of you, to keep your sister in your thoughts. Is she here tonight? I don't think we've met yet," Persy said, looking about her.

"No, she's—she's not out yet." Lord Carharrick folded the glove carefully and tucked it inside his coat. "May I get you another ice?"

Before escorting her back to the ballroom, Lord Carharrick accompanied Persy to the room where a maid looked after the ladies' wraps, so that she could change her gloves. They passed Pen and Lochinvar on the way.

Pen looked at her with a hint of alarm. "Are you all right? Not another ankle . . ."

Persy paused. Pen seemed really concerned, which was reassuring under the circumstances. She tried not to look at Lochinvar as she confessed, "No, I'm fine. I just needed a fresh pair of gloves, because I dripped coffee ice on the first pair. Where did Mama find the embroidered ones? Lord Carharrick would like to know for his sister."

Lochinvar cleared his throat quietly.

"Um . . . Piver's glove shop, I think," said Pen. "Let me see."

Persy handed her the remaining glove. Pen tsked over it. "Did you stain both?"

"Yes. Thanks, Pen, I knew you'd remember."

Pen and Lochinvar continued back toward the ballroom, and Persy got her fresh gloves. Lord Carharrick brought her back to Mama in the ballroom and took his usual unobtrusive place nearby.

"You are back late," Lady Parthenope commented after he left them. "I didn't think Maria de Courcy's supper worth lingering over." Mama was not overly fond of Lady de Courcy.

"I spilled an ice on my gloves and had to change them. Don't worry, my dress escaped," Persy reassured her. "It was Piver, wasn't it, where we got the embroidered ones with our initials? That's what I told Lord Carharrick."

"Yes. We shall have to go back for another pair, if you'll promise to take more ca— Lord Carharrick? Why did he wish to know?" Mama frowned slightly.

"For his sister. He took one, to show her. She's fond of gloves, he says."

A slow smile spread across Mama's face. "He doesn't have any sisters. Only a younger brother. The young rapscallion!" She gave Persy a smug look and patted her hand. "He just wanted to find an excuse to keep your glove."

"Whatever for?"

"As a token, of course."

"A token?" What was Mama talking about?

"A love token." Mama patted her hand again but mercifully did not say anything more. Persy sat back and wished she could melt into the floor.

No! This was absolutely *the* last thing she needed right now. Lord Carharrick couldn't be falling in love with her!

But what else could she expect? She'd been flirting with him just dreadfully over the last week or two, and he seemed to like it.

Lord Carharrick was a very eligible young man, heir to a comfortable fortune and an earldom in the West Country. He was also a choosy one, as this was his third season without having become engaged. It would be a feather in her cap to capture such a matrimonial prize.

But she didn't want to.

She knew that marriage in her social class was as much about fortunes and alliances as it was about love. She knew that she was lucky to have some say in choosing her husband, rather than having one picked for her as was done in so many other places in the world. That was what the season was, after all—a marriage market for the offspring of the aristocracy. Mama and Papa would heartily approve of her marrying Lord Carharrick, and she knew it.

But she still didn't want to.

She loved Lochinvar. And since she couldn't have him, then she

wouldn't have anyone. Oh, why couldn't she just go off somewhere and be a teacher like Ally, and not worry about finding a husband?

"Are you all right, my dear?" Mama's voice broke into her gloomy reverie. "I am sorry if I sounded harsh over your gloves. Accidents do happen, after all. We shall order you another pair. Perhaps two pairs."

"Thank you, Mama," Persy said dutifully, but she knew how unenthusiastic she sounded.

Another invitation to visit Princess Sophia arrived the next day. Charles and Persy were doing a Latin lesson when it arrived.

"You're getting awfully chummy with her, aren't you?" Charles asked as he read the note of invitation over Persy's shoulder.

"I wouldn't go quite that far, Chucklehead. She's quite old and a member of the royal family, remember. But she does seem to enjoy our company," Persy answered as she refolded the note and put it aside to show Pen.

Charles rolled his eyes as he took his seat. Persy couldn't resist poking him with a pencil. "What's wrong with us going to visit a lonely old lady?" she asked.

"Oh, nothing. But at least you could do something about looking for Ally while you're there at Kensington taking tea with royalty. I'm starting to think you don't even care about her anymore." Charles snatched the pencil from her.

Persy rounded on him fiercely. "I do too care!"

"Then why don't you *do* something?" He looked at her, all sarcasm gone. "Come on, Persy. You and Pen have been so busy with dresses and balls and parties. Finding Ally is a lot more important than those."

Persy's throat was suddenly hot and tight. "I know it is," she said, and slumped in her chair. "But I don't know what to do. You're not a girl. You don't understand. I have to go to these parties and be charming and pleasant, because I have to convince someone to fall in love and make an offer for me. There's nothing else I can do. And I can't just saddle up a horse and go down to Kensington on my own to look for Ally, because I'm a girl. I'm not allowed to go even down to the corner of the street on my own. Don't you dare scold me anymore, Charles Leland." She turned away from him, blinking back tears.

"Aw, Persy . . ." She felt Charles pull his chair closer and put his good arm over her shoulder. "I didn't mean to make you feel bad. I know you can't help being a girl. I just wish you were a boy, so we could go off and look—" He broke off. Persy felt him stiffen like a pointer that had spotted a bird.

"What?" she asked.

"Perse, what if you *were* a boy?" His voice had gone high with excitement.

"What are you talking about?"

"I mean, what if you looked like a boy? What if we dressed you up like a boy in some of my clothes? Then me and you could—"

"You and I," Persy corrected automatically.

"We could sneak out sometime—couldn't you tell Mama that you're ill? Then we could go to Kensington ourselves and have a look around. The gardens are open to everyone, Papa said, and I bet we could find a door somewhere to get inside the palace. You could open a locked door, couldn't you?"

"Maybe . . . oh, Charles, I can't do that!" The excitement his words had sparked in her flared, then sputtered.

"Do you just want to let Ally rot, then?" He looked hard at her. "Stop thinking like a girl. London's ruining you. Two months ago you would've said yes right away. Now you're turning into a—a—"

"Jellyfish?"

"Yes! A jellyfish in gloves and feathers. You're just afraid of being caught, aren't you?"

Persy smiled without humor. "Well, yes, I am."

"But don't you see? If anyone can do it without getting caught, it's you. You could open a locked door into the palace, couldn't you? I'll bet you could do that from *here*."

He looked so crafty, laying on his flattery like so much sugar frosting, that her smile became genuine. He saw her smile and grinned. "Bet you could do it from here with your eyes closed!"

"Or else I could distract a guard long enough for us to slip past him and inside." Persy found herself getting caught up in his enthusiasm. "Do you think we could do it? Really? I don't look much like a boy."

"Why not? There's so many people in London, we'd blend right in. No one will notice a couple of boys larking about in a garden. I'll bring that boat Grandmama Leland gave me for us to sail on the pond—there must be some water or something in the gardens there. And if you braid your hair and we give you a high neckerchief and a hat to hide it, and if you, um, slouch a little"—he gestured delicately toward her chest—"then we ought to be able to do it."

Persy looked at him, biting her lip. It was a lunatic idea, and a highly improper one too. What if she were to be caught wandering around London dressed in boys' clothes, accompanied only by her younger brother? It would be a tremendous scandal, and would probably ruin her chances of making a grand marriage. That decided it for her.

"All right. I don't know how we will do it, but you're right, we've got to try. Not being able to do anything about Ally has been making me almost sick," she finally said.

"Yes! What about tomorrow?" Charles jumped out of his chair and began to dance a jig. A vase of peonies on the table teetered.

Persy caught it. "Do you think we can be ready for it tomorrow, what with clothes and everything for me? If we're going to do this, we've got to do it right."

"Of course we can." Charles stopped dancing. "We have to tell Pen about it. She'll help."

"No!" Persy said. Charles looked at her in surprise, and she continued in a quieter tone. "We shouldn't. We need to keep this to just us. She wouldn't be able to come with us, anyway—three would be too hard to sneak into the palace. And if we get caught, it's our problem. We don't need to draw her down with us."

Charles considered. "You're probably right," he said. "But it seems funny for you two to be having secrets from each other. You never have before."

"I know," Persy sighed. "I know."

Step one of their plan commenced almost immediately, to Persy's surprise. Mama came in a few moments later to check on their lesson. Charles showed her his neatly written translation of a passage from Caesar, and while she perused it (though Persy was not sure why, as Mama's Latin was extremely rusty) he turned to his sister with an anxious air.

"Why, Persy, you don't look very well. Are you sure you're all right?"

Persy stared at him. He winked back, and comprehension dawned on her. "Er, no, now that you mention it. I do feel a little . . ." She sighed and slid down in her seat.

Mama put down Charles's translation and gave her a sharp look. "A little what? Oh, Persy, you can't get sick now! There's a card party at the Gilleys' tonight that I promised we'd attend after dinner at the Lyons'. And tomorrow is the Duchess of Gordon's ball. We can't miss that."

"Cards?" Persy put a hand to her forehead. "My head is starting to ache so. Just the *thought* of cards makes it worse. And my stomach . . ." She gulped some air as Charles had once taught her and emitted a satisfactorily disgusting belch. Mama jumped and looked alarmed.

"I don't think you want her at the Lyons' dinner if she's going to keep doing *that*," Charles commented with an air of ghoulish interest. "It's positively horripilatious."

"But . . ." Mama sat down next to Persy and felt her forehead. "You do feel rather clammy."

"Perhaps I ought to stay home tonight. If I rest tonight and tomorrow, then I should feel better in time for that ball tomorrow," Persy suggested.

"Oh dear. Dorothy Gilley will be disappointed. And tomorrow we had some calls and some shopping planned. But you are probably right. You cannot go to the Lyons' if you're in danger of—well, you know what I mean. Why don't you go have a lie-down, dear? You have been working so hard tutoring your brother along with everything else that it is no wonder you're feeling seedy."

"I'll help her up to her room," Charles said, rising and offering

Persy his good arm with a solicitous expression that nearly convulsed her.

Lady Parthenope looked misty-eyed. "Thank you for being so concerned about your sister. You are all such good, dutiful children." She patted his shoulder, touched Persy's cheek gently, and shooed them from the room.

Persy was torn between guilt and laughter. She managed to hold in the latter until they were up the stairs and out of their mother's earshot. "You ought to be on the stage, you little devil!" she whispered at her brother.

"Good, aren't I?" He grinned. "You weren't bad, either. Bet you never thought you'd be glad I taught you how to burp on command. Maybe Eton's been worth it after all. Right, then. Tonight while they're all out we'll get your disguise ready, and tomorrow while they're shopping we'll go to Kensington."

13

$\mathcal{T}$he next afternoon, a pair of boys strolled down the path from the Round Pond in Kensington Gardens toward the warm redbrick façade of the palace. The taller of the two boys held a dripping model sailboat tightly to his chest. He walked with small, hesitant steps, which seemed to irritate his companion.

"You're not wearing a dress anymore, Perse! You've got to walk like a boy now," Charles muttered from the corner of his mouth.

"That's easy for you to say," Persy hissed back at him. "I feel practically undressed. It's hard to get used to having bare legs."

It was also hard to get used to the neckerchief tied untidily around her neck and the disreputable felt hat pulled down over her ears to hide her hair. Charles had given her one of his arm bandages to bind her chest with, but it felt very strange not to be wearing a corset in public. And the trousers had been abstracted from Papa's dressing room after a breathless few moments hiding from his valet, because Charles's had proved far too snug. Not that Papa's fit her terribly well.

"They're not bare. You've got to *try*, Persy. That's better. How about a little swagger, like this?" Charles demonstrated.

Persy giggled, and he shushed her. "Stop that! Boys don't giggle. You'd better just be quiet, and let me do the talking if we have to."

"All right," Persy replied in as deep a voice as she could.

Charles giggled.

"I thought you said boys don't giggle?" Persy croaked.

"I can't help it. You sound like a bullock with the quinsy." He gave her a small shove. She bumped into him and put out her tongue at him. This was actually starting to be a little fun.

"That's better. Now we look like boys." Charles kicked Persy in the shins.

"Ow! Do we have to be quite so realistic?"

"Yes. You can do it too—ow! Not *that* hard! Let's go this way. I don't see any doors here."

Persy looked up at the looming building. "Ally could be behind any of those windows," she murmured, and clutched the boat harder.

"That's what we're here to find out." Charles trudged purposefully along. Persy broke into a trot to keep up with him.

If anyone had told her just yesterday how differently the sexes moved, she would have scoffed. But now, unencumbered by corsets and layers of petticoats and long skirts, she could well understand the difference. There was a very good reason women and girls didn't run, with their lungs constricted and their legs hampered. Her new freedom was a little frightening, but given time, she thought that she could get used to it. Very used to it. In fact, she was not looking forward to resuming her regular mode of dress, and she knew that she would always have the memory of this freedom in the back of her mind somewhere whenever Andrews laced her into a ball gown.

As they rounded a corner to another wing of the palace Charles nudged her. "There," he said, pointing with his chin at a small door. "It's not a main entrance, so there aren't likely to be a lot of people around it."

"But it's more likely to be locked," Persy said, squinting.

"So? I'll bet you can open it. And it's in a sort of angle of the building, so we won't be as noticeable. Come on. We can put the boat in those bushes there, and come back for it when we're through." He looked around them, and Persy was grateful that gathering clouds had kept many strollers from the gardens that day. Would anyone notice a pair of boys trying to open a door into a royal palace?

"Charles! Wait a minute. I just thought of something." She dumped the boat into a bush and took him by the shoulders.

"What?"

"Don't wiggle. I'm going to see if I can put a cloaking spell over us both."

Charles gaped at her. "A cloaking spell? When did Ally teach you that?"

"She didn't. I learned it on my own. It's easy to cast but takes a lot of energy to maintain. I'm not sure if I can do it for both of us. Perhaps if we stay close, or hold hands . . ." She closed her eyes and muttered the words she'd read in one of Ally's grimoires. All at once a slight stuffiness surrounded her, and the twittering of birds and distant clomp and clatter of a passing carriage in the lane beyond the palace sounded muffled, as if there were a blanket over her head.

Charles's eyes widened. "I think it worked," he whispered. "Are we invisible? Does it cloak sound, too?"

"I'm not sure. The book wasn't clear on that point. We'd better be quiet, though, just in case it doesn't. And no, we're not invisible. We're just very difficult to see. If someone were looking for us, they'd be able to find us." She held on to his good hand and pulled him to the door. "You'd better hold on to me because the cloaking spell might not work if you let go, and I may need both hands to open this."

Charles nodded and put his hand on her shoulder, and they both turned to examine the door. No keyhole, so it must bolt from the inside. Persy breathed out a sigh of relief. "This will be easier than trying to enchant a lock. All I have to do is move the latch, or bolt, or whatever it is."

"Without seeing it?" Charles sounded skeptical.

"I may not be able to see it, but I know it's there. What it *is* isn't important. It's what I *do* with it that is. You've heard Ally say that many times. I'm not enchanting the latch so that it will move. I'm exerting my will to cause the door to do what I want, which is to open. How it chooses to do that is up to it. Do you understand?"

"Um, what if it decides to open by exploding, or falling to pieces or something?" Charles's eyes swiveled nervously around.

"It won't. A door is meant to open and close. That's its purpose. I'm just asking it to fulfill that purpose. It wouldn't open by exploding, because then it wouldn't be able to open and close anymore. Of course, if someone else were standing on the other side, willing it to stay shut, it might crack or splinter under the strain. We never tried anything like that with Ally, because she said it was a cruel thing to do to a poor inanimate object that couldn't help itself. Now, do you want me to open this door, or not?"

He still looked nervous, but nodded.

Persy turned back to the door and closed her eyes again. There was a faint grinding noise, as of metal scraping against metal, and the door sagged open a crack. Persy turned to smile at Charles, and almost lurched into him.

"Bravo, Perse!" Charles hissed. "Hey, what is it? Are you ill?" He pushed her upright.

"I just lost my balance. I'm all right," Persy muttered and held on to his shoulder for a moment. She had forgotten that she would be doing two spells at once, the cloaking and the opening. Sustaining more than one spell at a time was doable, but it took a certain amount of concentration. She took a deep breath, and the momentary dizziness subsided. "I'm fine. Let's go in and get busy, shall we?"

They found themselves in a long corridor. Charles peered down its length. "What do you think, Persy?"

"I think we need to open doors and look behind them. There's no telling where she might be." Persy paused to make sure the cloaking spell still covered them.

"Right ho!" Charles tucked Persy's hand under his good arm and pulled her down the hall to the first door in sight.

The first half-dozen doors were disappointing. Most opened to reveal stacks of broken furniture, or barrels and boxes, or merely emptiness and an odor of deceased mice. But at least no one came to disturb their search. At the end of the corridor Persy opened a final door, revealing stairs. "None of these rooms seems to be used for much. Let's go up."

"But at least we haven't run into anyone down here." Charles hung back.

"Don't get all hen-hearted on me now, Chuckles. You were the one who wanted to come search the palace while we had tea with the princess. Show some spinal fortitude, won't you?" Persy tugged on his hand. Had she and Charles changed places? After her timidity out of doors, she now felt a fierce sort of joy at sneaking around the palace, at actually *doing* something about finding Ally instead of moping at home.

Charles swallowed and followed her up the stairs, still clutching her arm. They had a brief moment of terror when a hod-carrying footman suddenly appeared on the stairs above them, but he passed them by without a glance.

"Golly, Perse!" Charles whispered after the footman's footsteps could no longer be heard. "Your spell's a stunner." But he maintained his death grip on her arm just the same.

The doors that lined this corridor were taller and more handsomely made. But again, most of the rooms behind them, though also larger and obviously once intended for living in rather than storage, were either empty or held a few pieces of dust-sheeted furniture. Their tall windows were covered with moth-eaten velvet and brocade draperies, shutting out the light. There was an aura of neglect about them that surprised Persy.

"This is where the heiress to the throne of England lives?" she muttered in disgust to Charles. "The plaster was falling off the ceiling in that last one, and most of them have cracked panes in the windows and at least a dozen mice or worse in each. Did you notice?"

"What about Princess Sophia's rooms? Are they as shabby as this?" Charles asked.

"Well, no. But they smell old, and the plaster on the fireplace in her drawing room is stained as if there's a leak somewhere. It doesn't seem to bother her." Persy scowled at a loose floorboard in the corridor. "But Princess Victoria should live someplace splendid and beautiful. It's only right."

"Maybe the king won't let her."

"No, that's not true. Papa told us the king would like it if she lived at court so that she could learn more about being a queen. It's her mother and that dreadful Sir John Conroy who keep her here, so that she won't be exposed to any 'evil influences.' But I can't think of any influence more evil than damp and dry rot, can you?" She peeked behind another door, wrinkled her nose, and slammed it shut.

"Shh, Persy. You're getting too loud." Charles tugged on her arm.

How long had Papa said it had been since a king had lived in Kensington Palace? Eighty years? No wonder it was falling into rack and ruin. It was a shame to let such a handsome old building deteriorate like this. It was a royal residence, after all, and a historic one, too. Hadn't William and Mary lived here after the Glorious Revolution put them on the throne? And Queen Anne?

And now another queen lived here—or at least a queen-to-be, Persy reminded herself. But she was half a prisoner in this tumble-down old building, thanks to the ambitions of her mother's crafty advisor. Persy remembered Sir John's bold manner and the unpleasant quirk in his smile when they met him in Princess Sophia's apartment. Her fingers curled around the knob of the next door, and she pulled it open.

To her surprise, this room wasn't dim at all. The draperies covering its windows had been pulled back, and cool cloudy daylight filled the space. Several pieces of less decrepit furniture were scattered about, and it looked reasonably clean. A small coal fire burned on the hearth to dissipate the damp, and the lamps were lit.

In the far wall was a closed door, and seated in a straight chair by it was a man, absorbed in a book. He looked up from his page, startled, and Persy choked back an exclamation of surprise and drew back quickly. It was the auburn-haired man with odd-colored eyes who had accompanied Sir John that day at Princess Sophia's—his secretary, Michael Carrighar.

"Who's there?" he said, staring at the door as he rose from his chair. With one part of her mind Persy remembered his Irish intonation and the peculiar way he had looked at her, while with another she tried desperately to figure out what to do. Surely he couldn't see them! That footman hadn't, back on the stairs. If they tiptoed out very quietly, he'd just think the door had opened on its own. That sort of thing happened all the time in drafty old buildings. He would see no one was there, and close the door, and go back to his book, so long as—

"Someone's there," Mr. Carrighar said slowly. "I know there is." His eyes searched the doorway and narrowed. "I can almost see you. . . ."

Once again, Persy was riveted by his strange eyes. She felt glued to the threshold despite Charles's frantic tugging on her arm. How could this man sense that she and Charles were there?

"Please wait. I should like to speak with you," the man said, and reached behind him to bolt the door. As soon as he had turned, Persy felt released. She turned and ran blindly down the hall, Charles hanging on her arm for dear life.

"Where?" he asked as they ran.

"I don't know. Anywhere!" Persy gasped. The sound of their footsteps on the scuffed wood floor no longer sounded muffled, and she realized that she had let go of the cloaking spell. No matter—Michael Carrighar had somehow seen past it, though imperfectly. Finding somewhere to hide was paramount, and the sooner the better. Any moment now he would realize that they had fled and come looking for them. And this time he *would* be able to see them.

"There!" She pulled them around a bend in the corridor and toward a pair of large mahogany doors that flew open in the face of her quickly hurled opening spell. They stumbled several paces into the new corridor before they were brought up short as the doors slammed shut behind them.

Like the other corridors they had searched, one wall of this one was pierced by tall mullioned windows. But between the windows, and all along the other wall, were tall, glass-fronted bookcases. Broad tables below the windows held green-shaded lamps, and dozens of high-backed mismatched chairs were scattered about. It looked like a very long, very thin library.

"Where—are we?" Charles panted, clutching his side. "What is this place?"

"I beg your pardon?" said a familiar voice behind them. Persy and Charles, still clutching hands, whirled around, and Persy just smothered a small scream.

Lochinvar Seton sat in a window seat just to the side of the door they had entered. He had a large book in his hands and a look of disbelief on his face.

"Lochinvar!" Charles nearly shrieked. He dropped Persy's hand and ran full tilt to the surprised man.

"Charles!" Lochinvar had managed to set down his book before Charles hurtled into his arms. "What are you doing here? Who . . ." He looked up at Persy, and his jaw dropped.

"We must hide, right now," she said in a mostly calm voice, wishing she could follow Charles's example and throw herself into Lochinvar's arms too. Was she relieved or mortified that he was here? Both, probably.

"But—it's—Persy!" Lochinvar stared at her over Charles's curly head, buried against his chest.

Just then Persy remembered her trousered legs and boy's hat. She flushed. "I'll explain later. Someone's looking for us. *Please!*"

Her urgency finally seemed to cut through his bemusement. "Down here," he said, and gestured them under one of the tables.

"That's the first place he'll look if he comes in here," she protested.

Lochinvar shook his head. "It will be all right. Quickly!"

Brisk footsteps could be heard approaching the door. Persy grabbed Charles and dove under the table, and Lochinvar sat down at it, casually slouching in his chair as if he had been reading there some time. She tried to ignore one of his feet digging into her knee, and heard him mutter something under his breath as the door opened.

"Oh," said a masculine voice. "I beg your pardon." It was Mr. Carrighar.

"Yes?" Lochinvar replied.

Charles tried to peer up under the edge of the table, but Persy yanked him back. She herself kept her eyes fixed on the floor as she waited to be dragged ignominiously out from their hiding place.

"You didn't happen to see anyone come this way in the last few minutes, did you?"

"I haven't seen anyone since the duke's butler let me in— No, that's not true. The footman brought in coal about ten minutes ago, but that's all." Lochinvar's voice was cool, with just a hint of interest. "For whom are you looking?"

Michael Carrighar ignored his question as he strolled toward the table where they huddled like rabbits in a hole. Persy could picture him straining to peer under it. "Are you sure? Not even a hint that someone might have entered? An opening door? Foot-steps? Or . . ." He trailed into silence, and Persy guessed he'd real-ized how strange such queries sounded. But what would Lochinvar make of them?

"Not a thing. It sounds as if you're looking for a ghost. Is Kens-ington haunted, then?" Lochinvar's voice held a smile.

His lightness of tone seemed to irritate the other man. "Not at all," Mr. Carrighar said shortly. "Good day, sir."

Persy saw his feet retreat from sight and heard the door click shut. She also saw that a long end of Charles's arm bandage had come loose and trailed a good foot from under the table. How had Mr. Carrighar not seen it there?

"You can let go of my ankle now, Charles," Lochinvar mur-mured. "I expect he's gone to look for you elsewhere."

Charles exhaled noisily and clambered out from under the table. Persy followed him more slowly and stood behind a chair to hide her legs.

"That's as scared as I've ever been. Thanks for hiding us, Lochin-var. You're a brick." Charles pantomimed wiping his brow and grinned up at him.

"My, er, pleasure. This is—I mean, would it be too much to ask why you were running away from that man? And how you got in here in the first place? And why?" Lochinvar glanced at Persy, and she saw him color. Well, if he was embarrassed by her costume, how did he think she felt? She gripped the chair in front of her more tightly.

"We ought to tell him, Persy," Charles said, gazing at Lochinvar with worship in his eyes. "Maybe he can help us look."

Persy swallowed and thought furiously, *Why, oh why, did it have to be Lochinvar who discovered us?* Charles had no idea how humiliating it was to be standing here in front of him dressed in boys' clothing, her legs exposed, obviously up to something nefarious. Her first instinct was to buy time. "Might we also ask what you're doing here?"

Lochinvar nodded, keeping his eyes carefully at shoulder level. "My father's an old acquaintance of the Duke of Sussex, whose library this is. Everyone knows the duke collects dictionaries and Bibles, but they don't know he also has a very fine collection of breeding books—horses, that is. Father wanted to look up a few things here, and the duke very kindly allowed me to come do his research and have a look around."

"Oh." Persy forgot about her legs for a moment. If Lochinvar had entrée to Kensington, maybe he could be convinced to help them search for Ally, as Charles had said. If she could manage to talk to him without melting into a puddle of embarrassment, that is. She chose her words carefully. "Thank you for hiding us. We—er, we weren't running from that man because we'd done anything wrong."

"No, of course not."

Why did he have to look so handsome standing there in a dark blue coat with his hands behind his back? "It was for a good cause. Really," she continued.

"Honestly, Persy!" Charles made a face at her and turned to Lochinvar. "We were looking for Ally."

Whatever Lochinvar had been expecting, it hadn't been this. His eyebrows shot up. "Miss Allardyce, here? Are you sure? How do you know?"

"We're sure. Um . . . someone told us she was here," Charles said. Persy gave a silent sigh of relief that he had the presence of mind to lie.

"Thus the, ah, disguise." Lochinvar didn't look convinced, but he was probably too polite to challenge them. "Where's your sister?" he asked. "Or was it just the pair of you?"

"Just us," Charles replied. "Persy thought it would be easier for just two of us to sneak in, and she didn't want to get Pen in trouble too if we got caught. But you aren't going to tell anyone, are you? Not even Pen? Please? And will you help us get in again so we can look some more?"

"I can't quite stroll into it anytime I wish. But if Father sends me again, of course I'll look. And I'll try to make sure he sends me soon." He looked down at his boots, and Persy saw that he was smiling. "So you disguised yourselves and sneaked in? That took a lot of courage."

At least that didn't sound too loverlike. Maybe her chilly treatment of him had begun to work. "It was the only way we could think of getting in. And we should probably think about getting out soon before Mr. Carrighar comes back. If you'll excuse us . . ."

Lochinvar had started to bundle up his papers. "I'll help you. You'll need a lookout, won't you?"

"Oh, we couldn't think—"

"Who did you say that man was? Mr. Carrighar? You knew him?"

Persy knew she should grab Charles and leave now, without Lochinvar, but she couldn't. This had seemed to be a fine adventure when they started, but now she was . . . well, *scared.* "Pen and I met him once, taking tea with Princess Sophia. He works for Sir John Conroy, who is part of the Duchess of Kent's household. We disturbed him in a room on the other corridor."

"That's odd. The duchess's suite is in this end of the palace, but nowhere near that corridor, according to the duke's butler. He gave me a brief tour when I arrived." Lochinvar stopped sorting his papers and looked thoughtful. "So why should one of the duchess's employees be here?"

"You don't suppose . . . ," Charles whispered.

Persy frowned. "That he has anything to do with Ally? I doubt it, Chuckles. We probably just disturbed him taking a break when he shouldn't have, that's all. It would explain his being overset. *I* shouldn't like to get on Sir John's bad side."

Lochinvar peered out the door then motioned them out. Persy wished she could put up the cloaking spell again, but it was impossible now that Lochinvar was with them.

"Which way did you come in?" Lochinvar whispered in her ear.

She pointed down the hall and tried not to shiver at the feeling of Lochinvar's warm breath on her ear. "That way and down some stairs. But I don't think we should go back that way, just in case Mr. Carrighar's there."

"Good point." Lochinvar thought for a moment. "All right, let's go this way. It will take longer, but will probably be safer." He held out his arm to her. "Charles, hold your sister's hand. Let's keep close, and tread as lightly as you can."

Persy nodded, feeling both tenser and calmer at the same time. It was comforting to let someone else plot their sneaking about for them. It was also nerve-racking to have Lochinvar take her arm and draw her close to his side, far closer than was usual or proper in public, so that her hip almost brushed his as they walked, without the usual buffering layers of skirt and petticoats. She swallowed hard and gripped Charles's hand till he wiggled his fingers in protest.

They tiptoed past more doors, through a small gallery, and down another short corridor. Lochinvar inclined his head toward the end of the passage. "I think there's a staircase there. It ought to lead down, and then we can find your door out again," he murmured. "Luck seems to be with us. I don't think anybody's—"

"No! I shan't listen!" cried a voice.

Persy clutched Lochinvar's arm. "Where did that come from?"

"I don't know. Come on." He set his mouth in a grim line and began to hurry down the corridor.

"It sounded like a girl," she whispered. "Who do you—"

A thump interrupted her. It sounded as if someone had banged a fist on the door a few paces ahead of them. "Damn it, child," snarled a voice, "you *will*."

Persy stopped dead. That second voice belonged to Sir John Conroy. She tried to let go of Lochinvar's arm, but he would not release her.

"What are you doing?" he mouthed at her, gesturing. "Come *on*."

"No—I have to hear." A sudden suspicion about the identity of the first speaker had seized her. She leaned toward the door, dragging Lochinvar and Charles with her.

"I don't know why I should stay and listen to you, Sir John. Anything you might wish to say to me can be said in my apartments, in front of Mama and Baroness Lehzen," said the girl's voice. It sounded close to tears, but still strong and clear, like the peal of a silver bell.

Persy stopped the exclamation that nearly escaped her lips. There was only one person that voice could belong to. "The princess," she breathed, more to herself than to Lochinvar or Charles. "That's Princess Victoria!"

"No," said Sir John. "This is between the two of us. And as your dear mama already knows and approves of what I have to say, there is little difference in whether we have our chat here, there, or on the steps of Westminster. Time is growing short, my dear girl. The—"

"I am not your dear girl. Address me by my proper title, if you please. And I don't believe you speak entirely for Mama . . . though if it weren't for your meddling, she and I might still be on speaking terms. Half the time I can't help wondering if you've bewitched her, she's become so unpleasant. If it weren't for my dear Lehzen, I don't know what I'd do."

Sir John's harsh tone turned soothing. "Foolish girl, your mama lives for you. Every waking moment she has is dedicated to your—"

"She lives for me inheriting the crown." The silver voice was tarnished with sadness and resentment.

"Why not? It is what you will do someday."

"She isn't my beloved mama anymore. You've turned her head so that all she can think about is what is due her as mother of the future queen—"

"Mother to the future queen who is still nine-tenths a child, for all that she turns eighteen in a few short weeks. What if—God forbid—the king should die tomorrow? Wouldn't it be far better to name your dear mama regent for you until you are twenty-one, and spend the next few years learning how to be a que—"

"So that you can be her closest advisor, of course," the princess said scornfully.

"I served your father the duke before you were born. He himself asked me on his deathbed to look after his dear wife and infant daughter." Sir John's grip on his equanimity seemed to slip ever so slightly. "If the duchess turns to me for advice, should it be wondered at?"

"We have had this discussion more times than I care to recall, Sir John. How many times must I say it? No regency. I forbid it." Had the princess stamped her foot?

"You forbid it? You're not queen yet, my girl. And don't be so sure of your powers. The king may yet decide that the country would be better off with a regent until you're older."

"The king will do no such thing, and you know it. He and Mama hate each other. He would never declare her regent."

Persy remembered Papa's explanation of the difficult state of affairs between the king and the princess's mother. So it wasn't just gossip.

Sir John was silent. Persy could picture him struggling to maintain his composure. "That may well be," he conceded, and his voice once again grew smooth and conspiratorial. "So you become queen. Can you honestly say that you are ready to bear that burden alone? You will need someone to explain the complexities of matters of state in terms you can understand—"

"My education has not been neglected. I am quite capable of understanding what my ministers would wish to discuss with me," the princess snapped.

"So you might think now. But I know better. You will need a private secretary to help keep up with it all."

"Sir John." The princess's voice turned from silver to steel. "I said no to you when I was so ill at Ramsgate and you actually forced a pen into my hand to sign a statement appointing you as my private secretary. I have said no many times since then. It appears that I will have to say it once more. I will do so very slowly, just to ensure that you understand me: no. And no. And no again."

"Your Highness—"

"I have never liked you, sir, and it is your own fault. You have always treated me in a rude and familiar way and kept me from associating with anyone but your own family. You say you seek only to serve, and I agree—you seek to serve yourself. What papers will I see slipped into a pile of routine paperwork if I name you my secretary? A patent of nobility for yourself? A pension or two or three? A few favors for others, bought and paid for?"

"See here, you miserable chit—"

There was a sharp cry from the princess. "Unhand me, sir!"

"Not until I've had my say. I've spent the last twenty years of my life in your family's service, and it's high time I got my reward. Now, will you please sign this paper?"

"Never!"

There was a silence. Then Sir John's voice came again, taut with compressed rage. "Rest assured that I will be your secretary whether you like it or not. The only difference is in how it happens."

"What do you mean?" For the first time, the princess sounded uncertain.

"Never mind. Are you quite sure? Do you refuse to sign? Very well." Footsteps moved toward the door. "Might I beg Your Highness's permission to leave?" Sarcasm oozed from Sir John's voice. The doorknob turned.

"Blast!" Lochinvar jerked Persy away from the door and yanked her and Charles into a window embrasure across from where they had been standing. He shrank back against the glass and pulled her roughly against him. Charles buried his head once more against Lochinvar's side.

The door opened and Sir John stepped into the hall. He did not look around but slammed the door behind him and stalked down the hall, back the way they had come.

Persy's sense of time seemed to stop. She waited for an indignant Sir John to drag them from their woefully inadequate hiding place, her stomach clenching and toes curling with tension and fright. At the same time she realized that her head was resting on Lochinvar's shoulder and her face was pressed against his crisp white cravat that smelled of starch and lavender water and clean healthy male. The edge of his jaw was a hair's breadth from her lips, and if she moved just the tiniest bit she would be able to brush a kiss there.

"He didn't see us," Charles whispered, unburying his head. "He just walked right past us and didn't see us."

"I expect he was rather too angry to notice much of anything," Lochinvar whispered back.

He dropped his arm, and Persy realized that he had been holding her in an almost suffocating embrace. Not that it mattered; she'd been unable to breathe anyway. She looked up at him and saw that he was pale, with a faint sheen of perspiration on his forehead. Was it from fear or from some other emotion?

Had it felt as wonderful to him as it had to her?

A low sobbing sound interrupted her feverish thoughts. "The princess!" she murmured, and turned toward the door. That beastly Sir John had left her in tears.

"You can't!" Lochinvar grabbed her arm. "Come on. Let's go." He pulled them out of the window recess and down the passage to the stairwell.

Persy cast one regretful glance back at the door but obeyed. She couldn't very well have gone in and comforted the sobbing girl, much as she would have liked to—not in her boys' clothes, in a place she had no right to be.

They made it down the stairs without incident and hurried down the corridor. Persy wasn't sure whether she was relieved or disappointed that their adventure was at an end. "There," she whispered, pointing to the door they'd entered by. But that didn't seem to be enough. "I—thank you, Lord Seton. I'm sorry we dragged you into this."

Lochinvar held up one hand. "Don't apologize. It was most, uh, interesting." He paused, then smiled crookedly. "You make a very handsome boy, but I think I would rather you stayed a girl." And before Persy could answer, he opened the latch on the door and pushed them out.

As Charles retrieved his boat from under the bushes, Persy glanced back at the door. Lochinvar still stood there, running his hands over the door panels with a slight frown on his face.

"What's he doing?" she wondered aloud.

Charles was back, thrusting the boat into her arms. "Probably checking the latch to make sure we don't sneak in again. Come on, Persy. I've had enough for one day. Dressing my sister up in boys' clothes and breaking into Kensington Palace! Wait till I tell them about *that* back at school."

"Don't you dare!" Distracted from watching Lochinvar, Persy aimed a clout at him.

Though they squabbled companionably all the way home to

Mayfair, Persy's mind was only half there. They had failed to find Ally, or even any clues as to her whereabouts. But the conversation between Sir John and the princess—she had heard the princess's own voice!—was truly shocking. And as for Lochinvar . . . something about his frowning examination of the door troubled her, but she could not say exactly what it was.

14

At their next visit with Princess Sophia a few days later, Persy let Pen do most of the chatting, which she fortunately seemed happy to do. Her lively accounts of the social events they had recently attended washed over Persy as she stared with heavy-lidded eyes into her teacup.

Persy had found it very hard not to tell Pen about their strange visit to Kensington. She desperately missed talking with her twin, and though Charles was proving to be more of a companion than he ever had before, it was not the same. And it was hard to endure Pen's aloofness even though it was her own fault. She only hoped that Pen wouldn't launch into another discourse on Lord Carharrick's attentions to her while they were here.

"Now, what were the flowers like at the Gordons' ball?" the princess demanded. "I hear the duchess spends hundreds of guineas on her greenhouses, which the duke hates because roses make him sneeze."

Persy watched the flakes of tea that had escaped the strainer settle at the bottom of the clear brown liquid in her cup. She'd managed to convince Mama that she was still too ill to attend the

Gordons' ball, and had spent the evening listening to Charles concoct wilder and wilder explanations for what had occurred at Kensington until she really did have a headache and went to bed early.

She sighed, but quietly. If only she could slip away and go look for Ally while Pen and the princess chatted. Would asking to use the necessary work? It would be a dreadful breach of etiquette, but she could plead an emergency. Oh, there had to be some way she could look for Ally while she was here!

The particles of tea swirled round and round in her cup, until she began to feel dizzy watching them. Ally, oh, Ally . . .

The princess's drawing room, the bright afternoon sun on the faded carpet, and the swirling specks of tea all receded. A sense of anxiety filled her, of foreboding and worry. Then, slowly, a room came into focus in her cup, a dim room with curtains mostly drawn—to keep out the light, or to prevent anyone from seeing in?

Close to the narrow slit of light was a small table. A few books, paper and pens, and a half-darned sock lay scattered on its top. And seated in a chair by the table was Ally. She looked thin and drawn, as if she had neither eaten nor slept well in many days, and wore an unfamiliar gown of gray linen, with only a narrow white collar to relieve its plainness. Persy felt as if she could almost reach out to the beloved figure, and opened her mouth to call to her. But then Ally spoke.

"Here? They're here, in the palace?" She sounded hoarse, as if she'd grown unused to speaking.

Another figure came into focus. A chill ran through Persy as she recognized the man's dark auburn hair and pleasant features. "They're taking tea with Princess Sophia," Michael Carrighar confirmed. "She met them when they made their curtsies to the queen a few weeks ago."

He was talking about her and Pen! Persy blinked, trying to put it all together—Ally . . . Mr. Carrighar . . .

"My girls . . ." The raw longing in Ally's face made Persy want to cry. "Please, Michael, let me see them! Just for a moment . . ."

Mr. Carrighar came to stand by Ally. He twitched the curtains open the merest bit farther and stared outside, as if he couldn't bear looking at her while he spoke. "I can't do that," he said quietly. "You know I can't. Not unless you've changed your mind. If you have, I would be very happy to—"

"No! How many times must I say it? I will not help you!" Ally exclaimed, her tired eyes flashing. Then, all at once, her mood seemed to change. She reached up and placed a tentative hand on his sleeve. "Michael, you know it is wrong. Refuse with me! Surely the two of us together could withstand him."

To Persy's surprise, Mr. Carrighar dropped to one knee beside Ally and took her hands. He raised one and brushed a kiss across its back. "If only I could, my dear. You know how I feel about this dirty task. But he owns me, just as he owns you."

Ally stiffened. "He does nothing of the sort."

Mr. Carrighar sighed. "But he does, dear one, he does. What does it matter, this little undertaking? She'll never know what has happened, he'll get what he wants, and then we'll be free. There's no other way—believe me, if there were, I would have found it. Help me, and then we can leave here and make a new life together. You can come home with me to Ireland—you would make an admirable professor's wife—"

"Michael!" Ally looked away. Mr. Carrighar snapped his fingers and produced a handkerchief, with which he gently dabbed at a tear that slid down her pale cheek.

"Melusine, I'm not sure if these weeks have been heaven or hell." His voice was now as hoarse as hers had been. "They've brought me sleepless nights of anxiety over what he might do to my family if I fail him . . . and they've brought me you. I must help him . . . and I must convince you too. I can't lose you now."

"And what if I refuse?"

Mr. Carrighar swallowed. "If you won't help of your own free will, I'll have to force you. Melusine, please don't make me do that. Better give in than be destroyed."

Persy gasped, and the scene in her teacup vanished. With a loud cry, she flung her cup away. Tea sprayed across her visiting dress, and the cup bounced unharmed on the carpet and came to rest under the tea table.

"My dear child!" Princess Sophia stared at her as Pen and the lady-in-waiting leapt forward with napkins and concerned exclamations. "Are you ill?"

Though Persy tried to stop them, tears ran down her cheeks. "Pen, it was Ally. I heard her," she whispered. "I *saw* her."

Pen stopped dabbing at her dress and stared too. "What? Did you . . . what did she say? Where—" she began eagerly, then glanced at the princess and the lady-in-waiting.

Princess Sophia followed her glance and frowned. "Mary, pray take away these wet napkins. I will ring when we want you." She pulled her own handkerchief from her belt and leaned forward to dry Persy's tears. When her woman had left with the wet linen, she turned to Persy and took her hand. "What was it, my dear? You can tell me."

Her voice was low and soothing. Persy needed comforting very badly just then. "It was—it was a sort of vision," she said.

Pen handed her a fresh cup of tea. "Are you sure you should—"

"Yes, I'm sure." She turned back to the princess. "I don't know who else to turn to, and I hope—we hope"—she glanced at Pen—"that you can help."

"Of course! A vision, you say? How interesting! Do you often have them? What are they about?" Excitement overtook the princess's concern.

Persy sipped her tea and tried to frame her words carefully. "It was about our governess, who is missing."

Princess Sophia blinked. "Your governess is missing, and you're having visions of her? But that is amazing! Do you see her in these visions? Do you know where she is? She has not"—her voice dropped to a whisper—"*passed over*, has she?"

"No, no! We have reason to think that she's here at Kensington Palace," Pen said when Persy remained silent.

Princess Sophia laughed. "Oh my dears, that is quite . . . quite . . . goodness, you're serious, aren't you?" Her eyes, magnified by her spectacles, grew even wider. "Do you truly think she's here? But why?"

"It's hard to explain. But we're quite sure that she's being kept in this palace against her will. I hoped—we hoped that we could ask your help. But please, you mustn't tell anyone."

"Me? Really? What would you like me to do?" Princess Sophia asked eagerly. For a moment she looked more like a child of six than a woman of sixty.

"Look for her," said Pen. "We can't do that here, but you can."

"Well . . ." The princess drummed her fingers on her knee

thoughtfully. "I cannot search everywhere. I doubt my brother Sussex or the dear duchess would approve of my poking about their apartments. But anywhere else . . . your poor, dear governess! Who could have done such a dreadful thing?"

There was a knock at the door, and the footman scurried in. "Sir Jo—" he began to announce, but Sir John Conroy had already swept past him.

Persy cringed. She did not wish to explain her tear-stained cheeks or tea-spattered dress to this dreadful man, but couldn't hope he wouldn't notice them, for his lazy-lidded gray eyes seemed to see everything. She looked at the princess and hoped she could lie well on her feet.

"What do you think, my dear Sir John?" Princess Sophia crowed. "These dear girls have lost their governess, and think she's here in the palace! Is that not singular? Persephone has even had visions about it."

Persy saw Pen close her eyes and exhale, as if in pain. She herself would have cheerfully stuffed the princess's handkerchief into her royal mouth and jumped out a window. Hadn't they just asked the princess not to tell anyone?

But Sir John only raised an eyebrow as he seated himself opposite them. "You don't say? Well, there's no telling who might be lost in this old brickpile. I don't wish to offend you, ma'am, but I never did trust milord Sussex, even though he is your brother. I wouldn't be surprised if the missing lady were stuffed in a bookcase somewhere in his library." His tone was cheerful, even jocular.

Persy hastily buried her nose in her teacup at mention of the Duke of Sussex's library.

Princess Sophia tittered. "Oh, Sir John. Now really, my friends

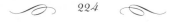

here have lost a governess and have asked me to look for her about the palace. You haven't seen her anywhere, have you?"

"Not I, ma'am. But I shall keep an eye out for her and put her to use if I do." The half smile that always seemed to hover around the corners of his mouth deepened. "I trust you'll forgive my interruption, ladies, but the Duchess of Kent wished me to ask the princess's opinion on her dress for Princess Victoria's birthday ball. Would you be so kind as to visit her later this afternoon? Such matters of state cannot be kept waiting."

Pen's eyes were wistful. "Princess Victoria's birthday ball. Mama is having one for us, too, but she had to put it off a week because they couldn't be held on the same night, of course. What color dress shall you wear, ma'am?"

Princess Sophia's eyebrows rose. "Why, I had nearly forgotten that you girls and dear Victoria have the same birthday. What fun! My goodness, you should be there to celebrate it too. Sir John, wouldn't the duchess be delighted to see that invitations are sent to the Misses Leland? I'm sure she would as a favor to me, especially when she hears about your birthdays."

Persy's irritation with the princess vanished. "Really, ma'am? Do you think she would invite us?"

"I'll make sure that she does." Sir John rose and bowed. "I've delivered my message, and I ought to be getting back. So many details to see to in these last weeks. I'm sure you understand, ma'am."

"Indeed I do, Sir John. Please assure the duchess I shall wait upon her shortly. And do not forget to take care of my friends' invitations." Princess Sophia nodded to him.

"Forget the two P's in a pod?" His smile was wide as he bowed again. "Not for the world. Good day."

After he had left, Princess Sophia beamed at them. "What fun this will be! Of course it will be the event of the season, and I am so happy that you will be there for it. I shall tell Victoria about it being your birthdays too when I visit."

Pen still looked transfixed. "Wait until we tell Mama!"

The invitations to Princess Victoria's eighteenth birthday ball arrived the very next day. Mama was slightly mystified but delighted.

"It was immensely kind of Princess Sophia to see that you girls were invited," she said as the three of them gloated over the thick, cream-colored cards. "We must see to your dresses at once."

"Face to face with your heroine at last. Will you be able to stand it without being translated to the Elysian Fields on the spot?" Papa grinned at them from the doorway; two of the maids could be heard whispering in the hall about the handsome livery of the footman who had delivered the invitations.

"We'll try not to levitate too much, Papa," Pen answered him.

From the deep chair by the fireplace Charles snickered. "I'd be careful about that, if I were you."

"Isn't there some geometry you ought to be studying, Charles?" said Persy in sweetly chill tones. But it was hard to be cross with anyone just then. They might even be able to meet the princess, to smile and exchange a few words with her, to touch her hand!

That night at Mrs. Cheke-Bentinck's party, Persy's mood was still high. Lord Carharrick, who had maneuvered her into joining a small group touring their hostess's celebrated orangery, commented on it.

"You seem different tonight." He paused under a lamp in the

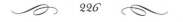

humid glass-walled room and turned her to face him. "Radiant. Not that you generally aren't, as far as I can see."

Persy laughed. Tonight she could, even at such foolish talk. "My sister and I have been invited to Princess Victoria's birthday ball. The king's sister took a liking to us when we were presented. She has asked us to visit several times, and saw to it that we were sent invitations. They arrived just this afternoon. Pen and I have always admired the princess—Victoria, I mean, though Princess Sophia has been exceedingly kind to us."

Lord Carharrick nodded. "Princess Sophia," he said slowly. "Not at the center of court by any means, but not without some influence, so it seems."

"She's a very kind and, I believe, very lonely old lady. She says that our company cheers her up," Persy said defensively.

Lord Carharrick held out his arm again, and they resumed their stroll through the banks of small citrus trees, laden now with small green fruit. The slates of the floor were cool through Persy's slippers. She shivered though the air was warm and damp. Lord Carharrick held her arm a little closer. "Your grandmother the Duchess of Revesby is in service at court, isn't she?"

"She's a lady-in-waiting to the queen," Persy agreed. Something about this conversation was beginning to annoy her but she wasn't sure why.

"A position of honor, and of some use politically to your grandfather, I'm sure, though personal service to the sovereigns is supposed to transcend such mundane considerations."

"Grandmama loves Queen Adelaide! She says she is a dear, kind person. She doesn't serve the queen just to gain favor for the family. She considers herself the queen's *friend.*" Persy suppressed an urge to pluck a handful of the hard little green oranges and throw them at him.

"Oh, I'm sure that she is. I admire her for her loyalty to the queen. But it is a fact that service at court can have beneficial, if unintended, side effects. You know your history well enough for that, I am sure." Lord Carharrick's assurances were quick and smooth and totally unsatisfactory. She opened her mouth to protest once more, but he hadn't finished.

"Service to the crown often runs in families. An acquaintance with Princess Victoria on your part now might prove to be a useful thing someday," he said, squeezing her arm ever so slightly. "I applaud your friendship with Princess Sophia, and I hope that it leads you on to even greater associations with the court in the future."

Persy nearly stammered with fury. "If you think we're toadying up to poor old Princess Sophia just to get at Princess Victoria—"

"I said no such thing, Persephone." When she tried to yank her arm from his, he turned her to face him and held her by the elbows. His eyes were dark and serious. "I admire you for taking the time to be kind to a lonely old lady. It shows your inherent amiability. And if your virtue should be rewarded someday, what is wrong with that? Who else could be more deserving?"

"But that's not it at all," she protested, and tried to pull away again. He ignored her and tucked her arm in his once more.

"A wife with connections at court can be a very valuable asset," he said, almost to himself. "It is very definitely something to consider. I wonder, Persephone, if your father will be at his club in the next day or so? Or should I direct a note to him at home asking if I might call upon him?"

 223

He had called her Persephone twice in the last three minutes. An icy breath of apprehension whispered in her mind. And mumbling on about wives with connections was an extremely ominous sign. Persy bit her lip and stared down at the toes of her slippers as they caught up to the rest of the group touring the greenhouse.

As they were about to leave the room Lord Carharrick paused and looked back at the rows of potted trees. "I shall always have a soft place in my heart for orangeries, after this evening. Perhaps, someday . . ." He smiled down at her.

Persy considered sneezing violently and saying she preferred fresh air and oaks, but couldn't bring herself to be so uncivil. So she bowed her head and let him lead her back to the dining room, where he was so solicitous in bringing her the choicest sweetmeats and ices that Pen, with Lochinvar in tow, stopped to ask if she had injured her foot once again.

"No, I didn't," Persy snapped. That line was starting to wear thin. "Thank you *so* much for asking, though."

"Just checking." Pen nodded at Lochinvar beside her. "We enjoyed our tour of Mrs. Cheke-Bentinck's orangery. Quite fascinating. It's amazing what you can learn in a greenhouse if you pay attention. How about you? Did you enjoy it too? We tried to catch your attention, but you seemed too absorbed in conversation to notice us."

"Pen!" Persy almost moaned. She thought frantically back over what Lord Carharrick had said to her amid the oranges and limes. Nothing blatant, at least that she could recall. It had been his tone and eyes that had spoken loudest. Where had Pen and Lochinvar been? There were all sorts of twisty little paths and nooks in the orangery for visitors to get lost in—Mrs. Cheke-Bentinck had a slightly interesting reputation—and the two of them could have been anywhere. Persy felt like crying.

"I am not overly fond of oranges myself," Lochinvar said, meeting her eyes. His face was careful and somber. Persy saw him slip a hand into his coat pocket and grip something inside it.

"Nor is Persy, I thought," Pen said, staring at her hard. "But tastes can change, can't they?"

She stared defiantly back. "Yes, they can. Is there anything wrong with that?"

"So long as it's a real change and not a stupid hoax. Ah, good evening, Lord Carharrick. Is that an ice for my sister? How lovely." Pen curtsied as he approached them. He bowed in return and turned to Persy.

"Thank you, but I think I've had enough ice for now. Won't you all excuse me for a few minutes?" Persy looked away from the delicate cup he offered her and pushed back her chair. She had to get away. From behind her she could vaguely hear Pen call out, "Persy, wait!"

The hall outside the dining room was mercifully empty of footmen. Persy ran blindly down its length and opened a door at random.

She found herself in a small, dark parlor, also blessedly empty. Crossing to the window, she leaned against it and rested her forehead against the cool glass. Pen and Lochinvar had overheard Lord Carharrick's conversation with her. What was wrong with that? It only helped in her campaign to chase Lochinvar off.

So why did she feel so wretched?

The doorknob rattled, and a sliver of light invaded the dark room. Persy turned and froze, hoping whoever it was would go away, and muttered the cloaking spell. It was turning out to be a remarkably useful—

"Perse, it's no use. I know you're there," Pen said softly, closing the door behind her. "Skip the spell."

Persy turned back to the window. "I would like to be alone just now, if you please," she said. To her dismay, her voice came out thick with unshed tears.

"No. You've been doing this enough. Come on, we're going to talk."

"I have nothing to talk about."

"Nothing at all? Nothing about Lord Carharrick wanting to call on Papa?"

Persy's hands clenched into fists. "You shouldn't have been listening. Do we have to talk about this now?"

"Yes." Pen had come to stand next to her in the window. "Persy, are you in love with him?" she asked quietly.

It was on the tip of Persy's tongue to say yes, but that would have been a bald-faced lie. She was so tired of lying to Pen. "No," she whispered.

"Are you sure?"

"Yes, I'm sure. I know he's wealthy and good-looking and will inherit his family's title, and I wish to God he were in Greenland right now so I wouldn't have to listen to his wooing anymore." The tears that had threatened before finally spilled over down her hot cheeks. "And I also wish you'd leave me alone and never bring this up again."

Pen exhaled and let go of her hand. "All right, Persy. I'm sorry, but I had to know." She handed her a handkerchief.

"Why?" Persy demanded and blew her nose.

"Because."

After a moment of silence, Persy finally looked at her. "Pen, I'm sorry. This . . . unpleasantness between us—it's all my fault."

It was Pen's turn to avoid meeting her eyes. "Maybe not entirely. I'm sorry too. But I think it will clear up soon."

"Why do you think that?"

She felt rather than saw Pen's shrug. "Maybe I'm becoming a seer. I'm going back to the ball now. You stay here for a while and pull yourself together." She squeezed Persy's arm and turned away. A second later, the door opened and closed once more.

Persy sagged against the window again. Would it be possible for them to call a truce now? Maybe Pen would stop making those irksome comments about Lord Carharrick. Maybe the painful, difficult silence that had risen between them would start to go away and they could be sisters again, and—

The door reopened. *Pen must be impatient,* Persy thought. "I'll be out in a—"

The words froze in her mouth. Light from the hallway was making a halo of the gold hair of the figure that stood in the doorway.

It was Lochinvar.

He closed the door and moved swiftly toward her. "Persy," he murmured.

"Lord Seton! I was just, um, leaving." She edged away from him and toward the door, nearly tripping over a footstool in her haste.

"Please wait." He closed the distance between them and caught her arm as she stumbled.

"Wh-why?" She tugged, but he would not let go of her.

"Because I want to talk with you."

"There's nothing you can need to say to m—"

"Yes, there is." He captured her other hand and drew her toward him, then kissed her softly, gently. His lips tasted faintly of strawberries and champagne. He paused for just a heartbeat—she was sure hers could be heard even out in the hall—and then kissed her again, a little less gently this time, and pulled her hard against him.

Persy knew she should leap back indignantly, slay him with a well-chosen word or two, then run shrieking from the room. But what she really wanted was to reach up and bury her fingers in his soft gold hair and kiss him back as well as she could. Just fainting was another option, but unfortunately she had never fainted in her life and was unsure how one went about it.

It's not you he's kissing, it's the spell, a small, cool voice in her head reminded her. That was enough to jerk her back to reality. She squirmed out of his arms and backed away toward the door.

"I—I think it's time for me to leave now." Her voice sounded squeaky and unnatural, even in her own ears. No wonder; she could hardly breathe. "There's been some kind of mistake."

Before he could say anything she slipped through the door and slammed it behind her, then ran for Mrs. Cheke-Bentinck's boudoir, where they had left their wraps on arrival. Mrs. Cheke-Bentinck's maid was there and kindly brought her a cup of tea and some eau de cologne when she confessed a sudden headache.

Persy lay back on a silk-covered divan and closed her eyes.

Lochinvar had kissed her—actually kissed her as if he really meant it. She tried to put it out of her mind but the memory of his mouth on hers, the lips smooth and firm and trembling ever so slightly . . . and his arms, straining to hold her closer . . . it had been wonderful and glorious and it could never, *never* happen again.

So all her sham indifference and pretending to be in love with Lord Carharrick hadn't succeeded in putting him off. That must have been one very strong love spell. Odd that it hadn't felt that way when she'd cast it—there hadn't been any of the usual tingling energy in her hands and shoulders and at the base of her throat that spell-casting often created. True, she'd come down with a headache immediately afterward, but she rather suspected that had been as much due to the Gilleys' punch as it was to intense concentration. But magic was funny sometimes.

So what should she do now?

It appeared that it was time to change her tactics, because subtlety obviously hadn't worked. She would have to lie through her teeth and tell Lochinvar, as kindly and as firmly as she could, that she did not and never would love him. She could say the same to Lord Carharrick, though at least she wouldn't have to lie. Then she could get on with the rest of her life, which would be bleak and lonely and miserable, but at least she would have done the right thing. The moral thing, even if it wasn't honest.

Somehow, the thought was not much comfort just now.

When it was finally time to go home, Mama scolded her. "Foolish child, why didn't you tell one of us you didn't feel well, rather than lurking up with Mrs. Cheke-Bentinck's maid all evening?"

Persy leaned back against the seat and shut her eyes. "I'm sorry, Mama. I didn't want to ruin anyone's evening."

Next to her Pen made a faint snorting noise. Persy peeked from the corner of her eye and saw that Pen was regarding her with an air of exasperation.

It didn't take more than fifteen seconds for that exasperation to come out after Andrews had helped them out of their gowns and they were alone in their room. "Persy, what happened?" Pen demanded. "And don't tell *me* any stories about a headache."

"I don't know what you're talking about. My head did ache." Persy tried for injured ignorance as she draped her petticoats over a chair to air. In truth it had been her heart that ached, but Pen needn't know that.

"What did Lochinvar say to you?"

Persy froze, glad her back was to Pen. How did she know about Lochinvar? She must have seen him enter the room, so it would be no good trying to refute it. "Lochinvar? Oh, he didn't say much of anything to me." He *hadn't* really spoken much, so that wasn't a lie.

"Persy, he was going in there to tell you he loves you. Didn't he?"

"Umm, well, no, he didn't." Not with words, he hadn't.

"Persephone Leland, are you being this dense on purpose?" There was a thud. Pen had stamped her foot. "He told me he kissed you. What do you think that means?"

"He *told* you that?" Persy turned and goggled at her.

"He's been trying to for the last few weeks, but you've been absolutely impossible. I thought it was because you'd decided you liked Lord Carharrick, but then you told me that you don't care for him. Now would you mind telling me what is going on with you?"

"Pen, please . . . my head." Falling back on her headache was completely cowardly, but Persy didn't much care.

"Oh, for God's sake." Pen spoke through gritted teeth. "There isn't any talking to you, is there?"

"No, there isn't. So just leave me alone right now, please." Without bothering to stop and plait her hair, Persy dove for their bed, curling into a ball as far on her side as it was possible to go and wishing, for the first time in her life, that she and Pen had separate rooms.

15

At breakfast the next morning Kenney brought in a letter for Papa.

"It was found on the front steps this morning when the maid went out to sweep, milord," he said, making it clear that he found such unorthodox delivery of a personal note highly questionable.

Papa took the note from Kenney's silver tray. "How curious. Thank you, Kenney." He picked up the butter spreader and started to slit the seal.

"A clean knife would leave it in more readable condition, dear," said Mama. "Thank you, Persy," she added, as Persy passed her clean knife to her father.

After last night's events, Persy had slept little and now had even less appetite for breakfast. She sipped her chocolate and toyed with the rest of her unsoiled cutlery.

"Oh, dear," said Papa, gazing at the note with a bewildered air.

"What is it, Papa?" Pen asked. She hadn't eaten much either, Persy noted.

"It's from Miss Allardyce. She is resigning from our employ, effective immediately." Papa stared at the piece of paper in his hand as if it were a new and possibly toxic species of mushroom.

"What?" exclaimed all three women at the table.

"It's not much of a note, really. Strange way to take leave of us, after all these years." He cleared his throat, took a sip of his tea, and read aloud:

Dear Lord Atherston,

It is with the greatest sorrow that I tender my resignation from your service, effective immediately. My current situation does not permit me to make this announcement in person, or to say a proper farewell to you and your family. I regret this deeply as well, and can only extend my sincere hope for your family's continued health and prosperity.

Your obedient servant,
M. Allardyce

There was a stunned silence after he had finished reading.

"Well!" Mama finally found enough breath to say. "Practically a member of the family for ten years, and that's how she says good-bye to us? Of all the ungrateful, unfeeling—"

"Is there a forwarding address on it, Papa?" Pen asked under her mother's tirade.

"No, there isn't. Seems a little odd. There's already quite a pile of her mail stacked in a basket in the hall—Kenney was just asking yesterday what he should do with it all. It doesn't sound as though

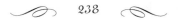

she intends to call for it, or for her belongings, either. Hmmph." He frowned and read the note to himself again.

"—ten years looking after you girls. I would have thought proper feeling would have dictated at least a brief visit but no, why should she exert herself just to say farewell to people who have given her their love and trust for such a long . . ." Mama was in full flow, like an Italian opera.

Persy's whole body felt numb, as if it were no longer hers. She met Pen's eyes and saw that she looked equally shocked. Whatever lay between them had to be put aside while they tried to figure out what this letter meant. Oh, why did everything have to happen all at once?

She rose and went to Papa, leaning casually over his shoulder. Pen rose as well and went to try to placate their mother, but her eyes remained on Persy.

"My goodness, Papa, this is dreadful! Might I see it? I just can't believe . . ." Persy held her hand out for the note, and he handed it to her. She took it in both hands and, as she had the other note they'd received from Ally, read it with more than just her eyes.

And felt nothing. There was no feeling, no sensation, no hint of emotion about this note. Not even a hint of Ally clung to it, though the word choice and handwriting appeared to be hers. It might have been written by an automaton or a ghost. The latter thought made her shiver.

She looked up at Pen and shook her head slightly. Pen's eyes widened, and she motioned Persy to change places with her. Charles watched them, his face pale and serious as he flexed his wrist and started tentatively to push his chair back with both hands. On the doctor's suggestion he had been leaving the bandage off his arm for short periods each day, to begin rebuilding its strength.

"It's you girls whom I feel the worst for. After so many years of caring for you, it is positively unnatural to leave without a word of fondness for either of you. . . ."

Persy put her arms about Mama's shoulders, thinking furiously. They would have to go see the Allardyces once again. But what would poor Mr. and Mrs. Allardyce be able to do? This note would only worry them further. Could she ask Lochinvar to find a reason to visit the Duke of Sussex's library at Kensington Palace again? Perhaps she could borrow Charles's clothes and go with him as a page or servant, and have another look around on her own. But after what had happened last night at the Cheke-Bentincks', she wasn't sure that she could look at Lochinvar, much less ask him to smuggle her anywhere. Oh, Ally . . .

That night at the Bridgewaters' ball, the last waltz of the evening was about to begin. Persy was cooling her warm cheeks against the marble of the window embrasure under pretense of looking out at Lady Bridgewater's gardens, hoping she could escape Lord Carharrick. She surreptitiously wiggled her toes inside her slightly-too-tight slippers. If she were lucky, in another few minutes she could go home and collapse into bed.

She had done her best to avoid him by forcing herself to be as conspicuous as possible and thereby attract other dance partners. Freddy Gilley and his friends had taken the bait and filled her dance card. Unfortunately they had also flooded her with stories from their Cambridge days, most of which involved the introduction of livestock into places where livestock were not usually welcome.

But Lord Carharrick had proved too tenacious. He managed to claim his two usual waltzes, during which he gazed down at her with shining, thoughtful eyes as he discussed his embryonic political ambitions, and had engaged her for a third dance that evening—something he had never done before. Persy was not sure of the propriety of allowing him to claim the last waltz of the evening as well as the two he had already taken, but neither was she sure how to refuse him without giving offense. Perhaps if she were lucky, Lord Carharrick would let this last dance slip his mind. Mama had already gone to ask Papa to see about the carriage, and perhaps she would—

"May I have this dance, Miss Leland?" said a voice.

Persy stiffened. No. Not tonight. Not now. She slowly turned to face her interrogator. Lochinvar stood before her, right hand already extended to take hers.

"But, ah, I don't think—that is—" she stammered.

"Thank you," he said, and propelled her out to the middle of the floor.

She caught a glimpse of Lord Carharrick staring at her, looking puzzled. She tried to signal an apology with her eyes; she didn't *want* to dance with him, but it was rude to stand him up like this. Then she saw Pen behind him, watching her and Lochinvar with a determined look on her face.

Before she could try to decipher Pen's expression, Lochinvar had already put his hand on her waist and swept her into the dance.

"Um, I'm afraid I had already promised this waltz to Lord Carharrick," she said.

Lochinvar's hand tightened on her waist. His hazel eyes were fierce as he gazed down at her. "To hell with Carharrick."

She blinked. How did one reply to such a statement? "Really, I—"

"Isn't that how you feel, too? That's what your sister said."

Persy nearly stopped dancing. Pen had told him *that*? She was going to have a lot of explaining to do when they got home. "I'm not sure that it's any of your business, sir," she replied as coolly as she could.

"It sure as hell is. Damn it all, I love you, Persy."

She was sure the orchestra was still playing, because they and all the other couples in the room were still dancing. But a sudden roaring in her ears had quite drowned the music out. "What did you say?" she whispered.

"You ran away the other night before I could say anything to you. After Pen told me you said you didn't love Gerald Carharrick, I knew I had to step in right away before anyone else did. And Pen said she'd flay me alive if I didn't clear this up tonight. I love you, Persy. You. Persephone."

Drat it, Andrews must have laced her corset uncommonly tight tonight because she was suddenly finding it difficult to breathe. But breathe she had to, because she had to put a stop to this once and for all. Even if it killed her. "Lord Seton, you are either drunk or having a colossal jest at my expense." Perhaps if she treated his declaration as a joke . . .

"I am neither. Are you?"

That stung. "Of course not! What a thing to say!"

"Then why won't you give me a chance? Look at me, Persy," he commanded.

His hazel eyes were almost green tonight. She couldn't look away, caught by the tiny gold flecks in their centers.

"I've always been in love with you. I was the one who insisted we ride over to Mage's Tutterow right away when I got back from the continent, because I wanted to see *you*. I wanted to see if you'd grown up from that girl who read books bigger than she was. You had, and you were lovelier and more you than ever. When I walked into that room and saw you with your eyes shut tight and your hair tumbling over your shoulders and the most comical look of determination on your face, I wanted to kiss you right then and there."

"This *is* a tease, isn't it? You've gone and made a bet with Freddy Gilley or someone that you'll convince me that you're in love with me."

"Look over there. I think Freddy's too busy convincing someone else about love to want to enter into such cruel games."

He inclined his head toward a nearby pair of dancers, and Persy saw that it was Sally Louder and Freddy, lost in each other's eyes. The sight was both touching and painful. Homely little Sally had found *her* love. Why couldn't she? She took a deep breath. It was time she stopped playing games.

"Lord Seton, I—"

"Please call me Lochinvar."

She shook her head. "Lord Seton, I can't let you go on thinking that you love me."

"But I do!"

"No, you don't. You only think you do."

"That's ridiculous. How can you know what I feel?"

"It's . . . it's hard to explain. But I know that you don't. I'm so sorry that . . . that this has happened."

"Persy, you don't understand. I want you to marry me."

That did make her stop dancing for just a few seconds because her legs nearly gave way beneath her. How those words made her breath come short with longing . . . and with pain.

"I can't," she whispered. "For several reasons. Someday you'll realize that you don't really love me, and then what? Do you want to trap yourself in a marriage like that?"

He bent his head so that he could look into her downcast eyes. "You're about to cry."

"No I'm not."

"Yes, you are. There's a tear at the corner of your eye—both eyes, now—"

She blinked hard. "It's just the lights. My eyes are tired."

"You're not fooling anyone, Persy. Stop this nonsense. All I've heard you say is that you think I don't love you. What about you? What do you feel?"

This was getting more dangerous by the minute. "I—my feelings are not important at the moment."

Lochinvar glowered. "They damned well are! All right, then. Tell me that you hate me. Swear by . . . by Miss Allardyce that you are completely indifferent to me."

She opened her mouth, then closed it. "No," she finally said, defiantly.

"Why?"

"Because I don't choose to."

He laughed. "You mean because you're an honorable person and won't perjure yourself. I already knew the answer anyway. When I kissed you last night, I felt it. You don't hate me. Admit it. Admit it or I'll kiss you again, right here in the middle of the ballroom." He tilted his head and leaned toward her.

"No!" she squeaked. "All right, I don't hate you!"

"Ha! So why the charade with Carharrick? Why this 'you don't really love me' nonsense? You can't run away from me this time, Persy."

"I will if I faint," she managed to whisper.

He looked alarmed for a moment, then shook his head. "No you won't. You're not the fainting sort, Persephone Leland. That's part of why I love you."

This wasn't working. He wouldn't listen to her. The only thing she could do was somehow put an end to this conversation, the sooner the better. Oh, why did the orchestra always make the last waltz of the evening twice as long as the others? As much as she hated it, it was time to act.

"Ow!" she cried, lurching suddenly to one side.

"What is it?" Lochinvar caught her. She couldn't help noticing he did so much more gracefully than Lord Carharrick had.

"I . . . my ankle. I think I twisted it again," she lied.

Lochinvar stopped dancing at once. "You're pale as a ghost. Is it the ankle you hurt before? Here, hold on to me and we'll get you to a cha—"

"No, I—oh, there's Mama and Papa. I have to leave now. Good evening." Without a glance or a word she turned from him, maintaining just enough presence of mind to limp noticeably as she hurried to Pen's side.

"What happened?" Pen asked, glancing back at Lochinvar. "Did he—"

"Hush. Take my arm and pretend to help me out. I'll tell you later," Persy replied in an undertone.

Back at the house, she and Pen maintained a studious silence as

Andrews helped them with their dresses and corsets and braided their hair for bed. As soon as the maid had left the room, Pen pounced. "All right, tell me. What happened? Did he tell you?" she demanded, her voice muffled as she slid her nightgown over her head. "I told him it was jolly well time he did."

"Oh, Pen!" Persy collapsed on their bed and burst into tears.

"What is it?" Pen sat down and pulled her against her. It was such a relief to lean against her sister and have a good hard cry that Persy couldn't answer for several minutes. Finally, after several frantic sniffs and a wild groping for a handkerchief, she drew a deep, shuddering breath.

"I can't. I can't marry him. He doesn't really love me." She sat up and rubbed her eyes. They felt curiously hot and dry after all those tears.

"What?" Pen's head snapped back in astonishment. "That's ridiculous! He adores you! And what about you? Don't you like him?"

"I love him," she said fiercely. "I haven't thought of anything else since he walked in on us dancing—"

"Neither has he," Pen interrupted. "So what's wrong?"

Persy leaned her forehead on her hands. "Because I've been an absolute idiot. I thought . . . I was afraid that maybe he was starting to like you."

"Persy, I have no interest whatsoever in Lochinvar. He's very nice and all, but . . ." She shrugged.

Persy nodded miserably. "I know that now. But I was so mixed up and afraid that I . . ." Slowly, stumbling over her words, she told Pen about the love spell. "So don't you see?" she finished. "He doesn't love me. It's the spell."

Pen was swishing the end of her braid over her cheek. "Why didn't you tell me all this sooner?"

Persy had been afraid of this question, but she couldn't evade it now. "Because I was . . . ashamed. I just couldn't admit to anyone that I'd done something so . . . so completely stupid. I've always been the good girl who studied hard and practiced her magic and was so proud of being good at it, better at it than—"

"Better at it than me," Pen finished. "Persy, I think you're overestimating this spell of yours. That night at the Gilleys' concert he was already talking nonstop about you."

"There's a big difference between talking about someone and proposing to them. Forget it, Pen, this is all my fault. And besides, what about his mother?"

"Huh?"

Persy grabbed her hand. "You heard Papa that time. Lochinvar thinks his mother was killed by a witch. He hates witches. What would he think if one day after we were married he walked in and found me starting a fire by magic or levitating to get a book off a shelf? He would hate me, and I would die if that happened. And what about if the spell wears off, and he realizes I'd trapped him into loving me?"

Pen shook her head. "You don't know that any of that will happen."

"No, but I can guess it will. When I cast that spell I was ready to give up magic if I could only have him. Lochinvar is who I love. But being a witch is what I *am*. I can either live a lie and give up my magic, or do without Lochinvar. If I marry him, we'll both be living a lie even though he won't know it."

"But—"

"But what, Pen?"

"I don't know. I'm trying to figure out some way to prove you're wrong."

Persy squeezed her hand. "Thank you. You're the best sister anyone could have. But you're not going to find a way for me to get out of this."

"There's got to be a solution. I just know there is. You don't understand—Lochinvar thinks the sun rises and sets on you. Please don't do or say anything final to him until we've had a chance to think about this."

"Nothing's going to change just because we think about it. It's . . . it's no use, Pen. Lochinvar and I—it will never happen." The enormity of what she was saying struck her, and she bowed her head. A tremor ran through her, and another.

Pen put her arms around her. "It's all right, Perse. Go ahead and cry."

"I t-t-told you th-that I wished w-we could stay thirteen," she sobbed into Pen's shoulder.

16

*T*wo mornings later, just as they were finishing breakfast, Lord Atherston paused at the dining room door. "Persy, might I have a word with you?"

Mama smiled and patted her lips with her napkin. Charles stared. Pen looked sympathetic. Persy felt herself flush with irritation and embarrassment, but she replied, "Yes, Papa," as meekly as she could, and followed him up the stairs to his study as if she were walking to her own execution.

Which, she thought bitterly, in a way she was. She had a fairly good idea what Papa wanted to talk to her about. Lord Carharrick must have made that appointment to speak with Papa at his club.

Bright May sunshine flooded Papa's study, brightening the deep crimson and green carpet and curtains. It was incongruous in this dark, masculine room, and Persy found herself wishing it were a dull cloudy day, to better match her mood.

Papa sat down on the small settee by the fireplace and patted the cushion next to him. "Hmm. Should I understand that perhaps you know why I asked to speak with you?" he asked, peering at her.

This was agony. "Papa—" Persy began.

"I'm sorry, dear. I should not engage in cryptic conversations about such a topic. Viscount Carharrick called on me yesterday to ask if I would approve his paying suit to you."

Her face felt as though it were carved from wood, and it was difficult to get her lips to move and form a reply. "I see" was the best she could do.

"He seemed quite sincere. Eager, even. I must confess I was a little taken aback. After all, you girls have only been out a few weeks. I suppose I've not had time to really consider what your being out in society implied." He gave her a shy smile and took her hand. "Carharrick's from a good family. Not as old as ours—his father's only the second earl—but still good. I've heard the estate in east Cornwall is quite a good one, and he seems to have some ambitions toward a political career. You could do worse."

He seemed to be waiting for a response. "Yes, Papa," she whispered.

"I wanted you to know that I gave him my permission to go on and do his best to convince you to accept him. If you think you would— Oh, I say, child, are those tears?"

"I'm s-s-sorry." Persy took his proffered handkerchief and buried her face in it.

"Should I have said otherwise? It seemed to be an honorable proposal and a suitable . . ." Poor Papa sounded utterly bewildered, but he put his arms around her and drew her to him. She leaned against him, just as she had always done as a little girl.

"That's n-not it. It's just . . ." Oh, what could she say to him?

Papa stroked her hair. "It is sudden, isn't it? That's what stopped me at first. But he seems very fond of you already, Persephone."

No, not Carharrick, not now, not ever ran over and over again through her mind in a mad little singsong. How could she tell Papa that?

"I can see you're more than a little overset by this," he said quietly. "Your mother and I would never force you to accept a husband that you didn't love, of course. But sometimes like is a reasonable basis for a marriage. Love often follows close on its heels."

"Papa, I don't think . . . well, I *don't* much like him. I can't really see that blossoming into love," she whispered.

Papa was quiet for a moment. "Well, he hasn't proposed yet, has he? But I wanted you to know what was in the wind, so that you could consider your answer when the time comes." He gave her shoulders a squeeze. "Why don't you stay here for a while and think about matters?"

"Thank you, sir," Persy responded, rising politely as he stood up. He kissed her forehead, gave her his usual slightly lopsided smile, and left the room, carefully closing the door behind him.

As soon as he had left, Persy cast herself down on the sofa. She was tempted to throw herself on the floor instead and shriek and cry and kick the legs of the furniture, but Ally's training won out.

So Lord Carharrick *was* going to propose to her. Maybe not tomorrow, or even next week. But soon—Papa had made that clear. The thought made her throat feel tight, as if an inexorable hand had closed on it. She would have to face that as well as Lochinvar. The imaginary grip on her throat tightened and turned icy cold.

She rolled onto her back and stared up at the ornate swags and interlocking shapes on the molded plaster ceiling. What was worse—dealing with Lord Carharrick, whom she didn't love and didn't want, or Lochinvar, whom she loved and couldn't have?

She jumped up and began to pace around Papa's study, avoiding the copies of famous Greek and Roman statuary that stood sentinel in every unoccupied nook. This was all her fault. She'd flirted dreadfully with Lord Carharrick, and he'd believed her. But she couldn't marry him. She would never consider marrying anyone but Lochinvar, and she couldn't marry him, either. What would Mama and Papa say after she'd refused Lord Carharrick and any other proposals that came her way? There was no way she could explain that since she'd refused her one real love, no one else would do. Pen and Charles would marry, but she'd be left at home.

Eventually, Lochinvar would marry too.

That thought was like a blow to her gut. How could she live at home and participate in the social life of the county, as she would have to, and see Lochinvar and whatever girl he chose to marry living their lives? There was no doubt he'd find someone else eventually; heirs to ancient earldoms married and begot heirs, and that was it. She would have to watch them dance at balls, and smile at each other across the table at dinner parties, and . . . She shuddered. There was no way she could watch that and stay sane.

So why not accept Lord Carharrick? She tried to imagine him sitting on the edge of his chair, eyes shining with enthusiasm as he described one of the new village schools on his family's estates or discussed new theories of education for farm laborers' children. She tried to picture reading books with him, arguing companionably about characters and motivations and the relative merits of Mrs. Gaskell and Mr. Dickens. But all she could see in her mind's eye was the avid interest in his eyes as he discussed her family's tradition of service at court.

Her skirts flared as she turned on her heel, knocking a small statue of the goddess Athena off its slender stand. She automatically pointed at it, halting its imminent fall, and waved it back onto its base.

Oh, why did she have to marry? For all Persy's privilege as a nobleman's daughter, it was women like Ally, who had to work, who had the freedom. Right now she would far rather be someone's governess than a marriageable young lady in society.

Someone's governess . . .

No. She couldn't run away and become a governess. It was impossible.

Or was it?

Charles had said more than once that she knew just as much about some subjects as his tutors at Eton. And her French and German were more than passable. Perhaps she could find a family going to the continent that needed an English governess.

"No," she said aloud. "I couldn't."

But Lochinvar was lost to her. All that was left was her learning and her magic. If not on the continent, could she go out and find magically talented pupils to tutor, the way Ally had? Maybe if she asked her, Ally's mother would be willing to help her find employment—hadn't she made a study of magical families?

Persy paced once more, feverishly thinking. Would the Allardyces help her if she told them about her plan to run away? Perhaps even let her stay with them for a week or two until she found a position?

She would need some days to pack up the appropriate clothes and other things—her books, or as many of them as she could manage. And she would have to sell her jewelry to have money to live on until she found work. The thought of selling Uncle Charles's beautiful pearls made her sad. She remembered little Sally Louder admiring them the day they'd been presented. Lucky Sally—for all her giddy simplemindedness, she'd found a man she could love and be loved by, even if he was Freddy Gilley. They would probably be perfectly happy together for the rest of their days, while Persy . . . well, at least she would have her self-respect.

The tall clock in the corner whirred softly, then chimed. Persy was shocked when the eleventh *bong* faded into silence. Papa had been true to his word and kept everyone away so that she could think in peace. He'd be aghast if he knew in what direction her thoughts had led her.

That made her pause. Papa and Mama would be horribly hurt if she ran away. But they'd be equally hurt when she refused Lord Carharrick and any other young man who proposed to her, no matter what Papa said about it being her choice. Far better they be hurt once, now, than hurt continually as she grew into an old maid. They would mourn her, spend a few frantic months looking for her, but in time they would get over her loss. They'd still have Pen and Charles.

Straightening her back, she went to the door. Kenney would be frantic to have the maid tidy up and the fire seen to, if it really was after eleven. She turned the key and stepped into the hall.

"I thought maybe you'd died or something," said a voice near the floor. "But then I heard you mumble to yourself and bang into something, so I assumed you were probably all right."

Persy stifled an exclamation as Charles unbent himself and rose from the hall carpet. "What are you doing there, Chucklehead?"

"Making sure no one bothered you. Pen said I should, if I had nothing else to do, and I didn't because you weren't there to work on my lessons with me. She wouldn't say why you shouldn't be bothered, though." He looked at her with bright, expectant eyes.

"Oh, didn't she? Thank you for standing—er, lying guard for me, but I've got a lot to do right now. . . ." Persy tried to push past him, but he held up his hand. The inquisitive expression on his face faded.

"Something happened," he said.

"No it didn't, Charles. I'm quite—"

"No! I mean, something happened to *me*."

An odd note in his voice stopped her. This wasn't one of Charles's jokes or exaggerations. "What was it?" she asked, more gently.

"I don't know. After you and Papa left, I went to sit in the window in the dining room, to—you know, watch the people drive by and look at their horses, maybe see if Lochinvar happened to go by with Lord Chesterfield . . ."

Persy's throat tightened. "And?"

"And I got this funny feeling, and when I looked outside, I saw someone coming up the steps with a note in his hand—just a boy, like someone would hire to deliver a letter if they didn't have a footman—"

"So?"

"So I ran to the front door and waited for him to knock. But he didn't. I opened the door, and he wasn't there."

"Charles—"

"But I saw him! He was really there. I didn't imagine him. I could see a place on the elbow of his jacket that had been patched with a piece of scarlet cloth, and that he was missing a front tooth. . . ." He trailed into silence, then gulped. "Could it have been a ghost?"

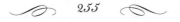

Persy put her arm around his shoulders. "I don't know, Charles. It might have been. But ghosts aren't anything to be frightened of most of the time—"

The knocker on the front door gave a brisk *rat-a-tat*. Charles started, then bolted for the stairs. Persy hurried after him, more concerned about his tripping and falling down than about the identity of the unknown caller. They reached the head of the stairs just as one of the footmen opened the door. A small, slight ragged boy stood there. When he saw the tall footman, he grinned. A gap in his front teeth was clearly visible.

"Miz Allardyce arsked that I bring this here note round," he said, holding it out. "It's fer Miz . . . uh, Miz Lee-land."

Persy launched herself down the stairs. "Thank you," she called. The footman took the note and, after a second's hesitation, fumbled in his pocket and handed the boy a coin. The gap-toothed grin grew wider, and the boy bobbed his head and turned to leave. Just before the footman closed the door, Persy saw a flash of scarlet. The boy's jacket was patched on the elbow with a square of bright red cloth.

She thanked the footman and took the note, which was addressed to the Misses Leland, and turned back to the stairs. Charles stood there looking shocked.

"That was him," he said, grabbing her arm. "That was the boy I saw. Was that magic? Did I see the future?"

"I don't know." Persy was already reading the note. "It's from Mrs. Allardyce. She wants us to come see her as soon as possible."

The next day, Persy, Pen, Charles, and Lord Atherston arrived at the Allardyces' shop once again.

Persy had not wanted Pen to accompany them, but there really hadn't been any way to prevent her. She had hoped to be able to ask Mrs. Allardyce to help her with her plan to run away, and having Pen about would make that almost impossible. It was bad enough having Charles along, but he would have forgotten his age and thrown a full-fledged tantrum if she'd tried to go without him.

She'd thought about whether or not to tell Pen about her plans, and decided against it. Pen would either try to dissuade her or try to run away with her. Neither was acceptable. Pen would probably be even more upset than Mama and Papa after she'd left, but it would be for the best. She'd find a husband and get over her hurt in time.

Mrs. Allardyce was waiting in the window. Persy saw her practically sag with relief when she noticed them climbing from their carriage. She was holding the door open for them when they arrived at the bookshop's entrance.

"Milord Atherston—Miss Persy, Miss Pen—I'm so grateful you came!" She clutched at Persy's arm.

Merlin Allardyce stepped forward, shooting his mother an annoyed glance as he did. "Lord Atherston! You honor us with your—"

"I wonder if you might help Papa," Pen said loudly, taking their father's arm and drawing him aside. "He can't find his copy of Marcus Aurelius at home and we thought you might find him a new one."

"Hmm? Oh, yes, I did lose it, didn't I?" Papa nodded vehemently. "Can't think where it got to."

Persy looked away. His old copy was tucked under a seat cushion in the drawing room, where she'd hidden it and then asked if he'd seen it anywhere. It had been the only way she could think of to get him to bring them here today. Just then she caught the eye of Lorrie Allardyce, who looked at her and suddenly grinned.

Merlin looked only too happy. "We have several editions, milord. If you would be so kind as to step up to the counter, I'll bring them to you." He scurried off. Mrs. Allardyce pounced and drew the remaining Lelands into the office.

"I'm so glad you came," she said again, showing them into chairs and seating herself between Persy and Pen. "If you hadn't, I don't know what I would have done! You're not needed here, miss," she snapped at Lorrie, who had sidled in behind them.

"Mm-hmm," Lorrie said, and took a chair.

"What's wrong, Mrs. Allardyce?" Persy asked, taking her hand. "Is it something about Ally?"

Mrs. Allardyce's shoulders sagged. "Yes—at least, it partly is. But mostly it's about you two girls."

"Us?" Pen exclaimed.

"The night before last, I had a dream. I'm a dreamer, you know—I often see things in dreams that come to happen. But this one was different. It was about Melusine—no, it *was* Melusine."

"You see things?" Charles breathed. "That's almost like what happened to me with your note . . . except I wasn't dreaming . . . at least I don't think I—"

Pen frowned him into silence. "You think she came to you in a dream?"

"I believe she did. But I couldn't talk back to her—it was as if she were making a speech to an empty room, not expecting an answer. She said—she said that you two were in great danger, and that under no circumstances should you continue to try to look for her."

"But that's ridiculous! We can't stop now!" Pen cried.

"Of course not!" Persy echoed. "Maybe it wasn't really her. Or maybe someone forced her to send the dream, and that's why you couldn't talk to her."

"I'd thought of that." Mrs. Allardyce sighed. "But there was no way for me to tell."

Persy extracted Ally's note of resignation from her reticule and handed it silently to Mrs. Allardyce. The older woman read it swiftly and frowned.

"She wrote it . . . and yet . . ." She hesitated.

"It doesn't feel like her. It doesn't feel like anything," Pen finished for her. "Just like your dream."

"I—I've begun to think it time we went to the constables, but we fear that they'll just presume she's run off with a lover. There's no evidence, after all. And if we bring Kensington Palace into it, they're just as likely to press charges on us for slandering the royal family. Oh, Miss Persy, Miss Pen, I just don't know what to do!" To Persy's dismay, the strong, practical Mrs. Allardyce burst into tears.

Charles produced his handkerchief and wordlessly handed it to her, then looked at Persy with wide, worried eyes. "Do something!" he mouthed at her.

"We're not giving up, Mrs. Allardyce," Persy declared. "What danger can there be for us? We'll keep looking. I promise."

Persy immediately cursed herself for promising. If she ran away now, she would be giving up the search for Ally. Would the Allardyces be inclined to help her run away if it meant abandoning the search for their daughter? Even if Pen and Charles hadn't been standing here, it wouldn't have been a good time to ask if they would take her in. Bother, this was going to be harder than she'd thought.

Lorrie picked up Ally's note. "Hmm," she said, tapping the edge of the paper absentmindedly on her hand. "You haven't found a maid yet, have you?"

"No," Persy said, startled at the irrelevancy of the question.

"What's that to do with anything? And besides, it's none of your business, miss. Go see if milord Atherston will take some refreshment, and be quick about it," said Mrs. Allardyce, blotting her tears. The steel in her backbone had evidently reasserted itself. "Have you spoken to the Princess Sophia yet?"

"Well, er, sort of," Pen said. "But I'm not sure that she—"

But Mrs. Allardyce grasped both their hands and said, "Bless you, my dears! Do you think you will be able to speak with her at the princess's ball? If you do, you must come again, the very next day."

Pen glanced at her. "We will, ma'am," she said. "The very next day."

Persy opened her mouth and closed it abruptly. Double bother! She'd hoped to leave that very morning for her new life, if she could convince the Allardyces to help. Maybe instead she'd come by herself that morning and ask their assistance.

Lorrie came back into the room. "His lordship said he'd be delighted, once I was able to drag them out of a book. I'll get . . . oh, my goodness." She stopped and looked hard at Persy. "You can't," she said. "It would ruin everything!"

"What are you babbling about? Come along, child! Glasses and the ginger spice brandy." Mrs. Allardyce shooed Lorrie up the stairs.

Just before they left, Lorrie pressed a tiny folded slip of paper into Persy's hand, frowned ferociously at her, then stared out the window at her as she and Pen and Papa and Charles got back into the carriage. Persy waited until she was safely alone in her room before she unfolded it and read the one word it contained: *Wait.*

$\mathscr{P}$ersy didn't have much time over the next few days to wonder what Lorrie Allardyce meant by that cryptic message. There were trips to Madame Gendreau's and a myriad of other shops to obtain the perfect accessories for their toilettes for Princess Victoria's ball, as well as the usual round of social events.

Gerald Carharrick's manner toward her grew alarmingly possessive. He had abandoned his former reticence and now hovered near her at balls, scowling openly at anyone who asked her to dance until even one of Freddy's less perceptive friends (which was saying something) commented on it.

Lochinvar was harder to deal with. She could not entirely snub him and refuse to dance or speak with him, but it was heart-wrenchingly impossible to dance with him and not see the hurt bewilderment in his eyes. Persy found herself paying careful attention during each second of time spent with him, storing up sensations and memories. Chances were, she reminded herself, that she'd never see him again once she left for her new life.

Whenever he tried to speak with her, she cast down her eyes and refused to answer. He turned to Pen, but he got little satisfaction there.

"He asks and asks what he did wrong," Pen whispered to her at one ball as they lurked in the retiring room set aside for the ladies. "He's miserable, Persy. You've got to do something or—or I don't know what will happen."

She looked carefully through her clothes press, making a list of what would be suitable to bring with her. Nothing too elegant, of course. Governesses were not supposed to be too well dressed. Madame Gendreau's confections of silk and muslin and lace would certainly not qualify as serviceable and sober, and she looked each one over carefully, saving their details in her mind to recall at some future date when she would wear only dull, plain, governessy dresses.

Hardest of all to contemplate was the gown Madame Gendreau made for her to wear to the princess's ball. Persy had been speechless with delight when Mama herself had carried the just-delivered bundle up to her and Pen's room and unpacked their dresses with reverent murmurs at Madame's genius. Hers was of pale blue satin that shimmered like an April sky, with a gracefully draped bodice and the new tight sleeves set with crystal-pleated poufs. Persy knew it would always remain in her memory as the last elegant dress she would ever wear.

The night before Princess Victoria's ball—and their birthday— was the Fothergill ball. Mama had nearly decided to refuse their invitation, but Lady Fothergill was an old friend. She compromised by deciding that they would attend but leave early, so that they could all rest up before the big event.

Late in the afternoon, a footman arrived at the house bearing a large bundle addressed to Persy. Kenney brought it to her as she sat with Pen and Charles in the library.

"Ewww. It sti-i-i-nks," Charles said, holding his nose and dragging out his words in a nasal whine.

"It does not." Pen craned her neck to watch as Persy unwrapped the gold paper from an enormous bouquet of roses and orange blossoms. A card was tucked among the flowers, but Persy didn't have to read it to know who'd sent them. Drat, drat, drat on Lord Carharrick!

Pen asked, "What are you going to do?"

"I don't know." Persy sat down and rubbed her eyes. Charles was right. The scent was overpowering.

"It doesn't look good, Persy."

"It doesn't smell good, either," Charles muttered. "Can we get rid of those horripilatious things before I bring my lunch back up?"

"Gladly." Persy swept the flowers up and deposited them with Mrs. Huxworthy, who loved flower arranging, then retired to her room. She would have to make it clear to Gerald Carharrick that future floral offerings were unwelcome—and the sooner she did so, the better.

She didn't have long to wait. Almost as soon as they arrived at the Fothergills' house that night, Lord Carharrick accosted them. "Good evening, Lady Atherston, Lord Atherston, Miss Leland."

Persy turned. Lord Carharrick stood behind her, staring at her with a peculiar intensity. As his eyes raked over her, a faint line appeared between them. "Will you give me the first dance, Miss Leland?" he asked.

At least the first dance was a quadrille, which did not permit much private conversation. "Yes, thank you," she said. Pen caught her eye and shook her head in sympathy.

He held her arm tightly while they promenaded down the

ballroom to join the forming set. The flowers had been a declaration of war, and now Persy felt like a besieged garrison, with Lord Carharrick as the barbarian horde at her gate. Why did he have to start wooing her in earnest here and now, of all times? Well, he could fight as hard as he liked, but she would never surrender.

"I'm rather sorry I engaged you for this dance," he murmured in her ear.

"Indeed?"

"It means that I can't claim the next one as well. I'd rather have you to myself in a waltz than share you in the quadrille."

Persy held her fan up to hide her involuntary grimace. He was being impossible. Should she be rude and put a stop to it now?

He glanced down at her. "You look quite charming tonight. But you always do."

"Thank you, Lord Carharrick." Persy's hands and feet began to feel cold. To her relief, the dance started. It would make further conversation more difficult, or so she hoped.

But it didn't stop him for long. "Did you get my flowers?"

"Yes, thank you," she said, trying to maintain an even tone. "They were lovely."

"I'm disappointed you're not wearing some of them tonight, Persephone."

Perhaps she could just pretend she hadn't heard him use her Christian name. "Pardon me?"

"I'd intended for you to wear them here. In your hair, perhaps. Isn't that the fashion these days?"

Persy nearly stood still as the petulance in his voice struck her like a clammy hand. "I'm very sorry, Lord Carharrick. But my dress—they would not have matched."

That seemed to mollify him. "Well . . . never mind. Another day soon I hope to be giving you a lot more than a few flowers." He squeezed her arm against his side as they promenaded between the rows of dancers.

"Lord Carharrick—" Botheration! She hoped he hadn't heard the irritated quaver in her voice and wrongly assumed it was caused by some gentler emotion.

They were now at the end of the quadrille line, waiting their turn to wheel back into the dance. "I wish you'd call me Gerald," he said, more loudly than she liked.

"But I—"

To her shock and surprise, he took her arm and propelled her into a nearby bank of palms. "The dance!" she protested. "It's only half over."

"They won't even notice we're gone," he said confidently. "And I wanted to speak with you now."

Persy seethed. They *would* notice—by leaving the dance she and Lord Carharrick had disrupted the figures—but that didn't seem to concern him. He still held her arm, pulling her into the palms until she felt as if they'd been transported into a jungle in deepest Africa, and then neatly maneuvered her so that her back was to the wall.

"My dear Persephone. Surely you know what I want to say to you," he said, gazing at her. "Isn't my heart plain to read in my eyes?"

If it was, then he must have a remarkably shrewd and calculating one. "I don't really think this is the time for—"

"I had some splendid news this week—news that I'm sure will interest you. Lord John Russell has accepted me as his assistant parliamentary secretary." His eyes gleamed as he spoke.

"Oh. Er, congratulations, Lord Carharrick. He is reputed to be a very clever man." Could this be all? Maybe she'd misconstrued his behavior and mistaken his excitement in his news for ardor.

"Clever, and up-and-coming. I'm sure he'll be prime minister someday. It's a very promising start to my own political career. Do you see that?"

She made herself nod enthusiastically. "Oh, yes. Quite. You are fortunate in finding such an excellent mentor for—"

"But a prudent man does not put all his eggs in just one basket, does he?"

"Well, no," Persy replied warily. This was evidently leading somewhere.

"Political advancement is about the connections and alliances a man makes for himself. Some do not always lead in a direction that is profitable or even desirable, which is why it is important to have more than just one. Do you agree?"

Her earlier annoyance with him had begun to reappear. "Um . . ."

"An astute man will look for those valuable connections in many places. Among the friends of his youth. In social venues." He captured her hand and raised it to his lips. "And if he is especially fortunate, even among the gentler sex."

Persy tried to withdraw her hand without being too obvious about it, but he held it too tightly. She wiggled her fingers in protest. "Lord Carharrick, I'm not sure I understand what you're trying to say."

"I *asked* you to call me Gerald." For a moment he frowned at her, then seemed to remember himself. "Oh, darling, I'm sure you do. You're just too modest to admit it. An utterly charming performance—you'll have the cabinet eating out of your hand at our dinners. You'll be able to worm anything out of them when you give them that demure look through your eyelashes, with just that hint of a blush—"

With a yank, she won the battle for her hand. "What do you mean, sir?" she cried, trying to step back from him. Unfortunately the wall prevented her retreat.

"Why, when we're married, of course. Who'll say no to a dinner invitation from the Duke of Revesby's granddaughter? And if your friendships in the royal family come to fruition—I applaud your acumen there." He chuckled. "We'll make quite a pair, with your connections and my—"

Good lord, the man was proposing to her based on her usefulness to his political career! This had gone far enough. "We'll make no such thing!" she said. "Lord Carharrick—"

"Gerald."

"No, not Gerald. *Never* Gerald. I can't believe that you think you can propose to me based on my political connections." She spat the last words with disdainful emphasis.

His face had begun to turn an alarming shade of red. "Believe me, your connections are but one of your attractions for me."

That was even worse. "No, sir. I do not wish to hear any more. I cannot—no, will not accept your proposal. If you will excuse me . . ." She tried to push past him, but he grabbed for her hand again.

"Why not, Persephone? You've seemed to find me attractive enough at all the parties we've been to these last weeks. Or have you?" His eyes narrowed as he looked at her. "I hadn't taken you for a flirt, but perhaps I was wrong."

Persy gasped. "Why, what a dreadful thing to say! I am no such thing!"

"Or was it something else? Like a game?"

"How dare you!" She drew herself up and stared down her nose at him.

"Oh, I dare. It *was* a game, wasn't it, just like the ones all girls play? Make nice with one man to attract the attention of another—"

"Lord Carharrick!" To her horror Persy had raised her hand as if to slap him. She forced it back down to her side.

"It's that damned pretty boy Lochinvar Seton," he said, voice dripping contempt. "I've seen how you look at him. Do you think I'm totally blind?"

Blast! Had she been that obvious? "I don't know what you're talking about," she mumbled.

"I thought you were an intelligent woman, Miss Leland. I'd looked forward to working with you to further my aspirations. And instead I find you're just as silly as any other girl in society, letting your head be turned by a handsome face—"

That was more than she could stomach. "Yes, he is handsome. He's the best-looking man in this ballroom as far as I'm concerned," she shot back. "What's more, he's smarter than any other man I've met this season, and he's not so wrapped up in himself and his *career* as some young men I might mention. Do you know what he's doing? Working on creating new schools for his father's tenants— actually accomplishing something for his fellow man instead of worrying about whom he knows and what use they might be to him. I'd far rather help him with that than throw dinner parties for a lot of stuffy old politicians. He's kind and modest and worthier of my love than you'll ever be."

"You're making a scene!" Lord Carharrick was now crimson, except for his mouth, which was white and pinched. He began to back out of the palms.

"Oh, and dragging me in here in the middle of a dance wasn't?" Persy felt positively giddy as the words rolled out of her mouth. Two months ago she would barely have been able to address him in complete sentences, and now she was striving to see just how unpleasant she could be to him. "Don't worry, no one can hear us. So I'll be blunt. I think Lochinvar Seton is worth ten of you, and always have. Now, if you'll excuse me . . ."

But he was already gone.

She slumped back against the wall and closed her eyes. There. She'd done it—perhaps even *over*done it—but there was no way he could misconstrue that conversation. All she could hope was that he didn't decide to get back at her by gossiping about it. Probably not—it made him look too silly, and surely his pride wouldn't permit his exposing himself.

Silly indeed. Who had been more ridiculous, him or her? Leaping to Lochinvar's defense like that after she'd been so vile to his face . . . it was a jolly good thing, as Charles would say, that he hadn't heard any of that conversation. . . .

The palms to her right began to rustle and sway. One nearly toppled into her, and she reached out reflexively to catch it before it fell. But another hand caught it and set it right, and a second later the hand's owner stood before her, breathing unevenly. He stared at her for several seconds more, his hazel eyes wide and unblinking and his gold hair tousled.

"Do you really think I'm worth ten of him?" he finally asked. "Really?"

No. This wasn't really happening. "What did you hear?" she whispered, backing against the wall again.

"All of it, I think. I saw him pull that little stunt in the dance. You didn't look happy, and I was worried about you." Lochinvar's eyes never wavered from her face. "So I edged in as close as I dared, just in case you needed rescuing."

No, no, *no!*

"I heard what you said to him . . . about my being worthier of your love. Was that what all this has been about? You didn't have to flirt with him to get my attention, Persy—you've had it all along. I told you the other night—I love you." He took a step toward her. "You're not going to escape me this time."

Personal teleportation would be enormously useful right now. But magic like that required concentration and time that Persy didn't have. She glanced quickly from side to side. Could she slither through the palms the way he had and make her escape?

"Persy." He was reaching for her. In another second he'd take her in his arms and there would be no escaping him—and no escaping herself. She had to do something, and do it *now.*

"*Repellere statim!*" she hissed, pointing at him with the fingers of both hands. It was the halting spell she'd practiced on Charles back at Mage's Tutterow, before she'd managed to twist her world into a disaster. Her desperation surged into it, giving it an unexpected power. It hit him full in the chest and froze him in place.

They stared at each other, Persy with her hands still raised, Lochinvar like a statue, arms extended toward her in an embrace that she suddenly realized she would never feel. She'd done magic in front of him—no, *to* him. No wonder he looked so dumbfounded. And horrified.

"Now do you understand?" she whispered. Then, because the shock in his eyes was too much for her to bear, she pushed past him and through the palms. She hurried past the dancers—the quadrille had ended and the waltz begun—and found Mama ensconced in a chair happily gossiping with Lady Gilley. She sank into a chair behind them, grateful that Mama was too busy to ask her why Lord Carharrick hadn't brought her back, and retreated behind her fan.

She'd accomplished what she'd set herself to do this evening—to permanently put off both Lord Carharrick and Lochinvar. So why did she feel so miserable and alone? If doing a halting spell on Lochinvar hadn't alienated him forever, nothing would. Why hadn't she thought of it before? If there had been one way to make him loathe her despite the love spell, this surely had been it.

Maybe that was why she hadn't thought of it.

Stop this! she told herself sternly. Loneliness was something she'd have to get used to if she was going to run away to be a governess. There wouldn't be any more young men vying for her attention. Wasn't that what she'd wanted, before she came to London? To stay quietly at home and dedicate herself to study?

She was getting everything she thought she wanted, and now she wanted none of it. The only thing she wanted now was to be one of those girls waltzing before her, with Lochinvar's hand in hers.

She saw neither Lord Carharrick nor Lochinvar for the rest of the evening, which was mercifully short, as Mama had promised, so that they would not overtire themselves for tomorrow. Both of them had probably gone home. She wished she could have done the same.

Instead, she danced with several young men, smiling and chatting so that no one could see her pain. This was what the rest of her life would be like—smiling through the emptiness. She might as well get used to it now.

"Persy?"

"Hmm? Coming, Ally." Persy blinked as Ally's voice drifted across the lawn to Grandfather's Folly. It was a hot day, and the shady summerhouse seemed to be the only place to catch a hint of breeze. Ally's call seemed distant and muted, muffled in the warm, muggy air. The usual hum of wasps in the Folly's roof nearly drowned it out. She must have fallen asleep—she'd been having the strangest dreams—

"Persy!"

Persy looked up. Ally was hurrying across the lawn. Her disheveled hair cascaded loose over her shoulders, and she wore a shawl over her dark afternoon dress. Now, what was Ally doing outside her room with her hair down, and why was she bundled in a shawl on such a warm day?

"Thank God! Oh, thank God I could reach you! I wasn't certain that I could. I've been trying and trying." Ally stumbled up the stairs of the Folly and leaned against one of the pillars, breathing hard.

"What do you mean, reach me? It's just a short walk from the house." Persy looked past Ally at the length of green velvet lawn edged with trees that separated the Folly from the house. Instead she saw a long, dimly lit corridor lined with doors. "Where did the grass go?" she asked, puzzled.

"It's not important now. Persephone, listen to me. I don't have much time. You must not, must *not* go to the princess's ball tomorrow at St. James's. You will be in grave danger if you do."

"Go to the ball?" Persy rubbed her forehead. Then she remembered. "Of course we have to go. It's Princess Victoria's ball. This is the only chance I'll ever have to meet her. I'd thought about running away before it, but I can't."

Ally glanced over her shoulder down the hall, which now appeared to be carpeted with green grass though the doors were still there. "Please, dearest child. You cannot—I beg you." Then she frowned. "What do you mean, run away?"

"To be a governess, like you. I've made a mess of everything, and this seems like the only way to fix it. I promised your mother I'd keep trying to find you, but you're back now. So I can tell her you're all right, and then she'll help me find someone to work for." Persy paused. "I suppose that means I could leave right away. But I just can't miss seeing the princess, and not wear my dress and everything. It's the last chance I'll have to be pretty, isn't it? Have you seen it? No, of course not. Come back to the house with me and I'll show it to you." She reached out to take Ally's hand, but Ally stepped back.

"Persy, stop talking and listen to me! Do not go to the ball! Something very *wrong* has been planned to happen there. I might be able to stop it if you don't come, but if you and Pen do . . . It's a trap, child. Do you hear me?" Ally's face was thin and white, and her hands twisted and clutched the ends of her shawl. It was so unlike her that Persy reached out to her once more, in concern.

"I don't know what you mean—" she started. Just then, Ally gasped.

"He's coming! Pray he hasn't heard—I must go. Please, Persy— tomorrow night—stay away. . . ." She turned and stumbled down the stairs of the Folly, nearly falling in her haste, and flew up the long, sunlit lawn.

"Ally, wait!" Persy cried, and tried to hurry after her. But her skirts held her imprisoned so that she could not move. She pushed and kicked against the layers of heavy fabric that held her back—

She sat up in bed, her heart pounding, perspiration making her nightgown cling to her back. The heavy coverlet was twisted about her legs where she had kicked it. Soundly asleep next to her, Pen whimpered and pulled it back up, then was still once more.

Persy lay back down and stared at the ceiling, glowing in the faint dregs of light from the hearth. She'd dreamed about Ally many times over the last weeks, but never as vividly as that. What could it mean? Mrs. Allardyce had dreamed about Ally warning of danger . . . had she made up her own dream, or had that really been Ally?

18

$\mathcal{M}$ama had decreed that they would spend a restful, quiet day today, in preparation for the evening. Rest and quiet were, however, relative terms. The entire household was awakened early in the morning by guns firing salutes all over the city, to ring in the birthday of England's heiress.

It wasn't until breakfast was nearly over that Persy emerged enough from her misery to remember that it was her and Pen's birthday, too. Kenney and Andrews and Mrs. Huxworthy the cook all filed into the breakfast room to present them with dainty gold-and-pearl bracelets, the gift of the household to them. Pen promised that they would wear them that very evening to the princess's ball, which nearly made the Hoaxer faint with joy. Mama gave them brooches set with diamonds, and Papa a purse with fifty pounds each to spend as they wished.

Persy knew the household staff was disappointed that their ball would not be on their birthday night—she had heard the Hoaxer waxing indignant about it to Andrews a few weeks ago. But Mama had planned their ball for the following week because it would not do at all to compete with the princess's ball. The poor Hoaxer would probably be even more upset if she knew that one of the daughters of the house would not be there for her own ball.

Persy still wrestled with the guilt born of that fact as she slipped upstairs to pack her running-away bundle. Pen was engaged in reading Charles's French exercise, and this would probably be her only chance to be alone all day.

Packing wasn't difficult. Three of her sturdiest, plainest dresses, plus one very sober dark silk dress for Sundays, would suffice for now. Fortunately the laundress had just returned stacks of clean linens, so fresh chemises and petticoats and stockings were ready. Persy wrapped everything in a sheet purloined from one of the guest bedrooms, compressing it as well as she could and tying it with the length of bandage she had borrowed from Charles when they sneaked into Kensington. The memory of that escapade made her smile sadly as she squeezed the air out of her bundle and poked and shoved it under the bed.

Later she would sneak it downstairs and hide it in the less-used reception salon. Then after the ball tonight, she would wait until the household was asleep, slip out of the house with her bundle, and begin walking to the Allardyces'. With any luck she'd make it there early, before too many shoppers had converged on Oxford Street. The money Papa had given her would come in handy—

"What are you doing?"

Persy would have jumped if she hadn't been on her hands and knees. She'd been so immersed in her thoughts that she hadn't heard Pen enter their room.

"Oh . . . uh, I—I dropped something and thought it rolled under the bed," she stammered. "Did Charles finish his French?"

"Well enough for now. What did you lose? Here, let me look." Pen swept up her skirts and prepared to drop down beside Persy.

"No! It's not there. I already looked. It was just—just, er—nothing important." Persy scrambled to her feet, grabbing Pen's arm to keep her from looking under the bed.

Pen stared at Persy's hand, then up at her.

"I'm sorry," Persy began, letting go of her arm. Tears came to her eyes. "Please believe me—it's nothing."

"Nothing, huh?" Pen snapped. "And so is the way you've been radiating wretchedness since last night? Something happened at the Fothergills', didn't it? I saw Lord Carharrick leave looking like he'd been beaten with a club after your dance, and Lochinvar left a few minutes later looking even worse. And then there you were, dancing and grinning like the Spartan boy with a fox under his cloak. *What happened?*"

Persy sighed. At least Pen seemed to have forgotten about the bed. "I just finally got rid of them both. For good. That's all."

"Both? What did you do to Lochinvar?"

Persy edged away from the bed. "I'd rather not talk about it just yet. It still hurts too much."

"Oh, Persy." Pen shook her head. "Why? I'm sure we could have figured something out—"

"Just like we did for Ally? No. I failed her, Pen. It's time I got at least one thing right. Now Lochinvar's free of me. He'll be far better off." She shrugged away from Pen's outstretched hand and fled the room.

She couldn't flee the memory of her dream of Ally as easily. It niggled at her mind like a cocklebur while she tried to concentrate on helping Charles with his maths in the drawing room that afternoon.

After her third mistake in simple addition, Charles poked his pencil at her nose. "Perse, you may be here but your mind isn't. What's wrong? Are you that excited about the ball tonight? Honestly, you'd think you were going to heaven or something, not just another ball. *Girls!*" He shook his head in simulated disgust.

Persy swatted his pencil away. "Stop it, brat. I've got a lot on my mind."

Charles opened his mouth to speak, then shut it. He regarded her so closely for a minute that Persy felt uncomfortable. "It isn't about Ally, is it?" he asked in an accusatory tone. "Because if it is, you'd better tell me. I thought we were partners when it came to looking for her."

Persy thought about denying it, but one look at his suddenly serious face stopped her. This search meant as much to him as it did to her. With a pang, she realized that her running away would affect him too. She couldn't give him the brush-off now. "In a way. At least, I think so."

"Have you heard anything new?" Charles's voice rose with excitement.

"Hush! No. That is, I don't think so. All right, I'll tell you," she said at his impatient squirm. "I had a dream last night that Ally told us not to go to the ball tonight, because we'd be in some sort of danger."

She braced herself for a blast of ridicule, but it never arrived. Charles's wide blue eyes grew even wider.

"She came to you in a dream? Like Mrs. Allardyce? But really came and talked to you?"

"I don't know. It was strange and silly, but somehow felt all the more real because of it." She told Charles what Ally had said, then continued, "But if she can do this, why hasn't she before? She could have come to me long ago and told me where she was, and then we could have seen about rescuing her."

"Maybe she couldn't. Maybe something happened that let her do it just this once. What if it was real? What if"—his voice rose another half octave—"what if you *are* in danger if you go to the ball tonight?"

"In danger of what? And from whom? It doesn't make any sense, Charles. Why should we be in any danger?"

"Why did Ally's mother dream it too? Why were there men watching our house for all those weeks?" he challenged. "Maybe they have something to do with the danger."

"And why did they stop just as abruptly?"

"People don't hang about watching other people's houses unless they're up to no good," Charles persisted.

"Look. Even if those men had anything to do with this, I doubt they'll be showing up at Princess Victoria's ball. Charles, don't you see? If Ally didn't really come to me in a dream, then there's nothing to worry about. And if she did, then that means she'll be there—remember, she said some evil deed would be done there that she would try to avert. If she's there, then I need to go look for her and try to help her if I can."

"That makes no sense at all, Persy. If Ally did come, then you'd be walking right into dang—"

"Ah, there you are." Mama marched into the room, trailed by Pen and, to Persy's chagrin, Lochinvar. "Tea, please, Kenney," she called over her shoulder.

Persy rose and curtsied as they seated themselves, hoping her dismay didn't show. What in heaven's name was Lochinvar doing here? Could she possibly find some excuse to leave the room?

"How's Lord Chesterfield?" Charles asked, as he always did.

"Very well, and expecting a visit from you if you can be spared from your lessons," Lochinvar replied. His smile as he spoke to Charles was genuine, but Persy could see the trouble in his eyes. Yes, she definitely had to leave the room . . . but drat it, *why* had he come?

"Rather!" Charles bent to his exercise book with determination.

"Were the crowds very bad?" inquired Mama. "We can actually hear them, you know, all the way from St. James Street."

"Bad enough for carriage traffic. It looks as if the whole city is out and about, in a festive mood. That's why I rode over on Lord Chesterfield," Lochinvar said. "Getting there will be a chore."

"Ah! So we'll have the pleasure of seeing you this evening?" Mama asked.

"I wouldn't miss it for anything, ma'am," Lochinvar replied. Persy stole a look at him and saw that he was looking at her. *Why?* she wanted to shout at him. *After what I did to you, how can you even bear to be in the same room with me?*

"Neither would the girls, of course. I'm surprised that the pair of them aren't already getting ready," Mama said with a teasing smile. Persy remembered her own secret preparations upstairs and felt herself flush. She was saved from anything more revealing by Kenney's unmistakably discreet knock on the door.

Instead of the requested tea he'd brought a message. "Pardon me, my lady. But the new lady's maid for Miss Persephone and Miss Penelope has arrived."

"What?" Persy and Pen said together.

Mama blinked at him. "The new lady's maid?"

"Ooh! Can I watch?" said Charles eagerly. Persy shot him a quelling look.

"But I've not engaged a new maid yet." Mama rose, looking uncertain. "You must excuse us for a moment, Lochinvar. Perhaps you could have a look at Charles's exercises. Girls, come with me."

Thank goodness, a legitimate excuse to leave, thought Persy. She hurried down the stairs with Mama and Pen to the front hall, where a straight, slender form stood with its back to them smoothing its hair in a mirror. Something about the set of the unknown woman's shoulders seemed familiar to Persy.

"Good afternoon, Miss . . . er . . . ?" said Mama as she reached the bottom stair.

The woman—girl, really—turned. Though she wore a small pair of spectacles on the end of her nose and had done her hair in a severe, scraped-back style, Persy knew her at once. It was Lorrie Allardyce.

"Good afternoon, your ladyship and misses," she said in a slightly croaky voice as she curtsied. "I am Clements. You will have received the letter that I would be arriving today." She shot a look at Persy and Pen that all but shouted, "Hold your tongues, please, and let me handle this."

"Ah, no," Mama replied, a slightly interrogative upturn in her voice.

"From Mrs. Forrest, at Tutterow village? I had worked for her sister-in-law, who is leaving for India next month. She was kind enough to write you to see if you were still looking for a maid for the young misses." Lorrie drew herself up, looking remarkably like Ally for a moment.

"Nooo, I don't quite recall, but there is a great deal of correspondence on my desk that I have not quite got round to," Mama said.

Lorrie tsked impatiently. "This is most irregular," she said. "Mrs. Forrest assured me that it was all arranged. Has the position been filled already? It will be most unpleasant to have to endure the ride on the stage again—"

"No, the position's still open," Persy said quickly, while Mama seemed to search for something to say. "It's providential that you arrived today of all days. Getting ready for the princess's ball will be so much easier now, Mama. Poor Andrews won't be run off her feet trying to help all of us." She gave Pen a meaningful look and prayed she wouldn't drop the ball.

"I'm sure we should be quite happy to give, er, Clements a try, Mama. How kind of Mrs. Forrest to think of us," Pen chimed in, right on cue.

"Well . . ." The mention of having Andrews to herself again made Mama's face brighten. "I feel quite awkward at not having known—"

"Nonsense, Mama. Letters go astray all the time. It will be just wonderful to have a maid at last, especially tonight. Shall I ring for Kenney?" Persy hurried to the bell before Mama could protest.

"I . . ." Mama looked at Lorrie, who gazed down her nose at the three of them, then at Persy, whose hand was already on the bellpull. A peculiar expression crossed her face, but before Persy could decipher it, it had vanished.

"Very well then, dear," she said. "Please do, then run back upstairs before Lochinvar thinks we have deserted him. I shall be along in a moment. Dear me, this is most extraordinary. . . ."

"Yes, Mama." Persy yanked the bell, smiled and nodded at Lorrie, then followed Pen back up the stairs.

"What in heaven's name is going on?" Pen murmured to her,

pausing at the landing. "What does Lorrie Allardyce think she's doing?"

"I don't know. We'll find out later, I'm sure," Persy whispered back as she kept walking. "Come on. Lorrie seems quite able to handle Mama without us." She opened the door of the drawing room.

"—just a dream, she said, but I don't think so. Ally wouldn't say there was danger for no reason," she heard Charles say in a low, urgent voice. The pair were at the table by the window, but evidently maths had been forgotten. Charles's face was red and earnest as he bent toward Lochinvar.

"Charles!" Persy gasped.

He jumped at the sound of her voice.

"What are you telling him?" she demanded, feeling tall and terrible as she advanced on him.

Charles rose, his face even redder. "I'm telling Lochinvar about your dream, 'cause you won't."

"What dream?" Pen interjected. "Persy—"

"It's not any of his concern, Chuckles, nor yours. You weren't invited to the ball. Please ignore him," Persy said, turning to Lochinvar. "He's making a mountain out of a molehill."

"Ally comes to you in a dream and says you're all in danger, and you want to ignore it?" Charles looked close to bursting.

Pen gasped. "You didn't tell me about that!"

"I don't know that it was Ally. I already told you that. It could just as likely have been indigestion," she shot back at him. "And even if it truly was Ally, I can't miss this chance to go look for her, and help her if she needs it—"

"Lochinvar helped us that day when we sneaked into Kensington Palace and he said he'd help us again. Maybe he'll know what we should do about tonight—"

"You sneaked into Kensington Palace?" Pen was starting to turn red. "What have you been doing behind my back?"

"It was my idea, but she didn't want to tell you," Charles told her. "We were trying to look for Ally."

"*Charles,*" warned Persy.

"You went looking for Ally without me?" The outrage in Pen's voice was almost tangible. She put her hands on her hips and scowled.

"If there's some possible danger . . . ," Lochinvar said.

"I didn't want you to get into trouble if we got caught." Persy tried to placate her. "I didn't care if I created a scandal dressing up as a boy, but you—"

"*You dressed up as a boy?*"

"She sure did." Charles nodded proudly. "She borrowed some of Papa's trousers and my jacket. Lochinvar said she made a very handsome—"

"Charles!" Persy groaned.

"*You* were there too?" Pen turned to stare at Lochinvar.

He coughed and reached up to adjust his cravat, as if it were suddenly too snug. "Er, well, yes."

"He rescued us when that man with the funny eyes came chasing after us, and hid us under the table in the duke's library." Charles now sounded positively gleeful.

"And no one saw fit to tell me?" Pen suddenly bore a remarkable resemblance to Mama in one of her more ducal moments.

"Is everything all right?" Mama herself came back into the drawing room, still looking vaguely befuddled. She halted and looked at the four of them.

Lochinvar was the first to recover. "I was just going to take Charles down to visit Lord Chesterfield, with your permission, ma'am," he said quickly.

"Thank you, dear boy. That is most kind of you. Charles, no obstreperous behavior, please. You may be leaving the bandage off your wrist these days, but it is still not as strong as it should be. Lochinvar, please don't let him misbehave with that horse."

"I promise." Lochinvar sprang to the door with alacrity. Charles needed no encouragement, either. They vanished before anyone could say another word.

"Girls, perhaps you will take a few moments to get acquainted with this Clements. I am sure I don't recall Mrs. Forrest's mentioning her in her last letter, but post does go astray, and her arrival today was fortuitous. It would be nice if we could keep a maid for you more than a quarter hour." She looked at them very hard for a moment.

"Yes, Mama," said Pen meekly.

Mama sat down on the sofa with a sigh and poured herself a cup of tea. "Do ring for Kenney on your way out, if you please. I don't think we'll be home if anyone else calls this afternoon. There is enough going on today as it is."

That was true, Persy silently agreed. She opened the door for Pen, who swept past her with a chilly glance that promised their conversation about Ally was far from over.

But before they had gone halfway up the stairs on the way to their room, Lorrie Allardyce appeared in the hall above them. "Oh, good. I was afraid I'd have to come and get you," she called.

Persy glanced around to make sure no one was hovering nearby. "Shhh," she cautioned. "Wait till we're alone." Once they were safely in their room, she locked the door.

Lorrie seated herself in the low chair by the fire and looked around the room. "Very nice," she commented.

"Er, thank you," said Pen. "Now, will *someone* tell me what in blazes is going on here?" She sat down on the end of the bed and glared at Persy.

"We weren't getting anywhere with finding my sister," Lorrie said calmly, as if addressing a small child. She had dropped the croaky attempt to disguise her voice and folded the spectacles into her pocket as she spoke. "So I decided that a little more leadership was needed on the premises."

"Perhaps if *someone* had told me we were actually searching for her, we might have got more accomplished." Pen was close to tears.

"I didn't tell you we were going to search Kensington Palace because I didn't want you to get in trouble if we were caught," Persy said, half pleading, half explaining. "If I'd been found dressed as a boy wandering about London, I would not have cared if Mama and Papa bundled me back to Mage's Tutterow in disgrace. I didn't want your chances for the season ruined if we got caught, but I didn't care about mine."

Pen frowned. "And then Lochinvar happens to find you and Charles wandering about the palace, and rescues you from someone, and you all keep it a merry little secret from me?"

"I made him promise not to tell you that we'd been there, because I didn't want you to be angry with us."

"You hadn't told her?" Lorrie asked Persy. "Well, no wonder she's in a pet with you."

Persy's head had begun to ache. "I told you, I didn't want you to get in trouble."

"Ally's my governess too, Persy. I love her just as much as you do. It wasn't at all fair for you to keep me out of it." She stamped her foot.

"I'm sorry. I thought—I mean, you seemed occupied with other things—"

"This isn't getting us very far on what to do about my sister," Lorrie interjected, rising from her seat to poke the fire. "Now, you said you would talk to old Princess what's-her-name tonight at the ball, right? Tomorrow we can see what she's had to say and plan our next steps."

"No, not tomorrow," said Persy before she remembered.

"Why not?" Pen looked at her.

"Oh—no reason. Tomorrow will be fine." Persy walked quickly to the window to hide her agitation. Idiot! She needed to be more careful or else she'd give her plans away.

"Hmmph," Lorrie mumbled.

Persy twitched aside the curtain and peered outside, waiting for the heat to die in her cheeks. A carriage rumbled past, and then a horse with two riders: Lochinvar, holding Charles before him as they trotted up the street on Lord Chesterfield. Charles wore an expression of bliss visible even at this distance. Well, at least Lochinvar didn't hate all the Lelands because of her.

"Why should he hate all of you?" Lorrie asked.

Persy turned and stared at her. Not even Ally had been able to read her that clearly. "How did you know what I . . . ?"

Lorrie shrugged. "Reading people is what I'm good at, magically speaking. I can't do it all the time or with everyone, but when it's as loud and clear as you were, it's easy. Why should this Lochinvar hate all of you?"

Persy looked at Pen, who crossed her arms over her chest and stayed stubbornly silent. "Because . . ." she began. "Because he has a prejudice against witches, and I deliberately did a halting spell on him at a ball last night."

"Persy!" Pen gasped. "You didn't!"

"Gracious!" Lorrie looked amused. "Why?"

"Because he . . . I . . . oh, it's a long story." Persy turned back to the window so that they wouldn't see the tears in her eyes.

"Because my sister is an idiot and did a love spell on him, and now she's doing her best to chase him away because she doesn't want his love if it isn't freely given." Pen sounded impatient. "But Persy, you—you let him know you're a witch! I can't believe that you—"

"It was the only way I could think of to put him off once and for all," she said, still staring out the window.

"That must have been a doozy of a love spell," Lorrie said thoughtfully.

"What do you mean?" Persy turned again.

"Most love spells only work if there's some natural inclination already in place between you and the object. You can't put a love spell on someone who doesn't know you, for example. Which one did you use?"

Persy sat down on the bed next to Pen. "It was one I found in Ally's room, with her books. A candle, some rosewater, a copper basin, ten spoons—"

Lorrie made a strange sound and sat up straighter. "And a pair of bootlaces?" she asked breathlessly.

"Um, yes. Is it a well-known one? Of course, Ally never taught—"
She stopped in astonishment as Lorrie Allardyce burst into peals of
laughter.

"Oh my goodness!" she said, gasping for breath. "I . . . oh!" She
dissolved again until at last she had to wipe her eyes on her sleeve.
"Oh dear. I'm *so* sorry. It's just that . . . well, *I* wrote that spell when I
was about twelve. It was a joke on my brother, Merlin—he was in
love with the girl in the apothecary shop across the street, and I just
couldn't resist. Rosewater makes him sneeze, you see, and Mama
had only eight silver spoons so he'd have to go find two more
somehow, and the bootlaces were just so silly. . . ." She giggled. "I
sent it to my sister afterward—I can't imagine why she saved it."

"But—the paper—it looked so old!" Persy felt as if the rug had
been pulled from under her feet.

"Of course it did. If there's plenty of anything in a bookstore, it's
bits of old paper. I took it from the back of an old medical book
that had been around forever. Dear, dear me." She wiped her eyes
again.

Pen, however, wasn't laughing. "So it wasn't a real spell, then,"
she said slowly. "But that means—"

"No, not real in the least—oh!" Lorrie's humor evaporated.
Persy felt the weight of their regard on her as a numb horror froze
her in place.

She *hadn't* enchanted Lochinvar into loving her. Everything he'd
done and said—his words, his kisses—had been *real*. He'd fallen in
love with her of his own free will. And she'd been dreadful to him
and done everything she could to drive him off, and it hadn't
worked . . . until last night. When she'd shown him that she was a
witch.

"Persy, I'm so sorry." Pen slipped an arm around her shoulders. "How were you to know it wasn't real?"

"If I'd known that anyone would ever find that silly spell and try to use it, I would never have written it," Lorrie declared. "Are you sure that you—that he—"

"I'm sure," Persy whispered. The memory of his eyes, wide with shock after she'd halted him, still haunted her. He had loved her— he had. If she hadn't been such an idiot after the Gilleys' party, they might now be betrothed—planning their wedding, stealing kisses when nobody was looking. . . .

This was it, then. She couldn't stay here and keep going out into society, where surely Lord Carharrick would snub her for what she'd said to him, if he didn't gossip about her heartless treatment of him . . . and where she'd have to endure Lochinvar's scorn and disgust. She would go to the ball tonight, and be gone before morning.

A knock on the door interrupted her gloom. "We'll be bringing in your bath in a moment," the housemaid's voice called. "Her lady- ship suggested you ladies might want it sooner rather than later."

"Why don't you go first?" Lorrie said to Pen before anyone could speak. She gave Persy a look that was as good as a command, and Persy was once more reminded of Ally. She followed Lorrie meekly down the hall to the small room that Mama had designated for their maid, when they finally found one. Lorrie's trunk was already there.

Lorrie perched on top of it. "Sit," she commanded, and pointed at the narrow chintz-covered bed. "And tell me why you want to run away from home."

Persy froze in midstep. "What did you say?"

"You heard me. I read it plain as the newspaper when you came to see us the other day. That's the other reason why I came today—to stop you. I need you around to help find my sister. Why *do* you want to leave, anyway?"

Persy swallowed hard. She wouldn't cry—she wouldn't. "It's just the best solution to—to a lot of problems."

"Hmmph," Lorrie said. "Bet my sister would be mad as a weaver if she knew."

"I can't help it!" Persy buried her face in her hands and burst into tears. Vaguely she felt the edge of the bed sag as Lorrie sat down next to her and slipped an arm around her shoulders.

"Lochinvar—he's the Lord Seton that came with you to the shop a few times, isn't he?" she asked gently.

Persy remembered Lochinvar's patient expression as Lorrie's brother preached to him about book bindings on their second visit to the Allardyces'. She'd been strongly tempted to kiss him for his kind forbearance, letting the ham-fisted Merlin keep him occupied so that she and Pen could talk to Mr. and Mrs. Allardyce. She nodded.

"Listen to me, Miss Persy. Don't run away tomorrow. Let's work on finding my sister. If we haven't been able to find her by the end of the season, you can leave—and I'll come with you."

"What?" Persy lifted her head and looked at her.

"I—well, to be honest, I ran away too. Partly to help look for my sister, but mostly because I don't want to get married, or let my brother boss me about the bookshop for the rest of my days," said Lorrie, staring down at her lap. "That's why I'm here as Clements. I want to make my own way without anyone telling me what to do. So if you decide you want to run away, I'll go with you. We can stay with friends of mine until we decide what we want to do. Between the pair of us, I'll bet we'd land on our feet just fine."

"You can't be—you'd do that? Really?" Persy wasn't sure whether to be disappointed, relieved, or happy, and settled for a mix of all three.

"Really," affirmed Lorrie. She held out her right hand and Persy solemnly shook it. They smiled at each other over their joined hands.

"Right." Lorrie nodded briskly. "Well, you go off to the ball tonight and see if you can't get that Princess Sophia to stop being a goose and be helpful. And I'll get that bundle under your bed put away so the housemaids don't find it, shall I?"

19

$\mathcal{A}$s their carriage inched into the queue of vehicles traveling toward St. James's, Persy gazed out at the masses of smiling men, women, and children lining the streets. No wonder Papa had wanted them to leave an hour and a half early for the ball. "So many people," she murmured.

"You and your sister aren't the princess's only admirers," he replied and patted her hand. "They've been lining up since dawn, wanting to catch a look at her on her way to the ball."

"I do hope Lochinvar and Charles will be all right." Mama took one last look at the crowds and lowered the blind on her window.

"What?" Persy and Pen asked at the same time.

"Lochinvar sent a note around after he and Charles went out on that horse of his, while you two were getting acquainted with Clements. It seems they got caught up in the crowds, and rather than trying to get him back, Lochinvar brought Charles home with him for the night. He assured me that his valet would take care of him while he attended the ball. I thought it a little odd, but I trust Lochinvar's good sense. And Charles deserves a bit of an outing after all these weeks. He does worship Lochinvar, doesn't he? I just hope he will behave himself." Mama sighed.

Papa smiled. "I am sure he will. He won't endanger his visiting rights with Lochinvar's horse. Stop worrying about the boy, and let us enjoy the evening."

Persy settled back in her seat and looked out at the crowds as their carriage crept toward St. James's Palace. She would rather have leapt out and run all the way up the mall than be stuck here, trying to contain her anxiety and excitement. Would Ally be there tonight? She tried to draw a deep breath but couldn't. Lorrie was as bad as Andrews when it came to tight lacing for ball dresses.

It was fully dark before they emerged from the carriage into the fine late-spring evening. There was an unusual glow to the sky from the illuminations that had been set up all over the city in celebration of Victoria's birthday, and a rumble of sound from the crowds that filled the surrounding streets. Joyous excitement filled the air, tangible as a London fog.

"Hurry up and wait again, is it?" Pen said, nodding at the queue of elegantly dressed people waiting to enter.

"Would you rather slip in a side door and miss seeing the princess?" Papa asked, opening his eyes wide in feigned surprise.

Pen frowned at him reproachfully and did not reply. All at once Persy's anxiety lifted, and she felt like shouting just like the crowds around them, or taking off her silk shawl with the deep fringe and waving it around her head like a banner. This was it. She would finally get to see Her Royal Highness, the Princess Victoria.

That is, if this line would ever move.

Fortunately, the line moved far faster than the carriages had. In less time than Persy expected they had moved past the powdered footmen in their splendid liveries at the door and through the hall to the long staircase leading up, up. . . .

Pen fanned herself furiously. "It's too hot," she complained.

On the contrary, Persy's hands and feet felt icy, though her face felt hot, too. The same feeling of distant unreality that she had felt at her first ball gradually enfolded her as they progressed up the staircase. She felt like a spectator watching herself and the others around her in their elaborate finery, a sea of rich colors and nodding plumes on the older ladies' headdresses. When she heard a distant voice announce, "The Viscount and Viscountess Atherston. The Honorable Misses Leland," it took her a moment to realize that it was talking about her. *Wake up, Persy. Don't float away now, or you'll miss everything.* She hurried after Mama.

They were approaching a small raised platform crowded with sumptuously dressed women. With a small start of surprise Persy recognized Princess Sophia among them. But instead of her usual slightly shabby and old-fashioned clothes, Princess Sophia wore an evening dress of the latest fashion in violet satin, with an embroidered tulle Italian cap on her faded gray-blond hair. Her usually dreamy blue eyes were sharp behind her spectacles as she surveyed the crowd, and she wore a small frown, unlike her usual placid expression.

"Look at Princess Sophia," Persy whispered to Pen. "She looks different tonight somehow, doesn't she?"

"Never mind *her,*" Pen shot back. Her voice trembled with excitement.

Then Persy saw her.

She was surprised by how tiny Princess Victoria appeared at

first glance. She was nearly a head shorter than Persy and Pen. *Why, Charles is taller than she is, and he's only eleven.*

But her smallness was deceptive. Though Princess Victoria's manner was appropriately modest and demure as became a girl of eighteen, Persy saw that it was merely a garment, a veil. Underneath that maidenly diffidence a majesty, an innate regal presence, lay in waiting. Unconscious of it though she might be, it was clear that she could fill the room with that presence if she so chose. But for now, she was content to be an eager young girl at her coming-out ball. Persy's heart swelled as she felt that royal aura, so concentrated in that small, slender frame.

Then she began to notice more. The princess's eyes, very large and very blue in her round face, shone with excitement, and when she smiled she showed a mouthful of white teeth. Her thick, light brown hair hung in fashionable ringlets on her bare shoulders, and her gown—satin with blond lace, Persy noted through her haze of hero worship—was exquisite. She smiled and nodded as guests filed past, and occasionally exchanged a quick greeting with acquaintances under the watchful eye of the Duchess of Kent. Persy remembered her beautiful, bell-like voice, and wished that she could hear it again.

"Drat! We aren't presented to her?" Pen whispered.

"No presentations tonight, or there wouldn't be any time left for dancing. I don't think Her Royal Highness wants that," Mama murmured back. "Dear me, Princess Augusta is getting stout. It's a shame Their Majesties were not able to be here tonight." She shook her head at the king's plump sister, who stood at the princess's left in place of the queen.

"The king is not at all well," Papa replied in the same low

voice. "But determined to live until this day. At least he has had his wish."

Almost before she was aware of it, they had passed the royal dais. Persy saw Princess Sophia's face light up when she saw them, and her frown smooth out as if in relief. Was she that happy to see them? Persy curtsied to her and was rewarded with a broad smile.

Mama led them farther into the ballroom and somehow managed to find a group of unclaimed seats.

"We saw her. We finally saw her," Pen said in hushed tones. Her eyes were positively starry.

But Persy felt somehow let down. Seeing the princess was at once thrilling and disappointing. To have been so close, without having a chance to meet her eye or touch her hand—it just wasn't fair. This would probably be the only time she would see the princess in her lifetime. Governesses were not received at court.

Pen's elbow dug into her side. "Look," she whispered.

Persy looked and wished she hadn't. Lochinvar was making his way through the crowd toward them. "Quick! Where's the necessary?" she said, trying to dodge behind Pen.

But there wasn't time to flee or even to hide. Lochinvar was there bowing to Mama and Papa before she could do anything. She was barely able to return his mumbled greeting or to meet his eyes, gold tonight under the glitter of the many candles in the great ballroom. She watched as he led Pen out for the first quadrille. He looked almost feverish, eyes too bright in a very pale face. Had he been taken ill? He'd seemed well enough that afternoon, trotting down the street on Lord Chesterfield with Charles.

She sat down next to Mama in one of the chairs. Princess Sophia had been terribly provoking when they'd told her about Ally, telling the whole tale to the odious Sir John after they'd sworn her to secrecy, but maybe she'd gone looking for her—she'd seemed very interested and eager to help. Would it be possible to speak with her this evening? Was Ally herself somewhere here tonight? Had her dream been real?

A couple promenaded past her seat. Persy recognized the richly dressed dark-haired woman from the royal dais: It was the Duchess of Kent, Princess Victoria's mother. Though her mouth curved in a smile, her eyes were peevish and anxious as she surveyed the room. She clung to the arm of her escort, who also wore a slight smile below his wary, darting eyes. When the cold eyes settled on Persy, the faint smile spread wide.

Persy bowed her head as Sir John Conroy's grin touched her. She knew she should feel grateful to him for ensuring that they received their invitations to this ball, but the only emotion he roused in her was aversion. Something about his shrewd, calculating eyes, as if gears and wheels spun behind them, reminded her of Mr. Babbage's calculating machine that Papa had told her about. She remembered the overheard conversation back at Kensington and shivered. The poor princess had withstood this man for years. How could anyone doubt her mental strength and resilience?

She sat staring at the fan in her lap long after Sir John and the duchess had passed. Only whispers of "the princess!" made her lift her head to watch Princess Victoria make her way to the center of the ballroom, led by the Duke of Norfolk's grandson for the opening quadrille of the ball. As most of the dancers were also trying to watch her, the orchestra was soon accompanied by a low, constant murmur of "I beg your pardon" and "So sorry" and "Did I hurt you?" If she hadn't felt so sad, she might have laughed.

Lochinvar and Pen passed too, and something about Pen's creased forehead and stiff posture as she danced the figures caught her attention. Oh please, Pen wasn't grilling him about the trip to Kensington or, heaven forbid, talking about *her*, was she?

She was even more surprised when, after leading Pen back, Lochinvar turned to her and without speaking held out his hand. She stared at him.

"Lochinvar would like to have this waltz with you, Persy, if you please," said Pen behind him in a patient voice. She sounded like Ally correcting Charles's table manners.

For one fleeting second Persy thought about refusing. Why was he asking her to dance? Why was he even acknowledging that she existed? "I—" she began.

But Lochinvar was nearly pulling her out of her seat by then, and it was too late. As they took their place on the floor, she saw Pen peer anxiously after them.

Oh, why had Pen made her do this? She wished the strange watching-from-above sensation that she'd had when seeing the princess for the first time would overtake her now. But it stubbornly refused to, and she was forced to be very much there, staring at Lochinvar's mouth as she always did when they danced. She had come to know it well after all these weeks of balls; right now it was tense, the lips pressed tight together.

As she watched, the lips parted and then closed. A few seconds later they opened once again.

"Might I ask you a question?"

She looked steadfastly at his mouth, and hoped her voice wouldn't shake. "Perhaps."

"Why have you been trying to put me off?"

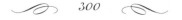

Was he about to denounce her? "I'd rather not say. In fact, I'm not even sure why you have asked me to dance this evening."

He swallowed. "Because . . . because I have something that I need to say to you."

She laughed, even though it hurt to. "Under the circumstances, I can't imagine that there's anything left for us to say to each other."

"Persy!" He looked angry, and gripped her waist so tightly that she was sure he'd snap a bone in her corset. "Will you please listen to me—"

At that instant, Pen was suddenly at her side. She grabbed Persy's arm and yanked it out of Lochinvar's grasp.

"Perse! Look!" She spun Persy around and pointed to an open door in the far wall of the ballroom.

Ally stood there.

20

At first Persy thought she was going to faint. "Ally!" she gasped, ignoring the irritated looks from the couples trying to waltz around them.

"Come on, Persy! We've got to go to her!" Pen yanked on her arm again and took a step toward Ally.

Ally stared at them from the doorway, beckoning. Her face was pale and her expression anxious, even at this distance. Had she escaped in the confusion of the evening? If so, they had to get her away to safety before she was found again. Persy pulled away from Lochinvar and hurried after Pen's billowing pink skirt.

"No!" Lochinvar grabbed her arm. "Persy, wait."

"Let me go! It's Ally!" She pulled away from him and turned after Pen again, darting and weaving through the dancing couples.

"Persy, it's not really—"

His voice was lost in the music and the angry mutters of the dancers they dodged around. Pen banged full tilt into a dancing couple and nearly fell.

"See here, young woman!" said the man, red-faced.

"Your pardon, sir." Pen regained her footing and tossed the

apology over her shoulder. Persy caught up to her then and grabbed her hand.

"Pen," she said as they dodged and wove. "What about my dream? Ally said—"

"I don't know. Please excuse us, sir, ma'am," she called as they plowed past an elderly couple who jumped out of their path, looking terrified.

A few dozen feet from the door, Pen stopped. Persy just had time to see it slowly close.

"What is she doing?" she panted.

"I don't know. Come on!" Pen threw herself at the door.

In a second's time they stood at the end of a long corridor paneled in dark wood. Persy could still hear the orchestra playing and the reverberation of dancing feet and conversation from the room behind them. But here it was still and quiet, with not even a footman standing by to apprehend trespassers from the ballroom. Halfway down its length a small lantern set in an alcove cast a pool of dim light.

Pen still clutched her hand. "Ally," she moaned. "Oh, where did you go?"

"Pen, Lochinvar said—I don't think he saw her."

"Then he couldn't have been looking in the right place. You saw her, didn't you?"

"Yes." An image of Ally's haunted eyes flashed before her.

"Then let's go. She's got to be here somewhere."

A movement caught Persy's eye. She looked up and saw a skirted figure just disappearing around a turn at the end of the hall. "There!"

Pen didn't bother to answer. She seized Persy's hand again and ran.

That turn led to a short passage, more a jog than a hallway in its own right. When they came to its end, they found another long hallway like the first, lined with doors and dimly lit with small lamps set at intervals down its length.

"Ally!" Pen shouted, just as they saw her disappear through a door at its end.

"Why is she running away from us?" Persy gasped for breath and mentally cursed Lorrie and her tightly laced corset.

"I don't know. But we won't find out unless we catch up with her." Pen was already halfway down the hall.

That door opened to reveal stairs. They hurried up them and into another corridor much like the others. There were no foot-men, no servants, no lights but the infrequent lamps, and no sign of Ally.

"Pen," Persy whispered as they peered down this new hall. "Doesn't this remind you of something?"

"Umm, no . . . blast it, where did she go? Should we have gone down?" Pen tugged at the door nearest them. It was locked.

"Listen! Our dream, back at home—before we came to London—when we first thought there was something wrong about Ally."

Pen paused after trying the next door. "You're right," she said slowly. "I'd almost forgotten." Her eyes widened as the details returned to her. "It looked just like this, didn't it?"

"What do we do?"

Pen bit her lip. "Keep looking. What else can we do? You take that side of the corridor and I'll do this one." Pen motioned with her hand and went to the next door. It too was locked.

Persy swallowed, remembering the sense of dread and danger she had felt in her dream. She tried three knobs that all stubbornly refused to turn. Were all the doors locked? At least that would mean that if one opened, then Ally would probably—

"Perse!" Pen hissed. "Over here!" She pointed at a door slightly ajar.

Persy hurried over to her, and after they exchanged one more anxious look, Pen pushed it open.

The room was brighter than the corridor. Persy had to blink while her eyes adjusted to the stronger light. Funny place for candles, though, set on the floor in circular patterns like that—

In front of her Pen let out her breath in a whoosh and sprinted across the room. Persy caught an impression of empty space, furniture pulled up against the walls . . . and a still figure neatly laid out in the middle of the bare floor, her hands folded on her breast. It was Ally.

Pen already knelt beside her, yanking off her gloves and lifting Ally's hand. Candles flickered around her, casting weird shadows. "Ally," she called softly. "Are you all right? Wake up, Ally! Persy, help me!"

Persy took a step forward, then froze. Right at her foot was a thin, chalked line. She followed it with her eyes and saw that it formed a large circle that took up most of the room, with candles set at intervals around and within it. The fine hairs on the back of her neck stood up.

"Persy, come on!"

"Pen," Persy said carefully. "I want you to come here first."

"What are you talking about? Don't you see it's Ally? She's fainted or something, and I can't lift her on my own." Pen smoothed Ally's hair and glared up at Persy, breathing hard.

"I'm not coming in there, Pen. Don't you see it? Didn't you feel it?" She gestured at dancing shadows cast by the candles and the soundless hum of energy that flowed around them. A thin reek of burning herbs—she caught the scents of ginger, basil, and clove—came from braziers set in the corners of the room.

"Feel what?" Pen followed her hand, but Persy could see by her wild eyes that she didn't understand.

"The circle, the candles—Pen, please come to me. Please." She made her voice as calm as she could.

Perhaps it was the last "please" that did it. Pen looked at her and then at the limp Ally, then gently set her hand back down. Persy noticed that Ally's head was resting on a small folded cloth, and that her skirts were carefully and modestly draped. It was clear that she hadn't fallen there, but had been deliberately placed. Spiky, angular figures had been chalked on the floor around her.

That was when Persy realized just how afraid she was.

Pen clambered to her feet. "All right, I'm coming. Then will you come and help me—"

She stopped dead, as if she had hit a wall, and felt the air in front of her. "Persy! I can't! There's something . . . I can't get past it."

It looked to Persy as if she were pressing her hands against a pane of glass that stood between them. She could see the soft skin of Pen's palms flatten against the invisible barrier.

Pen slid her hands up and down and then moved sideways, making a circle as she did. "I can't," she said in a small voice. "There's something all around here. I can see the circle on the floor around me, where the barrier begins. It must be magic, then. Oh, why didn't I feel it?"

"It was a trap. Ally warned me in my dream about danger, and she was right. But we didn't know that she'd be the bait." Persy felt sick watching Pen explore the invisible walls of her prison. "If I'd been the first one in, I would have done the same thing."

"No, you wouldn't. You knew there was something wrong right away. I felt you hesitate, and I wanted to grab your arm and drag you with me. Thank God I didn't." She stopped feeling the circle and looked at Persy, her bare shoulders slumping. "Can you get us out of here?"

"I don't know. I need to see what kind of spell it is. Is Ally all right?"

Pen knelt beside Ally again and touched the base of her throat. "She's breathing, and her heart is beating. But slowly—so slowly. It's like she's in some kind of trance." She smoothed her dark hair. "That wasn't Ally we were following, was it?" she asked softly, staring down at the beloved face.

"No, it couldn't have been." Persy walked around the edge of the circle, counting candles and peering down at the chalk marks. Here and there different colors of chalk had been used to draw a braided pattern unlike anything she had seen before, but all the candles in this circle were black. Of course. Black candles were for protection. Someone had gone to a great deal of trouble to prepare this. "I guess that's what Lochinvar meant when he said 'It's not really . . . ,'" she said absently. "I was too far away to hear the rest, but it must have been 'It's not really her,' or something."

"How did he know? And who were we following, then?"

"I don't know. Maybe no one. Just an image, to draw us up here." Persy rubbed her eyes as she stared down at the circle. A few feet within it, another circle had been drawn and set with copper-colored candles, interspersed with black. Within that circle was another, set with purple and black candles, and within that one yet another, with candles of orange and black.

"But why would we see it, and not him? How would he know?"

Persy straightened and looked at her. "I don't know. Unless . . ." She took a breath. "Did you ever . . . *tell* him anything? About magic, and Ally, and . . . us?"

"Of course not! I know better than that," Pen replied indignantly.

Persy resumed her examination of the circles. The elaborate braided patterns gave her the shivers though the designs were beautiful. They contained some power that she could sense but not identify. Ally had not taught them much about ritual magic. She had always said that rituals were useful only as a focus. It was the power of the person performing the ritual that mattered.

Whoever had prepared this ritual was evidently very powerful. Persy could almost see the shining web of magic that hung in the air over the circle. Would rubbing out part of the chalked lines or extinguishing a candle break its power? That was risky, as Ally had once explained—released from its bonds without focus, the power contained in a circle might explode like loose gunpowder, and Persy didn't want to risk Pen or Ally getting hurt in the blast.

Then where was the person who had prepared this magic? And why had Ally and they been brought here?

"Persy, listen! I hear someone coming." Pen sat up straighter and stared at the door. "You don't think it could be Lochinvar, do you? Could he have followed us?" she added hopefully.

Persy held her breath and listened. Footsteps, yes—but more than one set of them was approaching. She heard a female voice murmur something, and a male voice give a monosyllabic reply, and a third voice chuckle unpleasantly.

Pen heard them too. "Quickly! You've got to hide!" She looked around her and pointed at a table. "There—under there!"

"Too easy to see." Persy cursed the shimmering pale blue of her dress as she looked around the room. Then she noticed heavy curtains on the far wall that must cover a window. She darted around the edge of the circle and slipped behind the folds of heavy silk, flattening her petticoats as she did.

"Persy, your feet!" Pen's voice teetered on the edge of panic.

"Blast!" Persy stared down at her shoes. What could she do? Then she remembered the cloaking spell she had used when she and Charles sneaked into Kensington. Taking a deep breath, she muttered the words, and felt the familiar stuffy sensation surround her as the spell took hold. It fluttered and wavered around her, and she realized that the magic circle was pulling at it, trying to suck up her spell like a sponge. Was that what it was? A circle to hold magic power, like a reservoir?

A few seconds later, she heard the door open.

"Well, well! What have we here? Why, if it isn't one of the P's in a pod. Quite properly in a pod now, aren't you?" said a mocking voice.

Persy stifled an exclamation as she recognized it.

"But just one P?" Sir John Conroy continued. "Why is this? Where is your sister, girl?"

"Now, Sir John, this is my friend, if you please. There's no need to tease or be uncivil." Princess Sophia sounded peevish.

"Sorry, ma'am. Old habits, and all that," Sir John soothed. "What happened, Carrighar? Where is the other one?"

"I don't know, sir." Michael Carrighar sounded puzzled. "They're both here tonight, aren't they?"

"Yes. I saw them both myself. Where the devil is she, then?"

"Perhaps you would be so good as to tell me what is going on here," Pen said. Persy could picture her sitting by Ally, her back ramrod-straight and her nose high.

"What is going on here?" Sir John echoed. His voiced was punctuated by footsteps, drawing closer as he spoke. He must be pacing around the perimeter of the circle. "A great deal, Miss P-in-a-pod. We're offering you a chance to be of enormous service to your country."

Persy reached up and unpinned from her breast the diamond brooch Mama had given her. Then, holding her breath, she carefully scratched it at eye level across the curtain that concealed her. The heavy silk, rotted from years in the sun, split under the pin. She stuck the pin haphazardly back into her bodice and peered out with one eye through the narrow slit she had cut.

Pen sat just as she had imagined her, looking every inch the granddaughter of a duke. Only the grip she kept on Ally's hand betrayed her tension. Beyond her, hovering by the door, Princess Sophia frowned at Sir John, who paced around the circle with his hands behind his back. Persy moved her head to one side and just caught a glimpse of Michael Carrighar standing by the table Pen had told her to hide under. She breathed a silent sigh of relief that she hadn't.

"Of service to my country? How do you mean, sir?" Pen prompted him.

"My dear Miss P—"

"My name is Miss Leland, if you please."

He shrugged. "My dear Miss P, you know why we are here tonight, do you not? Why all of London is out there clogging the streets and creating a public nuisance? All this fuss just for the birthday of a young girl barely out of the classroom—a girl who might find herself Queen of England any moment now—"

"And what's wrong with that? Please, ma'am . . ." Pen turned to Princess Sophia.

"No, my dear. You must listen to Sir John. He is a very clever man, you know, even if he does sometimes tease too much." Princess Sophia simpered at him. He paused and bowed to her.

"Thank you, ma'am. Tell me, Miss P. What would you think if you or any girl your age was suddenly called upon to rule England? Could you do anything but make a mash of it? Hmm?"

"Surely this is the king's business, not yours," Pen ventured.

Sir John snorted. "The king is a moribund old wreck with the brains of a daffodil, girl. And all anyone else sees, from Lord Melbourne and the cabinet down to the merest linkboy in the street, is that Victoria's young and tolerably pretty and unlike the vulgar old men who've ruled this country for the last half century and more. They're just as happy to see a stupid young girl as a stupid old man on the throne, and expect blue eyes and nice manners to suffice for a monarch. Pah!"

Sir John stopped and jabbed his finger at Pen to emphasize his words. Below him, candle flames fluttered and danced.

"Please be careful, sir," Mr. Carrighar called.

"But *I* know better. I know that if she's to survive as queen, she needs a firm hand guiding hers. What *would* happen if the king were to die tomorrow? Victoria would collapse after two days as queen, unless there were someone next to her to help shoulder the burden."

"Someone like yourself," Pen said slowly.

"Yes, someone like myself," Sir John agreed. "Someone who could guide her, train her, lead her gently into her role. Her mother and I have tried to explain that for her own good she should either request a regency or take a private secretary to assist her. But she has always refused to even consider it. I have served my country in many capacities, Miss P. I sacrificed a very promising career in the army because Victoria's father asked me on his deathbed to watch over his daughter. By being Victoria's guide until she can manage on her own, I can keep my promise and keep serving my country."

It was an inspired piece of oratory. Persy wondered how often Sir John had practiced it before his shaving mirror. So, it seemed, did Pen.

"Just till she can manage on her own?" she mused. "Somehow I can't imagine that you'll be content with ruling England in her name for only a year or two, Sir John."

His face darkened. "Enough, girl. You know nothing of these things."

"Enough to know that I don't believe you'd ever let go of power. So what has any of that to do with my governess being kidnapped and myself being held here?" Pen snapped.

"It was time to take more drastic measures. Because that chit won't take me as secretary of her own free will, I must force her. With magic."

Persy froze. So did Pen.

"Ah, that has gotten your attention, hasn't it?" Sir John's anger was replaced once again by self-assurance. "My associate Mr. Carrighar is the son of a distant relative back in Ireland. He came to my notice not long ago, as did some, ah, shall we say, less than savory behavior of his elder brother's. Their father is a proud and upright old gentleman, well respected in Cork. If it were to get about that his son and heir had ruined his own cousin—how old was she again, Michael? Fourteen?—then I don't know what would happen to him. When Michael came to me asking for help in covering up his brother's lapse in judgment, I was delighted to do so, provided that he, in turn, help me with my own problem. Which he was quite qualified to do."

"He's a wizard," Pen said quietly.

"Well done, Miss P! He is indeed. The best wizards in Europe are Irish, so they say. So you see, it was very simple. I would fix Michael's problem if he would use his magic to fix mine. He made an excellent beginning, but it seems that it was beyond Michael's power alone. He could create the structure of the spell that would control Victoria, but required more magic to actually supply the power for it. Rather like having a lamp without the oil. It was most fortuitous that on an afternoon off, he happened upon a most unusual bookstore owned by a most unusual family. I don't think I need to say any more, except that fate can work in mysterious ways." He smiled and bowed his head in a mockery of piety. "We have enjoyed having Miss Allardyce as our guest, haven't we?"

It took all of Persy's will not to leap out of her hiding place and slap him.

"But it didn't work! Ally would never agree to help you do such a thing!" Pen's outrage was palpable.

"No, she wouldn't, though Michael did his best to persuade her. We knew that we'd have to take her power from her. But that presented more problems. According to Michael, some of her power would be lost if it were not freely given. Which meant that we again had a deficit . . . until we remembered you. Your Miss Allardyce could not help letting slip that her pupils were magically talented as well as charming." He bowed ironically to Pen. "Her Highness the Princess Sophia has been a friend to me in the years I have managed her affairs along with Victoria's. She invited you to Kensington so that Michael could size you up, and we were delighted when he reported that with your help, too, we would be able to accomplish our plan. All we had to do was lure you here, courtesy of a small illusion by my colleague, and—"

"Time, sir," Mr. Carrighar said quietly. He had been busy at his table during Sir John's speech though Persy could not quite see what he had been doing.

Sir John consulted his watch. "Very well, Miss P. Enough idle chatter. I should like to know where your sister is, if you please."

"She's not here." Pen looked away from him.

"I can see that, you insolent little chit. Where is she?"

"I don't know. We got separated when we were looking for Ally. I came up here, and . . ." She shrugged.

"I see." Sir John frowned. "Your Highness, if you would be so good as to begin the next act of our little drama and convince your niece to accompany you here? In the meanwhile, I shall find the other Miss P and pitch her into the circle. Will that do, Michael?"

"Yes, sir."

"Michael here is sad at losing the company of your Miss Allardyce," Sir John explained to Pen as he went to the door, a touch of malice edging his words. "I think that he has become fonder of her than he ought to these last weeks. Ah, well. You might want to take a moment to say your own farewells to her, Miss P."

"What?" Pen's face was white.

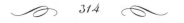

"Perhaps I wasn't clear earlier. We were forced to take your governess's power because she wouldn't cooperate. Unfortunately, her life will probably go with it. With a witch as powerful as she, the two become inescapably intertwined, so Michael tells me. Oh, don't worry. *You* should survive this evening, though we don't expect your magic to. Your sister may not, since her powers seem to be stronger and more developed than yours. But you can't make a cake without cracking eggs, now, can you?"

He crooked his arm to Princess Sophia, and led her to the door. A foot from it they stopped dead, as if they had walked into a wall. Sir John tried to reach for the knob, but an invisible barrier kept him from moving. "Carrighar," he called, his voice tight with irritation.

"The ward, sir. I'm sorry. But you said to make sure no uninvited guests arrived." The wizard stepped past him and swept his hand through the air in front of the door as if drawing aside a curtain.

"How will I get back in?" Sir John peered into the air as if he could somehow see the protective spell that had guarded the door.

"You could knock and announce yourself, sir."

Sir John gave him a black look and left the room with Princess Sophia.

It took all of Persy's will not to run to Pen, who was staring down at Ally with tears trickling down her cheeks. Then Pen lifted her head and looked at the curtain where Persy hid. Persy caught the glint of determination in her eye as she turned to Michael Carrighar, who was adding something to one of the braziers.

"*Must* you do that?" she asked, rubbing her eyes. "It's smoky enough in here."

"Yes," he said shortly, gliding over to the others and doing the same. Persy caught a stronger whiff of burning ginger.

"Sir John can't be the most pleasant employer."

Mr. Carrighar hesitated, compressing his lips as if biting back a reply, then shook his head. Pen was trying to distract him, Persy guessed—to keep him from completing his preparations for the spell that would bind Princess Victoria to Sir John. Was there anything she could do to help?

She turned her head to examine the window behind her and felt the same shield of magic covering it that must be covering the door. But even if she could get past the protective ward, open it, and clamber out without his noticing, the drop to the ground was at least forty feet, and she was not sure she could manage a hovering spell right now in her state of mind.

Pen tried again. "Isn't it risky, attempting this here? Why did Sir John choose tonight?"

"He thought it would seem natural, the princess announcing her new secretary on her birthday. And it was a good way to guarantee your presence." Mr. Carrighar picked up a crystal goblet and poured water into it from a pitcher. "Now please stop trying to distract me, Miss Leland. It won't do any good."

"Why don't *you* just stop? You must see that this is wrong. Are you willing to harm innocent people just so that Sir John can satisfy his greed?"

He paused to look at her. "What does it matter? Sir John will not harm the princess. He'll get what he wants and she'll be none the wiser."

"And England will be—"

"To hell with England," he growled. "Only the people I love matter."

"Like her?" Pen stroked Ally's forehead. Mr. Carrighar's angry face grew bleak.

"If *you* really loved her you would help me," he said more quietly. "If you willingly give me your power, it will go easier on you all. You would just walk from this room with a headache, no more. Your sister would probably survive. And if you could convince her to give her power as well, it—it might keep Melusine from losing her life. At the least it would make her passing a less painful one." He gestured at Ally and looked quickly away.

Persy's mind galloped. He would take Pen's power, and hers, and Ally's. Pen would lose her magic, but not her life. She herself would suffer more, but might survive. But Ally . . .

So what if she did willingly help him? Pen would still be Pen without her magic, she would still be Persy—and Ally might live. How important was her magic, compared to that?

Who else knew she was a witch? No one that mattered, really—not her parents or friends. The Allardyces would think her magic a small price to pay for their daughter's life. And Lochinvar . . .

She had not been willing to give up her magic for Lochinvar after all. But if she gave it up for Ally, the barrier between her and him might be removed. She could have him after all and live the life she'd dreamed of, by his side.

Her hand crept of its own accord for the edge of the curtain. All she had to do was step out from behind it and into the circle, and let him drain her magic. It would be so easy. . . .

Pen's voice stopped her. It was sharp and incredulous. "You

would kill Ally? I saw your face just now. If you have the least bit of feeling—"

"The least bit? What do you know of feeling, you—you *child*? You love this woman as your teacher. I love her as I love my own soul. I have the rare choice of killing either my father or the woman I would marry if I could. I cannot kill my father, so . . ." His voice dropped, and he reached down to stroke the blade of the long, sharp knife that lay among the magical paraphernalia on the table. "Rest assured, I do not plan to outlive her by long."

Persy saw Pen take a deep breath and straighten her back once more. "I have never been as good a witch as I could have been, Mr. Carrighar. I never practiced the way my sister did, and it shows: She *is* far stronger than I am. I know I disappointed Ally deeply because of this. But I did learn one thing from her, the most important thing—what power I have, I will use for good."

He looked at her, his jaw clenched. "Miss Leland—"

"Giving you my magic might or might not save Ally. But even if it did, she herself would never forgive me, because I will have used it for ill. As I see it, sir, the only way for me to do good with the little power I have is not to give it to you. I know Ally would think it the right decision. What does she think about *yours*?"

"Silence!" he roared, and pointed a trembling finger at Pen. She grabbed at her throat and coughed, then tried to speak. No sound passed her lips.

That was the final straw. Persy flung aside the curtain that concealed her.

"You leave my sister alone!" she cried.

21

$\mathscr{M}$ichael Carrighar's head whipped from side to side as he searched the room, and Persy realized that she was still covered by her cloaking spell. With an impatient gesture she brushed it away.

In the circle, Pen covered her face with her hands.

Mr. Carrighar stared at her, and an unwilling smile touched the corners of his mouth. "The other Miss Leland, here all along. I should have noticed your concealing spell. But my attention has been elsewhere, as you might guess." He gestured at the circle. "Then again, I might not have noticed. You are talented, Miss Leland. I felt that when we met at Kensington. But it isn't to be wondered at. You are *her* pupil, after all." His gaze moved back to the pale, sleeping Ally.

"Let us go, Mr. Carrighar. Let *her* go. There's still time while Sir John is away," Persy urged him.

"I can't. You heard me just now. Help me. With your power, willingly given, she might live. For the love of God . . ." His hands clenched into fists.

"No. My sister was right. Ally would never forgive us, even if she did survive. You're wrong, and someone has got to stop you." Persy pointed at one of the candles in the outermost circle. It tottered and started to fall.

But he was too fast for her. His own hand shot out in a sharp, chopping motion, and the candle steadied.

"That was ill done." The wizard's brows drew together in an angry scowl. "You should know better than to disrupt a circle spell of this magnitude. Someone might get hurt."

Persy couldn't resist a grim laugh. "Worse than they will if I don't try to destroy it?"

"You can't, Miss Leland. I won't let you." He stepped away from the table and toward her.

"It's not a matter of letting." She summoned the pitcher of water from the table and tried to upend it over the chalked pattern of the circle.

"*Frigus!*" he snarled, and the water fell harmlessly to the floor as glittering pellets of ice. "I'm warning you."

"Warn away, then." She backed around the circle as he approached, careful not to let her skirts even brush the edge. Should she try the candles again? He had been angry when she'd tried to knock one down. Would blowing them out work? "*Boreas, Auster, extinguite!*" she cried.

"*Pacamini!*" He spread his hands in a smoothing gesture as a curl of wind fluttered the candle flames. "What do you think you're doing? Only a fool would summon the north wind indoors."

"It almost worked, didn't it?" Persy couldn't resist taunting back.

"This foolishness won't get us anywhere. You can try all night to break my circ—"

"Thank you. I think I will."

Even in the candlelight, she could see him flush with annoyance. "This is not a parlor game."

"I wasn't joking." Persy kept backing away from him, bits of spells and magic ricocheting in her head as she groped for ideas. If she could stall him, keep him at bay, then maybe she'd be able to think of something. But if she stalled too long, Sir John might come back. She wasn't sure she could keep both of them away from her. They would force her into the circle, and she'd be caught. They would strip Ally's magic, and Pen's, and hers . . . the very thought of it made her shudder. Having her magic taken from her would be like being flayed alive.

Very well then. Sometimes the best defense was offense. She took a breath and tried to focus on Mr. Carrighar's eyes. *"Dormi,"* she whispered.

But she had forgotten something. As she narrowed her focus, his odd eyes, one blue, one brown, jarred her attention. She blinked, and the spell dissipated.

"So?" he said softly. "Switching tactics, are we? Will you attack me instead? Ah, Miss Leland, that is not wise. Please don't make me hurt you. I know how much Melusine loved you. For her sake—"

"*Loved* me? She's not dead yet!" Stung, Persy sent a blast of pure force at him. It hit him in the shoulder and made him stagger but not fall. With a circular motion of his arms he gathered the remaining energy of her spell and sent it into the circle. The candles burned a little brighter, with an eerie, unnatural bluish tinge.

"Keep it up," he called to her. "If I can't take your power one way, I'll take it another. You must have realized what the circle is by now, haven't you? Every time you throw out some unfocused magic, the circle will absorb it." His voice changed, became low and soothing. "You're like a moth beating against a lampshade. Save yourself the trouble and go into the circle, child, and let us get this over with. The ritual preparations are nearly complete. When the princess arrives we could have it done in a matter of seconds, and none of us will have to suffer anymore."

Persy wrapped her arms around herself, hunching her shoulders and breathing hard. The weird shadows cast by all the candles were giving her a frightful headache. Her angry blast at him had been a foolish waste of energy. Attacking him directly would not work, it seemed. Then what—

A flash of magic startled her. She dodged and shielded herself from the sudden force that tried to yank her off her feet and into the circle. "I thought you said you didn't want to hurt me?" she accused.

"I'm not trying to hurt you. But I cannot vouch for Sir John when he gets back and finds that you were here the whole time while he searched for you. He doesn't like being made a fool of." He took a step toward her, then another. "You're weakening, you know. Just being in the presence of a spell circle like this will draw your magic off. How much longer can you dodge me? How much time do you have before Sir John comes back? Go to your sister and your teacher. I promise it will be quick."

Persy backed away from him and tried to keep from trembling too visibly. Even if she wanted to attack him right now, her shaking hands would probably send the spell uselessly into the ceiling or floor, or worse yet, into the circle. She would have to find some other way to deal with him.

"Time grows short," he said again, and gave her another magical shove. This one nearly overbalanced her into the circle. With a cry she leapt back from the candles.

"Please, Miss Leland. I don't want to have to do this to you."

"Fiddlesticks," she muttered. "You're probably enjoying yourself."

"I assure you that I'm not."

Something in his voice made her look at him more closely. She saw with a flicker of surprise that he, too, was breathing hard. Why? Could he be tiring too?

But that made no sense. He was a trained wizard, and a powerful one. Up to now he'd been toying with her like a cat with a mouse.

She dodged another magical push and watched him. He *was* tiring, his auburn hair dark with sweat where it fell into his eyes. But why?

Then she remembered: the circle. Sir John had said that much of Mr. Carrighar's power was bound into the making of the circle. That was why he needed their magic too—to fuel the spell. Theoretically, he *was* weakened—weaker than she was, perhaps. But she couldn't be sure.

Persy risked a glance at her sister, still clutching Ally's hand as she watched them. Pen looked at her, and then at the door. Then she did it again.

She was trying to tell Persy to escape.

But she couldn't leave Pen and Ally alone, at the mercy of these desperate men.

Or could she?

Mr. Carrighar needed her. Without her magic in the circle for him to draw on, Sir John's plans would fail. The easiest way for her to foil him and save Ally and Pen, then, would simply be to leave.

If she could just get out of this room and hide somewhere . . . or better yet, find someone to help—a footman, anyone.

Sir John hadn't been able to leave the room until the ward had been lifted. Surely if she threw all her remaining power into it—focused it directly at the protective ward so that it couldn't be redirected back at the circle . . .

The door was behind her. If she could just move another few feet around, she'd be in the perfect position to dash for it once the ward was down. Could she do it before he stopped her?

"It's no use, girl." He stopped and cocked an ear toward the door. "Do I hear footsteps out there? Believe me, you don't want Sir John—"

"*Damn* Sir John!" Persy shouted, and pointed at Mr. Carrighar.

He threw his hands up before him in a shielding gesture, but not before she saw the satisfying look of shock on his face at her unladylike language. Before he could react, she swung around and reached both hands toward the door.

"Open!" she bellowed, not even bothering with the focus that spell-casting in Latin usually gave her. She felt an icy shock as her power cut through his ward and struck the door. It flew open, crashing back against the wall.

Persy felt as though it had slammed into her as well. She fell to her knees, gasping. She had put almost everything she had into that one word, and it had ripped the breath from her lungs and the strength from her legs. This made the headaches she got after too much practice feel like a gentle caress.

She tried to stand, to run, but everything below her knees seemed to have melted. Well, if she had to, she would crawl. She wouldn't give up now.

"No!" Michael Carrighar roared. She looked up through the tears of weakness that had sprung to her eyes and saw him rush around the circle toward her. She saw his mouth open, saw him start to form words, saw a mist of power condense in the air around his hands as he spoke. She saw him extend those faintly glowing hands toward her.

"I'm sorry, Ally," she muttered, and bowed her head. "Sorry, Pen. I tried." Then, because she was a duke's granddaughter and Ally's pupil, she straightened. At least she could meet her fate face to face.

But no blast of magic arced like dark lightning at her. Instead, she saw a small wooden stool hurtle through the air from behind Mr. Carrighar as if launched from a cannon. It walloped him over the head, then clattered to the ground.

The wizard swayed, his eyes round with shock, and the spell he had been about to hurl at her melted into the air.

Persy blinked. How had that happened? Had she done that?

It didn't matter. She drew up the last spark of her will and cast a feeble halting spell at him.

It was enough. Her magic, unfocused and weak though it was, finished what the chair had started. He fell heavily to the ground.

In the instant of his falling, Persy felt a commotion in the room, an invisible maelstrom where the circle had been. Without his conscious will to sustain it and lend it structure, the circle was collapsing.

"Duck, Pen!" she tried to shout. Magic swirled and eddied around them, lifting her hair and drying the tears on her cheeks like a physical wind. Sound that was not sound roared in her ears. But before she could even lift her hands to shield her eyes, the magic drew itself into a point, then vanished with a loud pop. All the candles in the circle went out, all at once.

And then, Persy collapsed too.

"She *fainted*? Oh, honestly—*girls!*" Charles's voice oozed disgust.

"Shut your mouth, Chucklehead, or I'll shut it for you." Pen's voice was hoarse, as if she had been crying.

Persy didn't bother opening her eyes. "Let's see you manage all that while laced into a corset, Chuckles," she muttered.

Chuckles?

She sat up, which was a bad idea. Her head felt like an overripe melon. If she wasn't careful, it would probably roll off her shoulders onto the floor and smash into a pulpy mess. She groaned.

"Not another word, idiot." Pen slid a steadying arm around her shoulder. "Not you, Perse. Him."

Persy winced at the movement. "Charles?" she said, and finally got her eyes open.

Though the room was dim now that all the candles were extinguished, lit only by the glowing braziers and by one small lantern, she could plainly see that her brother indeed squatted next to her, wearing a grin too large for one boy's mouth. "Hello, Persy. What did you think of my magic?" he said.

She shook her head and immediately regretted it. "What happened?"

"I told you *I'd* be the one that figured everything out. Lochinvar and I were standing outside the door, trying to figure out how to get in and rescue you, when it flew open on its own, and I looked in and saw that man about to hurt you, and I just felt like I wanted to *whack* him one, good and hard. Then I saw that little stool there, and . . ." He shrugged eloquently. "And it just flew up and hit him over the head. It felt *great*," he added.

Pen gave him a quelling look. "You broke through the wizard's ward and got the door open, Persy. I looked up and saw our dear delinquent brother standing there with his mouth open, and then everything happened at once. I'm sorry, Persy. I tried to help you. I tried to send you what magic I could while you fought him, but I c-couldn't even touch it. It was like it was frozen inside me—"

"And then I did magic to save you," Charles chimed in, speaking in capital letters and underscores. "I saved you and Pen and Ally—"

"Ally!" Persy cried, suddenly remembering. Ally in the circle, and Pen . . . and Michael Carrighar . . . but what was Charles doing here? Had he really done magic? She scrambled out of Pen's arms and back toward the circle. What she saw stopped her.

Lochinvar knelt by Ally, supporting her as she slowly sat up. She looked dazed but clear-eyed as she smiled at Persy. "You did it," she whispered, her face shining with pride. Lochinvar looked up at her too, but the lantern on the floor behind him threw his face into shadow.

"I . . ." Persy began to wish that she were still in a faint.

"Aren't you glad I told Lochinvar about your dream?" Charles hadn't stopped talking. "He was worried about you, so he took me back to his house and we borrowed some livery from the coach-man and he brought me with him as his page, in case something bad happened—"

Pen snorted. "As if you'd be in the least useful."

Charles smoothed his too-large postillion's coat. "Well, I was, wasn't I? And I did magic, you and Lochinvar saw me—"

"Shhh!" Both Persy and Pen lunged for him.

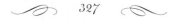

"What's wrong?" Charles asked, looking astonished. "Oh, don't worry. I told Lochinvar all about magic and you two and Ally and everything when we went riding on Lord Chesterfield. That's why he brought me along tonight."

"Charles," Persy moaned. "What have you done?"

"Excuse me," said a voice. It was light and silvery and girlish, and Persy recognized it at once. "I was looking for—oh, dear me. Is everything all right? Aunt, come see. Was this what you wanted me to see? Who are these people?"

Next to her, Persy felt Pen stiffen as she looked behind her. Then she scrambled to her feet and curtsied deeply.

"Yes, in here, child—oh!"

Persy turned just in time to see Princess Sophia's bespectacled face peep around the edge of the door. She looked at all of them, ending with Michael Carrighar's motionless form on the floor, and her jaw dropped.

"What have you done?" she cried. "Oh, you've ruined every-thing! Sir John—I must find Sir John and tell him." She gave them all one last tragic look and withdrew. Hurrying footsteps could be heard retreating down the hall.

Just inside the door stood Princess Victoria in her dress of white satin with lace. She held up a small lamp and gazed about her with a frown.

"Victoria," called another voice. A thin, middle-aged woman with sharp features and kindly eyes now hurried into the room. "It wass most strange," she said in German-accented English. "Princess Sophia behaved very oddly. Why, she slammed right in my face that last door. If I had not stopped to listen, I might not haf found— Heavens, what is all this?" She surveyed them with raised eyebrows. "Is not that Sir John's secretary on the floor?"

Princess Victoria took a wary step toward him, holding her lamp before her. "I think it is, Lehzen. How very odd. Is he ill?"

"Your Highness. If I might explain?" With Lochinvar's help, Ally had risen. Now she tottered over to Michael and knelt by him, brushing his hair off his forehead and laying her hand on it. "He is not ill, ma'am, not in the usual sense. A very great evil has been averted tonight, one that was aimed at you. Though this man would have done you harm, he was only a tool in his master's hand."

"*Mein gott!* That Sir John!" The woman Princess Victoria had called Lehzen—Persy guessed that it was her governess, the Baroness Lehzen—put her arm around the princess's shoulders. "Tell uss," she commanded. "What did Sir John do?"

Persy leaned her head against Pen and sighed, not sure if she should dare attempt to stand as well, as was proper in the presence of the princess. It was nice to sit back and let Ally explain things, with a word from Pen now and again to clarify matters. Ally's explanations—Sir John's plans, his blackmailing of Michael Carrighar, her kidnapping, and Persy and Pen's roles—washed over her like the tide. She had made enough decisions and done enough talking for one evening—for a whole year of evenings, it felt like. She could quite cheerfully lay her head down and sleep through till tomorrow, right here on the floor, lulled by Ally's voice—Ally's *dear* voice—explaining what had gone on.

"A magical duel? Really? This girl here?" said Princess Victoria, looking at her.

Oh, bother. Now she would have to stand. Were it anyone but Princess Victoria . . .

But before Persy could clamber inelegantly up on her own, a pair of hands closed on her waist and lifted her easily. She turned in surprise and met Lochinvar's eyes, very close to her own.

They were very dark now, a sort of teal color that matched his beautiful waistcoat, and his hair shone gold even in this dim light, like the—like—drat it, why wouldn't he say something instead of looking at her like that?

He was reaching into a pocket and pulling something from it. Without a word, he handed the something to her. Persy turned the soft little bundle over and wished she could sit down on the floor again.

It was her glove—one of the gloves she had stained with coffee ice at Lady de Courcy's ball. She could see her initials embroidered on the hem. Lord Carharrick had asked for one and Pen had taken the other to examine the stain. Persy had forgotten that she hadn't given it back. So how had Lochinvar gotten hold of it?

The ring finger of the glove was wrapped in strands of red thread—seven strands, she counted. Under the thread, bound to the finger, was a lock of bright gold hair.

Behind her, Pen uttered a small surprised sound. "So that's why you wanted it. But that means you—"

"I don't understand," Persy mumbled through the ringing in her ears.

"I've carried this around with me for weeks, but I've never said the words that go with it," he said, and met her eyes. "Do you know what it is?"

Persy swallowed. "It's a love spell—an old country one," she managed to say. "I read about it in one of Ally's books. But—"

"You're correct. But I never could finish the spell, no matter how tempting it was. What good would it be for you to love me because of this and not because you really wanted me of your own free will?"

Was she hearing things? Or had falling hurt her head, and now she was hallucinating, scrambling the events of the last weeks into nonsense? "But it's magic!" she cried, staring down at it once more. The lock of his hair was very bright against the white of her glove, as bright as the gold embroidery thread that spelled out *PL* on the hem.

"Why shouldn't I use magic?" he asked. "I came by it honestly enough. My mother—"

"Your mother was killed by a witch's curse. Papa said it was just a silly rumor, but . . ." Her mouth felt too dry to continue. The room felt like it had before—charged with a mysterious, perilous energy. But there was no spell circle around her now. Only those eyes, dark tonight and filled with their own magic.

"Mother didn't die from a witch's curse. If only there *had* been a witch with her, when she . . ." He sighed and shook his head, then squared his shoulders before he spoke again.

"Persy, my mother *was* a witch. That silly rumor got started later, God only knows how. If she'd lived, you and she might have— might have been friends."

Lochinvar's mother, a witch? This was more than Persy could comprehend right now. But Lochinvar hadn't finished.

"I inherited some of her power but there was no one to train me. Only when I got to Cambridge did I start to learn the rudiments.

I don't even know if this love spell would have worked. Pathetic, isn't it?" He smiled sadly.

"You . . . doing magic?"

"Yes, me. How do you think he"—Lochinvar jerked his head at Michael Carrighar—"didn't see you under that table at Kensington Palace? And after that, when Sir John passed us in the corridor? I'm not very good, but I was able to cast a sufficient cloaking spell. I'm surprised that you didn't notice it."

That almost made her laugh. As if she'd been capable of noticing *anything* when he'd held her against him that day. She felt like she had to shout in order to be heard over the sound of her heart thudding in her breast. But when she spoke, her voice would only come out in a whisper. "Then you don't hate witches?"

"No, Persy, I don't. Especially not one witch in particular." His voice was light, but his face was more serious and intent than she'd ever seen it. "I was afraid that *you* would be put off by it . . . and when you did that halting spell on me last night, I was too flabbergasted to do anything but stand there and stare. I called this afternoon hoping to see you but too much else was going on, and I couldn't get a moment alone with you. And then Charles told me about your governess and I was . . . well, I was madder than hell because of your charade and just wanted to get away and figure out what we could do to protect you, so that afterward I could yell at you good and proper and then ask you to marry me again. I should have known that you were far stronger than I could dream of being, but I had to do something to protect the woman I love." He put his arms around her and pulled her against him.

"Now zhen, sir . . ." Baroness Lehzen stepped forward with a disapproving look on her face.

"Sshh!" Princess Victoria grabbed her arm and pulled her back. "I want to see what happens."

Persy let her hands creep up to rest on his shoulders. Was she truly hearing this? "You don't mind that I'm a witch? Really?" she whispered.

Instead of answering, Lochinvar bent his head and touched his lips to hers. He drew back and looked at her, then kissed her again. It was different from those kisses at Mrs. Cheke-Bentinck's: This time, she knew that he was kissing her because he wanted to, not because she'd made him. She closed her eyes and, just as she'd longed to, buried her fingers in his hair and kissed him back.

After a while—it was hard to say just how long—someone cleared her throat rather pointedly. Lochinvar lifted his head and looked at Persy with satisfaction.

"There. Does that answer your question?" he asked, smiling. "I've kissed you in front of your brother, your sister, two governesses, and the heiress to the throne. So if you don't want your reputation irretrievably ruined, you'll *have* to marry me. And I can stop carrying this glove around with me, can't I? Or do I have to say that spell after all?"

She buried her face against his shoulder. "No, Lochinvar, you don't need to say it."

"Ohhh." Princess Victoria sighed happily. "That was better than an opera! Wasn't it, Lehzen?"

Charles walked up to her and solemnly offered her his arm. "I don't think we're needed here anymore, Your Highness. May I have the honor of escorting you back to the ballroom?"

22

AUGUST 1837—BUCKINGHAM HOUSE, LONDON

*H*onestly, tea with royalty again? Why can't I come this time? She liked me too, after all. She said so." Charles frowned ferociously at them as the carriage drew up to the front entrance of the Lelands' Mayfair house. He had not returned to Eton, begging to remain home until September, after Persy's wedding.

"Because this is a girls-only tea party, Chuckles," Pen returned as Ally climbed inside the carriage. She had been invited specially with them in order to visit the Baroness Lehzen.

"We'll tell her you send your compliments," Persy added.

"Oh. That's all right, then," Charles said gruffly and turned away. But they had both seen the look of happiness in his eyes. It seemed their little brother had taken something of a fancy to the Princess Victoria.

Queen Victoria, now. Only three weeks after her coming-of-age ball, poor King William had peacefully died, happy in the knowledge that he had lived past his niece's eighteenth birthday. The slender girl with the large blue eyes had slipped into her role as queen as if she had been born to it. Which, Persy reflected, she had been.

A few weeks ago she and Pen had read in the paper how the men of the late king's Privy Council, men learned and famous, men tempered by battles both military and political, had been awed by the majesty of their tiny new queen at her first council meeting. Sir John's malicious stories had found their mark, and all the council members had heard about her immaturity and ignorance verging on feeblemindedness. Instead they found her dignified and confident, aware of her youth and inexperience but prepared to work. "She not merely filled her chair," the Duke of Wellington was reported to have said, "she filled the room."

"I hope that will put paid to Sir John's poison," Pen had said, folding the paper with a satisfied snap.

"I'd rather something put paid to Sir John," Persy had replied, and moved closer to Ally on the drawing room sofa. They had been nearly inseparable since the princess's ball.

"Something already has." Ally squeezed her hand. "The queen took her throne without him."

"That's not quite what I meant," Persy objected.

"I know that. But sometimes picking up one's life and proceeding as if nothing had occurred is the best revenge of all." Ally had smiled, looking both wicked and wise at the same time.

That was more or less what happened, with a few surprises.

Lochinvar had presented himself at their door at the unheard-of hour of nine in the morning after the ball to ask Lord Atherston for Persy's hand. Papa had emerged from their interview looking confused but happy, both of which sensations became universal in the household when the bell rang yet again and Ally appeared in the drawing room doorway.

Persy was slightly worried about what Mama's reaction would be when Ally came back. Poor Mama had been dumbfounded when Persy told her about Lochinvar's proposal, and Persy supposed that it was not surprising. So when Ally had curtsied her greeting after being announced by an astonished Kenney, Persy kept a close eye on her mother. Indeed, Mama blinked and did not speak for several seconds, a sure sign that she was taken aback.

Pen spoke instead. "Mama, we hope you'll take Ally back as our governess for a while longer. She didn't mean to leave us—it wasn't her fault at all."

Mama didn't answer.

"I should like to explain my absence to you, your ladyship, but I am not sure that you would believe my story," Ally added quietly. "All I can ask is your forgiveness and understanding."

Mama gave her a keen look. "I see. I am assuming, then, that it had something to do with your magic?"

In that instant, an Indian in full battle dress declaiming Shakespeare in Russian while dancing a jig could have materialized in the middle of the dark blue Brussels carpet, and none of them would have noticed. Persy was not sure that she wasn't still in bed dreaming, but one look at Pen's and Ally's astonished faces banished that thought.

"Mama—you knew?" she managed to ask.

"But how—?" Ally gasped.

"Well, of course I did. I'm not entirely inexperienced when it comes to magic, you know." Mama picked up her embroidery, a funny little smile hovering about her mouth. "Why do you think I hired Miss Allardyce in the first place? Your grandmama Leland warned me when you were born that magic ran in the female side of the family, so I made sure that you would have a governess who understood you. I was concerned that all this had something to do with magic and had started to make inquiries on my own, but I didn't want to worry you girls."

Persy looked at Ally. It was her turn to be speechless.

"Magic is not something that should be much discussed," Mama continued. Yes, amusement definitely lurked in the corners of her mouth. "Especially in public. I merely kept an eye on matters and saw that Miss Allardyce had you girls well in hand. Of course I should like her to return. We'll have a great deal of work ahead of us completing Persy's trousseau in time for the wedding. Dear me, I must send a note to Madame Gendreau. Won't you excuse me?" She folded her embroidery and rose from her seat.

"Mama," Pen said. "What did you mean, you're 'not inexperienced with magic'? Are you—"

"Of course not, dear. But that doesn't mean I haven't run across it before. I'll tell you about it some other time." She smiled reminiscently and swept from the room, leaving Persy and Pen—and Ally—agog.

The next several weeks were spent in a flurry of shopping once again, interspersed with social events that had not ceased, including their own ball. Persy no longer dreaded them, because Lochinvar would be there, waiting to claim the first dance with her and as many as he possibly could after that. And she and Pen were finally free to giggle over all the evenings' events, with the amusing addition of Lorrie.

But perhaps the most surprising event occurred late in July.

The main part of the season had ended, and the parties and balls had slowed to a trickle as fashionable London society left for their country houses to avoid the city's heat and smells. Mama and Ally had taken advantage of the lull to complete shopping for Persy's trousseau, but even with that excuse Ally seemed to be out of the house a good deal more than seemed necessary. Pen and Persy filled the empty hours between visits to Madame Gendreau (where they saw Sally Louder getting fitted for her own wedding dress) tutoring Charles not only in academics, but also in magic. His power was as yet small and weak, like a newly hatched bird. But like a hatchling he was voracious, and practiced until his head ached and Persy had to charm away the pain. Lochinvar often joined them, and it was wonderful to watch him and Charles learn together, Charles imitating Lochinvar's every move like a worshipful puppet.

But Persy wanted Ally there, too. Happy as she was to think about her future with Lochinvar, she knew that it would mean losing Ally. Couldn't Mama handle the shopping on her own, so that Ally could be with them?

At lunch on that late July day, Ally surveyed them all. "My mother would be most honored if Persy and Pen—yes, and you too, Charles—could come to tea this afternoon. Would that be all right, Lady Parthenope?"

Mama had agreed that it would, and so they had all taken the carriage down to Oxford Street. Mrs. Allardyce greeted them warmly at the shop door, though her eyes narrowed when she caught sight of Lorrie, who had accompanied them. Persy saw that Lorrie affected not to notice, though she walked as closely behind her and Pen as she could.

Mr. Allardyce beamed as they entered, and even Merlin looked pleased, though he too cast dark looks in Lorrie's direction. Persy knew that they had not learned about her new position as their lady's maid until Ally came to see them the day after the princess's ball.

Then a fourth figure came forward to greet them. Persy had to stop and grab Ally's arm as panic rose in her throat.

It was Michael Carrighar.

He bowed to her and to Pen, and though his mouth smiled, his strange eyes reflected the trouble that must surely be evident in hers. She had nearly forgotten about him in the flurry around the wedding.

Ally put her arms around her and Pen's shoulders. "Girls," she said quietly. "I should like you to meet my future husband."

They stood in stunned silence. Charles stepped forward, looking outraged.

"Him?" he cried. "But I clobbered him! You can't marry him, Ally."

Michael bowed gravely to him as well. "You did indeed clobber me, sir. The lump you left me is only just gone down."

"I know you've only known him as an enemy. I did too, for a long time. I can't expect you to understand what happened between us at Kensington, and indeed it has taken me these months since then to sort out my own feelings for him," Ally said softly.

"Are you sure, Ally?" Persy could not bring herself to look at him yet.

"I'm sure, Miss Leland," he answered for her. "You don't know how happy I was to be bested by you—and your brother," he added as Charles moved impatiently. "You are a formidable witch for your years. But then again, you had the best teacher. I don't ask for your friendship yet, or even your approval. I know that I will have to work hard to earn them. All I do ask is that you believe that I love Melusine, with all my heart."

Mrs. Allardyce had bustled them to the table then, and Pen and Persy found themselves plied with enough of her best tea pastries and cordials to threaten the fit of all their new dresses from Madame Gendreau's. Fortunately Charles was able to maintain family honor and eat fully as much as Mrs. Allardyce could wish.

Before they left, Persy took a moment to draw Mrs. Allardyce aside and thank her for letting Lorrie stay with them.

"Well, so long as she does her job properly," Mrs. Allardyce conceded. "Lorrie is a flibbertigibbet through and through, but if being an abigail is what she wants to do . . . and if she's giving satisfaction . . ."

"She's most satisfactory, and is looking forward to coming to live with me after my marriage," Persy assured her.

"Lorrie in the country? Hmm." Mrs. Allardyce looked dubious. "Well, we'll see. You can always bundle her home if she doesn't suit."

Persy smiled. "I think we'll suit each other just fine."

As they clattered home in the carriage, Persy touched Ally's hand. "When I scryed for you, I knew—I could feel that something between you and Mr. Carrighar. . . ." She stopped, embarrassed.

"We had many weeks alone together—quite time enough for me to understand here at last was a man that I could love and respect. Feeling as I do about my father, how could I not understand his feelings for his? Love is a very strange thing indeed, Persy. As I'm sure you understand."

"Indeed," Pen echoed. "I hope that when I find it, it isn't so strange and difficult, though."

"Don't bet on it, Pen. I'll probably have to sort everything out for you, too," Charles said smugly, then clutched his stomach as the carriage hit a bump. After that, he kept his mouth firmly shut.

And now, the last surprise: this invitation to tea at Buckingham House with the queen. Persy leaned against the carriage door and wondered what it would be like.

"At least it isn't Kensington," Pen said, peeking around Ally to grin at her. "You don't think Sir John will be there, do you?"

"Don't even joke about it." Persy shuddered.

They were ushered into a small sitting room decorated with dozens of watercolors and countless bric-a-brac, and Persy realized as she stole looks around them that this must be the queen's own private parlor. She didn't have much time to examine her surroundings, for in less than a minute the queen herself came flying into the room. A small King Charles spaniel yipped and danced close on her heels. Following at a statelier pace was Baroness Lehzen.

Pen and Persy and Ally at once sank into curtsies. The queen went to them and, taking their hands, greeted them each with a kiss.

"I should be curtsying to you instead," she said, her beautiful eyes wide. "If it weren't for you I'd probably still be back in the schoolroom at Kensington, agreeing to all manner of ghastly things because *that man* wanted them. And Lehzen here would be back in Germany, starving in a garret somewhere. Dash, stop that! Sit down and be a polite doggy, if you please."

"I am sure you exaggerate, Your Majesty." Baroness Lehzen smiled as she scooped up the little dog. "But most grateful I alzo am to zhese ladies."

The queen led them to a sofa and made Persy and Pen sit on either side of her. "I would have liked to have you here sooner, but it has been *so* busy, you see. It was nice to see you at my drawing room in July, though. How is your dear little brother?"

Persy remembered the whispers they had heard among the august attendees of the queen's very first drawing room reception—the whispers that had grown to a near roar when the queen came forward and kissed them on both cheeks rather than holding out her hand for them to kiss, as was proper for their rank.

"Rather put out at not being able to see you, ma'am," Pen answered her. "I think he's developed something of a crush on you."

Queen Victoria smiled and colored. "He was quite charming. Will he be able to study magic now as well?"

"He will return to Eton next month for Michaelmas term. One of his masters is an old acquaintance of Lord Seton's, who is writing to ask if he might not be able to tutor Charles in magic—on the side, of course. We haven't told him yet, in case he spontaneously combusts from joy." Persy chuckled at the thought.

Queen Victoria laughed her silvery laugh. "I might see him sometime when I am at Windsor. Do you think he would like to come for tea?"

"I know he would, but we'd better not tell him or he *will* combust."

Tea arrived then, and the queen poured under Lehzen's watchful eye. She had taken Ally to a pair of chairs set a little to one side of the sofa.

"It must be most interesting to be able to do magic," the queen commented. "Was it frightfully hard to study?"

"Not for my sister, ma'am," Pen answered. "She was always the more studious of the two of us. Now I have to make up for lost time."

"Indeed?" The queen handed her a cup.

"I'm ashamed that she had to do most of the work the night of your ball. If I had been a better witch, I would have seen that circle and been free to help her," Pen said, her face sober. "So it has been decided that I will go to Ireland with Miss Allardyce and her husband next spring to study magic and, I hope, become as good a witch as my sister."

Persy smiled as Pen spoke. The queen must have noticed, for she asked, "Why do you smile, Miss Leland?"

"Because back in the spring, I would never have guessed that everything would turn out this way. I was sure that Pen would make a brilliant match and that I would go back to my family's home to devote myself to studying and magic. That's the way I wanted it to be, though I knew I would miss Pen dreadfully. And now, here we are." She met the queen's eyes. "It's Pen who is going on to study, and me who is getting married. I suppose the going-home part was close to right—Galiswood isn't more than a forty-minute ride from home."

Queen Victoria sighed. "That moment when Lord Seton proposed to you was *so* romantic. Was it really such a surprise to you? When is your wedding?"

"It certainly was a surprise, ma'am. I was sure he thought I was the last female on earth that he'd consider marrying. The wedding will be at the end of September, at Mage's Tutterow."

"Oh, I am sorry it won't be in London. I should have liked so much to be invi—but I can't do that sort of thing anymore, can I?" The queen's face fell. For a moment she looked like just another eighteen-year-old girl not allowed to attend a party she had looked forward to. "Will you write to me and tell me all about it?"

Persy gulped. The *queen* was asking her to write to her. "I would be honored—and very happy—to do so, ma'am."

Pen looked thoughtful. "I would imagine that becoming queen might have its less agreeable moments, on occasion."

"Well, yes, it does," Queen Victoria confided, with a glance at Baroness Lehzen, who was absorbed in conversation with Ally. "I am still learning what I can and cannot do. But on the whole, it has been wonderful."

"It allowed you to rid yourself of—of persons you did not want to have about you," Persy said quietly.

The queen shuddered. "Even after what happened that evening, Sir John still tried to importune me for a position. I haven't seen him since June and am quite looking forward to never, *ever* seeing him again. It is expected he'll be leaving the country shortly. And my mother . . ." She sighed. "She is my mother and I honor her, but it is such a relief to have room to *breathe* and learn how to be myself without her hovering over me." She set down her teacup and cleared her throat softly. At once, Baroness Lehzen turned to her.

"Now?" she asked.

"Yes, if you please," the queen said. She looked in turn at Pen and Persy, and Ally too, with a serious expression on her round face.

"Lehzen and I have discussed several times what the three of you did for me. I wish to reward you somehow, but I didn't know what we could do that wouldn't call attention to the, ah, unusual circumstances of your service to me."

Persy felt her own cheeks grow pink. "We don't need a reward, ma'am. We did what we did—well, because we've loved and admired you all our lives."

"Oh, dear." Queen Victoria's eyes grew bright. "Thank you very, very much. But I still want to do something for you, even if it is something only those of us in this room will ever know about. So I am founding a new royal order, like the Knights of the Garter or the Bath. But this one will be secret, and shall be given to recognize those persons who have performed magical services on my behalf."

Persy tried to look at Pen and Ally to see how they were receiving this, but tears blurred her vision. She felt for her hanky, remembering Ally's talk before they came to London. They *had* been able to do good with their power, and now that good had been acknowledged by the person who mattered most.

"Only I haven't been able to think of a name I like," the queen continued. "It will have to be Dames rather than Knights, of course. Dashy, no! You may *not* have a biscuit." She pushed her little dog away from the tea table and tapped him playfully on his upturned nose.

"Might I propose one, ma'am?" Persy asked as she dabbed at her eyes.

"Oh, yes, if you please."

Persy took a deep breath. "Call it DASH—Dames at Service to Her Majesty."

Pen clapped her hands. "The emblem could be a little figure of your dog. That way, if the name ever slipped out, no one would suspect it meant anything."

Smiling, the queen leapt up from the sofa and ran to a shelf. She returned with a sketchbook and pencil. "Like this, perhaps?" She drew a quick cartoon of the little dog, not begging for a treat as he had just now, but stretched out like a heraldic lion couchant, his ears forward and alert and his tail held proudly erect.

"Almost," said Persy. "May I?"

The queen handed her the sketchbook and pencil, then laughed in delight as Persy added a little star at the end of the figure's tail.

"Perfect!" she cried. "He will have a sapphire for his eye and a diamond in his tail, and his collar will have DASH spelled out in diamonds, too. He will hang from a ribbon of light blue and gold, I think. Lehzen, you shall take this to the court jeweler this afternoon and ask him to get started at once. When do you return to the country?"

"Next Tuesday, Your Majesty," Ally replied. Her cheeks were pink, and she too had had to resort to her handkerchief.

"Very well, then. You must come back on Monday and we will hold your investiture. Please bring your little brother and Lord Seton as well, so we will have some audience to applaud you. I'm afraid we can't supply trumpet fanfares and processions for the occasion." Queen Victoria smiled and took their hands.

"That will be fine with me. I don't care much for crowds, ma'am." Persy grinned. "They make me nervous."

Pen rolled her eyes.